WITHDRAWN FROM
SANDWELL
LIBRARIES

D0542558

PRYDE AND THE INFERNAL DEVICE

A thrilling new adventure for Matthew Pryde

1805. England is in the midst of her war with France. Matthew Pryde, engineer at a coal mine in Kent, is regarded as the perfect 'spy' to send across the English Channel to investigate rumours that the French are digging a tunnel underneath the Channel. Matthew is accompanied by the mysterious Mr Black – and the rather unexpected addition of the unconventional Kate Denton – to France where they must investigate...

*Malcolm Archibald titles available from
Severn House Large Print*

Pryde's Rock

PRYDE AND THE INFERNAL DEVICE

Malcolm Archibald

Severn House Large Print
London & New York

This first large print edition published 2010
in Great Britain and the USA by
SEVERN HOUSE PUBLISHERS LTD of
9-15 High Street, Sutton, Surrey, SM1 1DF.
First world regular print edition published 2008 by
Severn House Publishers Ltd., London and New York.

Copyright © 2008 by Malcolm Archibald.

All rights reserved.
The moral right of the author has been asserted.

British Library Cataloguing in Publication Data

Archibald, Malcolm.
    Pryde and the infernal device.
    1. Napoleonic Wars, 1800-1815--Fiction. 2. Espionage,
    British--France--History--19th century--Fiction.
    3. Mining engineers--England--Kent--Fiction. 4. France--
    History--Consulate and First Empire, 1799-1815--Fiction.
    5. Historical fiction. 6. Large type books.
    I. Title
    823.9'2-dc22

    ISBN-13: 978-0-7278-7899-1

Except where actual historical events and characters are being
described for the storyline of this novel, all situations in this
publication are fictitious and any resemblance to living persons is
purely coincidental.

Severn House Publishers support The Forest Stewardship Council
[FSC], the leading international forest certification organisation. All
our titles that are printed on Greenpeace-approved FSC-certified paper
carry the FSC logo.

 **Mixed Sources**
Product group from well-managed
forests and other controlled sources
www.fsc.org Cert no. SA-COC-1565
© 1996 Forest Stewardship Council

Printed and bound in Great Britain by the
MPG Books Group, Bodmin, Cornwall.

Prelude

**French Coast
February 1805**

'Signal from the commodore, sir: investigate strange sail.' Midshipman Bright suppressed his shiver as the northeaster sliced through his reefer jacket.

'Acknowledge, Mr Bright,' Lieutenant Charles Pole ordered. Raising his speaking trumpet, he gave a string of orders that sent the hands to the braces and brought the brig closer to the wind. There was really no need for the trumpet on such a small vessel, but Pole had only been in command for two weeks and felt that he should emphasize his authority at every opportunity.

His Majesty's gun-brig *Stubborn* raised her head to the steep chops of the Channel, shook aside a hatful of spray and plunged on, bowsprit dipping and both masts bending with the weight of canvas. Lieutenant Pole stalked the thirteen paces from the mainmast to the quarterdeck, removed the spyglass from its bracket on the mizzenmast and peered ahead.

After eight years at sea, he could automatically compensate for the roll of the deck, but he could not recognize the type of vessel on which he focused. She was too large for a fishing boat, too low in the water for a coaster and bore a rig unlike anything that he had seen before. He wondered if she could be a Baltic trader; he had heard that they sported a variety of weird and wonderful rigs up there.

'What is she, sir?' Bright hovered at his elbow, shivering with cold.

Pole shook his head. 'I don't know yet.' This was what command was all about, making quick decisions, sailing into excitement and bearding Boney off his own coast. His sudden grin was infectious. 'Make more sail, Mr Bright! I want to close with that vessel!'

'Aye, aye, sir!' Mr Midshipman Bright always showed punctilious respect for the lieutenant, partly because of his rank, but also because Pole was his cousin and had brought him on board as a personal favour.

Pole watched as his men scrambled to make sail, their bare feet pattering on the deck and more canvas breaking out from the already straining masts. He would have to be careful not to overload her, but he knew by the feel of the deck that *Stubborn* had life in her yet. 'One point to larboard, helmsman!'

'Aye, aye, sir.' The helmsman was within six inches of Pole's shoulder, but he bellowed his reply as if he were steering a First Rate 120 and Admiral Nelson himself had given the order.

'What the devil is she?' Pole focused the spyglass again, trying to hold the strange sail in the circle of vision as both vessels heaved on the sea. He did not flinch as a rogue wave spattered

6

him with spindrift.

'Beg pardon, sir, but she might be a blockade runner, some of them have low masts with spreading canvas, so as not to be seen so easy.'

'You could be right, helmsman,' Pole answered absently, relapsing into silence when he realized that he was bandying words with a foremast hand. He cursed his thoughtless lapse into loquacity, for he was a lieutenant in the Royal Navy, commanding his own ship and with the King's authority to uphold.

That vessel was very low in the water and he still did not recognize the rig.

'Smoke, sir!' Midshipman Bright shouted, his voice breaking with excitement. 'She's on fire!'

'The devil she is!' Pole could see the smoke now, a dark smudge barely discernible against the grey clouds that clung to the horizon. 'Damned if I'll lose our prize! That's beer money out there, boys!' He had intended the resulting cheer, but wondered if it was bad for discipline. Without thinking, he reached for the ratlines and scampered aloft, throwing his legs around the crosstrees of the mainmast and balancing easily against the roll and pitch of the brig.

Up here his range of vision was enhanced, so the strange sail appeared closer and he could see a much wider orb of sea and land. There was the coast of France, only two miles to larboard, with the deepwater Baie de l'Isle safe under the bristling batteries that were Bonaparte's defence against the Royal Navy. He grinned to think that he was taunting Boney's vaunted coast of iron and bronze with perfect impunity.

Their quarry looked longer from here, a lean, lithe, low craft with two masts carrying that awkward rig and a third, thicker, mast with barely a scrap of canvas. The smoke seemed to be concentrated around that useless third mast.

She looked dirty, not with the salt-smeared weathering that was common after a hard voyage, but as if she had been deliberately covered in coal dust, like some Geordie collier. Pole glanced down at his own command, with the scrubbed white deck, and the immaculate rigging that the Bosun checked every day. He nodded his pride at the contrast, reflecting that if the strange sail was typical of Johnny Crapaud's standard of seamanship, it was not surprising that the Royal Navy commanded the sea. He wondered if she was perhaps carrying naval stores for the blockaded French warships, or grain for Boney's Army of England that was camped ready to invade.

'She's a Baltic blockade runner!' he yelled, hoping to be thought omniscient, as officers commanding Royal Naval vessels should always be. 'Run out the bow chaser!'

From this height, the men looked foreshortened as they worked on the six-pounder, ramming down the powder and loading it with solid ball before opening the gun-port and hauling on the ropes that thrust its ugly snout forward. Within minutes *Stubborn* changed from a questing terrier to a predatory hound, going in for the kill.

'On the upward roll, boys!' Pole controlled his excitement as he gave the order to open fire. He

8

felt *Stubborn* judder with the recoil, saw orange flame split the jet of white smoke from the cannon's muzzle, and for one brief instant he traced the line of shot before it disappeared into the distance. Raising his spyglass, he watched for the result.

'Over!' he guessed, although he had seen neither a splash nor signs of damage on their prey. 'Fire again, Mr Bright!'

The strange sail had altered course, so she was even more elongated, her masts slightly further apart. This time Pole saw a brief fountain of water where their shot slammed into the sea.

'Short and to starboard!'

Smoke gushed greasily from the vessel as she turned full circle and headed toward them, her sails shivering as she fought to keep the wind. 'She's coming this way, boys! She must be surrendering!'

The crew cheered. Crowded, under-gunned and slow, gun-brigs were not the most popular vessels in which to serve. The navy used them for the awkward tasks, such as probing into enemy anchorages or investigating unknown craft, but they were not fast enough to catch even a half-decent merchant ship and too weak to fight anything more powerful than small privateers. However, there were compensations; discipline was often less severe than in a larger vessel and there were occasional captures, which meant prize money to be squandered in a few hours of roaring riot.

Momentarily forgetting his cherished dignity, Pole waved his hat in the air. 'Let's get closer, boys, before she burns quite away!' He saw movement in the bow of the quarry, grabbed the backstay and slid down to the deck.

'Sir! Charlie! What's that?' Midshipman Bright pointed forward, where something interrupted the even swell of the Channel.

'I've no idea,' Pole stepped to the bulwark and peered over. 'It's like ... a burning boat, coming toward us.' He watched for a moment as the thing came closer. 'It can't be though, because there's no oars, and it's moving against the wind.' He shook his head. 'I've never seen the like before.' Raising his spyglass, he focused on the strange apparition. 'It *is* a boat, I think. Some sort of boat, but there's no sail.'

'It's coming close, sir. Should we not get out of the way?'

'I should say so.' Pole agreed immediately as his incredulity turned to alarm. 'Three points to starboard, helmsman, if you please, fast as you like.'

'Too late, Charlie! It's going to hit us!' Bright stepped back from the bulwark. 'Oh sweet mother!'

One

'Easy, there.'

Hauling at the reins, Matthew Pryde eased the dog cart to a halt. The wheels just touched the kerb of the cobbled street. He smiled at the shop with its familiar sign: *Charles Denton: Purveyor of New and Second Hand Books.* Somebody had been busy with a paintbrush recently, so the gold letters stood out clearly, while the multi-paned window displayed a variety of new and already read books. Looking upward, he admired the display of early geraniums in the windows of the flat above. Trust Kate to enhance her home with something beautiful.

Folding the reins, he jumped to the ground and took a deep breath of the bright air. May was his favourite month, with its almost perfect weather and with every field and tree bright with new growth, so he had enjoyed the short drive from Ottin Hall. It was even better to be back in Ashbourne, with the early sun casting morning shadows and bird call sweetening the air. He grinned; somebody else evidently thought as he did, for there were snatches of song coming

11

from the head of the street. He listened to the words.

We'll shake hands and be friends; if they won't, why, what then?
We'll send our brave Nelson to thrash 'em again!

Matthew sighed, his mood spoiled. Everybody seemed obsessed with warfare, battles and invasion nowadays. He shook away the darkness, refusing to allow songs of Bonaparte's war to ruin his day. With the much happier anticipation of seeing Kate surging within him, he knocked at the shop door.

There were raised voices inside, followed by ponderous footsteps and the drawing of bolts as the door slowly opened.

'Ah, Matthew, my boy.' Charles Denton smiled, adjusting the pince-nez spectacles that threatened to slide from the bridge of his nose. He looked as amiable as ever with his face florid and a badly tied cravat at his throat. 'Come in. She will not be long.'

Matthew bowed briefly, stepped past the crowded bookshelves, ducked under the raised flap that acted as a counter and entered the back-shop-cum-living space.

'Oh sweet Lord, you can't come in here yet! Father, you can't let him in! I'm not ready!' Kate Denton leaped back from the parlour table, both hands to her head and her eyes wide with indignation. Her brown hair was still in curl papers, save for that rebellious tendril that always coiled under her left ear.

'It's all right, Kate, Matthew doesn't mind,' Charles Denton soothed, shaking his head benignly.

'*I* mind, though,' Kate scolded. 'Father! You should have known better.' She turned aside from the circular pier-glass that she had propped up on the table.

'Shall I wait outside?' Matthew could not hide his smile. Kate looked even more appealing than normal in her green dressing gown with the lacy frills, especially when one sleeve was sodden wet where she had inadvertently trailed it in the basin of water that sat beside the pier-glass.

'Yes, yes, do that.' Kate pointed to the table, her sleeve dripping. 'I've found a new book about the latest steam developments for you. Read that until I am ready!'

Matthew lifted the book and retreated to the shop, smiling as Kate first railed at her father, then politely asked for his help in removing the papers from her hair. He was glad that Mr Denton was the object of her tongue this morning. Sitting on the chair provided for the patrons, Matthew looked at the book, although he lifted his head from time to time as Kate's light footsteps pattered in the rooms above and her voice raised in a snatch of song. 'Bonny Tawny Moor', he believed, although Kate was inclined to mingle the words of two or three songs together, hum the parts of which she was unsure and alter the tune as she thought best.

He was too absorbed in a diagram of William Symington's steam paddle tug to notice when the counter flap lifted again, and Kate had to tap her foot on the floor to gain his attention.

'Are you ready?' she asked, standing straight-backed and smiling, waiting for his approval. Short-waisted and narrow in the skirt, her cream gown was obviously new, and she must have spent many hours on the elaborate embroidery around the collars and sleeves. Emerging behind her, Mr Denton raised his eyebrows and nodded encouragingly.

Matthew stood and bowed. 'Miss Denton, I have never seen anything so handsome in my life. I would like to invite you to a ball, but must settle for the May Day festivities at Norrington.'

Kate's curtsy was brief. 'Yes, Matthew, but do you approve of my *gown*?'

He sighed. 'It will have to do,' he said, then laughed at the expression on her face. 'Of course I approve. It's the most beautiful creation I have ever seen you wear.'

'Oh, Matthew!' She pushed at him. 'You were teasing me!' Kate looked at Mr Denton. 'When did he learn to tease, Father? He always wore such a serious Friday face.'

'I believe that you taught him the art, Kate,' Mr Denton said. 'Are you not wearing your spencer? It's chilly for May.' He did not press the point when Kate frowned. 'As you wish. So now, if you are quite finished gathering compli-ments, perhaps we should all be moving?' He glanced significantly at his watch.

'Our carriage awaits,' Matthew said.

'You have a carriage?' Kate sounded excited.

'Nearly. I've borrowed Mr Lamballe's dog

cart,' Matthew explained.

'And how do you find working as an engineer in Kent's first coal mine?' Mr Denton asked, as he always did.

'The occupation is not the most demanding,' Matthew replied, 'but Mr Lamballe is an unfailingly generous employer, despite the meagre returns of his endeavour.' Matthew helped Kate climb up the steep step into the cart. Mr Denton nodded, climbing in the back as Matthew took the reins.

'You were fortunate in obtaining employment so quickly after your return from the north.'

'Yes, sir.' Only the previous year Matthew had completed his first independent engineering commission when he surveyed the site for a lighthouse off the Northumberland coast, and at the same time had discovered his real name and identity.

'If you hurry we will catch them beating the last of the bounds.' Kate adjusted her straw bonnet with its garland of daisies. She sat beside him, looking around as she clutched the ivory handle of her parasol. 'Come along, then.'

It was a three-mile drive from Ashbourne to the village of Norrington, and when they arrived the long street of single-storeyed cottages was lively with festivities.

'This is where I was born, you know,' Kate said proudly, as Matthew eased the dog cart into the only stables and asked the ostler to care for the horse. 'I still think of it as home.'

'I thought Ashbourne was your home.' Matthew could not think of Kate living anywhere other than above her father's bookshop.

She smiled to him. 'Home is where you were happiest,' she said, 'and my memories of Ashbourne are not *altogether* agreeable.' Before Matthew could ask for details, Kate clapped her hands together as a procession of gaily bedecked villagers filed past. 'Oh look! There's the tail of the May Day Parade! I never saw a better!'

Dressed in patchworks of various colours, two men danced in front of the open doors and peered through cottage windows. They approached Matthew, shook severed cow tails in his face and pointed to a third man dressed as a horse.

'You have to feed the Hooden horse,' Kate explained. 'It's beer money for the afternoon cricket match. Just put a farthing in its mouth.' She leaned closer. 'And don't tell me that you're *that* purse-pinched, Matthew, for I'll not believe you.'

The Hooden horse had a carved head with a cleverly hinged mouth that gaped open in expectation. Fiddling in his purse, Matthew extracted a halfpenny and fed the horse. An eager hand grabbed the money and the wooden head nodded in gratitude, before the trio pranced away in search for another victim.

'That was wise,' Mr Denton said quietly. 'If you had not paid up, the two ticklers, that's the men that support the horse, would have set about you with the cow's tails.'

When one of the ticklers began to chant, others in the crowd joined in:

16

'Feed the horse this day in May
Feed the horse for summer
Feed the horse this day in May
Or face an angry tickler!'

'It was worth parting with a halfpenny, then,' Matthew said, and allowed Kate to drag him along the street. She was laughing, exchanging greetings with every person she saw as Mr Denton panted in the rear and tried to maintain his dignity.

'Come along, Mathew, and I'll show you the Chopper.'

'What's a Chopper?'

Kate looked over her shoulder, tipped her bonnet forward and smiled. 'My, Matthew Pryde, what a sheltered life you have led at that school of yours. All mathematics and Latin grammar.'

Many of the cottages of Norrington were bright with flowers, and it seemed that every inhabitant was on the street, either watching or joining in the celebrations. Matthew had spent his boyhood in a London foundlings' hospital, where festivities were unknown, while his youth in Maidhouse College had been a mixture of austerity and torment. He was now twenty-eight years old and had never participated in such an event.

'Why is it called May Day when today is the thirteenth?'

'It's Old May Day, silly!' Kate had her hand on his sleeve as she pulled him along, cheerfully using the pagoda summit of her parasol to clear

17

a space before them. 'This used to be the first of May, before the calendar changed!'

'Of course,' Matthew murmured. He knew that he should be enjoying himself, but felt out of place in this atmosphere of senseless frivolity, and tense with the knowledge that today could be crucial for his future.

He looked uncertainly toward Kate; once before he had asked her to be his wife, and she had turned him down. Now that his finances were more secure, he would ask her again. He took a deep breath to control his nerves.

'Kate?'

'Not now, Matthew.' She tapped his arm with her parasol. 'Look: there they are!'

The tall and muscular man strode cheerfully in front of a gaggle of boys. He carried a large felling-axe over his shoulder and a pair of long clippers thrust through the belt of his breeches.

'That's the Chopper. His name is Edmund Gambill, he's the blacksmith and he leads the Boundary men. See the axe? He uses that to chop down any obstructions that have been placed around the village boundary, and the clippers to cut away any thorns or anything.' Kate leaned forward. 'They're keeping the parish boundary secure against any encroachment, you see.'

'I see.' Matthew tried to show some interest in this archaic ceremony. 'And the boys?' They each carried a long wand of peeled willow.

'They have to beat the boundary stones so they learn where the parish ends.' Kate grabbed at his arm. 'You drove so *slowly*, Matthew, that they're

18

nearly finished. If we hurry we'll catch them at the Gospel Oak at the edge of the Common.' She looked over her shoulder. 'Come on, Father!'

'You cut along without me,' Mr Denton said. 'I'll come at my own pace. Old age does not come alone, you see.'

The Gospel Oak thrust upward at the junction of two fields, its ancient branches spreading tangled shadows over both parishes. To the west was Norrington, to the south Old Ottin and to the east and north the common's rugged grass stretched onward toward the distant sea.

'There could be some mischief at this last marker.' Kate had relinquished her hold on Matthew's arm and pressed forward with the rest. 'Your Mr Lamballe owns the land on the Old Ottin side, and he's quite the *newcomer*. We don't know what he'll do.' She spoke over her shoulder, eyes bright. 'The villages quarrel rather a lot, you understand.'

There was a group of people waiting around a wagonette in the adjoining field, watching their approach. Matthew could feel the tension building, as if some ancient drama was about to be revealed.

Edmund the Chopper strode to the oak and laid both hands on the trunk. He raised his voice in a shout that must have been heard right around both parishes.

'Norrington has arrived! Do you greet us in friendship or in animosity?'

One man detached himself from the Old Ottin group. As tall as Edmund, he wore tight yellow nankeens, with a small-sword at his hip and a blue coat that fell to his knees. The elegantly embroidered waistcoat and powdered hair seemed out of place in this rural setting.

Kate slipped closer to Matthew 'Is that Mr Lamballe? He looks *very* foreign, doesn't he? He's as gaily dressed as a bullfinch in spring-time.'

Matthew nodded. For all her extensive reading, he guessed that Kate's idea of a foreigner was anybody born outwith eastern Kent.

'That's my employer, Mr Lamballe. He's a Royalist from France, an émigré.'

Kate pouted. 'Employed by a Jacques Bonhomme! I never heard of anything so queer.'

'He's no Jack Bonhomme, Kate. Mr Lamballe's a wealthy man.'

Kate's pout became even more pronounced. 'An émigré with blunt? That's a bit smoky; most of them haven't a farthing to scratch themselves with.'

Matthew began to tease her for using such common language, but she shushed him into silence. *'Watch*, Matthew.'

As Mr Lamballe stepped forward, the Norrington boys stopped chattering and huddled together. Kate spoke in a whisper that could be heard halfway across the common. 'If he chooses friendship, then all's bowman and it's beer and civil whiskers, but if he chooses animosity, then each boy will be beaten as a reminder to keep the boundary secure.'

'Welcome to you, people of Norrington!' The new landowner of Old Ottin spoke with hardly a twist of an accent. 'The parishioners of Old

20

Ottin greet you...' He paused for a moment, allowing the tension to build. The Norrington boys began to look apprehensive. *'In friendship!'*

There were cheers from the villagers, relief from the boys and a general surge forward as people from both parishes merged around the oak and spilled onto the common. On a signal from Mr Lamballe a host of servants delved inside the wagonette to produce kegs of beer and great trays of bread and cheese. Within minutes the people of both parishes were huddled together in good fellowship.

'Enchanté, Monsieur Lamballe,' Kate murmured, raising a very unladylike tankard of beer, then nudged Matthew. 'Just listen to the Banbury stories.'

'We'll beat you Ottins this time,' Edmund boasted, brandishing the curving cricket bat that he held. 'No doubt about it.'

'Beat us? When the devil's *blind*, man! You've not beaten us in twenty years!' The Ottin spokesman was lean and wiry, with his face darkened by weather. 'Mr Lamballe has promised a crown piece to every man when we win.' He smiled. 'Just as we'll win the stool ball.'

'The what?' Matthew asked.

'You'll see,' Kate promised, evidently enjoying her position of guide and adviser.

Matthew watched as the Ottin spokesman suspended a three-legged milking stool from the branch of the Gospel Oak and chose a team of eleven women. They gathered in a noisy group, exchanging raucous banter with their men and throwing challenges to their Norrington rivals.

Matthew took a deep breath. 'Kate,' he bowed stiffly, as if to a stranger, 'I would like a few minutes of your undivided attention.'

She mocked him with a curtsy before shaking her head. 'Not just now, Matthew, for I am to play for Norrington!'

Her joy stilled Matthew's impatience. 'Then I would like to speak with you when you are finished.'

Kate raised her eyebrows. 'Since when did we need such formality?' She chalked an image of Bonaparte's face on the seat of the stool, much to the delight of both sets of villagers. 'Let's have a target to aim it.'

'Hit the ogre hard,' Mr Lamballe agreed, standing at Matthew's side as the women took their places.

'I'd be obliged if you would look after this.' Kate handed Matthew her bonnet, shook out her hair so it cascaded in a curled brown mane around her shoulders, tied it back with a single ribbon and stepped determinedly forward. She accepted a long-handled, broad-headed bat and prepared to defend the stool against the Old Ottin attack.

'It's a curious game, women throwing a ball at a stool.' Mr Lamballe shook his head. 'I suppose it is like cricket, in a way. I hope that you have remembered that you are playing for Old Ottin today?'

Matthew nodded. When Mr Lamballe had ask-ed him to play he had agreed at once, without realizing the depth of rivalry between the two villages. It was only when Kate complained at his lack of loyalty that he realized his decision would be unpopular in Norrington. 'I'll be the worst player at the wicket,' he said.

'Oh, I think the boot will be on the other leg, Mr Pryde. You were educated at Maidhouse College, so you must be an expert cricketer.'

Matthew watched as Kate knocked the ball a good distance into the common, dropped her bat and ran around the marked area. The crowd roared their approval, with one girl squealing and clapping her hands excitedly. 'I think that Kate is far better at stool ball than I am at cricket.'

'I expect at least fifty runs from you,' Mr Lamballe told him gravely. He lowered his voice. 'It is strange to think that Bonaparte is little more than thirty miles from here, mustering his armies, and here we are watching women play village sports.'

Kate hit another ball and scampered forward, her skirts in a flurry and her hair, of which she was so proud, bouncing madly.

'There's my Katty!' Edmund roared, winking to Matthew. 'There's the proud gal of Norrington.'

The proud gal looked pleased at the praise, and struck the next two balls just as sweetly. Matthew shook his head as Kate tried another ambitious swipe with the bat, missed completely and stumbled forward. The ball bounced off Bonaparte's nose. 'And there's a corker for you, Boney!' somebody shouted.

The Norrington section of the crowd groaned

while the wiry Old Ottin spokesman smiled his approval and looked slyly at Lamballe. 'Nelson himself could not have done better.'

'Thank God for the Royal Navy,' Lamballe agreed, 'although their blockade seems to pose no problems for some mariners.' He nodded toward a small group of people who had appeared on the fringes of the crowd.

There were six of them, two women and four weather-beaten men who moved with the wary confidence of predatory cats. 'You're a gentleman, I can tell,' one of the women said, as she approached Matthew. She was perhaps in her late twenties, with cheeks brightened by a lifetime of sea breezes and eyes as clear and direct as a spring morning, 'and I'm sure your wife would appreciate a new shawl.'

Kneeling before him, she spread out a selection of silks and shawls that would have graced any shop in London's Bond Street. 'Best French silk,' she announced, 'at the lowest Deal prices.'

'Smuggled?' Matthew asked, about to turn her away.

'Of course,' the woman said, 'by Joss Page himself.'

Matthew had heard of Joss Page, the Deal owler who once boasted that he could smuggle the King of France past Boney himself, if His Majesty had not been fool enough to lose his head. 'I do not yet have a wife,' he said, 'but do you have a shawl suitable for a lady?'

The woman's smile caught him by surprise. 'Your sweetheart will find nothing better between here and Paris,' she promised. 'Now watch this.' Selecting one of her shawls, she carefully threaded it through a silver ring that she removed from her finger. 'As fine as gossamer,' she said, 'and fit to grace Queen Charlotte herself.'

Matthew smiled, picturing the shawl covering Kate's shoulders. 'How much?' he asked, and started at the price.

'Is she not worth it?' The woman spoiled her gentle smile by producing a clay pipe and jamming it, bowl-downward, between her teeth.

'Of course.' Reaching for his purse, Matthew was aware that Kate had joined him.

'What are you doing?' She was flushed and breathless, but had replaced her bonnet so her hair was nearly under control.

'Ensuring that my purse is even more pinched.' Matthew handed over the money, watching the woman's hands close over the coins without a qualm. He saw Kate's mouth open in a protest that ended as he placed the shawl over her shoulders.

'It's exceedingly delightful,' Kate said, looking sideways at herself. 'And I thought you an old screw with your money.' Leaning forward, she touched his face with a gentle hand. 'Thank you, Matthew. You can be the kindest of men, sometimes. Now, let's find a space where we can sit, for I am quite fatigued.'

Despite Kate's best efforts, Old Ottin had won the stool ball by a massive eight runs, and there was despondency among the Norrington crowd as they gathered to drink Mr Lamballe's beer and eat his bread and cheese.

'It's a tradition that the landowner of Old Ottin feeds the five thousand,' Kate told Matthew. She leaned against the trunk of the Gospel Oak, watching Edmund set up the wicket for the cricket match. 'It's also something of a tradition that Old Ottin beat us in everything. We haven't won the stool ball since I was small, and I doubt that even Father can remember us winning the cricket.' She slid closer so he could feel the warmth of her body. 'But you have something to say to me, I think? You wanted' – she deepened her voice in gentle mockery – 'a few minutes of my undivided attention.'

Matthew nodded. Now that the time had arrived, he felt suddenly nervous. He took a deep breath, knowing that his whole future happiness could turn on her reply. 'Kate...'

'Matthew Pryde? Where is Matthew Pryde?' Mr Lamballe's powdered wig was conspicuous as he ploughed through the crowd. 'We need you for the cricket, Mr Pryde!'

'Not now.' Frustration nearly made Matthew swear, but Kate smiled.

'It's all right, Matthew. I'm coming to watch you anyway, and I'll be waiting when the game is finished.' She patted his arm. 'Come along now, and remember to do your best, even if it is for Old Ottin.'

The crowd moved noisily on, to reconvene about quarter of a mile inside the common. Matthew looked around, realizing that this must be a traditional spot for the match. They were in a slight hollow, with springy turf much fertilized by the sheep and cattle of both parishes. To the north and west, cottonwool clouds caressed the sensual curves of the Downs, while the shingled broach spire of Norrington church pierced the horizon, just off centre from the Gospel Oak. Behind him, to the south, the irregular rim of the hollow hid the Channel, where Lord Keith's restless ships restrained the French.

The crowd had formed a circle around the wicket, with a definite gap between the Old Ottin and the Norrington contingents and tension crisping the air. Matthew sat beside Kate, as Mr Lamballe marched out to the striking crease. He cradled his bat and fought his frustration.

'Kate...'

'Not now, Matthew.' She brushed him aside, concentrating on keeping the score.

'But, Kate...'

'We can speak later.' She looked up, darting a brief smile. 'It's all right, Matthew, I'll still be here. I'm sure you can exercise patience for a little while longer.' She pulled her new shawl tightly across her shoulders, adjusted the angle of her bonnet and cut another notch in the stick.

Kate gave a satisfied chuckle as half the crowd cheered, and when Matthew looked up, Lamballe was walking away from his stance, shaking his head.

'Clean bowled, by God!' somebody yelled.

'*Merde*,' Lamballe said.

Matthew glanced at Kate, 'I wonder what that means,' but Kate hid her smile.

'Something not at all gentlemanly, I fear.'

'Ah.' Matthew grinned. 'I forgot that you spoke French.'

'A lady should be fluent in modern languages,' Kate told him with hardly a hint of ridicule. 'And you are *fully* aware that I am a lady.'

Matthew felt the colour rush to his face as he bowed toward her. On their very first meeting he had foolishly asked if she was a lady, with unfortunate results. She had tormented him with the memory ever since.

'In you come, Matthew,' Lamballe invited. He raised his voice. 'Now you'll see something, Norrington! Mr Pryde used to play for Maidhouse College!'

The lithe bowler grinned, tossing the ball from hand to hand with casual skill that Matthew could only admire. 'Take your stance then, Mr Pryde.'

The bat felt heavy in his hand, the curved end awkward to balance on the rough turf. Matthew looked down the length of the wicket, aware of the bowler's smile, more aware of the hushed crowd. A skylark called above, and Kate's voice sounded.

'Good luck, Matthew!'

The bowler padded backward, turned and began his run up to the wicket. He seemed to move slowly, his feet rising easily, before landing with a soft spring that flattened the individual blades of grass.

Matthew had been watching closely. He knew that the bowler always shortened his stride just before he released the ball, and he threw alternately to the left and right. The lark was still singing as the bowler reached the crease; his arm swung back, then the ball spun forward.

Matthew stepped forward, swinging the bat mightily, to hear the hiss of air as he failed to connect and the sharp click of leather on stumps. There was a yell of triumph from Norrington, Lamballe was shaking his head in disappointment and Matthew began the lonely walk back.

Old Ottin made a poor seventy-eight runs that innings, but Lamballe shrugged.

'Never mind, gentlemen, we'll knock them out for less.' He tossed the ball to Matthew, who nearly fumbled the catch. 'Let's see how good the bowling was at Maidhouse College. We've already seen the batting!'

Edmund had taken first bat, and looked very capable as he stood at the wicket. Matthew bowed politely, which brought an ironic cheer from the supporters of both parishes, tossed the ball into the air to show that he meant business and began his run-up. The ball felt heavy in his hand, although he knew it was less than six ounces, while the stumps, twenty-four inches high and seven inches apart, looked a ridiculously small target.

He reached the crease, swung his arm back and then forward, releasing the ball, which flew high into the air before bouncing just in front of Edmund. Matthew heard the crack of wood on leather and ducked as the ball soared past his head. The Norrington contingent's cheer drowned out the Old Ottin groans.

'Well hit!' Lamballe praised the opposition.

'Matthew!' Kate was not so sporting. 'That was useless! You're meant to be on their side, not ours!'

With his confidence shaken by the first ball, Matthew struggled to complete his over, feeling only shame as the Norrington strikers knocked his best efforts all over the Common. He could feel the disgust of the Old Ottin crowd, and heard somebody wonder if he was playing to lose for the sake of his sweetheart.

'You tried your best, Matthew,' Mr Lamballe was not a man to bear grudges, 'but I think we shall try a fresh bowler now.'

'You go to deep fine leg,' a man in moleskin trousers ordered, 'that's away over there, right out at the boundary, behind the striker.'

Matthew nodded, realizing that he was being positioned in a place where he was least likely to see the ball, and therefore unable to cause any damage to the Old Ottin cause.

For the next hour he watched as the moleskin-trousered man and a worthy by the name of Long Tom attempted to whittle away Norrington's strikers. The Norrington score mounted.

'Mr Pryde!'

Edmund had hit the ball over his shoulder, so it sped high and wide. Matthew watched its flight, instinctively calculating its probable destination. He took six steps backward, extended both hands and waited for its arrival.

The ball struck his hands with painful force but he held on, wondering why the crowd suddenly cheered.

'Well caught, Matthew Pryde!' Mr Lamballe was grinning, with one hand raised in approval. 'I knew you would not let us down!'

'So it's fielding you learned at Maidhouse!'

The moleskin-trousered man pounded his shoulder blades with a heavy hand. 'Come on, then, and we'll put you in silly midwicket. You can be more useful there!'

The crowd seemed friendlier when Matthew took his new position, much closer to the wicket. Now that he had reduced fielding to simple mathematics, he could relax and enjoy the match.

Matthew watched for a few minutes, working out the angle of ball and bat, then, ignoring a warning wave, altered his position slightly.

He saw moleskin trousers make his run, saw the ball bounce twice, saw the hitter step forward to meet it and he ran forward, ten quick steps that brought him to a small lump in the ground. Moleskin trousers was waving him back, shouting something as he jumped, but Matthew knew that the striker would hit the ball short and oblique; he had no choice, given the angle of the bowl, and simple mathematics dictated that the ball must come to this position. He felt the solid smack of leather in the palm of his hand, threw it back without thought and heard the satisfying crack as the Norrington wicket fell.

'Out!' The shout contained more surprise than triumph. 'It's a draw!'

Mr Lamballe was shaking his hand, half the parish of Old Ottin were surrounding him, asking how he knew where the ball was going, the elderly striker was banging his bat against the turf as if it had offended him and Kate was coolly totting up the notches for both teams, as if she was not already fully aware of the score.

'Seventy-eight,' she confirmed. 'It is a draw.' She looked at Matthew, her eyes expressionless. 'We might have won if you had muffed that catch.'

'Time for more beer,' Edmund announced gravely. He shouldered the bat with which he had done so much execution. 'And next year we will have Matthew on our team. He qualifies by his attachment to Miss Denton.'

Matthew felt himself colour as half the population of both villages smiled knowingly, and hands thundered on his shoulders as he moved toward Kate. She was suddenly smiling. 'I'm glad you did well, Matthew and I forgive you for having played on the wrong side. Trust you to be different; neither a bowler nor a batter but a fielder!'

'I have something more important to speak to you about,' Matthew said, guiding her through the crowd.

'More important than the May Day cricket game?' She tapped him teasingly with her parasol. 'Don't you know that your catches will be the topic of conversation for months to come?'

Stepping round a riotous rabble of children, Matthew led her to the shade of the Gospel Oak. She trotted at his side, occasionally throwing him a curious look.

'Kate,' Matthew began, and stopped. Now he had the opportunity, he did not know how to begin. He had rehearsed this moment for weeks, but with these bright grey eyes fixed on him, he felt the words drain away.

'Yes?' Kate prompted, eyes wide.

The colour rushed to Matthew's face. 'Kate. I once asked if you would marry me.'

'I remember,' she said slowly. 'We were both very young.' She opened her parasol and inspected the green silk.

'You said *no* to me then.'

'I remember that, too.' Kate had found something very interesting in the branches of the tree above.

'If I asked you again, what would you say now?' Matthew hated the tremble in his voice. He could feel a single tear of sweat slither from his forehead down to the side of his nose.

Kate closed her parasol and allowed her gaze to leave the tree. 'Matthew, my dear, *dear* Matthew.' She looked at him, one hand reaching out. He saw the shadows behind her eyes and knew what her answer would be.

'Mr Pryde!' The man was gasping for breath as he lumbered over the rough grass. Sweat smeared the dirt on the face and soaked through the stained clothes of a miner. 'You must come quickly, Mr Pryde. There are men trapped far in bye. They're at the deepest level and the pump has jammed.'

'Kate?' Matthew looked at her, but she pushed him away.

'Go, Matthew. Attend to your duty.' She turned abruptly away and he was left with the gasping miner.

Two

There was a crowd gathered at the pithead, men and women talking fearfully and looking down the wide shaft that descended into awful blackness. A host of rooks perched on the immobile drum that should have been hauling up corves of coal, while there was no sound from the Boulton and Watt engine that worked the winding gear. Anxious miners surrounded him as he slid from the dog cart.

'What's happening, Houghton?' He addressed the stocky overman that Mr Lamballe had lured from the Northumberland collieries with the promise of shorter hours and better pay. Houghton was responsible for the pit in the absence of Mr Lamballe, who had appointed himself mine manager.

'Roof's fallen, Mr Pryde.'

'Anybody hurt?'

'One drawer killed, Mr Pryde, but there are others trapped beyond the fall, or maybe underneath it.' Houghton drew an arm across his face, smearing a clear swathe through the dirt. 'We can't get close, though; the air is bad.'

34

Matthew nodded. There should have been three steam engines working constantly, but only two were in operation. 'What's wrong with the pump?' Without a constant new flow, the air at the bottom of the vertical shaft, the well of the pit, would become progressively more dangerous. Augmenting the horror of poisonous gases, the fear of a firedamp explosion haunted every collier.

Houghton shook his head. 'Don't know, Mr Pryde. I'm no engineer.'

'Show me,' Matthew ordered. 'And until the pump is fixed, nobody goes down.' There was no point in endangering more lives in a rescue attempt that was bound to fail.

'Yes, Mr Pryde.' Houghton hesitated. 'I stopped the winding gear, but some men refused to leave the pit bottom.'

Matthew sighed. He had learned that northern miners were tenacious, hard-working and tough, but few were overly educated. 'Get them up, Mr Houghton, as quick as you can.'

Opening the door of the engine house, he strode to the steam pump. It took him only five minutes to see that the mechanics were perfect, so the fault must lie with one of the boilers. He knew this machine as well as he knew his own face. Distantly aware of the echoing shouts as Houghton bellowed down the shaft, he concentrated on the pump. 'Seventy-four-inch diameter cylinder,' he intoned, 'ten feet long, with four boilers and cast-iron pipes.'

'Yes, Mr Pryde, if you say so.' Houghton sounded nervous. 'They're refusing to come, up,

Mr Pryde.'

'Leave them, then,' Matthew decided. 'And take a roll call. See who's missing.' He checked for a loose connection, swearing when he failed to see anything immediately wrong. 'There might be a blockage. Maybe a bubble of air.'

'The air down below will be getting badly foul, Mr Pryde.'

'I know that, damn it!' Matthew snapped. 'Have you done that roll call yet?' He waited until Houghton had gone before he uncoupled the connections, aware that every minute was vital. Before he had accepted this position, he had toured a number of northern mines, where every engineer and experienced miner had emphasized the dangers of bad air. It was imperative to keep the air circulating down the pit, for the deeper the shaft, the more likely that there would be a build-up of gases. There were various types, from choke-damp that would slowly suffocate a man, to firedamp that could lead to an explosion powerful enough to destroy the entire mine and its contingent of colliers. Foul air was possibly the worst of the miner's many fears.

Matthew worked on, testing every component, every nut and bolt, every moving part, for he knew that even the slightest fault could halt this mighty machine. The murmur of voices from outside increased as the news spread and all the colliery workers and their families gathered outside.

'What's he *doing* in there,' a woman wailed. 'Doesn't he know that my fella's down there?'

36

'So's my butty.' The deeper, male voice sounded angry. 'Bloody *gentlemen* don't care about us.'

At last Matthew found the fault, a very slight bend in one of the supporting cranks, just enough to prevent the machinery from use. 'Got you!' Reaching for a hammer, he tapped the crank straight again and ducked back when it began to move. It was frustrating that something so simple could cause so much trouble. He raised his voice. 'Right! Build the fires and get steam up again!'

Houghton appeared and shoved a piece of paper into his hand. 'There's over a score missing, Mr Pryde, but I don't know how many are just refusing to come up, and how many are trapped.'

Matthew nodded as he heard the huff of the steam pump awakening, so that life-giving air could again flow underground. 'Right.' He nodded to the banksman, who supervised the arrival and departure of coal and workers down the well of the pit. 'I need two lanterns and spare candles.'

'Are you going down?' Houghton sounded surprised.

'We are,' Matthew confirmed. He looked at the steam-powered winding engine that chuffed at the pithead. The great drums were motionless above his head. As soon as he had taken over the position, he had insisted on replacing Mr Lamballe's horse-powered winding gear with a steam engine, but he still felt nervous when he began a descent.

'It's a very wide entrance,' he said, as he always did. Mr Lamballe's pithead was nearly twice as wide as any that he had examined in Northumberland, with a consequent increase in the speed at which colliers could descend and coal could be brought up. Matthew pondered Lamballe's request for some form of device to carry a group of men, rather than have them travel individually. The idea was sound, if expensive, and he found the technical aspects fascinating.

Matthew attempted to concentrate on such engineering problems; anything to distract him from the swooping plunge into solid darkness. 'Get everybody back to work,' he ordered, 'except at the face where the rock fall was. There is no sense in people hanging around worrying when there is work to be done.' He looked upward at the great drum that would soon be turning as the winding machinery dropped him far down into the earth.

There was a hemp rope, two inches in diameter, attached to an empty corf, the wheeled wickerwork basket that carried coal. 'We go down two at a time,' he decided.

Unwilling to reveal his nervousness, Matthew stepped inside the corf, ignoring the dirt and coal dust that smeared his clothes. He grabbed hold of the rope for balance, waited for Houghton to join him and nodded to the banksman. 'Let her drop.'

As always, he found the mechanics of the descent fascinating, from the steam engine that drove the winding drums to the grooves down which the corf slid. He was no longer shocked at the speed of their descent, but still ducked involuntarily as they passed a corf that was already being hauled up. The few hundred-weight of coal that it contained did not seem worth the price of a human life.

As they slid into the black, Matthew remembered his first meeting with Mr Lamballe.

The wind had roared raw from the east, dragging heavy clouds across the Downs and clattering branches into a mad devil's jig. Matthew had huddled deep into his travelling cloak, jammed the tricorne hat firmly onto his head and guided his ancient hack through the pillared gates of the property. Orchards and parkland surrounded Ottin Hall, but the house was old and more dilapidated than Matthew had expected, with geese running loose in the cobbled courtyard and a host of slovenly servants. A surly stable boy accepted the reins.

'Pray come this way, Mr Pryde' – Mr Lamballe was a tall man, dressed ostentatiously in unfashionable knee-breeches and a silk waistcoat, but his handshake was welcoming and his manner pleasant as he conducted Matthew to an extensive library near the centre of the house – 'and I will tell you of my fears and desires.'

Waiting until his host had seated himself behind a vast mahogany desk, Matthew accepted his invitation to sit. Overhead, a brass chandelier swung slowly in the draught from a huge fireplace.

'You are wondering how I come to be here?'

When Mr Lamballe smiled, his eyes looked intensely blue. 'Of course you are. I would, if I were you.'

Matthew shook his head. 'I would not be so impolite, sir.'

'No? With your country at war and only twenty miles of water separating England from the Ogre of Europe? Politeness may be an English virtue, Mr Pryde, but sometimes it is misplaced.' Close to, Lamballe was older than Matthew had thought, perhaps nearer forty than thirty, with lines of strain around his mouth and eyes. 'I am an émigré, Mr Pryde, thrown out of my country by the Revolution and waiting my chance to return.'

Matthew nodded. 'Yes, sir.' He hesitated for a second. 'I was not sure if you were a French aristocrat, or perhaps came from one of the Channel Islands.'

'French, certainly,' Lamballe's smile broadened, 'but not of the aristocracy. Like yourself, I am of the bourgeoisie. A gentleman, rather than a noble.'

Matthew bowed from his seat. 'I understand, sir.' Hundreds of these scared refugees had fled from the Terror in France and now waited for Britain to create a revival of their fortunes. Most were penniless, but Mr Lamballe appeared economically secure.

'I was a financier,' Lamballe explained further. 'I dealt with money, and when I realized that there was trouble coming, I sent funds over to London.' He smiled, lifting both hands in the air as a gesture that Matthew would have described as thoroughly French. 'And thanks to your stock exchange, I have prospered in my exile.'

Matthew nodded. 'Yes, sir.' He was unsure how he felt about foreign refugees able to make money and buy property in England when he was struggling to survive.

'My manners! Do forgive me!' Reaching forward, Lamballe rang a small brass bell and ordered brandy and two glasses from the servant who arrived. 'Although I am parted from France, I still retain some contacts,' he said, 'and there is no finer maker of friendship than cognac.'

Matthew had never cultivated a taste for brandy, and allowed the liquid time to explore his mouth before swallowing. The fiery explosion always took him by surprise.

'So.' Lamballe seemed pleased at Matthew's reaction. 'France is like that. Nothing is what it seems.' He leaned back in his seat. 'And you will be wondering what possible business we have together?'

Matthew fought for his voice. 'I was, sir.'

'Coal.' Lamballe looked directly across the table to Matthew. 'Our mutual business will be in coal.'

'Coal?'

'Indeed,' Lamballe nodded solemnly. 'Only three things keep this country safe from the little corporal.' He held up three fingers. 'One is the Royal Navy, which guards the great moat of La Manche, your English Channel. The second is the will of the British people. And the third is money, which pays for the Continental armies

41

that constantly rise to fight the evil republic.'

'Perhaps,' Matthew conceded, unable to see which way the conversation was headed.

'Bear with me, Mr Pryde,' Lamballe said, 'and you will see that I am right. You build the navy with timber, much of which is imported – and therefore bought. The will of the people is bolstered by good food and prosperity – again, money. And what makes the money to buy Austrian armies and Austrian blood?'

'Trade?'

'Yes indeed. Trade and industry.' Lamballe nodded. 'You have the finest manufactories in the world, and the most extensive trading network. What powers these factories? Coal. And what keeps the people of London, centre of trade, warm in winter? Coal. And from where does that coal come?'

'Northumberland, mainly,' Matthew said.

'Yes.' Lamballe rose to his feet, brandy sloshing from his glass as he paced around the library. 'Most of London's coal comes from Northumberland. It comes down the east coast in colliers that sometimes sail in convoy and sometimes alone. Each collier carries an average of three hundred tons of coal, and there are around five thousand voyages a year. Five thousand ships carrying coal the entire length of England.'

'Yes,' Matthew agreed. Northumberland had supplied coal to London for centuries; he saw no need to elaborate.

'And without that coal, London would freeze, or at least suffer. Industry would lessen and there would be discontent. The North Country colliers keep strong the heart of England.'

Matthew nodded again.

'Well, Mr Pryde, Bonaparte is equally aware of this somewhat grimy Achilles heel to the powerhouse of his enemies. If you were he, would you not seek to slash this sooty vein? Would you not send privateers and warships to patrol the east coast?'

Matthew tried to put himself in the place of the French leader. 'Possibly,' he admitted.

'I would. Did you read any history during your education, Mr Pryde?'

Matthew nodded. 'A little' he said, cautiously.

'Then you will know that the Scots always targeted Newcastle. They knew just how valuable the coal trade was to London, and by capturing Newcastle they could choke London of its fuel. And now, even the Royal Navy help the French cause. In the last war, before the Peace of Amiens, the navy press-ganged nearly three thousand seamen from Newcastle and Sunderland. That is three thousand less men to man the colliers. And then there is the weather; did you know that in 1800, sixty-nine colliers were shipwrecked?'

Matthew shook his head. 'No, sir, I did not.' He sipped at his brandy, now more hardened to the taste and effect. 'But there are other pits, sir, other coalfields. Surely coal can be transported by canal?'

'Surely it should, Mr Pryde, but the Northumberland coal owners always delay the parliamentary passage of canal navigation acts. They guard their own interests by adding clauses that pile huge taxes on canal barges that carry coal. They maintain their monopoly of the London coal trade, with all the inherent disadvantages to England, and consequent benefit to *Bonaparte*!' Lamballe made the name sound like a curse.

'I see, sir.' Matthew watched as Lamballe slammed down his empty glass. 'But I don't quite understand where I fit in.'

'Then I shall bring enlightenment, Mr Pryde. I have two problems, you see.' Lamballe glared fiercely at Matthew. 'I have begun to dig for coal in Kent, but my methods are old-fashioned and crude. That is where you can help, Mr Pryde. You are an engineer.'

'I am, sir.'

'You are an engineering man, Mr Pryde, and I am a frightened man. At this minute Bonaparte is massing his men across the Channel. He has a hundred and sixty thousand soldiers poised to land in the Isle of Thanet, only a hatful of miles from here. If he invades, then I am dead.'

'We are all in danger, sir,' Matthew reminded.

Lamballe shrugged. 'Bonaparte *may* kill you, sir, but he assuredly *would* kill all the émigrés. So this is a personal war, Mr Pryde. I oppose the ogre out of self-interest, not from a love of England. I am honest, you see.'

Matthew allowed himself a tight smile. 'I see, sir.'

'There will be no mercy for men like me, and I hear that Bonaparte likes to place captured émigrés face-up on the guillotine. I have no wish to watch the blade descend on my throat, sir, so I shall spend every penny that I have in helping

44

this country that has given me life. For my own selfish reasons, you understand.'

Lamballe's smile was so genuine that Matthew grinned back. 'Not entirely selfish, sir, I am sure.'

'There are large coalfields on the opposite side of the Channel, Mr Pryde, and I believe that they extend to my lands.' The smile became even broader. 'A coal mine in Kent might even make me a profit, while saving London the expense and danger of the long sea passage from Newcastle.' He leaned forward. 'I would you to be the mine's engineer, Mr Pryde.'

'Sir.' Matthew shook his head. 'I believe you have been misinformed. Do not think me ungrateful, but I am no mining engineer.'

'Then *learn*,' Lamballe said simply. 'This is a completely new mine, Mr Pryde, so I need a man of vision and enthusiasm. Help me modernize and run my colliery and we will bloody Bonaparte's nose for him, we will save England millions in transport costs, provide thousands of Northumberland seamen for the Royal Navy and keep the wheels of commerce turning.' The smile returned. 'And more importantly, you will keep my head attached to my neck.'

Matthew stood up and took three paces to the long window. He looked out over lawns whitened with frost to a copse of tall winter-bare trees. An apple orchard ruffled downwards to a hop-house, outside which a shepherdess spoke with her sweetheart. For a moment Matthew contemplated what Bonaparte's infantry would do with such a scene, and the barbarity and horror that invasion would bring.

'You have your engineer, sir.' Even as he spoke, he wondered how much of his decision was influenced by patriotism, and how much by self-interest. Only regular employment would enable him to seek Kate's hand.

The corf slowed just before it reached the pit bottom, and both men jumped onto the damp ground. Matthew held up his lantern so the flickering light reflected on the iron railway that he had installed, and revealed that the roof was a good three feet above their heads.

'When I worked in Mr Ogden's pit in Northumberland,' Houghton said, 'he would never have allowed so much space. It's wasted effort, that's what it is.'

'Lead on,' Matthew said, and followed Houghton through a child-tended fire door and along the main roadway, which sloped gradually to the south and east.

'This is far too wide as well,' Houghton grumbled. 'Mr Lamballe should concentrate on the coalface, not on making luxurious tunnels. There's no profit in it.'

Matthew said nothing. He could not consider profit at a time when men were suffering and dying, crushed under thousands of tons of rock deep beneath the cliffs of Kent.

After only a few minutes underground, Matthew felt the sweat starting from his body as the combination of humidity and foul air pressed down upon him. He heard a constant murmur in the distance, distorted by echoes, the sound of

46

human voices uplifted in foul cursing and the drumming of iron picks against rock and seams of coal.

Houghton led him on to a side shaft, and then down a steep slope into a scene that Dante would have flinched from painting.

Crouching under headroom of something less than four feet, a stream of people hauled and pushed wickerwork corves up the slope. 'Putters,' Houghton explained, needlessly.

Matthew could smell their sweat before he clearly saw them, and lifted his lantern to make sure he kept out of their way. It was the putters' job to move the coal from the coalface to the foot of the pit, and they swore as they hauled and pushed the laden corf along the rails. Dressed only in a filthy chemise that barely reached mid-thigh, and a round cotton cap squeezed onto curled hair that could have been attractive in different surroundings, the first putter slipped, cursed and recovered.

The light glinted from the gold rings that dangled from her ears, and reflected from the leather belt that passed round her waist. Attached to the belt, a chain extended between her legs to the corf, clinking dolefully as if she were a convicted criminal rather than an honest colliery woman.

A young girl, known as a foal as she had not yet escaped from childhood, sobbed as she pushed at the rear of the corf. Light from the lantern showed that there was nearly as much stone as coal in the corf.

'Foul coal,' Houghton said. 'There's not much

profit in this pit.'

A few weeks ago, Matthew would have been shocked at Houghton's callous disregard of the women and young girls who worked underground, but now he no more heeded them than he did the male miners. They were as much part of the colliery as stythe or gullets.

'How far to the fall?'

The putters halted, gasping. The foal jerked a thumb downward. 'Twenty-score yards.' She coughed and spat a mixture of phlegm and coal dust onto the ground.

Nodding, Matthew continued. There was a vertical shaft ahead, and he backed onto a wooden ladder to descend. A tiny boy, eyes huge in the glint of the lantern, opened the ventilation trap and watched as they squeezed through and negotiated the wooden rungs. The boy seemed very lonely as they moved on, into the dark.

'Mr *Lamballe*,' Houghton injected a world of scorn into the name, 'wants to widen all these vertical shafts to make it easier. He would do better to concentrate on finding a payable coal face, or everybody will be idle.'

'I'm sure he knows what he's doing.' Matthew shuddered as the boy closed the trap and darkness sealed him like a shroud. The lantern seemed feeble as he felt for the next rung of the ladder.

This lower level had no railway, and the air was heavy and rank, despite the suction of his pumps far above. Mr Lamballe intended to increase the height and width of each of these shafts, and add some sort of lighting, but Matthew knew that the deeper the shaft, the more difficult became the problem of ventilation, with fire damp an increasing hazard. He moved on, bent double, very conscious of the weight of rock that stretched from an inch above his head to the surface.

There was the sound of upraised voices, and the chunk of picks on rock.

'Hello!' Lifting his lantern, Houghton looked ahead, where distorted voices reverberated from pressing walls.

'Who's there?' The nearest figure lifted a long pit-candle, dancing grim shadows around the tunnel.

'Mr Pryde and Mr Houghton.' Matthew could hear the strain in his voice. He moved on, crouching as the roof descended. About ten yards ahead, a group of naked and filthy men were huddled at the end of the shaft. Some were pulling at chunks of coal and rock; others lay on their side, hacking with picks. The nearer of two women lifted a hand. She wore only a pair of ragged trousers and her upper body was seamed with blue ridges, the relic of some old accident.

'My feller's under there!' Her voice wavered, high-pitched. She jerked a thumb to her companion, a foal who looked at him with tear-stained eyes. 'And this yin's faither.'

'Let's get them out, then.' Matthew hoped he sounded more confident than he felt. He could see that there was little space for the men working with the picks, so he arranged a shift system with two men working while the others rested. He ordered the women putters to shift the excess rock, and sent word for more corves, more putters and a supply of pit props, lengths of timber that would shore up the workings as they progressed.

With so many straining bodies crammed into such a confined space, the heat and lack of air quickly grew oppressive, so that Matthew laboured to breathe while sweat painted his clothes to his body.

'Move aside,' Matthew said at length, when the nearest hewer stopped for a rest. The man glowered over his shoulder, but obeyed. Matthew took his place, rolling sideways into the tiny space. A couple of hours ago he had been proposing marriage to Kate, but now he was hefting a pick hundreds of feet underground, attempting to hack a passage to trapped miners. He swung clumsily, shuddering at the jar of iron on rock. There was a tiny trickle of dirt from the mark he made. He swung again, terrified in case there was a further rock fall but more frightened to admit his fear.

'Short blows, Mr Pryde,' Houghton advised. 'Save your energy.'

Matthew nodded, already regretting the impulse that had made him take the pick. He was no pitman, he lacked the sinewy muscles developed by years of constant labour, but he had to help. There were people trapped under this fall. He hacked again, and again, sobbing with the effort each blow took. Within minutes the muscles of his arms were aching, his back seemed to be on fire and the pressure on his hip was intolerable, but he continued, blinking the sweat from his eyes.

There was a pattering sound above and he flinched as a shower of dust and small stones fell on him. He waited until the fall subsided, shaking with fear at the prospect of being buried down here, so far from light and air.

Matthew listened to the hammer of his heart, and then started again, driving the point of the pick into the rock, breathing in a mixture of tainted air and coal dust. He could feel the muscles in his arm trembling, and there were already blisters forming on both hands. There was another small fall of dust and stone and he froze, cowering.

'Work faster, man, or shift out of the bloody way!' The northern accent grated in his ears, and Matthew grunted.

'I thought the roof was coming down.'

'You'll soon know if it does,' the voice assured him.

Lifting the pick, Matthew strained into the dark. He hacked again, throwing the pick forward, blinking and coughing in the unseen dust. He was aware of men working close by, and of the rumble of wheels as putters shoved away corves of rubble and coal. His world had constricted to a few feet of rock, where fingers of light illuminated dripping water and the slight impression left by his pick. He had no idea how much time had passed when somebody touched his shoulder.

'My shift. Move over.'

Matthew rolled out, watched the putters drag away the meagre results of his effort and crouched against the weeping wall of the tunnel, watching the naked men work, and wondered how they could endure such a life. As the chunk of picks in rock continued unceasingly, he rested, lying uncomfortably on the filthy rock with his eyes open and his mind racing.

There seemed to be tremendous effort for the little amount of coal being produced. Perhaps they were not tapping into the main seam? Or was there something else? He shook his head, knowing that he could not spare the time to worry about such matters now. Somebody pressed a canister into his hand and he swallowed the tepid water. He closed his eyes, hoping to sleep, but his mind saw only the rock face and heard the grumblings of uneasy rock. He shivered as the sweat dried on his clothes.

'Right, Mr Pryde, if you are still willing?'

Nodding, he accepted the sweat-greased shaft of the pick and looked at the rock face. It seemed sensible to drag off the shirt and trousers that only hampered his movement, so he was as naked as his fellow hewers when he rolled to his position and worked on, nearly sobbing at the pain of his blistered hands. Twice he had to stop and call for a prop to support the roof. That was good. That meant that they were making progress.

Lantern light glinted on desperate eyes, on the sheen of iron picks, on sweating shoulders and foreheads. Occasionally he heard the sobs of the putter as she returned to seek news of her man. There was none to give.

'Stop!' Houghton placed a hand on Matthew's

shoulder. 'Listen!'

In the sudden cessation of work, Matthew was very aware of the harsh sound of his own breathing, the drip of water and the constant groan and wheeze of the steam pump. There was also something else.

'Can you hear it?'

At first Matthew was unsure what he heard, but then he realized that it was a faint but definite tapping.

'Water?' he hazarded, but was shushed to silence.

'That's my feller!' The putter was behind Matthew, her hand on his back. 'I know it is!'

'Reply to them,' Matthew ordered, and, using the tip of the pick, he gave three sharp knocks on the rock. 'Keep working, men!'

The knowledge that at least one of the trapped men was alive spurred on the rescuers, so they threw themselves at the rock, swearing with each swing of the pick. A man thrust Matthew aside. 'I'll be better here than you.'

The miners worked on, stopping only to drink from the canister of water that Houghton fetched from above or listen for the knocking from the trapped men. Matthew watched, unable to match their strength or stamina, but unwilling to leave until the men were rescued.

'Through! By the living Christ we're through!' There was no cheering, only a sense of exhausted relief as the words echoed in the stinking shaft.

Matthew had no idea what the time was when the breakthrough was made, but he crawled forward to help. The miners had hacked a hole through the rock fall, shoring the roof as they progressed. Now a blow of a pick had penetrated the final few inches.

The hand protruded weakly, one finger a crushed mess of bone and blood, but Houghton eased himself forward, shoulders scraping on the rock above. 'Out you come!' His voice was surprisingly gentle.

Somebody was swearing, a constant, sobbing sound that seemed to be drawn from deep inside his soul, and then Houghton wriggled backward from the dark hole, hauling a man behind him. Lantern light showed the bloody trail over the rock, but as soon as the miner's head and shoulders appeared, he began to wrestle free.

'I'm all right. Leave me be.' He pulled himself to safety and lay on the ground, gasping for breath, bloody, filthy but alive. 'There's more men back there.'

'We'll get them,' Houghton promised, and pushed into the hole again.

There had been five men trapped by the rock fall, and three survived. One had minor cuts and bruises, one a crushed hand and the third a badly broken leg. He screamed, once, as Houghton dragged him through the hole, then lay in defiant silence.

'That's Jeff,' the putter said, crawling up to the injured man. 'That's my feller!'

Using the blunt end of a pickaxe, Houghton broke a length of timber into a rough splint and fastened it along the man's leg. The putter hesitated for a second to look at Matthew, opened her mouth as if to speak, but shook her head, grabbed Jeff's arm and began to drag him along the shaft.

'Father?' In the agony of work, Matthew had forgotten the foal. Now she looked up at him, fingers folding around each other.

'He did not make it.' The hewer's voice was rough with concealed sympathy. 'Best get back to the surface.' He met Matthew's eye and shrugged. 'The wee bugger's an orphan now. Her ma died two years back.'

The girl looked at Matthew, eyes wide in a shocked face. 'Come on, then,' he said, lifting her up. There was no weight in her body. 'We can't leave you down here.'

'Her father's no loss,' a hewer said. 'He was an idle lush with ready nieves.' Noticing Matthew's look of bewilderment, he explained, 'He was a quarrelsome drunken bastard. She's better without him.'

One by one the miners left the rock fall and their dead companions. Few looked back. Stooping to lift his lantern, Matthew joined them and it was only when he came to the first ladder that he realized he was still naked. It seemed a small matter beside the death of two men.

'Others might not agree,' Houghton said, sending Jeff's wife back for his clothes.

Matthew dressed and, still carrying the young girl, clumsily ascended the ladders. When he came to the ventilation trap, the young boy was sleeping. Houghton shook him awake, cuffed him for his negligence and left him alone in the dark. The sound of his sobbing stayed with Matthew as he slouched onward.

'They won't thank you, of course,' Mr Lamballe said, standing beside the great winding drum and watching a slow succession of corves carry a mixture of foul coal and rock from the depths. 'You risked your life for nothing.' He sounded angry. 'You're too valuable to work at the coal face.'

Matthew clutched the orphaned girl tighter. He breathed deeply of the morning air, only now aware that he had worked the night away and he was so tired that he could sleep where he stood.

'And who's the child?'

Matthew shook his head. 'Her father died in the rock fall. I didn't know what to do with her.'

'Put her down somewhere, then,' Mr Lamballe said. 'No doubt somebody will claim her for the sake of her wages.' He smiled suddenly. 'Come, Mr Pryde, you have done a brave night's work. Just remember why we are here.'

'Yes, sir.' Matthew looked at the sleeping girl in his arms. He was here to help save Britain from tyranny, but it was hard to believe in liberty while children were worked to exhaustion in the fetid underground. He shook his head, unable to find an answer to such a philosophical question. It was more important now to get some sleep, and find somebody to care for the girl he still carried. Matthew sighed; and then there was Kate.

Three

Matthew leaned back in his bath, luxuriating in the warm water that lapped against his chest and the coal fire that blazed a yard from him. An abundance of coal was one major advantage of working in a colliery. If he had kept a maid, he could have had her heat the water and fill the bath, but instead he had done all the work himself, leaving the great copper kettle in the middle of the floor after he had emptied its steaming contents.

Every muscle ached, and the water stung the numerous small scrapes and cuts that he had collected down the pit. When he closed his eyes he could hear the groan of the steam pump and the hammering of iron picks on the rock. The images of dark tunnels and dancing shadows, of small boys with huge eyes and filthy women dragging corves of coal tugged at his mind, together with the constant questions of Houghton.

'Why does Mr Lamballe want such wide roadways?'

'How can Mr Lamballe make money with

such a meagre return of coal?'

Mr Lamballe had provided Mathew with a cottage a short distance from the miners' rows. Set behind a brick wall in its own small garden, it provided some privacy and a place to retire when his day's work was done, but was hardly suitable accommodation for a gentleman. As soon as he was able, Matthew intended to move to a larger house, somewhere he could be proud to bring Kate. If, indeed, she accepted his offer. He groaned; he had left her in a rush and had not thought to even send her a note apologizing for his long absence. What must she think of him?

Matthew did not hear the door open, but he did hear Kate's gasp of surprise as she stepped inside the room.

'Oh my Lord!' She stared at him for a second, with her face colouring to deep crimson, and then she covered her eyes with her fan and turned her back. 'Oh! Oh I do apologize, Matthew, I had no idea, I really did not.'

Hastily reaching for his only towel, Matthew pulled it over the top of the bath so that he was at least partially covered. 'Of course not, Kate, you could not have known.' He spoke rapidly, unsure if he was excusing himself for bathing, or Kate for walking in unannounced. 'I did not mean to offend you, Kate.'

'Offend me?' She turned around again, coloured once more and spread the fan to hide her entire face. 'It is I who have caused offence; oh, Matthew, pray excuse me. I promise you that I did not see anything that I should not. Oh my Lord, I hope nobody finds out, we will quite *ruin* our reputations.' She left the room in a flurry of skirts and petticoats, banging the door behind her.

'No, don't go!' Matthew stood up, splashing water over the floor, took a step from the bath, realized he was naked and draped himself in the towel before cautiously opening the door and peering into the tiny hall. 'Kate?'

Kate sighed. 'I'm waiting out here. Go and put some clothes on, please.' She shook her head. 'But finish bathing first, Matthew. You look as if you have been down a coal mine.'

Washing as quickly as he could, Matthew dried and dressed hastily, and when he opened the door Kate smiled hesitantly to him. 'I really should have knocked. Am I forgiven?'

'There's nothing to forgive,' Matthew said. He was embarrassed at having been caught in his bath, but knew that once she recovered from her initial surprise, Kate would not be offended.

Her smile chased away the last of his worries. 'Not on your side, certainly.' She glanced around his parlour when she entered. 'I think there is always something peculiar in the house of a man living alone. It always looks so, so *unfurnished*. Bare floorboards and bachelor fare.'

Matthew said nothing. He had two chairs, a table and his bookshelf, which was adequate for his needs. For a moment he wondered if Kate was hinting that she would accept his offer of marriage, but instead she sat gracefully on one of the chairs.

'The fire, however, makes even a room this primitive look comfortable.' There was the squeak of wood on wood as she dragged the chair over bare floorboards and closer to the heat. 'There are some who would argue that a fire is wasteful in summer, but I do not agree.'

'I like a warm room,' Matthew told her.

'Then we agree on that point. I also like a *light* room.' Kate glanced disapprovingly around the unpainted doors and dark plaster. 'But I did not come here to discuss decor, Matthew. Or to spy on you, however diverting it may have been to see the expression on your face.' She raised her eyebrows in mockery.

Matthew looked away, wishing that he had time to remove the bath, which sat as a cooling reminder of his mortification. 'So why did you call, Kate? Of course,' he added hastily, 'I am always pleased to see you.'

'I was worried,' Kate said frankly. 'When you dashed away so suddenly I believed that you were merely doing something of an engineering nature, but then I heard that you were down the mine, digging people out.' She shook her head as anger replaced the mischief. 'What were you thinking of, Matthew? It's not your place to crawl down mine shafts!'

'I didn't do much,' Matthew defended himself. 'There were men trapped—'

'And you thought that you would join them?' she interrupted him, half rising from the chair. 'Are you entirely crazed, sir?'

'Half crazed, perhaps,' Matthew said, appreciating the concern that fuelled her sudden anger. 'I had no intention of joining them, but Mr Houghton and I tried to help. Mr Houghton did

60

far more than I.'

'It is Mr Houghton's job to work down the mine,' Kate reminded, 'and yours to maintain the machinery.' Reaching across the table, she took hold of his arm. 'All the same, Matthew, I was very proud of what you did. Both in saving the men and in carrying away that child.'

'Carrying away the child?' Matthew had nearly forgotten about the girl who was still sleeping in his bed. 'I still have to find a home for her.'

Kate nodded. 'Well, Matthew Pryde, she will not be staying here.' Tapping his arm with her fan, she ushered him through to the bedroom and gazed down on the tranquil child. 'Her name is Emily.'

'How do you know that?' Matthew wondered.

'I asked,' Kate said, simply. 'And I will find a suitable position for her.' She pressed the fan to his lips when he protested. 'Hush, Matthew. It is better this way. Now, I did not mean to rebuke you, but I had to tell you how I felt.'

'And the other thing?' Matthew pressed his opportunity. 'The question that I asked you?'

Kate dropped her eyes as the vibrancy left her voice. 'Dear Matthew,' she said. 'I am sensible of your regard, and I have not forgotten your question. I promise that I will answer soon.' She looked away, her tone becoming brisker. 'This child needs a proper home. I refuse to let her return to the mine, so she must be trained in something more fitting. Oh, Matthew, you have given me so much work to do!'

'How soon?' Matthew ignored her counter. 'How soon before you answer?'

'Just as soon as I am able,' she said, allowing her voice to drop. She looked at him, her eyes large but shadowed. 'I am flattered – no, that is not the right word. I am, oh Lord, Matthew, I don't know what to say.' She leaned closer, holding his arm. 'Please bear with me, Matthew, for I fear that I must ask you to have patience.'

'I have been waiting patiently since last I asked.' He could feel the frustration of disappointment boiling inside him.

'I know.' Kate touched him again. 'Dear, *dear* Matthew, I know. But ... there are things that must be resolved.'

In the silence that followed she walked back to the parlour and stared out of the window, over the garden wall to the distant mine. 'Matthew, you know how much I love to see the theatre?'

'The play?' To the best of his knowledge, Kate had seen two plays in her life, both at the Assembly Hall in Ashbourne. He immediately determined to take her to Drury Lane or Covent Garden at the earliest opportunity.

'Indeed. Well, Matthew, Mr Lamballe is like a man playing a part. Everything is done to perfection, but nothing is as it should be. He lives and talks as if he addresses an audience.'

Matthew shook his head, aware that Kate was trying to divert attention from his proposal, but unsure how to react. 'I am not sure that I understand.'

'It is a strange thing, Matthew, is it not, for Mr Lamballe to dig a mine in a place with no history of colliery work?'

Matthew realized that he could not hurry her.

He must show as good a grace as possible. 'Mr Lamballe is trying to help the country, Kate, and he is good to his miners. Indeed, his colliery is finer than any that I have seen, with its wide roadways and large shafts. I visited five collieries in the north and none are as large inside, yet produce so little coal.' He spoke absently, watching her shape silhouetted against the window.

'It is a delicious mystery, is it not?' Kate spoke to the garden and although her voice was low, he could sense her tension. 'A Frenchman opening a mine in Kent? A Frenchman with a fortune to squander while other émigrés are *quite* purse-pinched?'

'Mr Lamballe explained all that to me,' Matthew said. 'He is afraid that Bonaparte will capture the coal convoys from Newcastle and force England to surrender.'

'And in the meantime Admiral Nelson will be standing in a corner, sucking his thumb? Or bouncing his dolly on his knee, perhaps?' She shook her head, turning to face him. 'It's too smoky by half, Matthew.'

'There's nothing *smoky* about it,' Matthew said. 'He's fighting Boney in the best way he can.'

'By digging holes in the ground and forcing children to work like *slaves*?' There was genuine passion in Kate's voice as she returned to the chair. 'I think Emily is the best example of Mr Lamballe's concept of liberty. If he were so interested in defeating Bonaparte, he could don a scarlet jacket.'

'He is in the Volunteers...' Matthew began.

'Well, if he were so interested in finding coal, he would not leave his precious pit to play cricket. I do not like your Mr Lamballe, Matthew, and I'd like to catch him and lay salt upon his tail.'

Matthew dismissed her fears with a shake of his head. 'You are quite wrong, Kate, really you are. Mr Lamballe is my employer, I cannot speak ill of him.'

'You cannot speak ill of a Frenchman?' Kate raised her eyebrows again. 'And where was he when the roof of his mine was collapsing and half his workers were lying trapped underground? Not where it mattered, I'll be bound! No Matthew, there is something not right about Mr Lamballe, and I mean to find out what!'

As soon as he smiled, Matthew realized that he had made a mistake.

'Are you dismissing me so easily, Matthew Pryde?' Kate stepped toward the door. 'I intend to walk up to Mr Lamballe right this minute and challenge him. I ask if you will come with me?'

Matthew shook his head. He had not forgotten how wilful Kate could be. 'No, madam, I will not. Mr Lamballe has business in London today, and will not be in Ottin Hall, so I fear that your journey would be quite wasted.'

Kate paused for a moment. She returned to the window, looking toward the winding drum of the mine rising above the proud trees. 'And how long will Mr Lamballe be absent, pray?'

'He told me two days,' Matthew told her.

'Time enough for you to curb your temper and straighten your thoughts.'

'No, sir. Time enough for us to enter his study and find out exactly what Monsieur Lamballe is doing here.' Kate sounded triumphant.

Matthew shook his head. 'Enter his study? Kate, we cannot do that. It is not the act of a gentleman.' He lifted his head as Emily awoke with a whimper.

'A gentleman, Matthew?' Kate left the room, returning with Emily at her side. The girl stared around the room. 'And is it acceptable for a *gentleman* to enslave a child? A coal mine with no coal, a Frenchman with plenty of money, and strange *gentle*men in grey cloaks asking questions during the Old Ottin cricket match.' Kate shook her head. 'Too smoky by half, I said, Matthew, and I will be looking at Monsieur Lamballe's study, whether you come or not!'

'Then you will be on your own, madam, and I shall visit you in the hulks. They say it is hot in Botany Bay!'

Four

Kent
May 1805

'What *would* Mrs Grundy say? You will ruin your reputation, going out in the night to meet a man!' Matthew hissed as Kate slid from the shadows. With her dark green cloak bundled up high and the tricorne hat pulled over her head, she looked more like a highwayman than the daughter of a respectable bookseller.

'My reputation is entirely my own concern,' she replied, before relenting. 'I told Father that I was attending the women's debating society meeting. We do have one in Ashbourne, you see. It is where we bluestockings gather to put right the wrongs of the world.'

'And does your father allow you to attend?'

'My father does not *own* me, Matthew.' Her reply was fiercer than he expected. *'Nobody* owns me.'

'And Emily?' Kate had taken the girl away that morning.

'Tucked up in bed. We will train her up as a servant until we can provide for her education.'

Matthew peered at her through the dim of the summer evening. 'You are a queer little vixen,' he said.

'Maybe so, but I do not carry a travelling bag when I break into houses.' She pointed at the leather bag in Matthew's hand. 'What is that?'

'Tools,' Matthew told her, briefly. 'Or did you think we would simply walk through an open door?' He was quite pleased at her glare, for it told him that she had not thought out the details of her plan. She needed him.

They had met at the northern boundary of Ottin Hall, a quarter of a mile from the colliery and beyond the view of the village. A previous owner had erected a high wall around the policies of the Hall, but this particular section had been neglected, and wandering cattle had tumbled the stone, allowing easy access.

'I'm not sure we should do this,' Matthew voiced his doubts once more. 'It could be the gallows if we are caught.' He thought of the fatal drop and the choking swing as the hempen noose tightened around his throat.

'It was only transportation yesterday,' Kate reminded him, mockingly. 'Surely the penalty has not increased overnight? But rest assured, Matthew, we will not get caught, and we will discover this man.'

'And if there is nothing to discover?'

'Then I will offer you my apologies. But I cannot foresee that event.'

Matthew sighed. He felt sick at the thought of betraying Mr Lamballe's trust, but the alternative was worse. If he did not agree to Kate's request she was quite likely to make the attempt herself, and however fond he was of her, Matthew knew that she was not capable of such an endeavour. Anyway, he could never allow her to take the risk alone.

'Come on then, Kate, and keep quiet, for goodness' sake.'

'I hope there are no man traps,' Kate warned chillingly, as they entered the ragged apple orchard from which the blossom had already faded. 'You know how severe the game laws are.'

The thought of jagged metal teeth clamping around his leg increased Matthew's fears, but he eased between the trees, keeping to the shadows as he approached the house. An owl hooted eerily, and there was a shimmer of light and a brief burst of laughter from the servants' quarters. The sound encouraged him, for undisciplined servants might neglect to close all the windows, or even leave a door unlocked.

'Look at the size of this property,' Kate said. 'How did M. le Frog manage to purchase such a house? He's hiding something.'

'He made money on the stock exchange,' Matthew told her, 'and we are on a fool's errand.' He contemplated the wide swathe of parkland that stretched to Ottin Hall and took a deep breath to control the rapid hammer of his heart.

'If so, Matthew, then I am the fool, not you.' Her hand sought his in the dark, and she gave a little squeeze of reassurance. 'Thank you.'

Matthew looked over his shoulder, no longer surprised by her abrupt change of mood. He knew that he would break into a hundred houses if she wanted him to.

'We'll be best to try the east wing first,' he

said. 'It's furthest from the servants' quarters. The windows will doubtless be locked, but it is the quietest part of the house, so I doubt anybody will hear us there.' He emphasized his smile so she could see it in the gloom. 'Are you ready?'

She nodded, but he could hear her shallow, nervous breathing.

'Keep close, and don't look up. We don't want anybody to see our faces.'

Holding the bag carefully so that the contents did not clatter, he led her in a tense dash across the parkland to the house. He heard her quick steps pattering on the grass, heard the rustle of her clothes and then they slammed against the wall, sheltering in the shadows.

'Are you all right?'

'Of course I am. Come on!'

From his previous visits to his employer, Matthew was aware of the general layout of Ottin House. He knew that most of the rooms were hardly used, and hoped that the servants were as negligent in checking the security as they were in their other duties.

'Damn!'

'I beg your pardon, Matthew?'

The easternmost door was firmly locked, and it took only a little pressure to tell Matthew that there were bolts at the top and bottom. He began to work along the walls, checking each window in turn, with Kate silent at his side. Twice they heard the hoot of an owl, and once a high-pitched screech caused Kate to grab at his arm.

'I think somebody's watching us.' Her breath

tickled Matthew's ear.

'It's only a vixen,' he reassured her.

'Not the fox, you jobberknowl! There's somebody else out there!'

Matthew looked round, one hand gripping the heavy jemmy that he hoped not to use. He saw nothing except the dim shapes of trees, their branches spreading to the night like a beggar's supplicating fingers. 'Keep watching, Kate, but pray you are mistaken.' He smiled, trying to reassure her. 'If it's anybody, it will be some maidservant greeting her lover.'

He moved around the walls, testing every window and door, but there was no easy access. 'We'll have to do this the hard way,' he decided, and led Kate back to the furthest window. 'We'll use this one.'

'But it's barred!'

'They all are,' Matthew said. 'They're all barred, and they have shutters on the inside. The servants are not as wretched as I had thought. Now you keep watch.' Again he accentuated his smile to reassure her. 'You are what they call my *crow*, my lookout.'

The window was about four feet high, with vertical metal bars set into the stonework every six inches. Behind the bars was the glass of the window, and behind that a set of wooden shutters.

'How will you get in there? Maybe we should just go home.' Kate had obviously not expected such difficulties.

'This is my department,' Matthew told her. 'You remember that your Cousin William taught me the engineering business?'

Kate nodded. 'Of course.'

'Well, he was a very thorough teacher. When I was his apprentice, he sent me to a locksmith for three months, and I learned how to design thief-proof locks and windows. I also learned about their weaknesses.'

Opening his bag, Matthew produced a length of strong hemp rope and a short metal bar. As Kate neglected her duties to watch him, he looped the rope over two of the bars, thrust the metal bar between the strands and rotated it slowly. The tighter the rope twisted, the more pressure it exerted on the bars, so after a few minutes they began to move slightly, with the one on the left bending inward.

'It's working,' Kate squealed excitedly in his ear.

'You're my crow,' Matthew reminded her. 'You're meant to be keeping sentinel.'

'But this is more interesting,' Kate said. 'I've never seen you housebreaking before.'

After a few minutes Matthew began to work the left bar, pulling it backward and forward until it loosened and he could haul it from its position. It came out with a small shower of mortar. 'Hold this.' He handed over the bar. 'Put it down quietly.'

Looping the rope over the next bar in line, he repeated the procedure until he had created a hole large enough for them to crawl through.

'But there's still glass, and the wooden shutter.' Kate waited for him to perform another miracle.

'Simple,' Matthew said, enjoying the wonder in her face. Producing a small, sharp knife, he cut into the putty around the bottom pane and pushed until he felt movement. It took only two minutes to remove the glass, and inserting his hand through the hole, he released the window catch and shoved up the sash.

'Now the shutters,' Kate said. 'And if you can't find a position as an engineer, you can always turn to burglary.'

'If I do,' Matthew whispered, 'I will certainly not employ you as my lookout! Keep quiet, can't you?'

The shutters presented more of a problem. Made of solid Baltic pine, they were closed on the inside of the window and fastened with a catch. Matthew pushed, hoping to find that they had not been securely locked, but there was no give at all.

'Hand me my bag,' he ordered, and took out a brace and bit. Kate watched as he attached an adjustable cutting head and placed the brace against the shutters. Turning the brace like a giant compass, the head cut into the wood, gradually carving out a circular hole about four inches in diameter.

'Hurry up!'

Matthew realized that the night was passing, but he knew of no other way of defeating wooden shutters. Hoping that the noise of the blade would not carry through the house, he continued, gasping at the strain on his arms.

'It's working,' Kate said, then gave a small shriek as the circle of wood clattered to the floor.

Matthew swore, cringing, as the sound reverberated through the night. A score of bats exploded from the eaves far above. He thought he heard a questing voice, and Kate's hand squeezed his arm. She was trembling. 'Are you all right?'

When she nodded he realized that she was attempting to repress her laughter. 'You've been telling me to keep quiet all night, and then you make as much noise as you possibly can,' she said. 'Don't you think that's funny?'

Matthew decided it would be better to say nothing. He waited for a few moments, but nobody came to investigate the noise. Glaring at Kate, he thrust his arm through the hole and drew the bolt that secured the shutters. After that it was the work of a second to open them and crawl inside the house, taking the bag of tools with him. Kate followed, still suppressing her nervous laughter.

They emerged into dense darkness with a stone-flagged floor beneath them.

'I can't see anything,' Kate said, but Matthew delved into his bag and produced a small metal lantern with a single small glass lens. Striking his tinderbox, he lit the oil-fed wick and directed a narrow beam of light around the room. Heavy wooden tables lined three walls, while unmarked boxes sat solidly on a shoulder-high shelf.

'It's an old kitchen,' Kate decided.

'Used for storage,' Matthew said, and realized that Kate was clinging to his arm. 'Are you all right? It's not too late to get out.'

'No.' She shook her head. 'It's just that I

hadn't expected it to be so dark.' Her fingers curled around his biceps. 'I don't like the dark very much.'

'A fine time to realize that now!' Matthew said, until he realized she was trembling. 'Are you sure you want to continue?'

'No,' Kate said frankly, and then, 'yes. Yes. Come on.'

'Brave girl,' Matthew said, feeling a surge of renewed affection. He handed her the lamp. 'Hold that for me, please.' Closing the window, he pulled a piece of dark paper from his bag and placed it over the hole in the shutters, which he closed and bolted. 'If anybody should look in now, they won't see anything. Are you ready to move on?'

Their footsteps echoed eerily as they moved out of the kitchen and into a short corridor. Stone stairs circled upward, with ornate wrought-iron railings for support. 'Watch for the lamp,' Matthew warned. 'It gets really hot after a while.'

'How do you know?' He heard the forced brightness in her voice. 'Do you often break into houses?'

'Only at night-time,' he told her.

There was a square hall at the top of the stairs, with a great brass lantern hanging from the wall, and another set of stairs heading upward. Dark portraits gloomed at them, ugly in the slanting lantern light. They moved slowly, one cautious step at a time.

'What's that?' Kate's hand squeezed inside Matthew's elbow as something moved above them. He stopped, instinctively crouching to

74

make himself smaller. 'It's only a mirror,' Kate said, and pushed him upward.

The stairs changed direction at a square landing on which a long-case clock sat silent, its single remaining hand pointing permanently at six. They continued to a long corridor that ended at an archway. 'The library is through there,' Matthew remembered. 'That's also his study; let's end this foolery.'

Matthew had never used the picklocks that he had brought, so he was very glad, if surprised, to find that the key was in the library door. It turned easily under his hand.

'Hardly the action of a guilty man,' he pointed out, ushering Kate inside the room and closing the door firmly behind him. 'Now, I have no idea what you expect to find here, Kate, but I will help you look.'

Kate flashed the lamp around the room, its spot of light glinting on glass-fronted bookcases, a battered mahogany desk that was piled high with papers and documents and what looked like a hand-drawn map of the estate, set up on an artist's easel. 'I'd like to spend time in here,' she said, allowing the light to settle on the largest bookcase.

Thankful that the room was in the centre of the house and so lacked windows, Matthew lit one of the candles that sat on the desk. 'We'll save our oil,' he said, extinguishing the light in the lamp. 'We might need it later. Anyway, we'll make sure that the metal does not get too hot.'

In the light of the single flickering flame, they

began to search through the documents on the desk.

'Look for anything unusual,' Kate ordered. 'I don't know what, but there's something very smoky about that man. He pretends to be the frankest, kindest, most amiable creature there is, but he does it too much brown, I fear.'

Matthew did not reply. He felt like a traitor, probing the private papers of his employer, and twice suggested that they should leave, as there was obviously nothing here.

Kate shook her head. 'We've come this far, Matthew, and I will not leave until I am satisfied.'

'And if he is innocent?'

'Then we have wasted a night and you have demonstrated your ability as a thief. It is always an alternative career should nobody care to employ you as an engineer.'

The first pile of papers related to Mr Lamballe's request for a new turnpike from Old Ottin connecting to the Ashbourne and London road.

'I see M. le Frog has been writing a lot to Admiral Springer,' Kate sounded suspicious. 'He's the local magistrate, you know.'

'I know,' Matthew said. 'He's also the Member of Parliament. Mr Lamballe's trying to persuade him to drive a turnpike road from the mine, so that the coal can reach London quicker. It's all very sensible, and completely above board.'

Kate shook her head. 'I'm not sure about that. A canal would be better.'

'A canal would take longer to dig, and there would be more opposition from the Northumberland colliery owners.' Matthew ruffled through a sheaf of letters concerning new wine cellars for Ottin Hall.

'But a canal would be much more efficient,' Kate insisted, reinforcing Matthew's view that she thought she knew best about everything.

There were parliamentary minutes, books about mining, a pile of cheaply printed pamphlets entitled *Britons to Arms* that showed a brawny rustic thrusting a pitchfork into the prominent rump of a hastily retreating Bonaparte and a manual about training Volunteers, of which Mr Lamballe was a member. There was also a leaflet about dredging silt from harbours, and another about the new craze of ballooning.

'Maybe he intends flying over London to kidnap the King?' Matthew suggested sarcastically, but Kate responded with a glare so icy that it would have sunk a Greenland whaler.

'Here're his letters,' Kate said at last. 'All carefully written and ready to post.' Holding them to the candle flame, she read off the names. 'Admiral Springer. Mr Addington. Mr Fox. Albert Mathieu, whoever *that* is. Another for Admiral Springer and one for Admiral Keith.'

Matthew looked up from perusing the pamphlets. 'Say that name again?'

'Admiral Keith?' Kate returned to the letters, which she had discarded.

'No, the French one.'

'Albert Mathieu?' Kate held the letter up. 'Do you know him? Another émigré abusing our hospitality?'

'No, Albert Mathieu is not an émigré.' Mat-

77

thew shook his head. 'Could I see it, please?' He took the letter from her, feeling suddenly sick. Carefully folded and heavily sealed, the letter was on thick paper, with the name written boldly across the front in black ink. 'Albert Mathieu.'

'And who is he, then? Pray tell me.' Kate brushed away the wayward curl that dangled over her left temple.

'A French engineer,' Matthew said. He felt the sudden increase of his pulse as he looked at her. 'A French engineer with some very interesting ideas.' He weighed the letter in his hand. 'But what could Mr Lamballe want with such a man?'

Kate came closer. 'Can we open it?' The flicker of the candle highlighted her high cheekbones as she stared at him. She reached for the letter.

The deep voice sounded from beyond the pool of candlelight. 'I'd better have that.'

Kate stifled a scream and pressed a hand to her mouth. Matthew looked up, startled, to see a tall figure standing beside the door, his hair clubbed in a short queue and a heavy staff in his hand.

'Hand it over, if you please.' When the man closed the door and stepped closer, Matthew realized that he was no servant. The candlelight revealed a long grey cloak fastened at the neck and flowing over a dark waistcoat. The face above was stern.

'And who are you, sir, to be walking about inside this house?' Slipping the letter behind his back, Matthew prepared to bluster his way out.

'I would ask you the same question, if I did not

already know the answer, Mr Pryde. This is a strange place to find a mining engineer.' The stranger glanced to Kate. 'And Miss Denton, of Ashbourne, who cuts the notches for the cricket match.'

'I thought I heard somebody when we were outside.' Kate threw Matthew an accusing look, as if it were his fault that this stranger had caught them, then addressed the stranger. 'You were at the May Day festivities. You asked me about Mr Lamballe.'

The man gave a curt bow. 'John Black, at your service, Miss Denton.' He held out his hand. 'The letter, please, Mr Pryde?'

Matthew slid one hand inside his bag, feeling for his two-foot-long jemmy. 'As an employee of Mr Lamballe, I believe that I have a better right to the letter than you, Mr Black.'

'But do you have a better right than His Majesty?' Black thrust forward his staff so that the light reflected from the gilded crown at the tip.

'What?' Kate stared at the crown. 'What does this mean?'

Matthew shook his head, his mouth suddenly dry. 'It means that Mr Black is a Bow Street Runer,' he said. He removed his hand from the jemmy. 'But it does not explain why he is here.'

'His Majesty has granted me permission to be anywhere I will,' Mr Black's voice was edged, 'which is an authority I doubt you possess.' He raised a querying eyebrow. 'Do you, Miss Denton?'

Glancing at Matthew, Kate shook her head.

79

'However, having listened to a little of your conversation, I believe we may be following different trails to the same goal,' Mr Black said, more kindly, 'but this is neither the time nor place to discuss them. The letter, if you please?' Again he allowed the light to gleam from the gilded crown, and Matthew complied.

'We will leave this here,' Mr Black decided, replacing the letter after a brief glance. 'It is too well sealed to open circumspectly, and we do not wish to arouse suspicion, yet.'

'I do not understand,' Kate said. 'Who is this Albert Mathieu, and why should the Runners be interested?'

Black glanced at her. 'Sufficient to say, Miss Denton, that Albert Mathieu's ideas could put this country in more danger than it has been in since Duke William of Normandy landed. He is possibly the only man who could outmanoeuvre Admiral Nelson, and your friend Mr Lamballe has been helping his designs these past months.'

Kate stared at Matthew, who shook his head, struggling with this startling information. 'It seems that your suspicions may have been correct, Kate.'

'But you still have not told me who he *is*,' Kate complained.

'Come, Miss Denton, and you, sir,' Black said. 'We will discuss this at a more suitable venue, Mr Pryde. Shall we say Windward House, tomorrow evening at seven? Until then, Mr Pryde, I want you to continue with your duties as normal. Do not do anything to arouse suspicions.'

'Windward House?' Kate said. 'That is Admiral Springer's property.'

'Quite correct, Miss Denton. I am afraid I must ask that you join us, for it seems you are already embroiled in this affair. Until then, depart from this house as you entered, through a kitchen window, I believe? And say nothing to anybody, upon your honour.' He bowed. 'And now I must leave you, for a certain lady is awaiting my presence.'

Five

Windward House, Kent
May 1805

When Admiral Springer retired from the sea, he used the accumulated prize money of forty years to buy Windward House. He chose a position where he was surrounded by the ancient woodings and high hedges of Kent, yet was sufficiently elevated for the topmost floor of his house to have a view of the Channel. As the local Member of Parliament and Justice of the Peace, he was the most powerful political figure in four parishes, but Kate knew him as a customer of the bookshop and greeted him as a friend.

'Come in, Miss Denton,' Admiral Springer bowed as far as his enormous girth would allow, 'and you too, Mr Pryde. We live in grave times,

I fear, but that does not mean you are not welcome.'

Matthew admired the classical proportions of the newly built house with the wide steps that swept up to the front door and the pillars that stretched to include an arched fanlight. It was a different world from the miners' cottages that lay only a handful of miles beyond the woods.

Admiral Springer ushered them into a spacious front room whose windows overlooked the groomed lawn. Of the three men who stood to receive them, one wore the scarlet and gold of an army officer, the second pulled at the high collar of a clerk and the third was Mr Black, dressed in fashionably tight breeches and a blue waistcoat. The staff of office was tight in his hand.

The men exchanged bows, before Admiral Springer made the introductions. 'I believe that you have already met Mr Black of the Runners?' Matthew and Kate nodded agreement and the Admiral continued, 'This military gentleman is Major Sir John Jones, while this,' he indicated the man that Matthew had dismissed as a clerk, 'is Mr John Reeves, His Majesty's Acting Superintendent of Aliens.'

Matthew could not help himself from an impromptu bow and an exchange of glances with Kate. They were in distinguished company indeed.

Mr Reeves nodded, as if agreeing with Matthew's assessment. 'We have much to discuss,' he said, speaking in a slightly high-pitched voice, 'but I believe that Admiral Springer has something to show us first.'

'I have, sir. Pray come this way, gentlemen. And you, Kate.' Puffing mightily, the Admiral led them up a grand staircase, stopping for breath every few minutes. Four flights of stairs brought them to a domed glass room that contained the largest telescope that Matthew had ever seen in his life.

'Astronomy is a passion of mine,' the Admiral said, 'along with the study of geology and human nature.'

'If you could point your spyglass toward Mr Lamballe's mine, sir?' Mr Reeves watched as the Admiral adjusted the mechanism. 'Now, Mr Pryde, would you care to look this way?'

'Ladies first, surely?' Admiral Springer insisted. 'Boney may be the devil's child, but we shall not lose our manners for a mere gaggle of Frenchmen.'

'Quite right, sir,' Major Jones said. 'We shall not compromise our standards for any Johnny Crapaud.'

Reeves looked annoyed, but did not argue when Kate took her place at the eyepiece of the telescope. She allowed the Admiral to adjust the focus for her vision.

'What do you see, Miss Denton?' Reeves' impatience made it obvious that Kate's impressions were of small importance.

'Men working,' Kate said, 'steam engines, a road being constructed.'

'Quite correct,' Reeves said, 'and what is probably more to the point, what do you not see?' He gave a small smile, as if waiting for Kate to say something foolish. Matthew began to dislike Mr Reeves.

'Coal,' Kate said at once. 'Or rather, not enough coal to make the mine profitable.'

Matthew felt a surge of satisfaction as Reeves frowned.

'You are correct, Miss Denton,' Reeves said, grudgingly. 'And pray tell me, of what use is a coal mine without coal? None, madam.' He answered his own question. 'And why is that, Admiral Springer? Why is there barely a trickle of coal being mined?'

'Because that is all that is to be had, Mr Smith,' the Admiral replied. 'I said that my en- thusiasm for geology nearly equals my fascina- tion in astronomy, and I have studied the rocks of this part of Kent. They may bear some coal, but not in workable quantities. Coal seams, as you might know, run east and west, so the best way of discovering it is to search for evidence of coal in the riverbanks that run north and south...'

'Yes, yes, yes, Admiral.' Reeves held up a hand. 'It is sufficient that *you* know such things; we do not require a lesson in geology, however interesting the subject may be to some.'

'If there is no coal, then why is M. Lamballe digging a mine?' Major Jones asked the obvious question.

'That is what we wish to know, Major,' Reeves said. 'You may be aware that we record any aliens who land in this country, and watch those of whom we have suspicions? No? Well, I have had M. Lamballe observed for some time. Mr Black,' he nodded to the Runner, who lifted a single finger in acknowledgement, 'has spent many weeks in this area, following another line of enquiry. Mr Black, if you could continue?'

'Indeed, sir.' Black stepped casually forward. 'I was employed to observe Mr Houghton, who at one time was a member of the Friends of the People and the London Corresponding Society. You are all aware that both these groups have Republican and Jacobin sympathies?' He waited until everybody had acknowledged the fact.

'We like to keep watch on the known agitators, so when a French émigré approached Mr Houghton with an offer of employment, we immediately informed Mr Reeves, who ordered that we investigate Mr Lamballe.'

'And with what results, pray?' Admiral Springer asked. He bowed toward Kate. 'If you find this all too tiresome, Miss Denton, I am sure that you may be excused.'

'Tiresome? No, sir. Indeed you would have to a hire a great many wild horses to drag me away from what is a most fascinating meeting.'

Reeves grunted and looked away. He muttered something about 'bluestockings that interfered with affairs that were no concern of theirs', but Mr Black ignored him and continued.

'M. Lamballe arrived in England three years ago, during the late peace, and has spent considerable sums of money since his arrival, which is very unusual. Most aliens arrive penniless and remain that way, depending on the charity of the government to feed and clothe them while they wait for us to restore the natural order to their country.'

'I would be obliged, Mr Black,' Reeves was

frowning again, 'if you would keep to the matter in hand.'

Black gave a stiff bow. 'M. Lamballe claims to have been a member of the bourgeoisie, but our enquiries have revealed none of that name. Two years ago he started his mine and more recently he has requested Admiral Springer, as the Member of Parliament for the constituency, to initiate a bill for a turnpike direct to London. We did not understand why he should wish a coal mine in an area with no history of coal.'

'And that is where you became involved, Mr Pryde.' Major Jones spoke for the first time. 'I am responsible for organizing defences against the proposed French invasion, and Mr Lamballe's activities concern me greatly. I wish to know why he recruited you, Mr Pryde?'

'To improve his efficiency,' Matthew replied. 'When I arrived, his mine was operating by horse and muscle power. I have ensured he has modern steam pumps and steam winders, as well as a mechanical system to keep the air pure underground.'

'What are conditions like down his mine? Is there much evidence of coal working?' Black was busy at the telescope, taking notes as he watched.

Matthew considered for a moment. 'He has dug fairly deep, and seems to be concentrating on a single roadway, with few of the side tunnels that I saw in the north.' He hesitated. 'He has found coal, certainly, but I do not believe that the deposits are sufficient to pay for the mine.'

'That is because he is digging in the wrong

86

place, damn the man!' Admiral Springer sounded pleased that his suspicions were confirmed.

Kate glanced at Reeves. 'Sir, does this have a connection to the letter that we found? What exactly do you think Mr Lamballe is trying to do?'

'Until yesterday, madam, we were dumbfounded' – Reeves took over the conversation again – 'but your little escapade has opened up a most troubling possibility.'

Matthew exchanged glances with Kate, who pulled a face. He hoped that his suspicions were mistaken. 'Pray continue, sir?'

Reeves sat down as pedantically as he spoke. 'Let us consider the situation. We have a Frenchman, masquerading as an émigré, who is digging a great tunnel in Kent. We also have a French army poised only thirty miles from where we sit. We know that Bonaparte is desperate to invade, for the man has even attempted to bribe the smuggler William Johnson to pilot the Boulogne flotilla.'

'I was not aware of that.' Jones looked concerned, until Reeves shook his head. 'Johnson refused, and was thrown into a *very* uncomfortable prison for his pains. However, the very fact that Bonaparte made the offer reveals his lack of confidence in his own navy.'

The Admiral grunted and began to scratch himself in a most personal place until he remembered that Kate was present and hastily dropped his hand.

Reeves continued. 'We now have the name of a French engineer, Albert Mathieu.'

'An engineer?' Admiral Springer looked from Reeves to Jones and then to Matthew. 'I see by your expressions that I should be alarmed. Pray tell me why?'

'Before I elaborate, I think we should retire to somewhere more comfortable.' For the first time that evening Reeves showed some concern for Kate. 'It must surely be cold for Miss Denton up here.'

The Admiral's library was large, with a number of welcoming armchairs spread out amidst low tables and shelves of books. Pictures of ships adorned the walls, and various nautical implements were scattered on the floor, as if left there by a departing crew. 'Find a seat, Miss Denton, and you, gentlemen. Damn it all, I thought I could swallow the anchor and doze away my retirement and here's a little Corsican corporal ruining everything for me. Why France had to grab that troublesome little island I don't know.'

A sharp order saw a tray of drinks brought in, with decanters of brandy and a selection of wines. 'I suppose you expect rum,' Admiral Springer said, 'but I am afraid that I must disappoint you. Can't abide the stuff myself, and I would not inflict it on anybody else.' He eased himself into the largest of the chairs and patted the seat of the chair nearest to him. 'You sit here, Kate, my dear, and console me with your beauty.'

Kate bobbed in a small curtsy. 'Hardly beauty, Admiral.'

'You don't think so? Well, best let me be the

judge of that, although I am sure that Mr Pryde would agree with me?' The Admiral waved his hand. 'Well, sit down sir, and tell me about this French engineer fellow!' He indicated another seat, so he was positioned between Matthew and Kate with his legs spread out before him.

'Yes, sir.' Matthew sat down, feeling his face colour when he realized that everybody present was waiting for him to speak. 'Albert Mathieu,' he began, 'is possibly one of the most enterprising engineers in France. Only two years ago he proposed digging a tunnel to link England with France.'

'A tunnel linking England and France?' Kate shifted her seat. She leaned across Admiral Springer to hear better. 'Is such a thing possible?'

'Albert Mathieu believes that it is,' Matthew said. Since finding the name the previous night, he had read all that he could about the Frenchman's idea. 'It seems that the proposal is not new, but was first mooted about fifty years ago. However, Mathieu has gone one step further and actually prepared plans for the scheme. He proposed two tunnels, one starting in France and the other in England, joining at the Varne sandbank, which lies about eight miles south of Dover. Mr Mathieu recommended a staging point here, so that horses could be refreshed. I believe that Bonaparte was quite enthusiastic about the idea.'

Major Jones was hunched on his chair with his hands under his chin. 'Ventilation, sir? Foul air is the devil of every mine. How would this tunnel be ventilated?'

'By chimneys, I believe, Major,' Matthew told him. 'Reaching from the roof of the tunnel to the surface of the sea.'

'Good God,' Mr Black said, and refreshed his glass from the decanter, looking slightly bored. He sighed and softly quoted the lines of Charles Dibden:

'The French are all coming, so they declare,
Of their floats and balloons all the papers advise us
They're to swim through the ocean and ride on the air
In some foggy evening to land and surprise us.'

'Well, sir, it seems that Bonaparte has another plan of invasion.' Mr Reeves stood with his back to the cold fireplace, legs apart and an expression of intense worry on his face. 'Would you agree, Mr Pryde? You are the only man here with personal experience of Mr Lamballe's mine. Is it possible?'

'An invasion by tunnel?' Ever since he had read Albert Mathieu's name, Matthew had contemplated the idea with horror. From time immemorial, England had faced the possibility of invasion by France, but the Royal Navy had remained an invincible defender. On a dozen occasions the French had made great schemes for armies to land on the south coast and capture London, but always the Channel crossing had defeated them. Now here was Bonaparte, a formidable soldier with a large and experienced army, proposing to march under England's defences.

'I hope not.' Matthew shook his head, remembering the extreme width of the main shaft and Houghton's comments about the excess roof space and spacious tunnels. What had seemed like a waste of money now took on more sinister connotations. He explained what he had seen, speaking slowly. 'But I am no military engineer. I believe that Major Jones is better qualified to reply.'

'Is it possible, sir?' Reeves insisted on an answer.

'That, sir, we do not yet know.' Major Jones stepped forward. 'There are many problems involved in mining and tunnelling. Foremost are the worries of keeping the roof from collapsing, and of keeping the air pure. The latest advances in steam technology may well have overcome the latter, and Bonaparte does not need to construct a tunnel that lasts for years; only one that remains intact long enough to bring an invading army to these shores.' He frowned. 'Thirty miles, say, at four miles an hour. Eight hours' march.'

'That is for the vanguard, the forlorn hope. They will need reinforcements, supplies, horses and artillery. The tunnel must last longer than a matter of hours. It would take days to bring over an army on such a narrow front.' Reeves grunted. 'Thanks to Mr Pryde here, the French may have made a good start on their preliminaries, with the best modern machinery, but perhaps we are chasing a wild goose.'

'And perhaps not,' Mr Black said, examining his glass, which seemed to have emptied itself, a situation that he soon remedied. 'Consider the evidence, sir. We have a French émigré with seemingly unlimited funds. We have the same French émigré digging a deep mine in an area with no history of mining, and consorting with known agitators. Then we have a hundred and sixty thousand French soldiers poised to invade, and a French engineer who proposes a tunnel.'

'It seems fairly conclusive, sir,' Admiral Springer said. 'It's a bad business.'

Matthew shook his head. 'So how can we find out for certain, sir?' He was aware of Jones exchanging a glance with Reeves, who gave a short nod, as if of approval.

'We must learn if there is a corresponding tunnel on the French side of the Channel,' Mr Reeves said, quietly. 'That will be proof enough, I think.'

'Of course,' Kate nodded. 'You will have a contact over in France.'

Mr Reeves shook his head. 'Not yet, Miss Denton. We have our agents in France, but we do not have anyone sufficiently qualified to differentiate between a simple coal mine and a possible tunnel under the sea.'

'So will you have to send over somebody who has the necessary qualifications?' Kate asked.

'That is exactly what we will do, Miss Denton.' Reeves looked grave. 'We will need an intelligent, resourceful man with a knowledge of engineering, who is unknown to the French.' His smile was brief and precise as he nodded toward

Matthew. 'There are few such men in England.'

It was Kate who spoke first. 'Are you asking Matthew to become a *spy*, sir?' She recoiled in horror at the idea. 'Surely there are engineers within the army who are better fitted for the job?'

'There are artificers in the army, but not many, and none that can be spared. The men we have are fully employed in building Martello Towers and a tunnel through Dover cliffs, and preparing a military canal across the Romney Marsh.' Mr Reeves looked over toward Major Jones. 'As you are aware, we do not know if Bonaparte *is* planning a tunnel, or if we are leaping to douse a fire that has not even been laid.' He lowered his voice. 'I am asking Mr Pryde to serve his country, madam, in a post of great danger.'

Lifting the decanter, Matthew poured himself a generous glass of brandy. He was fully aware that spying was not the occupation of a gentleman, so that any army officer would be quite within his rights to refuse such a post, but Mr Reeves' mention of danger had been clever. If he refused now, it would seem as if he was afraid.

Casually lifting his official staff from the floor, Black smoothed his left hand along the shaft. Candlelight glinted on the gilded crown on the top. 'You were brought up in a foundling hospital, Mr Pryde, and only the charity of a born gentlemen enabled you to have a decent education at Maidhouse College. Is that not correct?'

Matthew swallowed as Kate laid a light hand on his arm. Sometimes he forgot that he clung to his position by ragged fingernails, and if he were to be exposed, then it was unlikely that anybody would seek to employ him in his professional capacity. 'That is correct.'

Black nodded. 'Even so, neither I nor anybody else can order you on such a risky operation. That is the advantage of living in this England of ours.' He put his lips to the gold crown of his staff in a gesture so dramatic that it was almost French. 'Bonaparte claims to have given France a coast of iron and bronze, while the *Moniteur* says that the Kentish men are fleeing at the very sight of the campfires of the French army.'

'Come, Mr Black.' Mr Reeves stood up. 'Mr Pryde is a true-born Englishman. He does not need to be reminded of the threat to this country.'

'Of course, sir.' Mr Black touched the crown again. 'We are all aware of Boney's army just waiting to pounce, just as Mr Pryde will be aware of his part in helping Mr Lamballe improve his mine.' He shook his head sadly. 'If such intelligence were to spread, there would be few positions available for him in England.'

Mr Reeves produced a ponderous gold watch from his waistcoat pocket, opened the cover and concentrated on the face. 'I shall have to leave you, gentlemen, for I have a rather pressing engagement with the Prime Minister.' He glanced at Matthew. 'I am sure that you will shortly come to a decision, Mr Pryde, but may I remind you that His Majesty would be eternally grateful for your help, and would think favourably on you if any situations occurred where an engineer might be employed.'

94

Matthew nodded. He was being given a stark choice. He could refuse, and face a future of unemployment, for Mr Black and the Runners would ensure that his humble origins and involuntary involvement with the French were broadcast nationwide, or accept and have a benevolent government throw the occasional crumb to him. He glanced at Kate, and knew that there was no choice. An unemployed engineer could not support a wife.

'I'll do it,' Matthew agreed. Kate's gasp twisted something deep inside him.

Admiral Springer stepped forward, hand outstretched in congratulations. 'Well done, sir, and I assure you that yours is the decision of a true gentleman!' The Admiral was grinning as he pumped Matthew's hand, while Major Jones contented himself with a quick military nod.

'You will be leaving within the week, Mr Pryde,' Reeves said quietly. 'Mr Black and I have already made the arrangements.' He glanced at Kate. 'It would be best if you refrained from speaking of this matter to your father or anybody else, Miss Denton. These things are best kept quiet.'

Matthew said nothing. He knew that Kate was trying her best to be brave, but he saw that she was trembling.

Six

Matthew heard the dispute the second he entered the bookshop. It was so unusual for Charles Denton to shout that he raised his hand to still the entrance bell and stopped to listen.

'Think of your reputation, Kate! You cannot continue as you are, meeting Matthew unescorted, walking to gentlemen's residences without a female companion, living as free as a man-about-town.'

'Oh, what *would* Mrs Grundy say?' Kate taunted, then retaliated with more heat. '*Why*, Father? *Why* cannot I live as free as a man? Am I not as *good*?' She was angry, but Matthew also heard the hurt in her voice.

Mr Denton's reply was inaudible, but Matthew thought that he had better announce himself by rapping on the counter.

'Ah, Matthew.' Mr Denton appeared visibly agitated, with his cravat uneven and his pince-nez glasses perched near the tip of his nose. 'Kate and I were just discussing family matters.'

'Of course.' Matthew bowed. 'I am grateful that you can spare the time to speak with me.'

'Oh, fustian nonsense, Matthew! We've known

96

each other long enough to dispense with the formalities, surely. Come on—' Lifting the flap that acted as both a counter and a barrier to the back shop, he hesitated for only a second. 'You might find the atmosphere a little frosty, I am afraid. It was quite an animated discussion, and family matters can be quite delicate.'

Kate bobbed in a mocking curtsy. 'Why, pray enter sir, and join our *amiable* conversation.' Her glance toward her father could have frozen molten lead.

'I'd prefer to face the French,' Matthew said. The expression on her face killed the smile before it reached his mouth.

'So I believe.' Lifting a pile of garishly covered broadsheets, she stopped on her way to the front shop. 'I don't like selling this babble,' she complained, 'but it's nearly the chief of our trade, and we must stock what the customers want.' She showed him the top copy, which was decorated with a picture of a grotesque Bonaparte hanging from the edge of a basket, while suspended above, a balloon drifted to distant clouds.

This little Boney says he'll come
At merry Summer time,
But that I say is all a hum
Or I no more will rhyme.

Some say in wooden house he'll glide
Some say in air balloon,
E'en those who airy schemes deride,
Agree he's coming soon.

'They don't mention a tunnel,' Kate said, and, ducking her head, pushed past him. 'I wish that I had never got you to go on that foolish errand to Mr Lamballe's house. Then you would never have been going away!'

As Mr Denton stared, Matthew followed. 'It's hardly your fault, Kate. It's just the way that things have worked out.'

'What things?' Mr Denton demanded. 'What foolish errand, and who is going away?'

'I am, sir.' Matthew decided that it would be best to keep as much to the truth as he could. 'Mr Lamballe's mine is not producing sufficient coal to be economical, and I am going to visit another mine elsewhere.'

'I see.' Mr Denton nodded his understanding. 'You are engaged on a business trip, searching for ideas for improvements. I would hardly class that as a foolish errand, Kate.'

Kate opened her mouth to retaliate but obviously decided it would be better to keep quiet. She looked at her father. 'I do not think that it is a good time for Matthew to be away. Not with the French threatening to invade.'

Mr Denton straightened his pince-nez. 'Well, Miss Kate, I am sure that I can do nothing to alter the situation. What can't be cured, must be endured. Or perhaps there *is* a partial cure?'

Matthew felt only confusion as Kate coloured and bustled into the shop. Carrying a small wooden box of books, Mr Denton followed her. When he whispered something in her ear, she shook her head violently, until he prodded her with a podgy finger. She sighed, shook her head again and eventually banged down her broadsheets. 'I'm not ready yet,' she protested, keeping her head low. 'I don't know what to say.'

Realizing that he was intruding on a continuing dispute, Matthew took a step backward. 'Perhaps it would be best if I were to leave,' he suggested, winking at Emily, who was watching from behind the table, nervously rubbing her hands together.

Kate nodded, then straightened up. 'Before you go, could you help me here, please, Matthew?' Her supposed request was more like a demand that brooked no refusal, so Matthew sighed and looked at Mr Denton.

'When my daughter commands, Matthew, who are we mere men to deny her?' He watched, half-smiling, as Matthew followed Kate through the parlour and into a small back room. His voice followed, pitched deliberately loud. 'Come, Emily, you and I will put away these books.'

'You have not been down here, have you?' Kate indicated a small trap door in the stone floor and waited for Matthew to pull it open. A flight of steps disappeared into darkness. 'This is our book store, where we keep the spare stock and those volumes that either have not sold or which are not currently popular.'

A faint smell of dust and mould greeted Matthew as he lifted a lantern and slowly descended into a store that seemed to have been hacked out of stone, a deep cellar that thrust twenty yards under the building. His lamplight pooled on the spines of piles of leather-bound books.

'Straight through,' Kate ordered, 'and I'd be obliged if you could keep the light in front of me.'

There was an inner door of plain elm, with a tarnished brass handle and a heavy iron bolt that Kate struggled to draw. The scrape of metal on metal echoed in the store. 'Inside here.' Her voice sounded strained.

The lamp revealed a small room, with a stone floor and ceiling. Bookshelves lined three walls. Matthew squeezed against the furthest shelf so that Kate could enter. He could feel her trembling.

'What is the matter, Kate? Is it the trip to France? I am sure that it will be well.'

She shook her head, but Matthew saw her brush something from her eye. Clearing a space among the books, she placed the lantern on one of the lower shelves. 'Could you lift that book from the top shelf, please? Take care, for it will be dusty.'

Stretching up, Matthew took down the volume that she indicated. It was large, with dark leather covers. He blew off the thick coating of dust and cobwebs.

'Thank you.' Kate held the book in both hands for thirty seconds before opening it at an illustration on the central page and placing it on the back shelf. The lantern shone on a scene of horror from Dante's *Inferno*.

'Have you ever wondered why we do not sell Gothic romances?' Kate asked. 'There is a demand, and a good profit.'

Matthew shook his head.

'No.' Kate answered her own question. 'And have you ever wondered why I do not speak about my mother?'

Matthew nodded. 'I have wondered, but I did not want to hurt you by asking.'

She looked at him, with the lantern light reflecting from her eyes and highlighting the determined set of her lips. 'I should have thought of that.' She nodded, gave a brief smile and touched his arm. 'Yes. You're the kindest of men, Matthew and I apologize, for I had not considered that.'

Matthew said nothing. He knew Kate well enough to realize she was building up to something.

'Can you remember what you did for Emily in Mr Lamballe's mine?' Kate's voice was soft, as if she were speaking to herself. 'You carried her up from the dark and took her home.'

The lantern flickered, casting strange shadows in the small room.

'That was a good thing to do.' Kate's voice was so low that Matthew had to strain to hear it. 'You are a pippin, Matthew Pryde.' She continued before he had time to reply. 'Can you guess why I have brought you here?'

'I cannot,' Matthew said.

There was a few minutes silence before Kate spoke again. 'When I was small, my mother used to bring me here when I had been naughty. Oh, I was a terribly naughty child. Sometimes I could not eat my dinner, and sometimes I did not read well enough, and once I even spilled some milk on my dress.'

'What a horrible little girl you must have been.' Matthew shook his head, smiling. 'A veritable sinner, no less.'

'Yes. So Mother must have thought. Every time I did something wrong she would bring me down here, with a backboard, a short candle and this book.' There was a long pause, but, realizing that Kate was reliving bad memories, he put a supportive hand on her arm. She did not shake it off.

'She would make me kneel, with the backboard on, and the candle burning in front of this book, open at this picture.' Kate allowed the light to play on a Gothic woodcut with images of Satan and the suffering of the damned. 'She said that if I made a noise, or told Father, the figure in the book would come alive. Then she would leave me, closing and bolting the door. I could hear her footsteps receding, and the trap door closing, and I was alone down here, with the candle and the picture.'

Matthew looked again at the picture, imagining the terror of a young girl locked alone down here. 'It is no wonder that you are still scared of the dark.'

'After a while the candle would go out, but I knew that the devil was still there, and I would cry softly, for I was too afraid to make a noise.' This time it was Kate's hand that crept closer, finding and squeezing Matthew's with such desperation that he nearly pulled away. 'I am still afraid of the dark, Matthew, desperately, terribly afraid, but even more afraid of having somebody else controlling me. Like Mother did.'

'I understand.' He squeezed back, overwhelmingly grateful that she could put her trust in him.

'Do you?' Kate's voice rose slightly, but whether in anger or uncertainly, Matthew could not tell. She turned toward him, more vulnerable than he had ever known her. 'The dark was worst, but sometimes she would put thimbles on her fingers and slap me, and then there was the rhubarb bottle...' There were tears on her face, but she allowed herself the consolation of only a small embrace before wriggling free. Her voice was firmer as she spoke again.

'She was a martinet, Matthew, and she ran us all, Father included. We could neither speak, nor write, nor read, nor even go to church without her approval. Father and I tried to help each other, but Mother dominated us both. We walked on eggshells for all my childhood, and I cried when she died.'

'She was your mother,' Matthew said, attempting to support her.

'Yes, Matthew, but I was not crying through grief; I was crying through relief. Once she died, our lives, Father's and mine, improved dramatically.'

'I understand more,' Matthew said. He did not say how much he envied her relationship with her father. He also felt despair churning within him as his hopes of marriage contracted; it was obvious that Kate was comparing a husband to her domineering mother.

'If we have children, Matthew, you must promise that they will not be treated so.'

'Of course I promise,' Matthew said, and

realized the implications of her words. He took a deep breath, feeling slightly sick. 'Are you agreeing to marry me?'

'I certainly would not marry anybody else,' Kate said, 'not after you dragging me into this dark room on my own! What *would* Mrs Grundy say? My reputation will be in tatters!' Her laugh sounded slightly hysterical, but he held her close until her lips sought out his and they kissed. She was soft and slightly salty and entirely Kate.

'I fear that I will be a very poor wife,' Kate started, but Matthew kissed away her words.

'But I must keep the shop,' Kate said, after a long time, 'for I have to care for Father.'

At that time Matthew would have promised her the moon and sun, had they been his to give, so he nodded.

'What will your father say?' Matthew wondered. He remembered the fragments of conversation that he had heard, and guessed that Kate had already discussed the situation with him.

Kate's giggle was reassuring. 'I can just imagine.' She deepened her voice in a poor imitation of Charles Denton. 'So you have come to a decision after so long, Kate, my dear. I suppose I will have to pay for the wedding, damn your eyes, and that will be more expense.'

Matthew hugged her again, unable to quite believe that she had accepted him. 'Last time I asked your father,' he reminded, 'he refused permission.'

'Last time you were a boy still articled in an apprenticeship,' Kate reminded. 'And anyway, this time I will speak to him first.' She giggled girlishly. 'Everything will be all right now.'

'Of course it will, as long as we are together.' Matthew agreed. 'You'll never be alone in the dark again.' He glanced at the picture, suppressing a shudder, as a flicker of the candle seemed to put a leer on the devil's face.

'Not any more,' Kate said, and squeezed his arm. 'Come along, Matthew, let's go and tell Father to give his permission.'

Matthew woke with the sensation that a hundred little demons had escaped from the pages of Dante's book and were engaged in a competition to break into his head. He groaned, rubbed his temples and tried to sit up. The movement increased his pain so he sank back to the pillow.

He was not sure where he was or how he had got there, but when he eventually forced his eyelids apart, blinking at the terrible light that stormed through the closed curtains, he realized that he had slept in the armed chair in Mr Denton's front parlour.

'It was rack punch that did it, sir.' Emily hovered over him, her bright eyes an insult to his agony. Even after a few days away from the mine, she seemed to have grown an inch in height and matured five years. 'But Miss Kate said that this would help.' She proffered a glass holding some disgusting mixture. 'Raw eggs in milk.' She thrust the glass under his nose, smiling. 'And I can't tell you how happy I am for you both, sir. Drink.'

'Take it away,' Matthew begged, but Emily refused to leave. 'Miss Kate told me that you must drink this, sir. She said that I was to stand here until you did, or she'd know the reason why.'

Matthew looked up. Miss Kate. That was his intended; the thought was suddenly terrifying. 'How is Miss Kate?'

'Every bit as bad as you are, sir.' Stepping closer, Emily put the lip of the glass to Matthew's mouth. 'Come on now, sir, and drink it all down.'

Unable to resist, Matthew obeyed, hating the determination in Emily's face as much as he despised the weakness that kept him lying in the chair. He heard movement from the bedrooms above, Mr Denton's heavy footsteps and the lighter patter of Kate. 'I shall have to rise,' he said, quickly checking under the covers to ensure that he was decent. The thought of meeting Kate when he was unwashed and unshaven spurred him to forget his headache and the churning in his stomach, so he shooed Emily from the room, made a quick toilet at the ewer and basin and eased his head out of the back window to allow the morning air to wake him. He heard the bustle as Mr Denton manoeuvred the stairs and Kate helped Emily set the table, but then the raw eggs did their duty and he had to leave the room.

'Are you sure, now?' Matthew heard Mr Denton's voice as he returned to the parlour. He hesitated outside the door, hating himself for eavesdropping, but unable to make his presence known.

'Of course I am sure, Father.' Kate sounded tired. 'Matthew is a good man. I will never find a better.'

'Of that I have no doubt,' Mr Denton said. 'But are you absolutely certain that you wish to marry him?'

Kate's reply was inaudible, and then Mr Denton spoke again. 'I know you too well to believe you, Kate. I know that you are not *entirely* sure about your choice of husband. We shall see what can be done.'

Scuffing his feet along the floor to give warning of his impending arrival, Matthew threw open the door. He forced himself to smile, although he felt nauseous at the thought that Mr Denton doubted Kate's commitment.

'Well, my boy?' Mr Denton sounded as cheerful as ever, despite the ice pack that he wore on his head in lieu of a wig. 'Have you come to your senses and decided not to take Kate off my hands?'

'Indeed not, sir.' Matthew could not help himself from grinning across the table at Kate, whose face had a distinct green tinge. She smiled back, wincing.

'What do you mean, *sir*?' Mr Denton sipped at the cup of tea that Emily placed in front of him. 'You're family now, in all but name. Damn it, man, you've been that for years, it just had to be agreed. You know that I look upon you as a son, so we'll have none of this *sir* nonsense. It's Charles from now on, or I'll refuse to answer you.'

Matthew looked to Kate, who raised her eyebrows but said nothing. 'Thank you, sir, Mr Denton.' He had to force himself to say

'Charles', but immediately he did so, Mr Denton thrust out his hand.

'Well said, Matthew. And well met. An engineer for a son, and even better, a good man. By God, sir, you make me proud, if you don't mind me saying so!'

Matthew regretted the impulse that made him shake his head. For a moment he wondered if he should tell Mr Denton everything that had recently transpired, including the impending trip to France, but a slant of sense persuaded him to keep quiet. Such an admission would only worry his prospective father-in-law, and put Kate in a very awkward position.

'However, now that you are betrothed, it makes things much easier for your forthcoming journey north, does it not? I do understand that you must investigate other mines to search for possible improvements, and these business journeys can be quite tiresome when one travels alone.' Mr Denton placed a podgy hand on Matthew's shoulder. 'Of course, it would be quite unthinkable for a single lady to travel even with a respectable gentleman, but as long as all the necessary proprieties are observed, there can be no objections to a man travelling with his intended.' Mr Denton beamed at his own magnanimity. 'I know that I can trust you to preserve her honour.'

That word 'trust' cut deeply into Matthew's conscience as he realized that Kate must have told her father that she was to accompany him on a trip to the northern mines. This amiable gentleman had welcomed him into his home and family, and he had responded with deceit that involved his daughter. Matthew glanced at Kate, but she just smiled happily back.

'And when exactly do you intend to go, my boy?' Mr Denton asked.

'Very shortly, Father.' Kate spoke for Matthew. Her look warned Matthew to keep quiet.

'Yes, Charles,' Matthew confirmed, hating himself for lying. Kate could accompany him as far as an inn in Deal, and would wait for him there when he performed his mission to France. He forced a smile. 'I assure you that I will treat her as a gentleman should.'

Mr Denton met his eyes. 'Of that I have little doubt, Matthew. I am more interested in discovering if she welcomes that treatment.'

'Father!' Kate began to scold, until Mr Denton raised his hand.

'No, no, Kate, let there be no secrets among the three of us. I am pleased that you have assented to Matthew's proposal, but I suspect that you still harbour doubts.' When he looked up, his expression was as hard as Matthew had ever seen. 'The experience of travelling is a great discoverer. I hope that you will meet each other's expectations, but if not, then you still have a career, Matthew, while Kate has a home and an independent income.'

Matthew nodded, his emotions confused. On the one hand, he wondered if Mr Denton approved of him as a future son-in-law, and on the other he was still elated that Kate had finally agreed to marry him. Compared to her assent, the impending trip to France was small beer.

Seven

Deal and the English Channel
June 1805

'It's like looking out from the stern cabin of a ship.' Kate stood in the front parlour of the Dolphin Inn at Deal, overlooking the beach. 'The sea is so close.'

Matthew smiled at her, unable to believe that she would soon be his wife. Although Mr Denton's words lurked in his mind, he did not doubt his feelings for Kate. She leaned forward, twisting her head to look out of the bow window, and that elusive twist of hair escaped, as it always did. Smiling, he reached out to push it back, and she momentarily put her hand on his. The simple touch thrilled him.

'Do you have everything you need, Matthew?'

Matthew nodded. He had been over the arrangements a score of times with Mr Black, who was going to accompany him. He went through his list. 'Joseph Manton pistol, map of northern France, French-made clothing, spyglass, paper for taking notes.' He shook his head. 'I was going to take a French primer, to help me with the language, but I will have to rely on Mr Black for that.'

Kate shook her head. 'I do wish that you spoke French, Matthew. You need a translator over there, and I put little faith in Mr Black.'

'I will just keep my mouth shut,' Matthew said.

'And Mr Lamballe? Will your sudden absence not raise his suspicions?'

'I gave him the same story that we fed your father, that I must travel north to investigate another mine.' Matthew stroked his club pigtail. 'I still find it hard to believe that he may be working for Bonaparte.'

'Take care over there.' Kate nodded seawards to the unseen coast of France. It was unseasonably dull, with a cold wind that lifted the top from the Channel swell and spread white spray across the beach. Beneath a clinging mist, the sea looked chillingly dangerous.

Matthew was no seaman. His previous nautical experience was limited to a couple of trips from the Northumberland coast to the Black Corbie, and the prospect of sailing the Channel, thick with French privateers, was unnerving. He forced a grin. 'I'll be in good hands,' he said. 'The Royal Navy will take care of me.'

'The Royal Navy are not involved, Mr Pryde.' Mr Black had slipped quietly beside them. He shot the cuffs of his frilled white shirt as he peered out the window. 'We have quite another method of transport.'

'You're not going by balloon, are you?' Kate's tone was teasing, but her eyes were deeply troubled.

'Nor by tunnel,' Mr Black reassured her. He

nodded outside, where one of the Deal luggers approached the beach. 'There's our vessel, Mr Pryde.'

'Good God in heaven!' Matthew stared. 'We can't cross the Channel in that!'

The lugger appeared long and clumsy as it approached the steeply shelving shingle of the beach. As Matthew watched, its bows rose abruptly and the two masts tilted backward until they were at a frighteningly sharp angle.

Kate withdrew her breath sharply – 'She's going to capsize!' – but the vessel merely skimmed the surface of the shingle, hissing to a halt as the crew swiftly furled the lugsails. Within a minute, half a dozen people were crunching across the beach.

'Some of the best seamen in the world, the Deal mariners,' Mr Black said, quietly. 'We often use them for operations such as this.'

'I thought they were all smugglers,' Matthew protested.

'Many of them are,' Mr Black said. 'Can you think of better experience? After a lifetime of avoiding the revenue cutters, what do the French matter?'

Kate squeezed Matthew's arm. 'You've to take care now, Matthew. Remember that you're an engineer, not a Hector or an Ossian.' Her eyes were troubled.

Matthew forced a smile and looked out to sea. Closer than London, France was just beyond the mist that hugged the waves closely as a shroud. 'Oh, go to Bath with you, Kate. I'll be in good hands.' Black was there to keep him right on the language and all the bureaucratic documentation that Continental Europe believed was necessary. He deliberately lightened his tone. 'I'm quite looking forward to kicking Boney's shins, spoiling Fouché's plans and helping Britain win the war.'

'All that and back for Saturday,' Mr Black agreed. He bowed to Kate. 'I don't expect we'll be more than a few days. A week at most, and then you can lie content with the knowledge that Mr Pryde has done his duty.'

'I'd prefer him safe with me,' Kate said sadly. 'But a week is bearable, and then all will be bowman and we have much happier arrangements to make.'

'Indeed.' Black bowed again, showing an elegant leg. 'I have yet to offer my congratulations, Miss Denton, and you, Mr Pryde. I am sure that you will make an excellent marriage.'

Kate met his bow, but her eyes were troubled. 'I wish I had never voiced my suspicions, Matthew.'

'Everything will be all right.' Black leaned closer to pat her arm. 'All we have to do is find anything resembling a tunnel in the Pas de Calais, or in the surrounding area, and look out for any signs of anything unusual. Mr Pryde will not have to indulge in any heroics.'

'No heroics,' Matthew promised. He could not even hit a cricket ball, for goodness' sake; did this man seriously expect him to battle Bonaparte's hordes?

Mr Black continued. 'Now, attend, Mr Pryde, if you would be so kind. We will be landing only a few miles from Boulogne, where Boney has men under arms, so we will need to be careful. You must do exactly as I say. I have arranged for a boat to call at the rendezvous in three days' time at full tide, and every day after that for the next two weeks.'

'Two weeks?' Kate looked up in alarm. 'You said one week.'

'And let's hope that even that was a pessimistic forecast,' Black reassured her. 'But it's always better to make sure. Now, Mr Pryde, once we find this mine, and I am sure that we shall, I want you to take as many engineering notes as you can – the kind of engines being used, quality of workmanship, that sort of thing. The sort of technical details that laymen such as me would not understand.'

Matthew nodded. Taking notes of engineering details did not trouble him.

'When do you leave?' Kate asked.

'On the ebb tide tomorrow,' Black told her. 'So in the meantime, let us eat, drink and be merry. Have I ever told you of the first time I was in France? Back in '93, it was, during the Battle of Toulon when a certain young major named Bonaparte was besieging Fort Mulgrave. I was a young ensign at the time and...'

'I am sorry, Mr Black,' Kate stifled a deliberate yawn, 'but I am fatigued after our journey.'

'Of course. Then I must regale Mr Pryde.' Black made himself comfortable between them both, signalled for another bottle of port and began. 'We held the harbour and the town, but the sans-culottes were pressing hard. I was leading a patrol into the countryside when four Johnny Crapauds attacked me. Desperate villains, full of bile and Republican spirit. I shot the first, spitted the second and the third ran away, but the last one had more courage and fought me, man to man. It was a hard tussle but I pricked him on the shoulder and he dropped.'

Black shook his head, as though at a pleasant memory. 'So there I was, with my sword dripping, and three of the moosoos lying on the ground. Two were dead as a doornail, but the other was only wounded. He waited until I turned my back and then he threw himself at me!' Rising from his seat, he brandished his glass, to the consternation of one of the other customers. 'He nearly got me, too, but I parried his thrust and cut his throat, by God...'

'Indeed,' Kate said, 'that's most interesting. You are a veritable Hector, sir.' Lifting her fan, she yawned again, 'I think it is time for me to retire and leave you gentlemen to your conversation and port. I bid you good night.'

When Matthew rose, she pushed him back down on his seat. 'It is all right, Matthew. I suspect that Mr Black has more need of an audience than I have of an escort. I am certain that I can safely climb a flight of steps.' Her smile was as mocking as he had ever seen, but she leaned forward and touched the top of his head with her fan. 'Good night, my love.'

He watched her as she withdrew, but she did not look back.

Cool air caressed his face as Matthew listened to

the beat of surf and the drag and suck of receding shingle. He slithered down the sloping beach, glad that Kate was still safe in her room, for he knew that an emotional parting would have unmanned him, and now he could concentrate on the matter in hand.

'In you get.' The Deal boatman spat a stream of tobacco-coloured liquid into the sea. 'Lively, now.'

Matthew clambered into the small boat with Black sitting opposite, his face set and his long grey cloak pulled high over his chin. The tricorne hat was jammed over his eyes.

Shivering in the chill of the pre-dawn, Matthew wondered if summer would ever arrive this year. He looked to the east, where flashes of phosphorescence revealed breaking waves.

'Careful there!' Black against a grey-streaked sky, the lugger loomed overhead. A swaying lantern revealed the name *Tern*, and then the wind snuffed out the light. To Matthew's unpractised eyes, the lugger's masts seemed to be precariously raked, with one central and the other stepped very far aft. Rough hands dragged him uncompromisingly on board and relieved him of his bag. 'Sit there, keep your head out of the way of the boom and keep quiet.'

Matthew did as he was told, marvelling at the silent efficiency with which the men thrust out clumsy sweeps to push them clear of the beach. The long hull raised barely a ripple as it sat in the shallows, and then the sweeps dipped and pulled.

'Fly for me, *Tern*!' The words from an unseen

116

mariner were strangely poetic, but suited the sudden surge of speed as the hull hissed through the water, with a white bow wave grinning beneath the bowsprit.

Matthew glanced astern, where the huddled roofs of Deal crouched under the dull English sky. He bid a quiet farewell to freedom, and lifted a hand to Kate, quietly sleeping so close by. Suddenly he felt sick; he wanted to jump overboard and swim back, but already *Tern* was a good quarter-mile from shore and moving fast.

He saw somebody hustling Mr Black below, realized that there was another passenger sitting slumped under a vast boat cloak in the stern and wondered how many spies this lugger was taking to France.

Wiry men hauled up the two lugsails with hardly a word exchanged and *Tern* headed into the high swell of the Channel, with spray spattering on board and a single seagull hovering astern. Briefly, Matthew wondered if Coleridge's Ancient Mariner had viewed his albatross with as much melancholy as he did that white bird, shuddered, and hoped that Kate would not be too angry when she woke to find him already gone. Simultaneously, and perversely, he wished that he had said goodbye.

It was too late now. Kate would be rising, rushing down to see him. Matthew imagined her disappointment and hated himself for his selfishness. He shook his head, forcing himself to focus on something else.

He noticed that the sails were darker coloured than normal, presumably so they could not be seen at night, while the masts were lower, and supplemented by the sweeps that were now neatly stowed just inside the bulwarks. Glancing astern, he saw the rising sun glint a last salute to the white cliffs and took a deep breath. He was on his way to France as an agent of the government. He was sailing into danger and might never return to Kate, so soon after they had become engaged.

God, but he felt sick.

'Here, have a sip of this.' Black slid down at his side.

Matthew accepted the flask willingly. He had expected rum, but it was French brandy and none the less welcome for the bite. 'Thank you.'

'We're making good progress,' Black said. 'No, don't sit up.' He pushed Matthew down as the seamen worked the sail and the great boom swung past, a few inches above their heads. 'These hackboats are fast as the devil,' he said, 'but they were hardly created for tall men.' His grin was unexpected. 'I'm afraid that we are surplus to their real purpose.'

'Smuggling?'

'Of course. This is an owler's boat, built by Ransom and Ridley of Hastings to the specific requirements of Captain Page, who uses it purely for the free trading.'

'Joss Page?'

'He's the best,' Black confirmed.

Matthew nodded. It was logical. He remembered the shawl he had bought at the May Day festivities. Joss Page had carried that from France, no doubt in this very lugger. The connection with Kate, however tenuous, assumed vast importance for a few minutes as *Tern* thrust across the Channel.

In common with everybody in Kent, Matthew was aware of the activities of the smugglers, who carried gold to France in return for luxury silks and brandy. It was said that Deal smugglers helped the French economy to survive, but there were few women in southern England who did not possess some article of French clothing in their wardrobe. 'So why is Captain Page helping the government?'

'Admiral Springer gave him a stark choice. If he carries agents over to France when and where required, then no notice will be taken of his activities. If he refuses, then the Press will take him and his entire crew.'

Matthew nodded. That was also logical. Nobody wanted to be pressed into the Royal Navy. 'Where are we now?'

'Passing over the Goodwin. Can't you smell the sands?'

Matthew sniffed but could smell nothing but salt water and tar. He swallowed hard when the boat gave a more than usually violent heave and his stomach reacted in sympathy. He glanced up when there was the unmistakable sound of female laughter from below. 'A woman?'

Mr Black nodded. 'That'll be Betsy, the captain's sister. She acts as mate as well.' He smiled. 'If you'll forgive me, I must pay my respects.' He rose unsteadily, grabbing at the low bulwark for support and touched a hand to his hat. 'One must keep friendly with the ladies,' he said, 'for they are the key to success.'

They were far into the Channel now, with the white cliffs a distant smear and the wind kicking the top from waves that rose on either side. The seagull was still following, its wings spread as it hovered on some invisible current of air, and Matthew fought a returning spasm of nausea. Cold spray spattered inboard.

'Sail approaching from larboard.' The words were laconic, but a young man, perhaps in his late twenties, with a face tanned brown by the wind and hands so large that they appeared deformed, shinned up the mainmast with amazing dexterity. He extended a spyglass.

'Naval brig,' he shouted. 'Starboard the helm, and keep a watch.'

'Will she board us?' Matthew asked, and the man shook his head.

'She could no more catch us than fly to the moon, mister.' He replaced the spyglass in its bracket by the mizzenmast. 'Your first trip to France, I hear?'

Matthew nodded.

The man's grip seemed to crush the bones in Matthew's hand. 'Joss Page.'

Matthew bowed. So this was the famous Captain Page; he had expected a man pickled with age and experience rather than this virile youngster with the clear eyes of a saint and the strength of a Hercules. 'An honour, sir.'

'You'll be all right. Johnnie Black's a good man, if he keeps away from the ladybirds.' Captain Page winked. 'He's trying it on with Betsy now, I hear. That's one woman who will teach him right from wrong, I'm telling you.' He glanced around. 'Not much navy today. The Frog fleet is away in the West Indies, I hear, with Nelson piling on all sail in pursuit, and the whole of Europe holding its breath for the outcome.'

Matthew tried to smile. 'And what will the outcome be, Captain Page?'

Page shrugged his shoulders. 'Why, sir, Nelson will meet the French and smash them, as he always does.'

'So do you think there will be an invasion? You seem to know these seas as well as any man.'

'Invasion? Look around you and tell me what you see.'

Rising to his feet, Matthew tried to balance on the gyrating, lurching deck. 'The sea, dozens of distant sails, and the coast of England.'

'Aye, now look again.' Taking Matthew's arm in a painfully powerful grip, Page slowly turned him in a complete circle. 'There is a clutch of Ramsgate trawlers, catching fish for the London market. And there is a coaster, carrying God-knows-what to God-knows-where. And that one? Rice from the Mediterranean, northward bound for Leith or Dundee. And over there?' Captain Page pointed toward the North Foreland. 'More coasters, galliots, fishing busses, hoys, brigantines, sloops, a wherry or two, three Deal luggers like ourselves, a cutter, two snows and that solitary Royal Naval brig.'

'Yes, there are many vessels out here,' Matthew agreed, 'but I fail to see your point.'

'That is because you take these things for granted, Mr Pryde. Tell me, how many of these vessels are French?'

Matthew shook his head. 'I could not tell you, Captain.'

'I could, Mr Pryde. Hold up a handful of fingers and take away five. How many do you have left?'

'Why, none.'

'And that's how many Frenchmen there are on the Channel today.' Page spat over the side. 'I do not say that the French will not come, Mr Pryde, but I do say that they will not come by sea!' His laughter echoed over the lugger, but Matthew felt a chill hand of fear clutch him. He wondered if, even as they sailed so confidently across the Channel, French miners were hacking out a tunnel hundreds of feet below, every day carving their way closer to the fertile fields of Kent.

'I see your point, Captain Page,' he said. Only the Royal Navy had ever thwarted Bonaparte; he was not a man to accept defeat, so would devise a method of circumventing Britain's defences. Suddenly Matthew realized just how important his mission might be. He must succeed; he must stop Bonaparte's mad design.

'And now, Mr Pryde, I expect that you'll be wanting to go below,' Captain Page invited. 'And meet the third member of your party.'

'We have no third member,' Matthew said, confused.

'Indeed you have,' Captain Page said. 'And a very insistent person, too, I hear. This way.'

* * *

There was a single hatch leading below, and a stern cabin that reeked of tobacco smoke and brandy. Black looked up as they entered, and unwrapped his arm from the waist of the young woman who must have been Betsy Page. She lowered a clay pipe from her mouth and glowered at them from under a tangle of hair.

'You're Betsy Page?' Matthew started, recognizing the woman who had sold him Kate's shawl.

She ignored him and railed at her brother. 'Can't you leave me in peace for five minutes? The boat doesn't need me now!'

'My apologies, Betsy,' Captain Page did not sound in the least apologetic, 'but it is time that Mr Pryde met our other passenger.'

'Ah,' Black stood up, 'maybe I should leave, then.'

'You stay right where you are, mister,' Betsy ordered, 'and continue what you were doing.'

The third occupant of the cabin huddled beneath the swinging lantern, still shielding his face with a hooded boat cloak. He nursed a heavy glass as if his life depended on the contents.

'Mr Pryde,' Captain Page said quietly, 'this lady will be accompanying you.'

'Lady?' Matthew repeated foolishly. This voyage seemed destined to overload him with surprises.

The figure in the corner straightened up and tossed back the hood. Kate grinned at him, her eyes full of mischief.

Eight

**Northern France
June 1805**

For a long moment, Matthew stared at her. 'What do you think you are doing? You're not coming to France.' He heard the heat in his voice. 'It's far too dangerous!'

'Do you think I would let you go alone? You can't even speak the language!'

They glared at each other as Betsy Page leaned back, holding her pipe and grinning. 'Don't mind me, I like a good argument. Married, are you?'

'Not yet,' Kate told her, briefly.

'No? You act as if you are.' Betsy winked at Matthew. 'If she's like this before you wed her, Mr Pryde, just imagine how much fun you'll have later.' She chuckled and grabbed hold of Black. 'You come with me, Johnny boy. Leave them to work things out in peace.' Eyeing Matthew up and down, she winked at Kate. 'Nicely turned leg, Katty, my gal. I like a nice calf on my men, and a shapely breech!' Her laugh filled the cabin, as Kate looked away in obvious confusion. 'Enjoy your fight.'

'Wait!' As soon as the cabin door banged shut,

Kate held up a single finger. 'Before we begin, what is your objection to me coming along with you?'

Matthew frowned. 'You might be killed.'

'And don't you think that I am also worried that you might be killed?' When she put her head on one side, Matthew saw that she was trembling and his anger immediately dissipated.

'Yes.' Matthew shook his head, struggling to understand. 'But I am a man. It is my duty to go.' He tried to explain. 'Kate, I am responsible for you and I don't want you here. It's not right that you should be in danger.'

'Oh, for God's sake! Did you not listen when I poured out my heart to you in the cellar?' Her anger easily matched his. 'I told you that I would make a poor wife, and so I will. A good wife does as she is told, Matthew, but I cannot. I must do as *I* think best, not as others think best for me.' Extending her hand, Kate brushed imaginary dust from his shoulder. 'Can you grasp that? You may wish to change your mind, Matthew, and find another wife. I would, if I were you ... Can you remember that I said that I do not want anybody to control my life?'

Matthew nodded. 'I remember, but...'

She put a hand to his lips. 'Please. Let me talk. That includes even you, Matthew. So if I choose to sail to France, then I shall do so, not as your responsibility, but on my own.'

Remembering the snatch of Mr Denton's conversation that he had overheard, Matthew searched for words, but Kate pulled her cloak closer and pushed past him. She paused at the cabin door. 'If you want to withdraw your offer of marriage, Matthew, I will understand, but I will still come with you to France. I have made my decision, and married or not, you are my man, until you decide otherwise.'

Matthew felt himself gape as the door closed. When he had considered marriage, he had thought of a conventional wife, who would manage his house and bring up his children. He had not considered a wife with such radical ideas, but then, he had been attracted to Kate because she was so different. He sat down on the seat that was still warm from her body, thinking about the other women that he had met. They had seemed so predictable, so much like each other that it was hard to differentiate one from the other. Only his sister Grace had possessed any sort of character.

'What have I fallen into?' Matthew shook his head, not sure what to think. Only one thing was certain: whatever she believed, Kate Denton was not coming with him to France. He sat for some time, trying to make sense of his feelings.

'Kate!' Only when Matthew ran onto the deck did he realize that they were already approaching the French coast. There was a long headland thrusting toward them, fields smearing green beneath a heavy sky and the clustered dots of settlements.

'Over here, Matthew.' Kate was standing by the mainmast, staring toward France. She held his arm when he approached. 'It is strange to think that just a few miles away, the ogre of Europe is waiting.'

'Those are the Heights of Ambleteuse.' Black joined them and indicated a prominent ridge. 'It is said that Bonaparte often stands there, gazing toward England as he plots his invasion strategy.'

Kate suppressed a shiver. 'Is it wise to sail so close?'

'We will keep offshore,' Captain Page said, quietly. 'Out of range of their gun batteries.'

'Have they many?' Kate wondered.

'Too many,' Black replied. 'Bonaparte has planted batteries on every headland and overlooking every harbour. He wants at least one field gun to every league of coast. Partly they are to defend the coastal traffic, and partly to guard the Boulogne Flotilla; that's their invasion fleet.'

'Now you see why I don't want you coming to France,' Matthew reminded Kate, but she said nothing.

'Look!' Black handed a spyglass to Matthew and pointed toward land. 'In that bay there.' At first Matthew saw nothing, then he saw row after row of open boats, fastened side by side just off shore. They bobbed up and down with the swell, an ominous reminder of Bonaparte's intentions.

'Invasion barges,' Captain Page said. 'These ones are small *péniches*, but there are also larger *prames*, every one armed with its own cannon. I saw one towed into Deal harbour a year or two back, complete with fifty Frenchmen. Arrogant buggers, boasting that they would not be prisoner long, for Bonaparte would soon be over to release them.'

'Aye, maybe he will, and maybe he won't,' Mr

Black said, quietly. 'But he's not over yet.'

Matthew nodded, but he thought of the great hole that Lamballe was digging under the Kent countryside, and the wide tunnel probing under the Channel. 'Let's hope that he never is,' he said.

'That there is Boulogne,' Captain Page pointed to a town that seemed to huddle against the coast, its church spires thrusting toward the sky, 'and I hear that between here and Calais are tens of thousands of French soldiers, all watching us.'

Kate smiled. 'I would think that they have other things on their mind apart from us, Captain Page.'

'Perhaps so,' Captain Page agreed, 'but all the same, I think it would be best if we moved away.'

A stream of orders saw the lugger haul further out, minutes before white smoke jetted from the shore and there was a sudden fountain of water two cables-lengths to starboard. The flat report of the cannon sounded seconds later.

'Just warning us off,' Captain Page said quietly. He glanced over to Black. 'Boney's a bit jittery nowadays, Mr Black. I'd be careful, if I were you.'

Matthew had stepped back. 'Were we in danger, Captain Page?'

'Not even a little bit. These French gunners couldn't hit a bull's arse with a cricket bat, but neither could you, if I remember.' The sudden grin was disarming, 'I watched you at the May Day match.'

'The danger starts when we leave *Tern*,' Black said. Lifting his spyglass, he examined the coast. 'Pray that God grants us success, for I have no desire to see London in flames.'

Kate shivered, but shook away Matthew's attempts to drape his cloak over her. 'That won't help,' she told him.

An unseasonably cold day had ended in a clouded night that provided perfect cover for a surreptitious approach to France. Captain Page ordered the sails furled and rowed *Tern* parallel with the coast, each member of the crew hauling slowly as Betsy stood at the tiller, pipe clenched upside down between her teeth.

Matthew felt slightly disappointed at France. Where he had expected great fortifications and armed guards, instead *Tern* eased past a quiet bay that would not have been out of place in Kent. Mist shrouded a rocky island half a mile offshore, while sounds of military music drifted like sugar coating a poisonous pill. Matthew shivered; he must make sure that Kate was not permitted to land in this country of soldiers and secret police.

'Baie de l'Isle,' Captain Page said. 'It's a strange place this, overlooked by high headlands and with water deep enough for the entire Channel Fleet. You'd think Boney would fill it with invasion barges, but instead he throws up a couple of defensive forts and neglects it. He's certainly no seaman, whatever his island roots.'

'Are there no troops on the island?' Matthew wondered.

'Sometimes.' Page gave casual orders that curbed *Tern*'s speed, so the sweeps barely raised a splash. 'Boney shipped in scores of workmen during the Peace when he planned to build a harbour of refuge, but he never got it finished, so I hear.'

'I see.' Matthew lost interest. He watched as *Tern* passed the bay and steered northward for quarter of an hour before slithering onto a muddy strip of beach. There was a line of dunes, with bent grass blurry in the dark and wind lifting a haze of sand. Yellow light blinked from the windows of a nearby village, and the barking of a dog ended in a high-pitched yelp.

'This is where you disembark,' Captain Page said, quietly. 'Mr Black, I will be here on Friday, high tide, and every two days thereafter. If you are not here within a fortnight, then you're on your own.'

Matthew saw Kate stepping on deck and knew that he must act quickly. Once she was ashore, he would be unable to protect her.

'Kate' – he lunged forward, grabbing her arm – 'you're not coming.' He held her tight to still her struggles. 'Captain Page, please keep this woman on board.'

'Keep her on board?' Page shook his head, all amiability gone as he proved why he was the master of this smuggling lugger. 'It's too late for cold feet now. I've got a cargo to collect. Now enough of this shilly-shallying! The longer we stay here, the more chance that Johnny Frenchman will come.'

Black had already slid over the side. He looked

back from the beach. 'What's the hold-up? Come on, Mr Pryde, and you, Miss Denton.' His voice was urgent. 'We can't stay here!'

'Matthew! Let go!' Kate injected venom into her voice and eyes, but it was Betsy Page who moved swiftly to Matthew's side and rapped his knuckles with a marlinspike. The sudden pain made him loosen his grip and Kate wriggled free, following Black over the side. She padded up the beach.

'Come along, Matthew,' she whispered, gaily, and he had no option but to follow, cursing quietly.

Moving with a crouching trot, Black led them off the beach and into the darkness of France. There was a strip of ragged furze that tore at their clothing, then a field of some indifferent grain, swaying slowly in a northerly breeze.

'I hope that you're satisfied,' Matthew hissed, 'putting yourself in danger just to show your independence.'

'And you're so clever, spying in France when you can't speak a word of the language!'

Black extended a hand. 'Would you two keep quiet? Save the fighting for the French.'

Keeping low, they skirted the field, passing a solitary cottage that stood outside the village. Matthew swore as a goose complained at their approach, but there was no sign of life from the cottage.

'They are afraid to leave,' Black explained, 'in case we are soldiers out plundering for food. Keep close, now.'

Matthew felt the rapid pounding of his heart as

he heard voices, and then a faint snatch of French, and glanced at Kate. She ignored him, lifting her skirt as if in disdain as they crossed a rough road. Her look should have chilled his blood, but instead he felt simmering anger that she had placed herself in danger.

'There's no need for you to get into a high dudgeon,' she hissed at him. 'I told you I was coming.'

'Wait.' There was urgency in Black's command. 'Lie down!' Matthew obeyed, stretching full length on the ground amidst the grain, and pulling Kate down at his side. She did not object. 'Listen, and for God's sake, keep quiet.'

At first they heard nothing, then the sound drifted on the wind, a drumbeat, low in the distance but steadily increasing in volume.

'What's that?' Kate whispered.

'Boney's soldiers on the march.' Black sounded more curious than concerned 'They're still some distance off, but getting closer, so let's find somewhere safer.' Rising to a crouch, he guided them to a small copse of trees about thirty yards from the road and ordered them to lie down.

The drumming grew louder, accompanied by a shrill piping, and the ground seemed to vibrate underneath them. Matthew peered into the gloom, aware that something was happening but unsure what it was. He saw something long, white and irregular flickering past and realized that it was the trousered legs of a column of marching infantry, their tunics invisible in the dark.

'Part of Boney's army.' Kate sounded calm.

132

'Sshh,' Matthew warned, but she snorted her disdain.

'Don't shoosh me, Matthew Pryde! They're all of thirty yards away. Do you think they can hear me above all that noise they're making?' She raised her voice, deliberately taunting. 'Lord, but I hate the French!'

The drumming faded as the head of the column passed, and the regular vibration of feet continued for five minutes before it died away. Matthew let out a long breath, but it was Kate who began to stand up.

Black pushed her back to the ground, shaking his head violently. He put a finger to his lips.

There was movement in the field, a muttered snatch of conversation, with the French words somehow sinister in the dark. Wood snapped, startlingly close, and an explosion of rough laughter echoed among the trees. A man loomed through the dark, stinking of sweat and tobacco, muttered something and lumbered on. The sound of splashing followed by an ammoniac reek told Matthew that somebody was urinating close by. He put an arm around Kate, who was stiffly immobile at his side.

A slight rustle directed his attention to Black, who lay beneath a bush, with a pistol in his hand. Matthew followed his example, pulling the Joseph Manton from within his cloak. The feel of the walnut grip was reassuring, although Matthew hoped never to have to fight.

A man tramped past within touching distance, his white trousers loose and torn, his black boots scuffed. Carrying his musket with the assured confidence of the veteran that he probably was, he spoke loudly to an unseen companion, stooped to gather dry sticks and moved on. After a few minutes others joined him, plunging straight into the cornfield with no thought for the farmer who owned it. Their voices gradually receded.

'That was thrilling,' Kate said, but Black placed a hand over her mouth, shaking his head.

'Keep quiet,' he urged, 'and keep still.'

Matthew became aware of that rhythmic drumming again, and another small party of men marched past, their white trousers making them appear like a gigantic caterpillar striding along the road. There was a jingle of bridles and bits, a rattle of hoof beats and a company of cavalry appeared, followed by the low rumble of a unit of artillery, their cannon short and sinister behind large-wheeled carriages.

'How many are there?' Kate wondered.

'These are just the ragtag and bobtail,' Black said. 'Stragglers hurrying to Boulogne to rejoin their regiments.'

Matthew glanced at Kate and clutched his pistol, praying that they might discover the mine quickly so they could return home. Cricket on the common seemed an impossible memory.

They lay there all night, enduring a drizzling rain that seeped under their clothing before fading with a dawn that brought more soldiers. A regiment of cavalry jingled along the road, with the morning light picking out the gold braid on their uniforms and reflecting from their steel breastplates.

'Cuirassiers,' Black whispered. 'Boney's serious about this, isn't he?' He raised a hand. 'Listen.'

Above the clopping of hooves and the rattle of equipment, Matthew heard thin music, jaunty, cheerful, and defiant. 'What's that?'

'The "Ça Ira",' Black said, and they listened to the tune that had led the French to a hundred victories on battlefields all across Europe. Black put words to the music:

'A ça ira ça ira ça ira,
Les Aristos a la lanterne...

'They say that Marie Antoinette used to strum the tune,' he said. 'I wonder if she plays it on her celestial harp?'

The music grew louder, and then Kate drew in her breath. Marching four abreast, the French infantry filled the road. The column seemed endless, rank after rank of marching men carrying their muskets any which way, their moustached faces ominous under giant cocked hats with the national cockade that Kate called a 'badge of rascality' ugly in the morning.

'They're not going to stop,' she said quietly. 'They conquered the Alps and all the armies of Europe. What is twenty miles of sea to them?'

'Twenty miles too many,' Black said. He was quietly counting, timing and writing notes in a small pocket book.

After the column came carts, loaded with bags and chests, ammunition, food or bottles of wine.

'At least the soldiers' wives don't have to walk.' Kate pointed to the rear of the convoy, where women gossiped together or lounged in listless boredom, arms draped over the sides of the carts that swayed slowly along the road.

'*Cantinières*,' Mr Black corrected drily, then explained, 'prostitutes.' He looked at Kate, as if expecting shock, but she nodded.

'Very sensible,' she approved. 'Better that way than rape.'

Matthew looked away. Kate always had the power to surprise him. Behind the carts straggled a disorderly collection of camp followers, men and women, some carrying children, others dragging their feet in near exhaustion.

'That's the wives now,' Black said. 'And there we are, all part of Bonaparte's army of invasion.'

Matthew felt a renewed chill at the words. If their fears were correct, then these soldiers, and tens of thousands like them, would be marching through the fields of Kent, descending on Old Ottin and Norrington with musket and slaughter, sweeping aside the half-trained Militia and pressing on to London. He wondered how the Volunteers would fare against such men. Oh, they would fight, he knew. They would rally bravely behind their gaudy colours and march forward in confidence, but could they cope with the plunging shot of a battery of French twelve-pounders? Would they stand when faced with the reality of bone-splintering death and the unbearable agony of dismemberment and mutilation?

He closed his eyes briefly, trying to imagine men such as the Old Ottin cricketers standing in line across the common, muskets held in steady hands as the heady drum-roll of veteran French infantry rattled to the honest English sky.

The mental image altered, as more French appeared, emerging from Mr Lamballe's mine, to crash into the rear of the Kent Volunteers. Matthew pictured the French marching across the neat fields, pillaging Ashbourne as the inhabitants fled, with Mr Denton dying in the burning shambles of his shop.

'We can't let it happen,' he said. He glanced over to Kate, lying bravely at his side with her face white and her lips pressed together.

'We won't,' she told him. 'We'll find their damned tunnel and close it off.'

Matthew squeezed her arm, not sure whether to be shocked at the first curse he had heard her utter, or proud at her courage.

She inched closer, flinching as a twig snapped audibly beneath her. 'Matthew, I know that you do not want me here, but I am here, and so are you, so let's just make the best of it.' She held out her hand, and that curl was no longer playful as it hung loose around her left eye. 'Truce?'

Matthew nodded. 'Truce,' he agreed, 'but I'm still out of humour with you.'

Her smile took him by surprise. 'You can shout at me later, when we are married.'

'That seems to be the last of them,' Black said, after half an hour had passed with only a heavily laden country cart rumbling on the road, 'so let's move on.'

They rose stiffly, now very aware of the presence of Bonaparte's army, and headed inland, away from the coast. Matthew studied the countryside, noting that the fields were larger than those in Kent, while the villages were smaller, more unkempt and with a more guarded atmosphere. There were reminders of the military everywhere, from discarded haversacks to small bodies of foragers, and even the air tasted different, somehow, in a way that he could not explain.

After twenty minutes, Black changed direction again, moving northward, parallel with the coast but keeping away from the roads. They trudged, seemingly for hours, along the edges of vast fields lined with fruit trees whose growth had been stunted by the unseasonably cold summer. Familiar bird song sugared the sky, but Matthew could hear the distant tread of military boots, marching to the coast.

'This will do,' Black ordered. They stood on the crest of a slight rise, overlooking a solid farmhouse. At one time it had been painted white, but time and weather had removed most of the covering so that it was now a dirty grey, with patches of timber work showing through the plaster.

'Those soldiers made us a bit late,' Black said, 'but we should be all right here. Wait.' He slipped away behind a row of slender poplar trees, and Matthew saw him emerge on the earthen path that led to the farmhouse. He rapped on the wooden, peeling door, waited for a reply and nodded to the woman who appeared. She was about forty, with a comfortably rounded body and dark eyes.

Matthew saw the woman put both hands to her

mouth, before beginning a rapid conversation with Black, which seemed to continue when both entered the house. The door closed quietly behind them.

'She's checking with her husband,' Kate told Matthew, as if she was privy to their conversation. She moved closer, as if seeking reassurance. 'Do you really mind me being here?'

'I'm worried about you.' Matthew was pleased that she had asked the question.

'I would be more worried if you had been alone,' she told him frankly, then sugared her words with a smile. 'I do not want to lose you; I've heard how the French mademoiselles can turn a man's head.'

Matthew shook his head. 'I've heard that they do as they're told.'

'Really? How utterly unimaginative of them.' Her smile taunted Matthew until he looked away. 'Mr Black is waving us in.'

A mixture of cooking and farmyard smells greeted them as they entered the house, and Matthew noticed that Kate inspected the interior closely, although there was little enough to see. The door opened directly into a stone-flagged room, with simple, sturdy furniture, while a picture of a young man in military uniform adorned plaster walls. A goat stretched lazily on the ground, closer to the central iron stove than the unglazed window.

The man beside Mr Black was slender, with shadowed eyes.

'You cannot stay here long,' he said slowly in heavily accented English. 'Bonaparte is building up his forces daily; the soldiers may call here at any time. Already they have taken over most of the farms in the area.'

'We will be three days at most,' Black said, 'and then we will leave.' He gestured for Kate to come forward. 'This is my travelling companion, Miss Denton, and her intended, Matthew.' He bowed toward the Frenchman. 'M. Durand, and his wife Suzanne.'

The Frenchwoman appeared from a shaded corner of the room, her clogs clattering on the flagstones. Close to she looked younger than forty, with a finely featured face and tired eyes. Her camlet jacket had faded from red to a dull pink, but the patches were so neat as to be barely noticeable and her apron was crisply white.

M. Durand nodded to Matthew, but bowed splendidly to Kate. *'Enchanté*, mademoiselle, and welcome to France.' His smile appeared genuine. 'It is not perhaps the best time to visit, with the Republicans in charge.'

There was nothing mocking in Kate's curtsy. She spoke in French, accepted Durand's hand and raised it to her lips. As Durand smiled, Suzanne responded with a volley of French that seemed to batter at Matthew's ears, while Kate lifted a hand in protest. She said something that caused Suzanne to slow her speech, and for a few moments they spoke together like old friends.

'Suzanne says that we cannot stay because the soldiers sometimes come to plunder,' Kate told him eventually. 'That is why the goat is inside the house. The soldiers have stolen the rest, and many of the geese and chickens.'

Matthew nodded. 'I understand. Our presence would put them in danger. What would the Republicans do if they found us here?'

'These people are Royalists,' Black interrupted. 'They will accept the danger in the name of the King. *Vive le Roi!*'

Neither M. Durand nor Suzanne responded to the appeal to their loyalty, so Kate tried again, speaking slowly, but emphasizing her words with outspread hands as Suzanne shook her head and Black raised his voice. Matthew allowed the goat to nuzzle at his legs.

'I have told them three days,' Black said. 'The decision has been made.'

'Could you keep quiet?' Kate glared at him. 'You cannot just order these people into danger.'

'It is their duty,' Black said, but Kate stepped toward Suzanne, shaking her head, and the Frenchwoman smiled. Matthew wondered at the secret affinity of women, but when Durand lifted his shoulders in resignation and produced a bottle, he nodded and accepted the brimming glass.

'To France,' Durand said quietly. 'And peace between our countries.' For a second Matthew wondered if drinking to France was treason, but when Durand added, 'And peace from women,' he grinned his acknowledgement and drank.

'Matthew, Mr Black,' Kate switched easily from French to English, 'Mme Durand has agreed that we can stay for two nights, but we have to remain in the barn, out of sight. After that we must find somewhere else. An *estaminet*, perhaps?' She shook her head at Matthew's blank expression, and explained. 'An *estaminet* is an inn.'

'You can't sleep in a barn,' Matthew complained, but Kate shook her head.

'What did you expect to find in the wilderness, men in soft garments? A couple of nights in a barn will not harm me. Or you, and no doubt Mr Black is well used to such hardships.'

Black did not look very pleased at Kate taking the initiative, but he made no objection as Durand led them through a side door and into a cobbled courtyard. There were low outbuildings with sagging doors, a pile of manure against one wall and a general air of despondency, but Matthew was glad to see that the barn was fairly clean. There was straw in the stalls and a large brush leaning against a trestle trough. Motes of dust floated in the beams of sunlight that filtered through the gaps in the high roof.

'Choose a corner,' Durand offered, 'and perhaps rest for a while.'

After the nervous excitement of the Channel crossing and spending a night hiding from the French army, the thought of a couple of hours' rest was very appealing. Matthew moved toward Kate, hoping to make her comfortable, but she was already nestled into the straw with her cloak pulled over her face. Sighing, he curled into a corner and checked the priming of his Manton. If he could not help Kate, at least he could protect her if the soldiers came.

He awoke with the sensation that something was

wrong, but before he spoke Kate pressed a finger to his lips. She lay at his side, with her brow furrowed and straw sticking to her hair and festooned over her green cloak.

'Soldiers!'

She gripped his arm, hip pressing against him as she pointed through a gap in the barn door. Matthew saw movement, a flicker of blue.

'Hide yourself,' Black's voice was taut. 'Don't move until I tell you.'

The stalls were empty of animals but there was high-smelling straw and dark corners replete with cobwebs and furtive rustlings. A solitary chicken rose, squabbling, and settled on the lip of the trough. Black slid to the ground, swearing softly.

Matthew crouched behind a solid shelf of wood, started when Kate crept close to him and felt her hand slide into his. Belatedly remembering that she was afraid of the dark, he gave a reassuring squeeze, before thumbing back the hammer of his Manton.

The sound of voices rose, the French words unintelligible to Matthew's ears. For the first time he wished that Maidhouse College had taught modern languages as well as the classics.

'The soldiers are asking for food, but Suzanne is telling them that they have none to spare,' Kate translated. Matthew could feel her trembling, but whether with fear or excitement, he could not tell.

Somebody laughed and there was a gush of cold light as the barn door opened. A soldier burst in, flinched as the chicken rushed past him but recovered with an embarrassed laugh and removed his cocked hat. His hair was brown and very short above a young, strained face, but there was nothing youthful about the manner he unsheathed his long bayonet as he kicked the door shut.

'He knows we're here!' Trying to still the trembling of his hand, Matthew pushed forward his Manton.

Kate released his hand and stretched to whisper in his ear. 'He's only after the chicken.'

The soldier moved toward them, making loud noises that were presumably intended to attract his prospective dinner. His kick had closed, but not locked, the door and a treacherous slant of wind thrust it wide open.

'Lord!' Matthew felt Kate's breath hot against his neck as sunlight illuminated all but the furthest corners of the barn. Matthew felt suddenly naked; the French soldier could hardly fail to see him.

Squinting along the barrel of the pistol, he began to apply pressure to the trigger. The Frenchman looked ludicrously young, but he represented the scores of thousands outside; he was the enemy and Matthew was resolved not to allow himself, or Kate, to be tamely captured. He could nearly feel himself being placed face down on the guillotine with the basket blood-stained before his eyes and the great triangular blade rasping in the grooves above his neck.

He felt the trigger move slightly; another few seconds and the hammer would fall, igniting the powder to send an ounce of lead toward the soldier. The noise would alert everybody within a hundred yards and he would have to scoop up Kate and run, ending any hope of finding the tunnel. He pushed forward the pistol, aiming directly for the centre of the soldier's body.

'Allez!' Matthew froze as Suzanne bustled in to the barn, shouting loudly. As she approached, waving her arms as if in anger, the soldier turned, flinching before her words. Suzanne shouted at him for a full thirty seconds, pushing him backward with the sheer force of her words, then pulled back her hand and slapped him resoundingly before pushing him toward the open door.

The soldier protested, one hand on his face, and Suzanne appeared to relent. Shaking her head, she dived into the barn, nearly trampling on Matthew's hand, searched for an instant and produced an egg, which she handed to the soldier, before shoving him outside. There was a hollow thump, presumably a bar being placed across the door to deter any further intrusion, and the voices receded.

'You're a regular out and outer, Suzanne,' Black approved, and prodded Matthew in the back. 'Come on, you've had enough sleep. We have a tunnel to find and an invasion to prevent.'

Matthew realized he was trembling as he uncocked his Manton and replaced it inside his cloak. He felt Kate's hand warm on his arm and wished that she were safe in England.

'He couldn't see us, of course,' Black said. 'Not coming from the light of day into the dark of the barn. Thank God none of us panicked.'

Matthew nodded. If Suzanne had not intervened, his shot would have alerted the French and ended the mission. Perhaps Kate thought she would be a poor wife, but he *knew* that he made a very poor spy.

Nine

On the 4th of June 1805, Admiral Horatio Nelson arrived at Barbados in his search for the French fleet. That same day the French Vice-Admiral Villeneuve weighed anchor from Martinique. His plan had been to draw Nelson away from the Channel, and it had worked. Ten days later Bonaparte decreed that Nelson's ships were 'in no state to make long voyages, and his crews are exceedingly tired'.

Northern France
June 1805

The soldiers had been arriving all day, formation after formation marching in, some tired and weary, others fresh and singing. There were cavalry with jingling stirrups, their helmets proud above braided hair, infantry in blue and white uniforms and artillery bouncing past on their carts with the snouts of cannon menacing in the fading light.

'Light six-pounders,' Black said. 'Mobile but

fragile-looking for field work.' He had spent the day noting regimental names and estimating numbers.

Matthew realized that Black knew his stuff. He had recognized nearly every unit by their uniform or standard, and had given an approximation of their history and strength.

'All destined for England,' Black said.

'But they have to get there first,' Kate reminded.

Matthew knew that if even a few thousand of these veterans arrived in England, they could do immense damage. 'Let's see if we can find that damned pit,' he said. They had intended to spend the day searching for the tunnel, but the roads were clogged with French military. They had to skirt the fields, dodging foraging parties and encampments of laughing, confident soldiers, cavalry with horses in such poor condition that Kate was moved to pity and bodies of men who spoke in languages that Kate did not recognize, but knew were not French.

'A polyglot army, this,' she said, quietly.

They moved quietly, a hundred yards at a time, with Matthew's heart hammering and even Black looking shaken at the evidence of French military might. 'If we could only get up high, we might be able to spy out the countryside,' Matthew suggested.

'Yes, or we could hail a passing soldier and ask him where the tunnel is,' Kate injected sarcasm into her voice. 'We may as well hang out a sign – British spies, show me your secrets.'

About to retaliate, Matthew saw how pale Kate

was and realized that her nerves must be strained. He did not know what would happen if the French caught an Englishwoman spying, but guessed that it would not be pleasant. 'Maybe you're right,' he agreed, appeasingly, and followed Black onto a cart track. Wheels had worn deep grooves on either side of a central ridge of grass, while a tattered hedge of gorse sheltered them from the offshore wind.

'This track leads to that rise.' Black pointed ahead, where a cluster of wind-tortured trees marked the crest of a long ridge. 'As Matthew rightly said, we might have a better view from there.' He lowered his voice, as if imparting a secret. 'Remember, if we find the winding gear we're halfway to success.'

Matthew plodded miserably onward, already hating the sordid, uncomfortable life of a spy, acutely aware of the unseasonably cold wind that sliced through his cloak and knowing that they had only a few days before *Tern* was due at the rendezvous. Again he heard the tramp of feet, but with a difference; there was a disturbing clanking, and no regular crunch of boots.

'Wait,' Black said, wearily. By now the march of soldiers was too familiar to worry about. They slipped to the side of the track, seeking shelter in the shell of an abandoned farm. The skeleton of an apple tree hung over them, stripped of leaves and ugly in death. A ragged column of men appeared over the crest ahead and crowded around a bend in the track.

'This lot are different,' Kate observed. 'There is no order.'

'Probably recruits,' Black told her.

More like a mob than a disciplined body, the men shambled downhill, round-shouldered and with their heads hanging in shame. Occasionally one would look up and stare at his surroundings. There was a mixture of ages, from the shockingly young to the seemingly ancient, and the only thing uniform about their clothing was its raggedness. Some were barefoot, others wore heavy boots, and all looked tired. They were all shaven-headed and shackled, with chains around their wrists and ankles, and the men in command wore dark uniforms, rather than the honest blue of the army. When a cart creaked in the rear carrying a collection of picks and lanterns, Matthew glanced at Black.

'Slaves?' he asked.

'Slave labourers,' Black confirmed. 'Petty criminals, deserters or perhaps men who have refused to accept that Bonaparte's way is the only way. Political dissidents.'

Kate shook her head slowly, her eyes soft with pity. 'No wonder we are fighting them. Thank the Lord for British liberty.'

Black's smile was cynical. 'Aye? Tell that to the convicts that we transport to Botany Bay.' When Kate looked confused he gave a short nod. 'But they look like miners, so we'll follow them.'

'Back down again,' Kate sighed, brushing mud from the bottom of her skirt. 'We're going in circles.'

'Welcome to the glamorous world of espionage,' Black agreed.

The slave labourers took a side track that slid around the flanks of the rise and plunged downward. The valley through which they passed was shallow, but dense woodland on either side seemed to press down upon them.

'Strange that the soldiers have not stripped this for fuel,' Black said, but Matthew was too intent on keeping his balance on the muddy road to reply.

There was the sound of hoarse orders and another group joined the first, ragged men merging together in shuffling hopelessness, the clank of chains their only drumbeat and the sting of the lash their alternative incentive to a marshal's baton.

'Ahead!' While Kate and Matthew were staring at the suffering men, Black had been scanning his surroundings. 'Look.'

About a quarter of a mile in front, thrusting to the sky from what must have been a deep depression, the winding drum stood dark against the wooded ridge. As they watched, it began to rotate, and Matthew could hear the hiss and groan of a steam engine.

'How did I miss that?'

'You were concentrating on the people,' Kate excused him at once.

Matthew shook his head. 'I'm not hear to watch people, but to discover the mine.'

'No,' Black disagreed, 'any semi-competent agent could find the mine. You have to decide whether or not it masks a tunnel to England.'

Matthew swore softly at the sudden reminder that the security of Britain depended on his judgement.

'You'll be fine.' Kate took his hand. 'Trust me; you'll be fine.'

'Wait.' Black put up a hand and moved them off the track into the shelter of a twisted tree. 'Watch for an entrance.'

Close to, the mine seemed more extensive than Matthew had at first thought. Set into the hollow, a collection of low buildings clustered within a tall wooden fence, at the gate of which the labourers had stopped. Heads down and shoulders bowed, they waited while dark-uniformed guards counted them.

After a few minutes, the guards pushed open the gate and the convoy shambled in.

'That's it,' Matthew said at once, 'this must be the place.' He indicated the wooded ridges on either side. 'It's hidden in this valley; that's why we could not see it.'

'It could be just a coal mine,' Black warned, but Matthew shook his head.

'So why the slave labourers? And where is the coal?' He pointed to the armed guards that gossiped casually stood at the gates. 'And why the fence and sentries?'

They withdrew to the closest of the overlooking ridges and, using Mr Black's spyglass, watched the operations for the remainder of a dull day. More groups of chained men arrived, while a constant flow of wheeled tubs carried spoil from the pit.

'They must be throwing that in the sea,' Matthew decided. 'There are no spoil heaps, nothing to give away the position of the mine.'

'We could have wandered for a week and found nothing,' Black agreed, 'if we had not chanced on the slave labourers.'

The guards on the gate were kept busy checking clumsy drays, some whose contents were concealed by tarpaulins, and others that carried lengths of timber.

'What are they?' Kate wondered.

'Props,' Matthew explained, 'to shore up the roof. Judging by the numbers, they must be making good progress.'

'Of course,' Black said quietly. 'The sooner they dig the tunnel, the sooner they reach England.'

It was Kate who produced food for them. 'Only bread and cheese,' she said, 'but a lot better than nothing.'

Black looked up. 'How did you manage that?'

'Not me.' Kate shook her head. 'Suzanne brought it this morning.'

'I'll be sure to thank her in person,' Black said. 'Such generosity must be rewarded.'

They ate quietly, watching the unceasing activity in the pit. At irregular intervals there was a muffled bang that seemed to come from beneath their feet, and Kate looked at Matthew for an explanation.

'Explosive,' Matthew said. 'They break up the rock with gunpowder, then clear away the spoil with pick and shovel, shore up the roof with timber and move on.'

'Is that not very dangerous?'

Matthew recalled the stories he had heard about miners dying underground, and his own limited experience of helping clear the rock fall. 'It can be,' he said.

'Boney doesn't care,' Black said. 'Not with so much slave labour, and if that should ever fail, he can conscript foreigners from all parts of his Empire. Human life is cheap to him.'

'Human life is cheap to the British coal-masters too,' Matthew told him, and wondered if such a statement could be construed as treason, given the peril that the country was in.

'I would like to know how long they have been working,' Black said, 'and how deep they have dug.'

Matthew pondered. 'They have to dig deep enough to reach beneath the level of the sea, and then to drive toward England.' He marvelled at the concept. 'Imagine a tunnel over twenty miles long, right under the Channel. A tunnel through which this whole army could march, emerging within forty miles of London, having bypassed the Royal Navy. Albert Mathieu was a genius to think of this.'

'We can't let them succeed,' Kate said quietly. 'We must stop them.'

The sound of the steam pump competed with the clatter of the winding drum as it hauled up more tubs of spoil, each one another bite toward the invasion of Britain, each one a twist of Bonaparte's imperial bayonet into the heart of freedom.

'All three of us?' Black injected sarcasm into his voice.

'We must do something.'

'That's not what we are here for,' Black reminded. 'We are only here to observe and report. No heroics, remember? Anyway, what would you have us do? Fill the thing in?'

'*I* don't know,' Kate sounded tart. 'I am not the engineer here, but I do know that we must do something.' She looked at Matthew, eyebrows raised hopefully.

'Look.' Black pointed toward the mine. 'There must be two hundred miners there, and fifty soldiers on guard. We just observe and report.'

'Wait,' Matthew urged. 'Somebody's coming.'

They watched as a clumsy four-horse diligence lurched over the track, rocking back and forth in a manner that must have been very uncomfortable for the occupants. The guards immediately stiffened to attention and a sergeant stepped forward, barking an order. Most of his men presented arms as two others threw open the gate. The diligence rolled inside the compound.

'Somebody's important.' Black sounded interested. He extended his spyglass. 'There's some sort of symbol on the door, but it's covered in mud. I'd like to see what it is.'

As the diligence slithered to a halt a few paces from the mine entrance the door opened and two people emerged. One was a slim man of about thirty, who carried a dark travelling cloak and a leather case. The bicorne hat seemed too large for his head, and the ribbon around his club pigtail was so badly tied that one end flapped around his neck. He waited for the second occupant of the coach to precede him.

She was a woman of around the same age,

soberly dressed in a concealing cloak that flowed from the black cravat at her neck to her ankles, but her tall bonnet with its huge black cockade hinted at suppressed flamboyance.

'She's a sweet-goer,' Mr Black approved as the woman stepped gracefully forward. 'A very tempting armful.'

Kate sighed, took the spyglass and focused on the woman. 'Look at her throat,' she said, handing the glass to Matthew.

'I can't see her throat,' he said. 'It's hidden under her cravat.'

'Precisely,' Kate said. 'It's hardly feminine, is it? Nor is the cockade, but we can allow that in France. Why the cravat?'

Matthew pulled a face. 'Maybe she's cold.'

'Matthew!' Frowning, Kate retrieved the spyglass. 'You've all the imagination of a mathematician! She's hiding something!'

They watched as the man and woman sauntered past suddenly attentive guards and approached the mine. 'I'd soon find out what's beneath that cravat,' Black leered. 'And what's under the cloak.'

'You are no gentleman, sir,' Kate reproved him absently. 'You have a commonplace mind.'

'Permit me to *enjoy* my commonplace mind,' Black said, taking hold of the spyglass and focusing on the woman. He stiffened suddenly. 'Oh sweet God in heaven!'

'Mr Black?' Kate touched his arm. 'What is the matter? Pray tell!'

'That woman...' Black spoke quietly as if his voice would carry the distance to the mine. 'I know her. She has changed, but ... dear God!'

'You know her?' Kate edged closer, her hand reaching for the spyglass. 'And who is she? Some old lover, no doubt? Pray tell!'

'She is trouble, Miss Denton. That is Citizen Peltier, the niece of Joseph Fouché and probably the most ruthless woman in Europe.'

'But you said that you *know* her, Mr Black,' Kate persisted. 'How would you know such a woman?'

'We have crossed swords before,' Black said slowly. 'Literally as well as metaphorically.' He passed over the spyglass to Kate, who immediately studied Citizen Peltier. 'If she is here, Miss Denton, then this mine is indeed important.'

'Is it usual in France to have such a prominent woman?' Kate wondered, but Black only shook his head.

'There is nothing usual about that woman, Miss Denton. She would be formidable in any country.'

While Peltier entered one of the buildings, the man signalled to the brakesman at the pithead. Leaving his work, the man immediately helped him into a waiting corf. Holding the cable with his left hand, the man nodded to the brakesman, who operated the drum to lower him down the mineshaft.

'So we have a notorious French agent and a mysterious man visiting a mine with no coal.' Black screwed up his face. 'Do you have any suggestions?'

'He could be Mr Peltier,' Matthew hazarded.

'No,' Kate said. 'I don't know who they were,

156

but they did not act like man and wife. He carried himself differently.' She shook her head. 'I recognize that man, somehow. There is something familiar about him, but I don't know what.'

'Familiar?' Black ridiculed her with a smile. 'Have you spent much time in France, then, madam?'

Kate coloured and looked away. 'This is my first time, but I recognize that man. I'd swear to that in a court of law.' She shook her head. 'That will worry me now.'

'Don't let it,' Black said, magnanimously. He raised his spyglass. 'There's the diligence returning now.'

The coachman had performed a wide turn and now headed back to the entrance, avoiding one of the timber wagons with some difficulty. The guards presented arms again.

'Interesting,' Mr Black said, soberly. 'Even Peltier's coach demands respect.'

'So tell me of your previous meeting,' Kate demanded. 'We must have something to pass the time, and I'd wager there is a good deal of romance and scandal involved.'

Black shook his head. 'You'd lose your money, Miss Denton, for there is neither one nor the other.' He was quiet for a long minute, as Matthew continued to study the mine and Kate waited impatiently.

'Come along, Mr Black.'

'I have already mentioned our meeting, Miss Denton. You have heard of the siege of Toulon back in '93? I was a very young lieutenant then,

157

with the Royal Marines. We held the town and the French, with a certain artillery major named Bonaparte, were trying to recapture it.' Black paused for a moment as Matthew pointed to a wagonload of timber arriving at the mine.

'For shoring up the roof,' he said.

Kate spared time for a glance. 'Fascinating,' she said, dismissively. 'Pray continue, Mr Black?'

'My colonel sent me inland with a small detachment to see what the Frenchies were up to, and I encountered a body of irregulars, as I have already said.' Black paused for a moment, searching for words. 'We fought, of course, but we were Royal Marines and they were only peasants with muskets and swords. We killed most of them; indeed, I thought we had killed them all.'

'And Citizen Peltier?' Kate probed. 'Where does she fit in?'

'Her brother was among them.' Black's voice was flat.

'But surely she cannot blame you for that?' Kate was immediately indignant. 'I mean, that was war. You killed him in fair fight!'

'People like Citizen Peltier do not need an excuse to hate,' Black said. 'Now I think we should be quiet and allow Mr Pryde to do his job.'

They spent the remainder of the day hiding above the mine, with Matthew taking detailed notes of everything that he saw.

Using his watch, he counted the tubs of waste that were extracted each hour, and compared the figure with those from Mr Lamballe's mine. If the miners worked at a comparable rate, then he could calculate the extent of the underground workings.

He used the spyglass to examine the steam machinery, estimating its age and capacity to pump water from the mine.

He watched another shift of miners shamble in, shaven heads bowed and chains clanking, and realized that the digging would continue by night and day.

'They're not going to stop,' he said. 'They will push on for ever.'

He could feel Kate's anger growing with every hour, but also knew that Black was correct. They were here to observe and report, not to try some jackass scheme to upset Boney's plans all by themselves.

'Air,' he said at last, lowering the spyglass. 'That is their weakness. That is where they may fail!'

'What?' Kate looked at him with renewed hope in her eyes.

'Every mine has problems. The three most prevalent are flooding, the roof collapsing and dangerous gases.'

'I see,' Kate nodded. 'And this mine?'

Matthew refused to be hurried. 'To combat flooding, mines use pumps. This mine has a fine steam pump for just that reason. To ensure that the roof remains in place, mines either leave columns of coal or use timber baulks as props. We have seen the timber arriving. That leaves gas. Mines fight the build-up of gas by pushing fresh air through the works, but the more extensive the mine, the more difficult that becomes.'

'I understand,' Mr Black said, 'but how does that help us?'

'Albert Mathieu's plan included air shafts that extended from the tunnel roof to the surface of the Channel,' Matthew reminded. 'I cannot see the Royal Navy allowing that to happen, but there must be an alternative. A pump that can thrust fresh air into the mine.'

'You said that there is a pump here,' Black reminded.

'A *water* pump,' Matthew corrected. 'For a mine of the size Bonaparte intends, a much larger machine is necessary.'

Kate shook her head. 'I'm not sure I understand. Does that mean this is only an ordinary coal mine?'

'No. None of the tubs have contained coal, and an ordinary mine would not require slave labourers.' Matthew jerked his head toward the workings. 'This is no coal mine; I am nearly certain that we have found Bonaparte's tunnel. But there must be a powerful air pump somewhere, and if we can find it, we have found the Achilles heel. If the pump can be destroyed, the mining will be delayed, perhaps indefinitely.'

'I thought that we were just here to observe, not to play the hero.' Kate's words were taunting, but her eyes were hopeful.

'We are,' Matthew said. 'But if we can find the pump and inform Admiral Springer, he could order a naval landing party.' He thought there was disappointment behind Kate's nod.

'Rather than devising tasks for the navy, you concentrate on finding the pump,' Black said. 'You are here because of your engineering knowledge, so now is your chance to justify yourself. We seem to have achieved our first objective. Tomorrow you will search for this air pump, and I will look at the defences.' His sudden grin was directed more toward Kate than Matthew. 'I think we can afford to congratulate ourselves; we have confirmed that the French are digging something, and whatever it is, it's not a coal mine; we know where their tunnel is located, and we may even have found a weakness. I think we can call that a good day's work. Now all we need do is discover this damned air pump. And that's your job, Mr Pryde.'

The burden of responsibility returned, pressing down on Matthew's weary shoulders.

'We'll have to get closer,' Kate decided.

They had watched the mine all morning, counting the constant stream of timber wagons entering the compound and the tubs of spoil emptied onto them for the return trip, one wagon every half-hour, following the same broad track toward the bay. Although Matthew had scoured the mine workings, he could see no sign of a steam pump.

'We? You're not going anywhere near the mine.' The idea of Kate putting herself in danger horrified Matthew.

'Quite right,' Kate agreed solemnly. 'It's far better for you to go alone, so when somebody asks you a question you can mime to him.' When

Matthew turned away, she goaded him with a superior smile. 'However, as I both look and sound French, perhaps I could go alone?' With the red camlet jacket and white apron that she had borrowed from Suzanne, Kate appeared no different to the local women. 'Shall we go?'

Adjusting the red Phrygian cap that he had jammed on his head in an attempt to appear French, Matthew ruffled his normally clubbed hair and sighed. 'God, I wish that Mr Black was here.' The Bow Street Runner had left early to scout the shore-based defences.

'It's a bit late for that,' Kate reminded him sweetly. 'So you'll have to put up with me. Let's just get on with this, shall we?'

Matthew sighed. He desperately wanted to find the air pump, for that was the key to the mine, but he refused to endanger Kate. He looked at her, all eagerness and determination, and wondered if every decision in their future marriage would be so complicated.

Kate broke his mood by nudging him with a sharp elbow. 'Something is happening.' She pointed to the road.

There was the sound of raised voices as the team of horses from one timber wagon became entangled with another. Horses brayed as drivers cracked their whips and shouted themselves hoarse in an attempt to unravel the mess, but the harnesses seemed to be ever more tangled. He saw one driver lean forward, overbalance and fall, yelling, to be trampled under the hooves of both teams.

'Come on, Matthew,' Kate urged. 'That's our

way in!'

'What?'

'The guards are watching the party. Nobody's at the gate.'

Leaving the ridge, they slithered downhill, dodging from tree to tree until they were within twenty yards of the fence. They stopped for a moment, ensuring that the guards were engrossed with the timber wagons before slouching closer. Matthew felt the same sick nervousness in his stomach as he had experienced as a youth knocking on the door of the rector's study. Controlling his shallow breathing, he winked at Kate, who was repeating a snatch of song, until she realized it was the English ballad 'Betsy Blowsy', and glanced guiltily at Matthew.

'Sorry,' she said. 'Now, I'll do the talking, you pretend that you're a mute, or a foreigner or something.' Shockingly, she grinned, as if at a joke.

'You've got bottom, I'll grant you that,' Matthew told her.

'I'm petrified,' Kate admitted, 'but I won't let Bonaparte invade Britain.'

A third wagon had appeared, completely blocking the road as it slewed to a halt beside the others. The sergeant of the guard was screaming abuse and waving his fist at the carters, who ignored him as they tried to attend to the fallen man.

'How is your driving?' Kate asked, quietly.

'No better than fair.'

'That will have to do. Here, wrap this around your mouth.' Kate produced the shawl that he had purchased at the May Day festivities. 'Maybe they'll think you're injured.'

'Allez!' The voice was sharp and feminine. It came from the diligence they had seen the previous day, and Citizen Peltier stepped down to survey the chaos. Adjusting her cravat, she pointed to the carters and issued crisp orders. Without hesitation, they dragged their injured companion to the side of the road and left him there, groaning, while they clambered back onto their wagons.

Under the flail of Peltier's tongue, the carters made rapid progress in disentangling the harnesses, and the first load of timber was soon creaking toward the mine.

Now knowing who she was, Matthew studied Citizen Peltier. As Mr Black had noted, she was a tempting armful, about the same height as Kate, with a remarkably clear complexion and a mouth whose apparent lack of symmetry made it all the more appealing. One side seemed lower than the other, and only when he worked out that a scar caused the deformity did he realize that she was pointing to him, her eyes narrow and shrewd.

Kate stepped forward, speaking slowly. When Peltier frowned and jerked a question, Kate shook her head and spread her arms wide in a gesture that Matthew had never seen her use before. After a few minutes' conversation, the Frenchwoman turned aside and Kate moved to Matthew's side. She was shaking.

'I told her that we were Dutch and you could not speak French.' She spoke quietly, with a shake in her voice. 'But we have to take the wagon along that road there,' she pointed past the mine, 'to the gun battery on the northern promontory. They need timber.'

Matthew stared. 'The gun battery? That's no good to us. We need to go closer to the mine!'

'Don't argue! Mr Black told us how dangerous this woman was, and she certainly has authority here. Did you see the way these soldiers jumped when she shouted at them?'

Matthew nodded. Aware that Citizen Peltier was staring at him, he hauled himself onto the wagon and tested the horses with a quick pull at the reins. With their ribs showing through dull skin, they were in such poor condition that it seemed a shame to crack the whip, but they took the strain and hauled willingly, if painfully slowly, along the ill-made road.

Citizen Peltier fingered the cravat at her throat as she watched them jolt past the gate, shouted something that Matthew could not understand and returned to her diligence.

'You concentrate on the driving,' Kate said, 'and I will examine the compound. Once we've delivered the timber we can maybe get inside for a load of spoil and have a proper look for your pump.'

Matthew grunted. He had never driven anything so large and clumsy as a four-horse wagon before, and needed all his skill to keep the horses pulling in the same direction. They plodded on slowly, hugging the boundary of the compound before striking for the coast. Unsure of his skill, Matthew drove slowly, watching for sudden dips

165

or subsidence that might tip the wagon over.

Matthew looked longingly at the sea. The mining compound was only quarter of a mile inland from La Baie de l'Isle, and they were climbing up a series of zigzag bends, each one steeper than the last, with the horses struggling to pull their load. 'Keep going, boys.' Matthew dismounted and walked beside the team, aware that his weight made little difference, but hating to see the animals suffer.

'Matthew! Look down there.'

They had reached the halfway point, with the bay dull and grey to their right. Matthew glanced over, and involuntarily stared. From this position he could see a constant stream of lighters carrying the spoil from the mine toward the barren island that stood sentinel against the sea.

'That makes sense,' he said, shaking his head in reluctant admiration. 'That makes a lot of sense.'

Captain Page had been mistaken. The French had not abandoned the island, but were actively developing it. Scores of slave workers were working to enlarge its perimeters with the mine waste, while a small group clustered around the central structure that squatted in a slight hollow, screened by trees that would make it invisible from the sea. Mist clung wetly to the island.

'What makes sense?'

'Albert Mathieu's plan for a tunnel had tubes carrying air from the surface and a staging post in mid-Channel.' Matthew controlled his excitement. 'Well, the navy would soon end that, but instead the French have adapted this island as a large air vent. See that thing in the middle? That's the steam pump, so we know that the tunnel is under there.'

'Are you sure?' Kate stared at the island. 'How do you know?'

'I don't,' Matthew admitted, 'I am putting two and two together and coming to a logical conclusion. There is the proximity to the mine, the slave workers, that building and the mist.'

'The mist?' Kate shook her head. 'I don't understand.'

'There is no mist anywhere else. It's waste steam from the pump.' Matthew grinned. 'When that woman directed us up here she could hardly have helped us more!'

Kate nodded. 'At least the mine is still a long way from England.'

'We don't know that,' Matthew sobered her. 'We don't know how far they have dug. But we do now know where the pump is.' He scrutinized the island, with its clanking workers and the uniformed soldiers that stood sentinel. 'And we know that it's guarded.'

The horses were reluctant to finish the ascent, but with loud shouting and the cracking whip, he pushed them on to the gun battery. Steam rose from their flanks when they halted, and they stood with exhausted heads bowed.

'Whatever virtues the French have,' Kate said quietly, 'caring for their horses is not one of them.'

'They can build good fortifications, though,' Matthew murmured.

Sloping stone walls rose sheer from the top of

the cliff, with neat embrasures in which lounged blue-clad artillerymen, smoking pipes and chatting languidly as they watched the wagon. When they realized that Kate was a woman, two or three raised a cheer and cried out loud remarks, to which she replied with laughter and a wave of her hand.

'They want to know if I have any sisters.'

Matthew touched the butt of his Manton and wished they were both safe in England. He hoped nobody asked him any direct questions.

The sergeant seemed surprised to see them, and quickly called a young officer, who scratched his head in wonder as he surveyed their load, and then indicated that they should bring it inside.

'He did not expect any timber,' Kate told Matthew, 'but he'll take it anyway.'

When soldiers hauled open the iron-studded wooden doors, Matthew urged the horses inside and looked around as a barking sergeant summoned a score of soldiers to unload the wagon.

The walls of the battery were of stone, ten feet thick and fronted by sloping earth that would diminish the impact of even the largest cannonball. Even worse, there were facilities for heating shot. Matthew knew that seamen feared red-hot shot, which could set their highly inflammable vessels alight. These artillerymen knew their job.

'Matthew,' Kate nudged him with a sharp elbow, 'look at the guns.'

As the sergeant blasted the men by sheer lung power, Kate sauntered to the parapet, dragging

Matthew with her and pointing out to sea, as if admiring the view, or commenting on the sails of the patrolling Royal Naval warships. She smiled to the young officer, spoke quietly and tapped the barrel of the nearest cannon as she glanced meaningfully at Matthew. Only then did he realize that it was made of wood, with a wooden carriage and a solid wooden barrel, painted black. He looked toward the bay, where the steam pump crouched on its shrouded island and the slow stream of lighters carried spoil under the protection of false cannon.

Matthew breathed out slowly as he realized the implications of their discovery. If the cannon in this battery were false, then it was quite possible that the corresponding battery on the opposite arm of the bay was equally toothless. With no effective gun batteries, the steam pump, which would control the air flow for the tunnel, was virtually unprotected against a naval assault.

There was no more than a company of infantry guarding the steam pump, and therefore the tunnel. Matthew felt impatience itching at him; he had to return to England with this intelligence, for once the Royal Navy knew that there were no shore batteries, they could sail in unopposed. There was no limit to the damage they could do.

Despite his elation, Matthew kept his face immobile as he left the battery, but grinned to Kate as soon as they passed the last sentry. 'How *did* you know about the cannon?'

'When you were driving in, two of the soldiers were carrying a gun barrel; a piece of iron that size would weigh a ton!'

Matthew looked at her with new respect. 'You're fly to the time of day, aren't you, little bluestocking? But do you know what this means?'

'Not exactly,' Kate said, 'but you seem excited. Tell me why, pray?'

'Because we've done it, Kate.' Matthew faced her, allowing the horses to pick their own route. 'We've found the French entrance to the tunnel and found their weakness. You see, if these coastal batteries have no guns, there is nothing to stop the navy.'

Kate nodded, immediately understanding. 'I see. Joss Page said that there's deep water in the bay enough to float a squadron of 74s! Nelson can bombard the steam pump and the island until there is nothing left.' She squealed, grabbing at his arm. 'Watch the road, Matt!'

'All's bowman, Kate. I've got it!' Matthew manoeuvred the wagon around a tight bend, hauling at the reins as the horses threatened to slither dangerously near to the edge of the road.

Kate did not hide her smile. 'So I was of some use, then? Despite your strictures.'

Checking that the road was relatively straight ahead, Matthew slipped his arm around her shoulder and pulled her close. The prospect of success dissipated any residual anger. 'We did it together, Kate. All we need do is survive one more day and we can sail home.'

'That will please Father,' Kate reminded. 'He'll be in a perfect fever of happiness when he hears we have been away in France, unchaperoned except for a Bow Street spy. And half the French army, of course. It will do wonders for my reputation.'

'Your father must never know we were over here,' Matthew began, solemnly, until he realized that she was teasing him. 'You are full of moonshine, aren't you? You take every opportunity to cut up my peace.'

Her laugh was careless. 'Is that not the job of a wife? If I ever stop teasing you, you will wear your Friday face every day of the week.'

'You are an impudent little rustic.' Matthew's pretence at annoyance seemed to amuse her even more. 'I'll expect better once we're wed, young lady!'

Her laughter came again, mocking. 'Young lady? I remember you still fresh from the schoolroom, Mr Maidhouse College. And I believe that I am older than you!' She put a hand to his lips. 'Hush now, for here is the house and you might get Suzanne all a-flutter if she sees you acting the goat.'

Meeting her eyes, Matthew grinned, enjoying the banter nearly as much as he enjoyed her company. She laughed openly. 'As Dr Pangloss would say, Matt, "Everything is for the best in this best of all possible worlds!" '

Leaning closer, she kissed him, just as the first roar came from the farmhouse.

'What's that?' Matthew slipped a protective arm around Kate's shoulders. There was the shrill yell of a woman, then the raised voices of two men.

'That sounds like Mr Black and Durand,' Kate

said, pulling free. 'They're arguing about something.'

The voices rose louder, joined by Suzanne's rapid French, and then there was the unmistakable bang of a door.

'We'd best go in and sort it out,' Matthew decided, 'before they kill each other, or attract the attention of the soldiers.'

Thrusting inside the house, they ran up the uncovered stone stairs to the upper floor, from where the noise emanated. The door to the Durand's bedroom was open and Suzanne knelt on the bed, both hands holding the covers to her chin and her clothing scattered around her. She was speaking quickly, shaking her head as Durand shouted at her. Clad only in his shirt, Black spread his arms wide and tried to intervene.

'Oh!' Kate gripped Matthew's arm, shaking her head. 'Oh, the stupid man! Durand's found him in bed with Suzanne!' She frowned. 'I always suspected that Mr Black was a bit loose in the haft, but not with a married woman!'

Their arrival only seemed to inflame Durand's anger. Lifting his hand, he slapped at Mr Black, who blocked the blow easily, but did not retaliate. Durand spoke again, as Suzanne wriggled backward from the bed, sobbing.

'Try and separate the men,' Kate said, 'and I'll look after Suzanne,' but as she stepped forward, Durand pushed Black out of the way and lunged at his wife. Matthew barely noticed Black ducking toward the door as Suzanne screamed and jerked backward. Letting go of the sheet, she fell naked from the bed, bounced up in an instant and pushed between Kate and Matthew. Still screaming, she ran through the still-open door in the wake of Black, her bare feet slapping on the floor.

'Wait!' Matthew put out a hand to stop Durand from following, but the Frenchman brushed him aside as he plunged after his wife, shouting.

'Mr Durand!' Matthew followed, clattering down the steps. He reached the parlour just as Durand caught Suzanne by the hair and pulled her violently to one side. Suzanne screamed, both hands reaching to her head, and Durand slapped her hard across the face.

Brought up to treat women with chivalrous respect, Matthew moved instinctively. He grabbed Durand's right arm and held it tight, glaring into the Frenchman's face. 'No, Mr Durand, you can't do that.'

Durand was lean but a lifetime of farm work had made him immensely strong. He pushed Matthew aside, threw his wife to the ground and kicked her hard in the ribs.

'Stop that! You hear?' Matthew tried again, but Kate was quicker, throwing herself at Durand, trying to smother him with outstretched arms as she spoke in rapid French. Durand's response was almost casual as he lifted his balled fist to punch at Kate, but Matthew leaped forward, smothering the blow and wrestling Durand back, just as Suzanne rose from the floor, shrieking.

'Matthew!' Kate tugged at his arm as the front door smashed open and a group of blue-coated soldiers thrust into the room. The leading man stared at the spectacle of squabbling men and women, said something to his companions and began to laugh, until Durand raised his voice.

The only word Matthew understood was *'Anglais'* but it was enough to change the attitude of the soldiers. The humour ended and they stepped back, raising their long muskets.

Suzanne screamed and tried to run for the door, but instead collided with the nearest of the soldiers, who staggered back, while the second instinctively stepped out of her way, glaring at Matthew.

Ripping himself free of Matthew, Durand grabbed at his wife, who ducked away, screaming, and again ran for the door, but a soldier levelled his musket and fired. The gunshot was deafening, ending all other noise, and Matthew coughed as white powder smoke filled the room.

'Matthew!' Kate grabbed at his arm as Suzanne crumpled to the floor. The soldier who had fired murmured what sounded like a prayer and dropped his musket. Lying naked on her back, with her arms spread wide and a bloody hole beneath her left breast, Suzanne gazed up at them from lifeless eyes.

'Anglais?' Ignoring the dead woman, the young officer who led the soldiers rested the point of his sword under Kate's chin. He spoke in quiet English. 'It would be better if you surrendered.'

Ten

France
June and July 1805

Even before Matthew reached for his Manton, he knew that it was too late. He saw the nearest soldier lift his musket, his thumb pulling back the hammer with practised skill. He saw the muscles in the officer's forearm tense, and his face harden for the thrust. He saw the terror flare in Kate's eyes and dropped his hand.

'All right, mossoo, you've won.'

Withdrawing his sword, the officer stepped quickly forward and removed the pistol from inside Matthew's coat.

'*Bon.*' He checked the priming. 'Joseph Manton, *merci*, monsieur. It is a fine pistol.'

'British made,' Matthew said, 'and it took seven Frenchman to capture it.'

The officer shrugged. 'And you surrendered without a fight, monsieur,' he reminded him.

Somebody shouted in Matthew's ear and pushed him in the back, so he stumbled forward. Somebody else yelled at Kate, who responded with chill civility and the French officer grabbed hold of Matthew's cloak and dragged him toward Suzanne.

'You see this woman? She died because of you English. Another French death because of Prime Minister Pitt's stubbornness.'

Matthew looked at Suzanne, remembering her fear and her kindness. 'We did not kill her,' he said. 'One of your men shot her.'

The blow to his stomach took him by surprise, and the pain drove him to his knees as the officer struck again, slapping his head so the Phrygian cap slid over his eyes. 'You English! You cause war after war and sit so arrogantly behind your ditch.'

Matthew heard Kate scream and jerked upright, but the officer struck him backhanded across the face. He lunged forward instinctively, catching the officer by surprise so they grappled on the floor with soldiers thumping around them, kicking out or crashing down with their musket butts. Matthew heard Kate yelling, he fastened his hands around the throat of the officer and hung on, unaware that he was shouting, repeating Kate's name again and again as the French soldiers alternately struck at him or attempted to pull him away.

Hands grasped his arms and shoulders, throwing him back from the officer as a horde of soldiers descended on him, punching and kicking until he slid against the wall, swearing, with his retaliatory blows ever weaker. Blood blinded him as he looked up, and Kate's mouth was open as she spoke, reaching toward him with two soldiers holding her back. He saw the officer reverse the pistol and raise it high, but could not avoid the blow that knocked him out.

At first Matthew did not know where he was. He seemed to be paralysed, unable to ease the agony in his hands or the cramp in his back and legs. He groaned at the pain that threatened to burst his head apart, and ripped into him when he tried to open his eyes.

'Oh God,' he said, quietly. 'I'm blind.'

The ground seemed to be rocking from side to side, while a remorseless drumbeat beneath him reminded him of the anvils of hell of which Dr Trueman had so often spoken at Maidhouse College.

'Is this death, then?' He was surprised at the strength of his voice, despite the taste of salt blood in his mouth.

'Oh, thank God that you're alive!'

'Kate?' Fresh waves of agony persuaded Matthew that he should not attempt to sit up. 'Where are we?'

'In a French diligence, carrying us into the bowels of Bonaparte's Empire.' Kate's voice was low. 'Now lie quiet if you can, you have taken a couple of nasty knocks and you've been unconscious for a full day.'

'Am I blind? I cannot see anything.' He tried to open his eyes, but the pain was too great.

'We are both tied hand and foot,' Kate told him with surprising calmness, 'and one of the Frenchies knocked you on the head so your face is covered in blood. It has caked solid over your eyes.'

Matthew fought another wave of pain, wriggled his wrists and ankles for a few minutes and decided that they were too well tied. When the thought came, it was horrifying. 'And you, Kate? Are you all right?'

'I'd be pitching the gammon to say that I was, Matthew. I'm fagged to death, and more than a little scared.' She stopped suddenly. 'Oh, I see what you mean. Yes, they did not interfere with me in *that* way.'

They were silent for a while as the diligence rumbled over the roads and the sound of horses became just another part of the torment of their existence.

'Matthew, what do you think happened to Mr Black? I did not see him once the French arrived. Do you think he escaped, or...?'

'I do not know.' Matthew had grown used to Black's easy confidence. He could not think of him lying dead at the point of a French sword, but the image of Suzanne came vividly to him. The French had not hesitated to kill her, woman or not. 'I fancy he will be all right. Maybe he is planning some mad rescue mission just now.'

Kate's laugh sounded false. 'That's just what I thought,' she said.

'Yes.' Matthew tried to roll closer, but he was fastened to the floor. 'You're a queer little vixen, Kate, but I wish you were not involved in this mess.'

'Oh? Don't you like my company, then?' She tried to taunt him, but her words lacked their usual sting. 'I'm frightened, Matthew. What will happen to us?'

He did not know. 'We'll probably be held for a few days and then exchanged,' he said, as the vision of the guillotine shadowed his mind. He could see that wicked triangle of steel poised above his neck, hear the hard voice of the executioner and the swish of the blade. It was worse because they had come so close to success. One more day and Captain Page would have taken them back home with their intelligence.

Matthew groaned; the Royal Navy could have sailed into La Baie de l'Isle and destroyed the air pump, maybe even brought down the roof of the tunnel, but not now. Black's amorous escapades had helped Bonaparte's plans, and handed Kate and him to the French.

That ride seemed to continue forever, with the occasional brief halt to change the horses. Twice Matthew slipped into unconsciousness, but the agony of cramp brought him back, and he heard a sound that may have been Kate sobbing, but he could not reach over to offer comfort. The agony of being unable to help her was worse than any of his physical aches.

Matthew did not know how long they had been in the coach when it eventually halted and the door crashed open. Loud voices assailed him; something cold slipped between his ankles, cutting him free, and rough hands jerked him upright.

'What's the meaning of all this?' He heard the croak in his voice as he was pushed outside, but his legs refused to work and he staggered, falling painfully on stone. Somebody lifted him and held him tight, hustling him forward. About to shout for Kate, he thought it better if he did not mention her name. Perhaps she could use her knowledge of French to escape. She might persuade them that she was not a spy. The thought gave him a little comfort.

Still unable to see, he was pushed up a flight of circular stairs, and guided inside a building in which every sound echoed and where clammy dankness gripped like a mantle of ice. Somebody yelled in his ear, a fist cracked against his head and he heard the rasp of a heavy door opening.

There were loud voices shouting guttural French, something hard banged between his shoulder blades and he fell forward, to be jerked upright and pushed onward, down a flight of steps. He staggered, swearing, but strong hands guided him, one step at a time, downward and ever downward until he thought he was back in Mr Lamballe's mine.

Harsh voices mingled with hollow echoes, there was the smell of dampness and chilling cold, a faint scream from somewhere, sudden heat as a lantern was pressed close to his face, then more steps, old and worn and greasy.

Matthew felt somebody cut the bonds from his wrists and groaned at the agony of returning circulation, but before he could move, his arms were stretched above him and secured by heavy bands. He heard the rattle of chains, something struck him hard in the stomach so he retched, and then there was a loud bang, the sound of retreating footsteps and silence broken by harsh breathing. He leaned against the wall behind him and swore, his arms already protested against their unnatural position.

'Matthew?' The sound of Kate's voice came as a tremendous relief. 'Are you there?'

'I'm here,' he said.

'Thank God.' There was silence for a few minutes, save for laboured breathing and a mysterious rustling that Matthew could not place. 'Is there anybody else in here?' Kate tried again, speaking in French, but there was no response. 'I think we are alone, Matthew.'

'Can't you see?'

'It's dark,' Kate told him, her voice trembling. 'So dark.'

Matthew moved toward her voice, but the chains jerked him back to the wall. He could only imagine her terror, scared of the dark, trapped in a French dungeon with no possibility of help. 'I suspect that Mr Black will be trying to rescue us right now. He'll probably have followed the coach all the way to wherever we are.'

'I was thinking the same thing myself,' Kate said. 'We'll be free in a couple of hours.' The rustling continued, louder now.

As a youth, Matthew had heard about people chained to walls, but only now did he appreciate the sheer torture of the position. When he slumped, the shackles bit painfully into his wrists, chafing the flesh and restricting the flow of blood to his hands. When he straightened up, he suffered cramp in his back and legs. He could not rest. 'Kate? Are you chained too?'

'Against the wall,' Kate said. 'Matthew, talk to me. Please. Don't leave me alone in the dark.'

Matthew realized that her fear of the dark would magnify everything that she was suffering. 'We're in this together, Kate. We'll pull through.'

'I'm still unclear what happened,' Kate said. 'Obviously Mr Black took a fancy to Suzanne, and Mr Durand discovered them together, but how did the French soldiers know where we were, or who we were? And where *is* Mr Black?'

'I expect the soldiers simply heard the commotion,' Matthew said, and added, 'We were not very successful spies, were we?'

'I think we were,' Kate defended herself, as he had hoped she would. 'We found out everything that we were supposed to, and more. It was Mr Black who let us down, with his inability to keep his breeches on! When we get back to England we can tell Admiral Springer about the wooden cannon. He'll send in the navy to destroy the French tunnel.'

'That's just what we'll do,' Matthew agreed. He heard Kate whimper, and there was the cheerless clank of her chains as she moved.

'Matthew, do keep talking. Please don't leave me in the dark.' Her voice was little more than a whisper. 'Can you imagine Nelson's frigates blasting away at these tunnel workings? Or the bluejackets and marines landing to destroy the pithead?'

There was a hint of hysteria in Kate's attempt at laughter. 'Knowing the Royal Navy, they'll probably press-gang all the miners. Hundreds of new recruits!'

Matthew agreed. 'Maybe so, but they might prefer to be French slaves than Royal Naval seamen; the conditions are much the same, except that they can get drowned at sea.'

They were quiet again, except for murmurs of pain and the rattle of chains. Twice Matthew heard Kate sob, and the knowledge that he could not help hurt him deeper than he had imagined.

He could doze, but not sleep, for the jerk of his weight on torn wrists was more agony than he could bear. He heard Kate humming 'Bonny Tawny Moor', and tried to join in, but the music would not come.

'Don't leave me in the dark, Matthew. Not alone.'

'I'm here, Kate.' He heard the catch in his voice.

'How long have we been here?'

'I don't know. Hours, I think.' Matthew slumped backward, biting his lip until the blood came. If he slept, he left Kate alone and awoke to even worse nightmares. He must stay awake for the sake of Kate.

The crash of the opening door made him start, and an avalanche of noise battered at his head. Harsh French voices echoed, rough hands grabbed at him, releasing him from the chains and dragging him away. He tried to struggle, but the agony of cramp crippled him, and he could do nothing as they hauled him from the dungeon, along a stone corridor and up a flight of stairs.

There was more noise, and then somebody threw a bucket of water over his head and savagely rubbed the blood from his eyes. He yelled, blinking in the raw light, and saw that he was in a windowless room of stone walls, with a groined stone roof. A dozen candles pooled light onto the desk along one wall, and four burly men thumped him painfully onto a wooden chair before expertly tying him down.

The man behind the desk studied a small sheaf of documents until Matthew was secured. When he did look up Matthew thought he looked like a benevolent clerk, with soft brown eyes and a high collar.

'M. Pryde, is it not?' The clerk spoke with hardly a trace of a French accent. 'A young engineer from London, I believe?'

For a second Matthew wondered if he should deny his identity, but he quickly realized that there would be no point. 'That is correct.'

'Good.' The clerk nodded. 'My name is Dugua, and I am here to decide what to do with you.' He was silent for a long time as one of the candles guttered in a draught and the breathing of the four burly men filled the room. 'But before I do, pray tell me why you have honoured us by your presence?'

'You brought me here,' Matthew said, and yelled as one of the men promptly slapped the back of his head. The benign clerk nodded.

'Quite so. We brought you here from a farm-house in the Pas de Calais, where you had no right to be. Pray tell me why you were in France, at a time when our two countries are at war?'

'We were at sea, fishing, when a storm drove us onto the French coast,' Matthew invented furiously. 'We were hiding until we could get back to England.'

'Quite so.' Dugua nodded to one of the burly

men, who backhanded Matthew twice. 'But to save you from further fabrications, I should remind you that Joss Page the Deal smuggler brought you over, together with the spy John Black and a young woman.' Dugua shook his head. 'It is a sad business, asking questions of a woman, but it needs to be done.'

Matthew looked up. 'She has nothing to do with this! She came over by mistake.'

Dugua sighed. 'It is regrettable when such mistakes are made, Mr Pryde, but they happen, and then?' He shrugged, reached sideways and lifted what looked like a string of shrivelled mushrooms. 'In war, terrible things must be done.' He looped the string around his neck and only then did Matthew realize that it was composed of severed human ears. 'Pray come with me, Mr Pryde.'

On Dugua's signal, two of the men lifted Matthew's chair and carried him from the room, up a flight of circular stone stairs to a courtyard into which moonlight flowed eerily. Torches threw jumping shadows as they sputtered from brackets in the walls, and in the centre was a structure that Matthew had heard spoken of with horror, but had never thought he would see.

The guillotine was smaller than he had expected, but every bit as sinister. About twelve feet high, the structure was of wood, with brass grooves for the triangular blade, which was poised high. At right angles to the upright, a wooden shelf lay ready for the victim. The whole machine was placed on a trestle table, and a soiled wicker basket sat ready to catch the severed head.

'The guillotine is really quite an effective device,' Dugua said, 'quick and efficient, but when it was first used, the crowd bayed for the return of the gallows.' Leaving Matthew's side, he walked to the machine and stroked the upright timber in a gesture that was vaguely obscene and indisputably disturbing. 'It does not have the same dramatic struggle, you see, the same spectacle of the criminal twisting and kicking as life leaves his body.' He faced Matthew, smiling softly. 'Or her body. You see, the Jacques enjoyed those few minutes, the shadowy time between life and death. But with Mme le Guillotine, it is just a simple *click* as the lever is pushed, then death. Instant and merciful.'

'A great improvement,' Matthew said, and Dugua nodded.

'Perhaps so.' He sighed again. 'It's this modern age, you see. We pander to speed and efficiency rather than spectacle and tradition. Sometimes I miss the old days.'

'It must be very hard for you,' Matthew said. He flinched as he saw a knot of men emerge from the far corner of the courtyard, carrying a bound and defiant Kate. He could feel her agitation as she saw the guillotine, but rather than increase, her struggles ceased. Matthew felt an immense surge of pride; Kate would not allow them to see that she was scared.

'It can be,' Dugua agreed. 'But we have to work with the materials that we are given. We can compensate; by ensuring that our clients are happy to go to execution, it provides such a merciful release from the torment of life.'

The men were pushing Kate forward, so that her face was pressed close to the timber of the guillotine. She looked toward Matthew, straightened her shoulders and, unbelievably, thrust out her tongue.

Matthew had never before witnessed such an action of utter defiance. Whatever happened, he knew that Kate would not be defeated. She had faced Bonaparte's utmost horror and responded with the most contemptuous gesture that she could. 'Are you going to kill us?'

There was no reply, but the knot of men thrust Kate beside Matthew before disappearing back inside the building. They were left alone in the courtyard with the skeletal structure of the guillotine before them and the grey walls thrusting all around. Shadows taunted them with a tasteless tango and when Kate looked at him, he saw the fear in her eyes, beneath the defiance and the anger.

'I love you, Kate,' he told her.

She nodded, forcing a smile. 'That's the first time that you've ever said that,' she said.

'You've always known, though.'

'Always,' she agreed calmly. 'But it's nice to hear it.' She looked up toward the guillotine. 'It's an ugly thing, isn't it?'

'Very functional, though.' As an engineer, Matthew could appreciate the efficiency of the machine, compared to other methods of execution. 'It will be a quick death.'

Kate was quiet for a few seconds. 'It's such a

waste,' she said, quietly, 'to die here. We would have made a good marriage.' She looked at him, twisting in her bonds. 'I love you too, you see.'

'I was never sure,' Matthew told her. 'There was always something hidden, somehow.'

'Not now,' she said. She tossed her head so that rebellious twist of hair flopped around her eye. 'Not ever again.'

There was the faint tapping of a single drum, and the men appeared, carrying a third bound figure that struggled and shouted in French.

'Mr Black, no doubt,' Kate said. 'So we can all die together.'

'And Bonaparte marches on.' Matthew felt sick. He was less afraid to die than frustrated that the French had defeated him. He looked to Kate. 'If I could send you home, I would.'

'I know that,' she said.

The drum continued, its single beat echoing from the tall walls. Matthew saw the men untie their prisoner, who lashed out at them, his voice rising as he stood before the guillotine. It was not Black, but the wirier figure of Durand, unshaven and with a badly bruised face. He pointed to them, shouting, as Dugua walked from a side door.

He had changed his clothes and was now dressed entirely in white, with an oversized cravat around his neck and black riding boots. A large pair of shears hung around his waist. Pushing back ornate cuffs, he approached Durand and spoke a few words.

When Durand cringed away, Dugua touched him on the forehead and pointed upward to the blade. He spoke quietly, smiling.

Kate translated for Matthew. 'He says that it will be better if Mr Durand lies still, so that the guillotine has a clean cut.' Kate's voice shook. 'So it seems that Mr Durand will be first, probably to increase our fear.'

'I'm damned if they'll see me scared,' Matthew vowed. 'But I wish you were not here.'

'Well, I am,' Kate told him. 'And I don't regret much. Only that we could not get our information to England, and that Father will never know what happened to us.'

There was a sickening fascination in watching the burly men throw Durand face down on the guillotine, where he writhed and yelled, kicking his legs until they tied him. He continued to shout, and Kate flinched.

'He says that Mr Black is a womanizing ... well, it's a word that I would not repeat, Matthew, but it's not very nice. He's blaming Mr Black for everything.'

Matthew stared as the burly men pushed Durand's body forward so that his neck rested directly beneath the triangular blade. The drum continued to tap as Dugua crouched at the side of the machine, speaking softly as he stroked Durand's head.

Durand writhed, twisting to glare at Dugua and shouted loudly, but Kate did not translate the words. Dugua stepped back.

'Monsieur Pryde and Mademoiselle Denton. You may think that we are merciless in thus executing M. Durand, but he is a traitor to France. He knowingly harboured enemies of the state. I ask you, what would happen if an English farmer did the same?'

A Tyburn hanging was just as ugly as a decapitation, and Matthew knew that an English crowd would enjoy the spectacle. He did not reply as Dugua pulled a small lever and the blade descended. There was a slight sound, like a knife chopping an apple, and Durand's head fell from his body to land neatly in the basket. Blood gushed from Durand's neck, splashing onto Kate, who made an exclamation of disgust.

'*Vive la France*,' Dugua said quietly, as the drum fell silent. The burly men untied the body and began to drag it from the machine. They were careless, smearing blood across the timber frame as they pushed what remained of Durand into one corner. Somebody lifted the still bleeding head, kissed the mouth in a parody of affection and held it high. Smiling, Dugua produced his shears and neatly clipped off Durand's ears.

'Oh sweet Lord,' Kate said, softly. 'These people are savages.'

Matthew wished that he could hold her, as much for his own comfort as for hers.

'So...' Dugua walked slowly toward them. He stood between them, looking from one to the other with the ears dripping blood onto his too-tight white breeches. 'Who shall be next? The handsome English engineer? Or the pretty young Englishwoman that he brought with him?'

Matthew felt his eyes drawn to the terrible machine that dominated the courtyard. He saw the sinister smear on the blade that the burly men drew back up, saw the battered basket that held Durand's head and could not suppress his shiver of horror. He did not know what was worse, to die knowing that he had failed in his duty, so that a horde of Frenchmen would march under the Channel to descend upon England, or to die knowing that he had failed Kate.

'Kill me, Monsieur Dugua,' he kept his voice as level as he could, 'but let the woman go. She is only here by mistake. She is no threat to you, or to France.'

'Ah,' Dugua nodded, 'chivalry from an Englishman? That is a rare commodity, and one that must be exploited. I shall make a bargain with you, Mr Pryde. If you tell me exactly why you are in France, who sent you and how you intended to return, I shall indeed let the lady live. If you do not, then...' He made a chopping motion with the edge of his hand.

Matthew felt Kate stiffen. 'You have nothing to say, Matthew.'

For a long moment, Matthew held Dugua's eyes as the frustration rose within him. He strained against his bonds, hating this Frenchman more than he had hated anybody in his life, but knowing that he had to make a decision. If he told Dugua what he knew, the French might order their army through the tunnel before Britain was ready. Whatever the outcome of the invasion, there would be terrible bloodshed in England, with God knows how many people killed. If he did not tell, then Kate would be placed on the guillotine, and he could not contemplate that horror.

191

'You have nothing to say, Matthew,' Kate repeated, then, raising her voice, she spoke slowly in French.

Dugua listened, smiling. 'Your lady tells me that you are a fool, Mr Pryde, with no knowledge of anything. Unfortunately, I do not believe her.' He sighed, nodded to one of the burly men and gave a brusque order.

'What?' Matthew struggled again, swearing. 'What's happening?'

The burly men moved unhurriedly toward Kate. While one clamped massive arms around her, the other produced a knife and sliced through the ropes that held her.

As if she had been waiting her chance, Kate began to fight, wriggling violently, kicking and biting, but her captors were obviously experienced in such reactions and held her tight.

'Leave her! Let her go!' Matthew heard his voice crack in terror as the men carried Kate to the guillotine. He tried to throw himself forward, but only succeeded in unbalancing the chair. He fell on the straw-strewn cobbles, kicking and swearing.

When the burly men placed Kate, quite gently, on the tray beneath that evil blade, she stopped struggling. A single drop of Durand's blood splashed beside her but she refused to flinch, and twisted her head in an effort to look at Matthew. 'You know nothing, Matthew,' she ordered, and began to sing.

Her voice was so hoarse that at first Matthew did not recognize the words, but then he joined in, allowing the salt tears to wash the congealed blood from his face:

'Rule, Britannia! Britannia rule the waves,
Britons never will be slaves!'

Kate's voice trembled at the end, and Matthew shook his head. Maidhouse had taught him to control his emotions, but great sobs racked his body as he watched Kate's courage. He could not betray his country, but still less could be ever allow Kate to suffer. He nodded to Dugua. 'No! Don't kill her.'

'What was that?' Dugua held up a hand and moved closer. 'Mr Pryde?'

'Matthew! No!' Kate screamed, twisting against her bonds, but then another voice joined in.

'Vive le Roi!'

Eleven

Paris
July 1805

There were half a dozen of them, ragged men in grey cloaks that clattered from one of the doors, and they carried swords and pistols. The first shot slammed into one of the burly men, and then the courtyard became a scene of desperation. Dropping Durand's ears, Dugua thrust a hand inside his waistcoat, produced Matthew's Manton, fired a single shot and ran back inside the building.

Raising a raucous yell, the attackers thrust forward, hacking at the guards with a zest that betrayed either desperation or long-contained frustration. The fight was short but immensely brutal and continued until the grey-coated men had massacred all the guards.

Unable to move, Matthew could only watch as the attackers butchered the dead bodies, shouting savagely as they chopped at them. The tallest strolled over to Kate.

'Sorry to be so long, Miss Denton, but I had to whistle up some local help.'

'Mr Black!'

'None other,' Black agreed. He sliced her free with the bloody sword that he carried. 'Have you had enough of France yet?'

'A long time ago!' Hurrying across to Matthew, she began to tug at the knots, until Black joined her and cut through the rope.

'We'll have to hurry,' he said. 'Dugua is nobody's fool so he'll rally his troops in minutes. This way.' Turning, Black gave a shrill shout and circled his hand in the air. The grey-coated men rallied to him, talking excitedly. One laughed as he licked the blood from the blade of his sword.

'Kate—' Matthew stumbled, screwing up his face at the agony of returning circulation. The situation had changed so rapidly that he felt giddy.

'Don't talk,' Kate looked dazed. 'Come on, Matt.'

Leading them into the side doorway by which the grey-coats had entered the courtyard, Black snapped an order and one of his men slammed a wooden beam across the door.

'That will delay them for a minute,' Black said, and strode along an echoing stone corridor. Matthew reached for Kate's hand, squeezed it once and ducked as the roof lowered.

'Servants' entrance,' Black joked. 'This place used to be a convent, before the Revolution banned religion. Now Fouché's secret police use it, as you know.' He turned abruptly right, into a small stone chamber. 'We go this way.'

There was a side door that led to a cloistered walk, much overgrown with weeds, and they emerged into a busy street.

'Where are we?' Matthew stared around him. He had thought they were deep in the French countryside, perhaps in some grim castle surrounded by the fields of downtrodden peasants, but instead they were in the outskirts of a busy town, with a mixture of well-dressed and tattered people on the pavement, while carriages mingled with the laden carts that lurched along the road. Drawn by two skeletal oxen, a *voiture* rumbled over the broken pave, with a ragged postilion flaunting his whip with pitiless glee.

'Paris,' Black told him.

'Paris?' Kate forced a smile. 'I've always wanted to see Paris, but not when I look quite so wretched.'

'We're not staying,' Matthew said, 'we're running for the coast.' He looked to Black for confirmation.

'I'm afraid not, Mr Pryde.' Black shook his head. 'We have one horse between the three of us, which won't be enough. We must hire more.'

'Did you not think of that?' Kate asked, fear sharpening her voice.

'I was rather more concerned with rescuing you,' Black told her, calmly. 'So, Miss Denton, you will see Paris after all.' He spent a few minutes with his followers, shaking their hands and joking before sending them off into the filthy tumbledown houses that seemed to stretch forever beyond the road. 'There are still Royalists to be found in France, you see,' he explained, 'if you know where to look.'

'And plenty of women too, Mr Black,' Kate reminded archly. 'Even if they are already *married*.'

'That was unfortunate,' Black admitted.

'And nearly fatal for us all.' Kate turned the screw a little more before she relented. 'However, you redeemed yourself by your daring rescue.' She dropped in a little curtsy that Matthew suspected was more mockery than gratitude.

Feeling as if he were walking into a robbers' den, Matthew kept very quiet as they walked toward the centre of Paris. They passed the Doric pillars of the Norman Barrier, rested in the shade of an avenue of magnificent elms and entered a city that seemed a world away from the sordid nightmare of the Terror or the mutilated corpses on Bonaparte's battlefields.

Save for the reminders of the military in a score of statues of victorious generals and the dragoons that ordered the traffic, the centre of Paris was a delight of ornate architecture and public gardens. Splendid equipages carried men in bright uniforms and women in clothes of such gauze-like inadequacy they appeared designed to tantalizingly reveal rather than respectably conceal. Kate favourably compared the rippling Seine to the muddy brown of the Thames, but distracted Matthew's attention from some of the bold-eyed Parisian women who surveyed him openly.

'You can't speak French,' she reminded.

'Indeed he cannot,' Black agreed, 'but some languages are more fundamental than speech.'

'It was your attention to *fundamentals* that caused us so much trouble,' Kate reminded him, sweetly, 'but you can make amends by finding us some food, and getting us back home.'

Shunning the restaurants with their tempting fare but watchful clientele who might work for Fouché, they toured filthy side streets with open sewers running beneath swaying lanterns until they found a cafe. There was little choice in the menu, but even stale bread was welcome, while the red wine eased away some of their tension. A pornographic print peeled from the bare plaster wall.

'So now,' Black sat opposite them on the bare bench, his face serious as he chewed, 'pray inform me what you discovered.'

Matthew told him about the false cannon in the batteries and the steam pump concealed in the centre of the island.

'The navy will love that,' Black said, eagerly leaning forward. 'Gun emplacements with wooden guns? Boney must have diverted everything to the Army of England; Nelson can sail in with the entire Channel Fleet!' He grinned. 'You've done well, Pryde, by God!'

'It was Kate who found the wooden guns,' Matthew reminded him.

Black nodded. 'Quite so. Once I get this intelligence to the Admiralty, Boney can kiss our arse, for he'll not see any other part of England!'

'Your mind remains commonplace, Mr Black.' Kate rebuked his choice of language, but Black snapped his fingers and ordered a second bottle of wine.

'We don't have time for this,' Matthew complained, but after Kate's ordeal he could not deny her a few minutes' pleasure.

'Oh, Matthew, after the war, will you show me Paris? I want to see the Place de la Concorde and the Consular palace of the Tuileries. And the Louvre, I would love to visit the Louvre.' She seemed to have lost some of her aversion to France as she clung onto his arm. 'Just imagine, we're not yet wed, and already we're on honeymoon.'

For a second he considered reminding her of their position, but when he saw the new lines of strain around her mouth and the horror that still lingered in her eyes, he held her instead. Her joy was frantic, her laughter verging on the hysterical, and when he pulled her close he could feel her tremble. There was no doubting Kate's courage, but she was paying a high price for daunting Bonaparte in his own city.

'When this war is over, then I promise you that we shall return to Paris, but with good clothes on our backs and in a carriage and four.'

'And we can see all the great pleasure gardens too? The Tivoli and the Frascati? Can we visit the theatres and maybe dance in the Palais Royal?'

Realizing that Kate clung to the prospect of future pleasure to help her through this time of trial, he smiled. 'We shall stay in only the best hotels, and behave like true English milords, bullying the waiters and demanding instant attention.'

Kate's giggle would have been more re-assuring had it not been so high-pitched and Black frowned to her. 'I'd be much obliged if you would keep your voices down,' he warned. 'Fouché's spies are everywhere.'

They stopped at a stable, and while Black haggled with the proprietor over the price of a hack carriage Matthew examined his surroundings. Away from the hectic elegance of the city centre, Paris was shabbier than he had expected, with less traffic in the streets and a great number of women wearing the red camlet jacket and apron that seemed to be a feminine uniform. Of the far less numerous men, many appeared to be injured in some way, either walking by the aid of a wooden crutch or bearing scars or patches that hinted at honourable wounds.

'It looks like a country at war,' Kate said, quietly. 'Everything is high-pitched, frantic, as if they were afraid that this could be their last day.'

Matthew nodded. Despite Bonaparte's order to re-open the churches, Paris seemed more pagan than Catholic, with its sophistication a facade beneath which horror crouched, whetting atheistic and Republican claws. His time in France had convinced him of the importance of Britain winning the war. He had seen the military build-up at the coast, so much larger than anything Britain possessed, and the slave labourers in their chains. He had personal experience of the secret police and the guillotine, and shuddered at the memory of Kate lying beneath the blade, afraid but defiant.

Matthew looked upward, wondering that the same sun that smiled over Kent should also heat the Republican fervour in Paris. Although only a few miles of water separated the two nations, everything here seemed strange, as if reflected in a distorting fairground mirror. He glanced down the street, where a clumsy diligence rocked over the pave, passing the small group of Parisiennes who did not seem to object when the coachman casually flicked at them with his whip.

Matthew shook his head, desperately looking forward to standing on the deck of the *Tern*, feeling the bite of sea air and hearing English voices again.

If they hired a coach here, a hard drive should see them at the coast tomorrow, and then it was only a short hop to England. He frowned, trying to work out how many days they had been in France, gave it up and hoped that Mr Black would know. He would take Kate right into the Dolphin Hotel in Deal and buy himself a pint of October and an honest English mutton chop. The thought made him smile.

Black looked tense when he emerged from the

stables. 'They only have one coach to hire, and it is already out.'

'Horses?' Kate enquired. 'Do they have horses?'

'It's a long ride to the coast, Miss Denton,' Black began but Kate interrupted him.

'Do you think I care about that?' Her voice rose as the memory returned. 'We were nearly guillotined this morning because you could not control your base passion, and now you are concerned about comfort rather than expediency? Get us some horses, Mr Black, or I shall!'

For a second Matthew thought Black was going to strike her, but instead he grunted and stepped back inside the stables. Kate looked at Matthew and raised her eyebrows. 'Sometimes people need to be reminded what is important in life.'

Matthew nodded, wondering again what married life would be like. He watched her for a second, realizing that she had always displayed a strong will, and remembering her words that she would be a poor wife. Perhaps he had made a mistake, catching a tigress by the tail, and he contemplated a future under petticoat government.

'Oh, Lord, Matthew, I'm frightened.' Kate quickly shattered his pessimism. 'Whatever happens, promise you won't leave me alone in this terrible place. Rather let me die first.'

'I won't leave you alone,' Matthew promised, as the ogre-wife of his imaginings dissolved and Kate returned, as steady, sensible and teasing as always, but now with a new vulnerability to balance her bravery.

'I wish we had married first.' Kate's words surprised him. 'Before we came here.'

Matthew reached for her. 'We'll have the banns read immediately we return to Ashbourne,' he promised.

'You don't understand,' Kate's voice trembled. 'I need...'

They had been too intent on each other to notice the diligence that had drawn up, or the passenger that had alighted. She strode past them and into the stables. There was the sound of a woman's voice, raised in surprise, and then Black appeared, moving quickly.

'For God's sake, run,' he ordered, urgently. 'We are discovered!'

Twelve

Paris
July 1805

'What?' Matthew looked up as the passenger from the coach appeared. 'Oh sweet Lord!'

Citizen Peltier crashed out of the stables, with the scar on her face drawing her lip down and her eyes hot with anger. For a long moment she seemed to stare directly into Matthew's eyes, but she turned, shouting, and pointed to the fleeing Black.

Kate gasped, one hand to her mouth, then she recovered and grabbed Matthew's arm. 'Run! Come on, Matthew! Run!'

Matthew ran. He felt Kate's hand drop from his sleeve so she could lift her skirt high above her ankles, and he hesitated, unwilling to draw ahead.

'Go, Matthew! Run!'

'Come on!' He grabbed at her, hustling her onward as he cursed their bad luck. Why did that woman choose this particular stable to visit, and why had Mr Black panicked when he could have surely just walked away?

Only a few moments ago he had been planning to buy a pint of October in Deal, and now he was flying for his life. He could hear footsteps beside him, hear the repeated cry of *'Anglais! Anglais!'* and saw people turning toward them, pointing.

'Matthew!' Kate pulled him into a side street. 'This way!'

He could see Black ahead, running as if Lucifer was on his tail, and then Kate stumbled again as her unfamiliar clogs caught on the cobbles. Matthew hesitated, grabbing at her, and somebody in a blue-and-white uniform was level with him, shouting in French.

'Kate!' He steadied her, prepared to fight, but the soldier ran past, ignoring them to concentrate on Black.

Kate looked at him, her eyes wild and her breath coming in shallow spurts. 'I don't understand,' she said, speaking quickly. 'That woman, Citizen Peltier, said to ignore the couple and catch the running man. It's Mr Black they want, not us.'

Matthew's immediate reaction was of mingled indignation at the French perception of his unimportance and guilty relief, but concern quickly followed. 'She must have recognized him,' he decided.

'What shall we do?' Kate wondered. 'Oh, Matthew, what can we do?'

There were shouts from ahead and the sound of a musket; a woman screamed, high-pitched, again and again.

'We must help him,' Matthew decided. 'No, *I* must help him. Kate – I want you to make your way back to England and acquaint Admiral Springer of all that we have found. I will try and rescue Mr Black, as he did us.'

'No, no,' Kate was shaking her head, clinging to him with her eyes pleading, 'don't leave me alone here. You promised you would not leave me alone.'

'But I must,' Matthew began, until he saw the extent of her fear. She was trembling, with her lips quivering and bright tears forming in her eyes.

'Not alone. Not in France. It's so dark.' When Kate shook her head the first tear fell, coursing down her cheek, and her hair bounced around her ears. 'Please.'

Matthew held her close. She had been so brave on the guillotine, but the prospect of being alone had brought back all her childhood terrors. She clung to him, sobbing, and Matthew knew that he had no choice. 'We will return to England together,' he said.

'But poor Mr Black?'

'Poor Mr Black is the author of his own misfortunes.' Matthew hardened his heart. 'And my concern is with you, not with him.'

'Can we not help him?'

'You are in no position to help anybody, Miss Denton.' The voice was so close that Matthew jumped, and Dugua was smiling at him over the barrel of his own Manton.

Matthew pulled at the chains that had held him so securely to the wall for so many days. His few hours of freedom made the confinement seem even worse, and he swore, kicking backward at the harsh stone.

'Don't take on so, Matthew,' Kate advised. 'Save your strength.' She forced a smile, with her teeth a flash of white through the deep gloom of the dungeon. 'At least we have seen Paris.'

'We'll see it again,' Matthew vowed, knowing how hollow his words must sound, 'but next time we will have won the war and we will not have to dodge our own shadows.'

'We will see it together,' Kate said, and the ugly clatter of chains ridiculed her. 'And maybe Father can come too. He has always expressed a wish to travel, but he has been too busy looking after the shop, and me.' She stopped, sighed, and Matthew knew by the sound that she was pulling at her chains in sudden frustration. 'Oh, Matthew, we'll never get out of here again. They'll ask you the same question, and then they'll kill us both.'

He heard the despair in her voice. 'No. No, Kate, we mustn't think like that. We must keep hope.'

'Hope? There is no hope, and Matthew.' He heard the sob in her voice as she rattled the chains. 'Oh God, this is my fault! If I had not insisted on you poking into Mr Lamballe's house we would be safe at home now.'

'There's always hope,' Matthew said. 'Mr Black may have escaped and could come back for us. Anything could happen.'

Kate said nothing for a long time, but Matthew could hear her clogs scraping over the filthy straw underfoot. 'Do you know what I wanted, Matthew? That day I agreed to marry you?'

'Tell me.' Matthew could feel some slack in the chain that held his left arm, and stretched up to make it as taut as he could. For the last few days, he had been working to escape. If he pushed alternately left and right for long enough, he might loosen the staple that held the chain in the wall. He knew the chances of success were small, but the effort gave him some hope.

'I wanted a wedding at Norrington, with the vicar and all the people that I grew up with. I wanted you and me and Father to be happy, and then for us to go on honeymoon to Tunbridge Wells.'

'All of us on honeymoon?' Even if he stretched on his toes, he could not reach the staple, but Matthew continued to work at the chain, pushing and pulling. He grunted when a tiny flake of mortar flicked past him. That was some progress. 'Your father as well?'

'Of course not, addle-head! Just you and me.'

The staple was definitely moving. Matthew could feel more play, so he pulled as hard as he could, swearing.

'Matthew, what are you doing?'

'Fighting this blasted chain. Tell me more about Tunbridge Wells. What will we do when we get there?'

'Oh, lots of things. We can stroll the Pantiles and listen to the concerts. We can take walks to the rocks and up to Sion Hill; I am told that it is very pretty up there. We can partake of the steel waters and improve our health, and maybe we can hire a carriage and go for rides in the countryside.'

Matthew heard Kate's voice fade to a sob as the dream faded and the reality of imprisonment deep inside France returned. Taking the strain on his arms, he began to climb up the wall, placing his feet against the rough stones, gasping at the pain but determined to loosen the staple.

'Matthew, what are you doing? Stop it: you will do yourself a mischief.'

'I hope to do this damned chain a mischief,' Matthew said, 'but you carry on. Tell me more.'

'When you get yourself established as an engineer, and I have full control of the shop, we'll have a house just outside Norrington. I know the very property. It's been empty for years, ever since the last tenant died, and the owner does not seem to care for it, so it should be cheap to rent.'

'Which house is that?' The strain seemed to be tearing his arms from their sockets, so Matthew leaped down, jerking at the staple as hard as he could. He yelled at the pain, but felt the chain slacken a tiny fraction.

'What on earth are you doing? Are things not bad enough that you should try to injure yourself as well?' Kate's voice was sharp.

'I'm trying to get us out of here,' Matthew told her. The manacle had rubbed the flesh from his wrists and blood seeped onto his hands. 'Keep talking.' He leaned against the wall, trying to control the waves of pain that ripped through him. 'Which house?'

'Worple Hall,' Kate said, quietly. 'Do you know it? It stands on a rise beside the old track by the fields, with a view to the sea in front and across the Downs to the rear.'

Matthew began to move his chains in a circle, hoping to increase the movement of the staple. The iron bit into his wounds. 'I do, but it's a bit tumbledown, is it not?'

'Yes,' Kate agreed, 'but what a situation! We would have dawn light in the morning, sunsets in the evening, and quiet walks through the lanes and fields.' She was quiet for a few minutes. 'And a library, Matthew. I would love a library of my own books, not just books to sell.'

There was no doubt that the staple was working loose. Matthew could feel the slackening of the chain, while every few twists brought down more flecks of mortar. Mr Black had said that this building had been a nunnery, so the Republican regime had probably added this refinement. 'I can't promise you anything, Kate,' he said, grunting with the effort of swinging and twisting the chain, 'but if it is possible, I will try and get Worple Hall for you.'

'No, you *still* don't understand. I don't want you to get it *for* me.' Again, there was a catch in Kate's voice. 'I want us to get it *together*. I must be a part of it.'

Matthew paused. Until that moment he had listened to Kate, but had not concentrated on her words. Now he began to understand. She would never be a conventional wife, seeking security through the labours of her husband and offering in return devotion, children and compliance. Kate wanted equality; the tribulations of her childhood had forced her into a search for independence that he had disrupted, so she was torn between her love for him and her fear of being dominated by another. Her constant teasing was an affirmation of her autonomy, a reminder that she was not merely an appendage but an individual in her own right.

He stopped working on the chain. Kate seemed to know what she wanted from life, but did he? He had concentrated on his engineering career to the exclusion of all else, treating Kate as a delightful diversion, an appendage rather than a partner. That was patently wrong and he was suddenly ashamed of himself. Kate had been his saviour during the black times at Maidhouse College, and Kate had travelled the length of England to help him discover his own identity; she deserved better of him.

'We will *both* be part of it, Kate. Whether we live in Worple Hall or elsewhere, we will *both* share the house, and the life.' It felt strange to make such promises while chained to the wall of a French dungeon. 'It will be our life, Kate, not just mine.' He was sensible enough to stop there, as Kate shuffled in the straw.

'By your leave, of course, Matthew.' There was bitterness in Kate's voice. 'Legally, you will own everything. Once we are married, every piece of property will be yours and every decision I make will be subordinate to your approval. You may allow me equality, but you will have the legal right to withdraw that concession at any time.'

'Indeed,' Matthew put an edge into his voice, 'but I cannot change the law, Kate, so you must learn to trust me.'

The silence stretched for minutes, broken only by Matthew's renewed attempts on the staple. When Kate spoke again, her voice was distant, as if she was musing out loud. Matthew nearly felt guilty at listening to her thoughts.

'It is hard to hand one's life entirely to another. One's feelings, one's hopes and finances, one's dreams and aspirations, one's soul, or the essence of one's happiness, all given in pawn. That is what a woman does when she marries; she bundles her life up in a package, places it in the care of a man who she often hardly knows and trusts in his goodness, charity and consideration.' There was another long silence before she spoke again. 'I am afraid, Matthew, that I will be back in the dark again, unable to move and crying silently in front of Hades.'

'Like you are here?'

'This is physical,' she replied at once. 'Physical pain is temporary; you know it will end, but being trapped emotionally is forever. I thought that I had escaped when my mother died, but she had placed the fear too deep. Perhaps I can never escape, perhaps I am trapped in that cellar for ever.'

'Except that you are not alone,' Matthew reminded. 'I am here.'

'But you are outside me.'

'Only until we are married.' Matthew had stopped working on the staple. Kate was more important than his freedom. 'Then we become one.'

'But does that really happen?' Kate's voice rose again. 'Father and my mother were never *one*, and I know lots of married people who do not appear to even *like* each other. Why should we be different? How can I know?'

Matthew thought quickly. 'You can't know, but you can trust. How many married people have been chained in a French dungeon together? Or have sailed in a smuggling lugger?'

After a long silence, the mockery returned to Kate's voice. 'Or have dined on bread and watered wine in a Paris cafe? So, how are you getting on with your chains, Matthew? Can you get us out of this place yet?'

'I'm working on it,' Matthew said. He did not know if anything had been resolved, but he certainly felt closer to understanding Kate. Now all they had to do was escape from a French dungeon, reach England and tell Admiral Springer that the French were indeed digging a tunnel, but it was vulnerable to naval attack.

211

Compared to soothing over the emotional concerns that seemed to beset them both, facing the physical world was a relief; practical problems could be solved by practical means.

The crash of the door opening and the yellow glow of lanterns interrupted them as a group of men thrust into the room. Once again the gabble of French rebounded from the walls, and Matthew's struggles were useless as he was unshackled and dragged out. This time the guards also brought a protesting Kate.

There was the now familiar succession of stone steps and corridors before they were hauled into a long room, lit by a high chandelier. There were five burly men standing against the wall, and Matthew wondered briefly if Dugua had a supply of replacements, until hard hands shoved him forward.

Two people sat behind a table, facing them. One was Dugua, with that obscene necklace of human ears, smiling slightly as he drummed a devil's tattoo with his fingers. To his right was Citizen Peltier, with a red cravat covering her neck and extending high onto her chin. After a few minutes the door opened again and two more men entered the room. Walking slightly slope-shouldered, the younger hurried to the table, murmured something to Dugua and took his place beside Peltier. Matthew glanced at Kate, for the last time they had seen that man he had been entering the tunnel, but his presence did not matter beside that of his companion.

The third man did not immediately approach

the table. Instead he stared at Matthew, nodding slightly, and then stooped to whisper quietly to Dugua, who nodded.

'Good evening, Mr Pryde.' Anton Lamballe gave a short bow. 'It is a pleasure to meet you again.'

Matthew felt the slide of despair but ducked his head in response.

'Mr Lamballe,' he said.

Dugua's fingers increased their tempo as he frowned toward Matthew, but it was the woman who spoke first.

'There are only two. Where is Black? Bring me Black.'

After a moment's delay two of the burly men left the room, to return a few minutes later with Black. Ignoring the chains on his ankles and the heavy bruises that disfigured his face, he bowed to Kate, then to Peltier.

'Miss Denton; Mademoiselle Peltier. I am delighted to meet you both again, although the circumstances are not of the best.'

'Mr Black.' Kate glanced toward the watching Frenchmen and dropped in a curtsy. 'It is good to meet a gentleman again, after being in such low company. The accommodation in this inn is not of the finest and the service is positively antediluvian.'

'Enough.' Dugua stood up. 'Mr Black, I assume that you are already acquainted with Citizen Peltier?'

Black nodded. 'It would appear so, although I cannot recollect the occasion.'

Peltier rose in her seat, one hand fingering her

cravat. Pointing a finger at Black, she spoke rapidly in French, which Kate translated for Matthew's benefit.

'I will remind you of the occasion, Mr Black. It was outside Toulon, in 1793. Do you remember now, Mr Black?' Peltier leaned forward until her face was only an inch away from that of Black.

Black met her eyes unflinchingly. 'I remember Toulon,' he admitted.

'And do you remember murdering my brother? And giving me this?' Still speaking, Peltier ripped away her cravat.

Matthew saw the scar that marred her neck and extended to her mouth as Peltier pointed to Black, nearly stretching across the table in her anxiety to reach him.

Kate continued to translate, with her voice shaking. 'She says that Mr Black mutilated her and left her for dead.'

Matthew looked at Black, who had suddenly paled and would have stepped back if the chains had not prevented him. 'It was a fair fight,' he said, speaking in English as he addressed Kate, and then Peltier began to shout rapidly in French.

Kate shook her head. 'This must be the occasion that Mr Black told us of, when he fought a group of Frenchmen outside Toulon. According to Citizen Peltier, the Frenchmen were only children, one a boy of fifteen, and the other his thirteen-year-old sister. This woman, Mlle Peltier, was the sister.'

'Not quite the hero, then,' Matthew mused. He

eyed Black, who seemed to be protesting his innocence. 'No wonder she hates him.'

Dugua banged the table. 'Enough! This hearing has only one function: to ascertain the identities and guilt of the three prisoners. Citizen Peltier has identified the prisoner Black. Does anybody identify the other two?'

'You already know who we are,' Matthew began, but Kate placed a placatory hand on his arm.

'It's all right, Matthew. They must have their appearance of legality before they murder us. Is that not correct, Mr Dugua?'

'Citizen Lamballe,' Dugua ignored the interruption, 'do you recognize this man?'

'That is Matthew Pryde,' Lamballe confirmed. 'I employed him as an engineer in my mine in England.'

There was a stir of interest at the table, with the mysterious man at the edge leaning closer to study Matthew. Kate looked at him curiously, shaking her head. 'I know you,' she whispered, 'I'm sure I know you.'

'In your opinion, citizen,' Dugua continued, 'is Mr Pryde a competent engineer?'

'He is, Citizen Dugua,' Lamballe replied without hesitation. 'Mr Pryde is a most competent engineer, and a capable and brave man.'

Matthew bowed in reply. It was always good to hear professional compliments, whatever the situation.

'Do not be so grateful, Mr Pryde,' Dugua warned. 'Citizen Lamballe, we discovered Mr Pryde close to our...' he glanced at Matthew before continuing, 'military mining establishment. In your opinion, would Mr Pryde now constitute a danger to the Republic?'

Lamballe seemed to hesitate before he continued, but when Dugua prompted, he nodded. 'Unfortunately, yes, Citizen Dugua. If Mr Pryde were released, he would make haste back to England with his intelligence. Our mining operation would be jeopardized.'

'Quite so,' Dugua nodded. 'And the woman?'

Lamballe coughed delicately. 'I am not sure why she is in France, citizen. Miss Denton sells books in a small shop.'

Matthew was aware that everybody at the table was looking at Kate.

'Perhaps she was hoping to buy more stock?' Dugua smiled at his own joke, but Peltier shook her head and spoke in rapid French. 'In English, please, so that our prisoners can understand.'

'I met these two at the mine. The woman, Mlle Denton, did all the talking. They are a team, and she acts as his translator.'

'Ah!' Dugua nodded. 'That I can understand. The English are too proud to learn another language.' He sighed, theatrically. 'Unfortunately it also means that Miss Denton is equally dangerous.'

'You had no hesitation in attempting to murder me even before you considered me dangerous,' Kate reminded him, but Dugua ignored her.

'Citizen Cusset, do you have any questions to ask?'

The man at the end started slightly, as if he had not expected to be included in the procedure. He looked at Matthew and spoke in quiet, hesitant French, which Kate translated.

'The gentleman would like to know if you had a solution to the problem of air circulation underground,' Kate said. She glanced from Matthew to the Frenchman, frowning.

'Tell him that it is a constant worry in our mines too,' Matthew said, 'but after we have won the war our respective engineers can get together and work out a solution.'

Dugua shook his head, so the ears on his necklace rubbed together. 'Won the war, Mr Pryde? You British are so keen to win that you will fight to the last drop of your allies' blood.' He held up a hand, counting off the fingers one by one. 'Austria, Piedmont, Prussia, Naples, Hanover; all allies of Britain, all defeated by France. And how many English soldiers died to defend their borders? None.'

Matthew began to speak, but Kate was the faster. 'It was France that was the aggressor,' she said, 'your Emperor of murder who caused the deaths. Bonaparte who bombarded the Paris mob. Bonaparte who butchered the people of Pavia and Jaffa, Bonaparte who turned his back on Christianity in Egypt and murdered his own sick in Palestine.'

'Enough!' Dugua thumped his fist on the table as Lamballe looked troubled, but Kate, once started, was hard to stop.

'I hear that his personal life is no better. Did he not seduce his own sisters? Is he not descended from a thief and a galley slave? Is his mother not a...' She stopped and glanced at Matthew. 'Now it is I who display a commonplace mind,' she said. 'I hope that I have not shocked you, Matthew dear.'

'Not at all, wife-to-be,' Matthew responded in kind, although he had been taken aback by the rancour of her assault. 'You speak only the truth.'

'Liar!' Dugua must have hurt his fist with his previous table thumping, for now he merely shouted. 'You shopkeepers provoke us into jumping the ditch, and very well, we *will* jump it. We shall plant the tricolour on what we leave of London, crush your pretty mercenaries aside and welcome the Irish peasants and English workers who flock to our banners of liberty.'

Matthew shook his head, trying to envisage Edmund Gambill and his fellow cricketers greeting the French as liberators. 'I am afraid you would be disappointed, Mr Dugua, even if you could cross the Channel.'

'As you may be aware, there are ways to circumvent even the greatest obstacle,' Dugua said, until Lamballe grunted a warning. He nodded. 'It matters little. We know enough about you, Mr Pryde, and your, how do you say it, your dolly? Your bird of paradise? Your lady of easy virtue?'

Matthew saw Kate colour at the insulting insinuations, but she kept quiet.

'So,' Dugua shrugged. 'You are both spies, and as such will be executed. Mr Black also.'

Although he had expected nothing else, the announcement of his impending death stunned Matthew. He stared at Kate, who was looking at

218

Cusset with her eyes narrowed. 'Kate...'

Kate smiled. 'I've said my piece, Matthew. Let us not show them any fear.'

'Silence!' Dugua's chair grated on the stone flags as he thrust it violently back. 'Take them away.'

Peltier pointed to Black. 'That one first,' she said, 'and I will pull the lever myself, and catch his head as it falls.' Her smile was as vindictive as anything Matthew had ever seen. 'As soon as I heard that Captain Page had landed Mr Black, I did not even inform Citizen Fouché before I hurried to trap him.' She nodded to Kate, who was still translating for Matthew. 'You see, Miss Denton, we know exactly what is happening in your Kent. We too have our spies. And I demand the pleasure of his death.'

'As you wish,' Dugua shrugged.

'Monsieur Dugua,' Cusset touched at his sleeve, 'Citizen.' He spoke rapidly, and Dugua, after listening for a few minutes shook his head.

'*Non,*' he said. 'They will all be executed at dawn tomorrow, for their information is too dangerous to reach England.' He waved his hand in the air. 'Take them away.'

'What did Cusset ask?' Matthew wondered, as they were manhandled back to their dungeon.

'He asked that you be kept alive so he could discuss things with you.' Kate gasped as the guards thrust her wrist back into the manacles. 'He probably wanted one of your fascinating discussions about algebraic fractions or geometrical parallelograms or such like.'

Matthew nodded. He waited until the door

slammed and began to work on his chains. He had one night to loosen that staple, and then it would be too late. He looked across to Kate, allowing time for his eyes to adjust to the dark.

'Matthew, I can't be brave any more. I nearly screamed last time I was on the guillotine. I can't face it tomorrow.' The very calmness of her voice frightened him, but he could not help.

'Just think of Tunbridge Wells,' he said, and hauled mightily at the chain. The staple gave way at once, showering him with fragments of mortar and pieces of stone and sending him forward so he sprawled full length on the ground, swearing. 'Devil take it!'

'What's happened?' Kate was all concern. 'Are you hurt?'

'Hurt? No, and nothing bad has happened, but listen for the guards coming.' Matthew lay still, partially stunned. He knew that he had loosened the staple slightly, but was astonished at such immediate success. He pushed himself against the wall, expecting the door to burst open and shouting guards to trample in, but there was no movement outside. He rose, wrestling with the manacles on his wrist. They were closed with a simple pin, which he extracted without difficulty, before dropping the chain on the ground. It landed with a chunk of iron.

'Matthew! Are you free?'

'Keep still.' It was the work of a minute to unfasten Kate's wrists and she collapsed against him, sobbing. They held each other for a long minute, and then instinctively pressed together in a lingering kiss.

'Come on,' Kate pushed him away, 'we haven't got time for that now.'

Matthew noticed her wincing whenever she moved her right arm. 'Are you all right?'

'Yes, I think so. These chains wrenched my arm.' She rubbed harder, and forced a smile. 'It'll be all right. What are we going to do now?'

'Escape,' Matthew said briefly.

'Can you get us out of here?'

Bending to the door, Matthew examined the lock. 'Yes. It's a very straightforward mechanism.' Extracting the pin from Kate's manacles, he inserted it into the keyhole and felt for the levers inside. 'We can thank your uncle for giving me a thorough apprenticeship. I was three months in a locksmith's shop, remember, so I know how these things are made.'

'Thank you, Uncle William,' Kate said dutifully, as Matthew manoeuvred the pin and listened for the satisfying click as the lock sprung.

'Actually, any self-respecting engineer can do this,' Matthew admitted. He opened the door slowly and eased out his head. He was familiar with the long stone corridor with the closed doors, but was surprised that there were no guards to be seen. 'It's safe,' he said. 'Come on.'

'What about Mr Black?' Kate wondered. 'We can't leave him here to get guillotined.'

Intent on getting Kate to safety and advising Admiral Springer of the vulnerability of the air pump, Matthew had forgotten about Black. He hesitated for a moment, remembering that it had been Black's dalliance with Suzanne that had led to their capture in the first place, but he already

221

knew his decision. Black had made up for his mistake by his rescue attempt; he could not be left as a sacrifice to Bonaparte.

'Of course,' Matthew tried to sound as if there was no choice, 'but we'll have to find him first.'

The corridor was long and gloomy, with a single guttering torch illuminating a score of doors, each one of which might contain Black. 'We'll try each door,' Kate decided, 'and if it opens, then he's not inside.'

'And if it opens and half a dozen French grenadiers charge out,' Matthew said, 'we can just apologize and walk away.'

Kate said nothing, but Matthew guessed that her look would have withered him if there had been enough light to see.

The first four doors opened to their push, each one revealing a dingy chamber similar to the one they had just left. The fifth was locked, and Matthew spent a few nervous minutes with his pin, but to judge by the smell and the scurrying vermin, the occupant had been dead for some time.

'Hurry,' Kate pleaded. She moved on ahead, pushing at the doors. All were open save three, and she tapped on each. 'Mr Black?' Her voice echoed along the corridor, and once again Matthew wondered at the laxity of French security. There was a decided lack of guards to police Bonaparte's vaunted Republic. 'Mr Black?'

'Who's that?' The voice was faint but recognizable and Kate signalled to Matthew.

'This one!'

Fighting the trembling in his hands, Matthew probed the lock with his pin. He felt for the mechanism, swearing softly as the bars failed to fall correctly. Sweat greased his palms and forehead, dripping onto the ground.

'Hurry,' Kate said, glancing along the corridor, 'please hurry.'

The distraction broke Matthew's concentration and he again failed to open the lock. 'Kate,' he tried to quell the irritation in his voice, 'could you look for a way out of here?'

'No,' she shook her head violently and stepped closer. 'Not on my own.'

'All right.' Matthew withdrew at once. 'Just keep watch, then.' He bent over the lock, trying to ignore her nervous breathing as he worked the bars. He could sense Kate's trembling, but could not help her. This time the bars fell into place and the lock sprang back. Matthew threw open the door and stepped inside.

'Matthew!' Kate's hiss made him start. 'There is somebody coming!' A lantern glimmered eerily at the end of the corridor.

'Sweet Lord!' Bundling Kate before him, Matthew closed the remaining doors and returned to the dungeon he had so recently left. He shut the door and placed himself against the wall, rattling the chains as realistically as possible. After a few moments he tensed at the sound of footsteps, but they passed without pausing. Taking a deep breath to control the batter of his heart, he counted a slow hundred before moving again.

'Matthew?' Kate looked up from the opposite

wall. Her eyes were huge.

'He's passed,' Matthew told her, and pulled out the pins that secured Black's hands. Black collapsed, groaning and rubbing at his arms and shoulders.

'We've no time for that,' Kate said sternly, 'come on!'

The corridor was deserted, with their footsteps echoing from the harsh stone. They moved slowly, stopping every time they heard a noise, and when they reached the circular stairs Matthew halted again.

'Come on,' Kate urged, 'what are we waiting for?'

'To listen,' Matthew said. 'If we meet somebody on the stairs we'll be trapped.'

'And if we stay here we'll also be trapped,' Kate reminded him. 'Let's get out of here, Matt. Please.' She sounded close to collapse.

The first step was the hardest, but once they had begun there was no return. Matthew could not recall the landings, from where corridors arrowed into terrible darkness, or the heavy wooden door that opened soundlessly to his touch. He moved on, with Kate immediately behind him and Black at the rear.

'Are we all right?' Kate asked.

'We're all right,' Matthew confirmed, raising his voice to inspire confidence. He saw Kate's frown as she looked at him, but moved on, one steep step at a time, keeping close to the central stone pillar around which the steps wound, and hoping not to meet anybody coming downward.

He froze at the sound of voices ahead, and

glanced frantically up. The stairs seemed to circle forever, before disappearing into blackness, but there was an opening a few steps up.

'Come on!' Moving quickly, he ushered Kate and Black through the door and pushed them along the corridor as the sound of voices increased.

'They might come this way.' There was a tremble in Kate's voice.

'In here!' Black spoke for the first time, pushing open a side door and sliding inside. The room was long and narrow, bare save for a wooden bench. An unglazed window revealed a dark sky, with clouds dragging across the stars. 'Stand against the wall,' he ordered, 'and don't look outside in case somebody sees you.'

Kate immediately pulled back from the window. The voices momentarily stopped, then restarted in the corridor outside their room.

'Please, Lord, don't let them come in here.' Kate shrank against the wall, hoping for invisibility.

The conversation swelled into angry words; a man and a woman that Matthew recognized as Mlle Peltier and Lamballe. He curled his fist into a ball, preparing to fight rather than return meekly to his chains.

'Somebody's upset,' Black said, until Kate hushed him with a wave of her hand.

'I'm trying to listen!' Her hand felt for Matthew's and squeezed slightly, then she pressed her ear to the door.

The voices rose higher, and Matthew heard his name mentioned, and the name of Black. 'What are they saying?'

'Ssh!' Kate flapped her hand again.

Peltier was shouting, her voice shrill, and Matthew heard a sound that could only have been the stamp of her foot on the stone floor.

'I can only hear bits,' Kate whispered, 'but it doesn't make sense. Citizen Peltier is saying that she wants to kill Mr Black, but Mr Lamballe says that Fouché forbids her to. I can't quite hear him for all the noise she's making.'

'Listen, then,' Matthew said.

'It would be easier if you kept quiet!' Kate rounded on him. 'Give me space!'

Matthew backed off, remaining within touching distance in case the French decided to burst through the door. He watched Kate bending forward to listen, her ear to the keyhole.

'Mr Lamballe is speaking again. "This way is better," he says, "this is the way it must be." But she's still arguing.' Kate looked back, shaking her head. 'They're moving away down the corridor again.'

'Good,' Black said. 'As soon as they've gone, we can get out of here.'

Kate cracked open the door to listen. 'They're still arguing, but I can't make out the words now. Whatever it's about, that woman wants to kill you, Mr Black.'

'So it would appear, but I intend to cheat her of the opportunity,' Black said, 'so the sooner we are away from this place, the better.'

When the voices faded entirely, they slipped out of the room and back onto the staircase.

Kate addressed Black directly. 'Did you kill a

fifteen-year-old child?'

'Of course not,' Black sounded angry. 'Peltier is either mistaken or lying.' He squeezed in front. 'Let me lead,' he said. 'For I may know the way better.'

The spiral stairs ended at the courtyard, where a solitary guard sat in a corner, pulling at his pipe until the bowl glowed red. He stood, stretched, and disappeared into a dark doorway.

'The Lord is watching over us tonight,' Kate said.

'Amen to that,' Matthew agreed. 'Could you just get Him to extend the time, so we can get safely home?'

'That's out of my hands,' Kate said, 'but I'll do my best.'

The feel of cold night air was a pleasure, but Kate averted her eyes from the guillotine that sat as a reminder of what tomorrow might bring. 'Hurry,' she pleaded, and kept close to Black as he guided them to the same side door by which he had entered on his previous dramatic rescue.

'It's open,' he said, surprised. 'I thought we would have to force it.'

'That's all right,' Kate giggled with relief, 'Matthew is good at locks.'

Still thankful at the lack of guards, they slipped through the dark corridors. Twice Kate thought she heard a noise and they shrank into the shelter of a door recess, but there were no guards, merely the ancient building creaking in the night.

'This is too easy,' Kate worried. 'Maybe they've set a trap for us.'

Matthew's rational mind rejected the possibility. 'Why? They already had us chained and helpless in limbo. The French are just thorough dunces.'

'Keep quiet!' There was venom in Black's hiss. 'Can you two not do anything without having a long discussion?' He held up his hand. 'The outer door is guarded,' he warned. 'Keep back.'

The soldier at the back door leaned against the wall, cradling a musket in his arms as a single candle pooled light all around him. With his cocked hat tilted forward and his moustache moving gently with every breath, he did not look the formidable figure whose companions had caused so much terror across Europe. Matthew held Kate close as Black eased forward, nearly invisible in the shadows.

There was a sound, a single cry of alarm from the sentry, and Matthew saw Black rise from nowhere, wrap one arm around the man's neck and pull back savagely. The sentry struggled, drumming his heels against the wall, but by the time Matthew moved forward to help he lay quiet.

'Is he dead?' Kate asked, staring at the sentry.

'He is,' Black confirmed indifferently. He checked the door and swore. 'It's locked.'

'That's Matthew's job,' Kate said, proudly.

'Or we could use this.' Matthew pointed to the massive key that hung at the sentry's waist. 'Let's hope that there's no sentry posted outside.'

The door opened smoothly onto an empty

road, where moonlight blinked through the swaying branches of an elm.

'Thank God,' Matthew said. 'Even Paris looks good tonight.'

'We're out,' Kate nearly sobbed, but Matthew noticed that she winced as she tried to move her right arm.

'And this time we're staying out.' Black had discarded any flippancy. He closed the door behind them and leaned against the wall. 'We'll need horses and then it's a dash for the coast.'

'A stables, then,' Kate said. 'And Matthew can pick the lock.' She seemed quite proud of his talent for housebreaking.

'Can you ride with your arm?' Matthew asked, bluntly.

'I'll have to,' Kate replied, 'because I'm not staying behind.' There was pain in her smile. 'I can ride pillion if I have to, but that will slow us down.'

'Can you ride astride?' Black was even more forthright. 'I doubt that a minor stables will stock side-saddles.'

Kate lifted her chin. 'If I *have* to lift my skirt up to my waist to ride a horse, Mr Black, I'll ensure that you are looking elsewhere first.'

'We have intelligence that must reach England.' Black's voice was harsh. 'I consider your attributes somewhat less important. But I warn you both now, if you cannot keep up, then I will leave you behind.'

'You already came back to rescue us,' Matthew reminded him, but Black shook his head.

'I did not come back for you, Pryde. I came

back to discover what you had found out. The security of England is paramount; our lives are not.'

'So shall we stop bandying civil whiskers and leave?' Kate asked sweetly. *'You* may wish to leave us behind, but *I* have no desire to have my ears decorate the neck of Mr Dugua.'

'This way,' Black kept to the shadow of the prison wall, 'and try to refrain from idle chatter.'

They had hardly left the walls of their prison when Black pointed ahead. 'God is certainly good to us this night,' he said, 'he has gifted us a dilly.'

The diligence stood a few yards from the corner of the street, with the coachman nodding on his box and his long whip thrusting to the sky. The four horses stood with their heads down, one pawing the ground in impatience and another whinnying softly as its tail flicked slowly from side to side.

'There could be somebody inside,' Matthew warned, but Kate rejected his caution.

'Then Mr Black will throw him out. Won't you, Mr Black?'

'With great pleasure,' Black agreed. 'Now follow me and for God's sake keep quiet.'

The coachman seemed to start awake as they approached, but rather than look toward them he dismounted, climbed clumsily to the ground and stamped his feet as if to restore his circulation. Black gestured them into immobility as the man stomped toward the shelter of the wall, both hands busy with his fly buttons. Matthew moved closer to Kate, protecting her from such sights.

The diligence was larger and heavier than an English stagecoach, but lacked any pretence at elegance. Little more than a clumsy box, it was dark painted with an indistinct coat-of-arms on the door and had three curtained windows on either side.

'God, but it's ugly,' Black said, 'and look at these wheels! Positively medieval.'

Matthew agreed; the iron-rimmed wheels at the back were nearly twice as large as those at the front, while the ancient thorough-brace suspension would ensure an uncomfortable ride

'Never look a gift horse in the mouth,' Kate reproved them, but she still hesitated before opening the doors. 'It might be occupied.'

'Check the interior, Pryde. I'll take the reins.'

There were two matching pairs, bays and greys, cross-cornered to give a chequerboard pattern, and as Black mounted the box and lifted the whip, Matthew jerked open the door and thrust his head inside.

He had expected something as stark and utilitarian as the exterior, but instead found a place of satin cushions and soft drapery, with a carpet on the floor.

'Clear,' he whispered, and extended a hand to help Kate in.

There was a jerk as Black released the brake, then they heard the crack of the whip and the diligence pulled forward. Kate gave a small whoop of delight and moved to the window, staring outside. 'Matthew! Look at him hop!'

The driver was following, his flies gaping open as he waved a massive fist at them, but the noise of the horses drowned his words. 'He looks upset.' Kate sounded pleased.

'He'll soon warn the others, though.'

'So we'll have to move fast.' Taking hold of one of the massive carriage cushions, Kate nestled into a corner, stretched out her legs and closed her eyes.

Black seemed to agree, for he cracked the whip again, sending the horses cantering through the dark Parisian suburbs. Rolling down the window, Matthew thrust his head outside.

'We'll drive in stages,' he shouted. 'I'll take over in an hour. Is that as fast as you can go?' For all the horses' effort, the diligence was hardly exceeding walking speed.

'It's a slow beast, this,' Black replied, yelling over the growling of iron wheels on the uneven pave. 'Do you know the way?' He was hunched forward, peering into the dark of the unlit street.

'I'll just follow the road!'

Black grunted and plied the whip so the horses lurched forward, sending the carriage smashing into a pothole. Matthew retired inside, closing the window to save Kate from the draught.

'We are about a hundred miles from the coast,' Kate told him, 'and we dare not change the horses, so it will be a long journey.'

'And a slow one, I fear,' Matthew said. 'A good English coach can make an average of eight miles an hour, with the occasional gallop of ten, but this monster will be much slower. Perhaps half that.'

'Four miles an hour?' Kate sounded disappointed. 'And we'll have to rest and feed the horses too, if we can't change them.' She gasped as the coach swung hard around a bend, throwing her against the window. She rubbed at her injured arm. 'That's about twenty-five hours' travelling time, and maybe another ten hours for rest.'

'More,' Matthew said, quietly. 'It may be a hundred miles direct, but we cannot afford to take the main roads; Dugua will alert the military and there'll be patrols everywhere. It's the byways for us.' He grabbed for support as the diligence crashed over a rut. 'And they will be even rougher than this.'

Once they were outside Paris, Black halted to light the lamps and Matthew took his place on the box, nervously handling the long whip. Save for Mr Lamballe's dog cart, the last equipage he had driven had been a racing curricle, and the diligence was shockingly slow and clumsy in comparison. He could nearly feel the horses strain to haul it along the potholed road, and used the whip far more frequently than he liked.

'Come on, boys! Use your muscle!'

The horses looked well, but rather than pulling straight, the bays set in opposite directions, one to the right, the other to the left, which upset the greys, made driving difficult and constantly rocked the coach. Matthew peered ahead, trying to make out the run of the road by the weak glimmer of the lamps. Beyond the pool of light, France crouched, dark and unfathomable. He swore. Clouds had concealed the stars, obscuring the road, yet he dared not slow down in case Dugua was pursuing. The bark of a dog only increased his feeling of isolation.

'Settle down there!' Matthew roared, laying the whip along the flank of the nearside bay. The animal jumped, but continued to pull badly.

The French would be aware of their escape by now, and Matthew pictured a squadron of cavalry galloping after them, swords loose in their hands as they cried vengeance on the British spies. He glanced to the rear, seeing shadows in the dark and hearing the drum of imaginary hooves.

That nearside bay was pulling awkwardly again, unsettling the grey so both horses veered to the left. Matthew compensated, hauling at the reins and swearing loudly. The lamplight glanced off the boles of trees, a constant avenue of poplars that flickered like the stripes of a thousand tall zebras, producing a near hypnotic series of light and dark.

There was the square yellow gleam of light from a cottage window, gradually enlarging, as they came closer. Matthew fixed his eye on the spot, intent on driving as far from Paris as possible. They drew level with the cottage, passed it and rumbled on with the great iron-tyred wheels crunching on the surface of the road. An hour passed and the sky began to pale so the lamplight was dimmer, creating monsters from bushes and soldiers from grazing livestock. Once Matthew winced when the light reflected from predatory green eyes, but he recognized the creature as a goat, and not some demon of the night.

He slowed when they came to a village, easing

the horses along a narrow, filthy road over which gloomed dilapidated tenements, rather than the thatched cottages of England. He flailed his whip at a pack of starveling dogs that bayed and ripped at the wheels of the coach, and sighed his relief when they rolled back among the forlorn fields.

By now dawn was cracking the eastern horizon, a band of bitter light gradually seeping across the sky. He could see trees silhouetted against grey clouds, and heard the raucous wakening of a myriad birds. Desolate behind its screen of tombstones, a church sulked through windows smashed in fratricidal hatred.

'Mr Pryde!' Black leaned out of the window. 'Pull in wherever it is convenient. We will have to rest the horses.'

Matthew drove until he found a field sheltered by a belt of trees, with a shattered mansion whose lord had surely given brief but bloody entertainment to the sans-culottes. He eased along a road now rutted and torn, and stopped behind a tall wall, topped with iron spikes. The crest of the one-time owner was carved into the stonework, but had been used as a target for missiles so it was chipped and forlorn, a relic of a fallen dynasty.

'Welcome to the Republic of France.' Kate eyed the ruins. 'Liberty, fraternity, equality and desolation.' She sounded tired, and held her right arm awkwardly, as if the pain was increasing. 'What was it Calgacus said? They make a desert and call it peace?'

'He was talking about the Romans,' Matthew

recognized the quote from Tacitus, 'but I see what you mean.'

The horses' flanks were steaming and their tails shaking with exertion as Matthew released them from the harness. Thankfully, the pump in the courtyard still worked, and he filled the stone trough, allowing the horses to drink while he wiped them down with the carriage cushion.

He pointed to the bays. 'These two are the very devil to drive. Blackguard French horses that cannot be taught to pull straight.'

'They managed very well.' Kate reproved his outburst. 'We must have travelled all of twenty miles at one stretch.'

'But we have much further to go,' Black said. 'We must leave the main road very soon, for Dugua and that devil Peltier will have the patrols out by now.'

'That devil Peltier?' Kate probed for more information, but Black shrugged her off.

'We'll allow the horses to graze and recover and hope that nobody takes a fancy to them. In the meantime, scour the place for food, and then we will try and rest ourselves. We'll set off in the evening.'

'In the evening?' Matthew did not agree. 'Will that not give the French time to catch up?'

'They'll expect us to keep moving,' Black said. 'Trust me on this.'

The house seemed to have been deserted for years, with rubble lying inside the rooms and thick dust layering smashed furniture. While Matthew led the horses to a large field that combined sweet grass with a plethora of weeds, Kate

236

and Black searched for anything edible. Their combined haul was an ancient hen and two eggs, only one of which proved inedible, and an ornamental fish that had swum as absolute monarch of its own small pond.

Hiding the coach inside the stable block, Kate pointed to the side panel, where a large yellow P stood out from the dark green body. 'I wonder who used to own this monstrosity.'

Matthew grunted. 'It looks like it was somebody important.'

'Oh God, I hope so,' Kate said. 'I hope it belonged to Bonaparte's brother.' There was no humour in her laugh. 'Serves them right for trying to guillotine us.'

As animals had soiled the ground floor of the house, they withdrew to an upper room to eat. Matthew watched Kate, in her ripped French peasant dress, biting into a leg of chicken so the juices ran down her chin, and wondered what her father would think if he saw her now. She looked up at him, face smudged with dirt, dark eyes pouched through lack of sleep and hair a tangled confusion, and smiled.

'You're still wearing that Friday face, Matthew. Eat; we're on our way home.'

Matthew nodded and bit into the scraps of meat that the wing afforded. It was a poor meal, but there was plenty of good water. He frowned at the weeping sores that the manacles had left on Kate's wrists, but she waved away his concern.

'It doesn't matter. I've had a lot worse.'

When they had eaten Black questioned them

about the mine. He listened as Matthew explained what they had found, with Kate interrupting to add details that he had forgotten, or to give her own opinion.

'Are you certain that the forts are virtually defenceless?' Black sounded amazed.

'Certain,' Matthew confirmed, as Kate nodded vigorously. 'They hold only one or two real cannon. The others are false – cut-down barrels painted black, stuck on wagon wheels and the like.' He smiled through his fatigue. 'Bonaparte must be running short of guns.'

'No.' Kate shook her head. 'He will be stripping his defences to take as many as possible to England.'

'If one fort is like that,' Black repeated Matthew's earlier thoughts, 'then we can assume that the other is the same. So the defences of the bay are a paper tiger.' He shrugged. 'Unless Bonaparte thinks there is nothing worth defending.'

'Well, that's hardly true,' Kate said, tartly, 'as the steam pump for the mine is right in the centre of the bay.'

'So you say.' Black's eyes fixed on Matthew. 'You are certain that you found the pump? There is no doubt in your mind?'

'None whatever,' Matthew said. 'Mlle Peltier sent us with a load of timber to the fort, and we looked down upon the island. The pump is hidden from the sea, but clear from the headland.'

'Oh yes.' Kate's smile was so charming that Matthew knew it was false. 'Matthew and I found the pump, and Admiral Springer would have the intelligence days ago, if you had only controlled your manly impulses!'

'Kate...' Matthew extended a restraining hand, but Kate was not inclined to back down.

'Yes, Mr Black, if you had not thrust your attentions on Suzanne, we would all be safe in England, and Admiral Nelson could be burning and destroying the pump and Bonaparte's mine right at this minute. Instead, we've been chained to a wall and threatened with death, while poor Suzanne and Mr Durand were killed. Quite horribly too, I may add.'

'So the pump is on the island within the Baie de l'Isle, and the fortifications are weak.' Ignoring Kate's outburst, Black repeated the essentials. 'Do you have any more intelligence, Pryde?'

Leaving Kate to rant, Matthew described everything he had seen. Black listened intently, nodding to show he understood the more technical details.

'And you are certain that this pump is crucial to the workings of the mine?'

'Indeed.' Matthew nodded vigorously. 'Without the pump, bad air builds up at the bottom of the mines. Sometimes it leads to explosions, and at other times to a noxious gas. The more powerful the pump, the safer the mine, at least as far as airflow is concerned. Of course, there is still the risk of the roof falling in.'

'Yes, yes.' Black waved him away. 'I am not concerned with the roof.' Standing up, he paced the room for a minute, with his hands writhing together behind his back and his feet ringing hollowly on the floorboards. 'I must work out what is best to be done.'

'Why, Mr Black, I shall tell you that!' Kate was not inclined to let him escape so easily. 'We must get this intelligence to England forthwith ... but only when the call of our breeches has been answered.'

Black stopped his pacing to look at her. 'Miss Denton, I understand your anger, but in my own defence I must say that I did not seek out the bed of Mme Durand. Rather my company was her price for allowing us to remain in her home.'

Kate lifted her chin, silent for once. 'If adultery was the price, sir, then surely a gentleman would have looked elsewhere for a place to sleep?'

'Perhaps,' Black said, softly, 'but if by doing that a gentleman condemned a lady such as yourself to more exposure to the French soldiery, who, I may remind you, are not renowned for their chivalry, would he then be correct? I had the choice, you see, of retaining my honour as a gentleman and putting you in discomfort and danger, or aiding my country by acting contrary to my wishes.'

'And you took the course that was contrary to your wishes,' Kate said, 'how very noble of you.'

Black bowed in acknowledgement. 'You are pleased to use sarcasm, Miss Denton. Pray consider the facts. You met the lady: she was hardly one to tempt Adam into sin, was she?'

'I liked her,' Kate started.

'I did not say that I did not *like* her, Miss

Denton. She was a likeable woman, but hardly a temptress. Good Lord, she must have been forty, if she was a day.' He bowed again, making a sweeping leg. 'Now if *you* had requested my company, there would have been no question.'

'There will never be such a question,' Matthew rose to Kate's defence, 'nor even a such thought, if you are indeed a gentleman.'

Black raised his eyebrows but said nothing. He resumed his pacing for a further ten minutes, then sighed and stared out of the window. 'I must do whatever is necessary. There is no help for it.'

'No help for what, pray?' Kate asked, but Black shook his head.

'I was merely thinking out loud, Miss Denton. You had both better take some rest while I watch for the French. Mr Pryde, I will wake you in about four hours, and you can stand sentinel while I sleep.'

At one time the mansion had boasted scores of rooms, but the lack of a roof had rendered the top floors uninhabitable. Matthew found what he thought had been a bedroom, with tall windows, but he was surprised when Kate followed him in.

'Is this decent,' he wondered, 'both of us sleeping in the same room?'

Kate shook her head, forcing a smile. 'Whatever would Mrs Grundy say? No, it is anything but respectable,' she agreed, 'but after all, we did share a dungeon and a coach.' She was smiling, but Matthew sensed that there were shadows beneath the flippancy.

'Are you all right?'

'I'm scared, Matthew,' she admitted frankly. 'I don't want to wake up alone in a strange room.' She lowered her voice. 'Still less do I want to wake up with a strange man *sharing* my strange room.'

Matthew returned to the levity that helped them over such difficult moments. 'So I am not strange, then?'

'Oh, very strange,' Kate told him, 'but I have grown used to you over the years.'

Matthew smiled, and then looked up abruptly as the full implications of her words struck him. 'Is it Mr Black? Has he made any improper advances?'

'No,' Kate shook her head emphatically, 'he has not, but ... but I do not like him, Matthew. He has a darkness in him.' She pointed to a corner of the room behind the ornately decorated door. 'Would you think me most indecorous if I slept over there?'

'Not if you behaved yourself,' Matthew told her, and added softly, 'You are safe with me.'

'I have always been safe with you,' she said quietly, 'and that is the only compliment that I will pay you this night.' Turning her back, she lay on the floor, twisting uncomfortably until Matthew fetched the blankets from the coach.

'Here,' he said, roughly. 'One beneath you and one above.' Removing his waistcoat, he folded it. 'And that will suffice for a pillow.'

Kate smiled, smoothing back her hair. 'Thank you, Matthew. You see? With you I am as safe as I would be as home, and snug as a bug.'

Nodding, Matthew withdrew to the opposite side of the room. He watched her wriggle into a more comfortable position, very aware of the curve of her hip as she lay on her side. That was Kate, his friend from youth, and if they succeeded in escaping from France, she would be his wife. The idea was unbelievable.

He tried to ignore the hostile miles that lay between them and safety, concentrating instead on Kate's breathing as she settled to sleep. When she moved again, one of her legs protruded from the blanket and he stepped across and covered her up, pulling the blanket up to her chin. She opened her eyes, smiled briefly and was sleeping before he completed his task.

'Dream sweet,' Matthew said. He looked down on her for a few moments before retiring to his own corner of the room and sitting on the comfortless floor. Somewhere outside a blackbird sang, the noise so nostalgic of England that he felt unutterably sad and very far from home.

Propped against the wall, Matthew knew that he could not sleep and prepared himself for a long day listening for the galloping hooves of French cavalry. He shivered at the thought of being caught again, and hoped that Black would keep a good watch. When he woke the light was already fading, the sky was alive with birdcall and Kate was bending over him.

'Matthew! The French have taken Mr Black!'

Thirteen

France
July – August 1805

'Matthew!' Her voice was urgent. 'Matthew!' She shook him again, leaning so close that her hair flopped loose to tickle his face. He looked up, unable to comprehend where he was.

'Kate?'

'It's getting dark outside and I can't see Mr Black anywhere. I think the French have captured him!'

'What?' Matthew sat up, rubbing at the stiffness in his back and neck from the uncomfortable position in which he had slept. 'When?'

Kate repeated her words, her eyes wide and worried. 'He's not downstairs.'

'Have you looked outside?' Matthew glanced out of the window. Untidy trees cast long shadows, while near-horizontal rays of sunlight revealed how much time had elapsed while he had been sleeping.

'No. The French might be there.'

'Right.' Matthew scratched his head, aware that his hair was unwashed, unkempt and probably stinking, while his face sported an ugly beard. He hated Kate seeing him so ungentlemanly. 'I'll have a look. You wait here.' He forced a smile. 'He's probably just gone to check on the horses.'

Kate's nod was unconvincing.

Lifting a length of wood as a makeshift weapon, Matthew slipped downstairs. Unsure whether he should shout or keep silent, he chose the latter as he checked each room, but there was no sign of Black. Neither were there any French soldiers. He swore in frustration, and knew that he must search outside.

Keeping in the shadows cast by the house, he ran to the field where he had left the horses. At first he thought that the French must have retrieved them, but a faint whinny from the far corner stilled his anxiety. Dim in the gloom, he saw horses grazing.

'Is he here?' Kate had followed him. Her subdued whisper made Matthew jump.

'No. I'll try the stables.'

With Kate a constant shadow, he ran to the stable block, now convinced that the French had spirited Black away. The diligence stood there, ugly and cumbersome and with that bright yellow P on the sombre paintwork.

'Mr Black?'

'Are you there, Mr Black?' Kate added her voice. 'The French have not taken him, Matthew. There are no horses, and no fresh horse droppings.' Trust Kate to be so practical.

'So what's happened, then? Maybe he has gone to find food?'

'Maybe,' Kate sounded doubtful. 'But ... Matthew – what's that?' She pointed to a note attached to the coach door. 'That was not there earlier.' Pulling it free, she retreated to the better light outside the stables before reading.

'What does it say?' Matthew stood at her shoulder. 'Is he all right?'

Kate read the note a second time before she replied. 'Oh yes, Mr *Black* is all right. Just listen to this:

My dear Mr Pryde and Miss Denton,

It saddens me to leave you in such a manner, but you will surely agree that the information you have found must reach England by the speediest means possible. Accordingly I have availed myself of the swiftest of the carriage horses, and will attempt to ride to the coast, there to make rendezvous with Captain Page. I know that you will understand that such intelligence is too vital to be delayed, and am assured that your natural wit and adroitness will enable you to escape safely from France.

Kate looked up. 'He has not even had the grace to sign it.'

'He hardly needs to,' Matthew said. He closed his eyes, feeling the sick slide of despair.

Kate slid her hand inside his. 'We'll still get home, won't we?'

'Of course.' Matthew raised his voice to emphasize his sincerity. 'We'll be faster without him.'

Kate looked at him, frowning. 'We both know *that*'s a bag of moonshine. How can we drive with only three horses?'

'Maybe we don't have to. How's your arm?' Matthew watched her wince when he tried to touch her. 'Can you ride?'

'Bare-backed? Without saddle or bridle? Maybe a man can do so, but it's hardly possible for a lady, Matthew. Despite what I said to Mr Black, I am not one of your centaurs that can emulate men by riding astride, thank you, and with only one working arm—'

'You cannot ride,' Matthew interrupted, 'in which case we drive unicorn. But first we'll lighten the coach of everything that we can. It's heavy enough for four horses, so much worse for three.'

'We'll *eat* first,' Kate accepted his decision without argument, which revealed how concerned she was, 'if Mr Black has left us anything in his anxiety to run away.' She raised her voice. 'He must have planned the whole thing, Matthew, ordering us to sleep so that he could escape. He's leaving us to die here.' Her chin came out in that stubborn streak that Matthew was beginning to recognize. 'Well, I won't.'

'Good. Neither will I, then.' Matthew watched her march away, hips swinging in indignation as she stormed into the house, banging the door behind her.

They tore everything they could from the diligence, throwing out all the internal fittings, from the wooden panels that lined the doors to the luggage boot. Working by the last light of dusk, and then by candlelight, they got rid of the spare curtains and blankets, the chest of liquors that Matthew wished he had found the previous day,

247

and all the internal seats save one. When they had finished, the coach was lighter, but still looked cumbersome as it stood beside the once-elegant stables.

'Not these,' Kate said, rescuing a couple of bottles from the liquor chest and smiling to Matthew. 'They won't take up much weight and we might need them later.' For the last two hours she had slogged alongside him, so sweat had sliced pale streaks through the grime on her face.

Matthew watched her admiringly, realizing that they had probably shared more experiences than most married couples who never left the security of their native parish, or strayed from conventional lives. 'What a long-headed girl you are, Katty.' He winced as she suppressed a gasp of pain. 'Is that arm still giving you concern? Maybe I should look at it.'

Kate instinctively flinched away, but eventually agreed that he could try to help. Ordering him to turn his back, she stripped off her outer clothing, replaced enough for decency and presented her bare arm.

'Be careful,' she said.

As gently as he could, Matthew inspected her. He had feared that her arm was broken, or even dislocated, but delicate probing reassured him that there was nothing seriously wrong. Her biceps and triceps were deeply bruised and he suspected there might be a strain, which would account for the pain. Both wrists were also badly scraped from the iron manacles, and one wound was weeping.

'I'm going to bandage this up,' he said, and

removing his jacket, began to strip off his shirt.

'Matthew Pryde!' Kate sounded shocked, but she neither pulled away nor averted her eyes. 'You'll catch your death.' Her voice was low.

Bare to the waist, Matthew saw that Kate was looking at him with an expression he had never seen before. He felt the colour surge to his face and began to apologize, until he realized that she was not offended. Before she could object, he ripped the sleeves off his shirt. 'Now let's get you bandaged up.'

'I must wash first,' Kate insisted, and led him to the water trough. 'As will you, Matthew, for you are not the sweetest-smelling flower in the field, and I am sure that I am every bit as bad.'

Only when they were as clean as circumstances permitted did Kate allow him to bind up her wrists, watching with a small smile on her mouth. She asked what he was doing when he ripped a long strip from the tail of his shirt and shook her head in mute protest when he explained that he was fashioning a sling.

'Get dressed again,' he said, and turned his back.

'You're a good man, Matthew Pryde.'

When she was ready, Matthew looped the sling around her neck and positioned her injured arm inside. 'That might help,' he told her. 'I don't think you're badly hurt.'

'Matthew...' Leaning closer, Kate put her left hand to his cheek, bent closer and kissed him softly on the mouth. 'Now get your jacket on again before you get too cold, and then please fix the harness up.'

It was a complicated task changing the harness from four horses to three. Matthew worked for an hour before he was sure that everything was secure, with one of the greys and a bay side by side nearest the diligence and the remaining grey on its own in front as the unicorn, or leading horse.

Night had carried a fine rain with it, so by the time he was finished, Matthew was miserably wet.

Kate handed him a glass. 'Hot brandy and water,' she said. 'I cannot think what it will taste like, but at least it will provide stimulation.'

He thanked her with a smile, swallowed half the glass in a single draught, gasped at the sting and handed her what remained.

'No. You finish it,' Kate said as he touched her injured arm. 'I feel terrible that I cannot help much. You will have to do all the driving yourself.'

'So let us be started.' Matthew finished the glass. The hot liquid exploded in his empty stomach. 'You and me together, Kate, and confusion to the French.'

'And to Mr Black,' Kate added.

Even with all the excess removed, the diligence was heavy for the remaining three horses. Matthew felt them straining as he cracked the whip, and cursed the rain that would add to their difficulty. 'Come on, there!'

The carriage lights gleamed on the familiar straight road with the regularly spaced trees, the same morose villages with the weeping roofs and flapping shutters and the same occasional mansion that sat shattered amidst sad fields. After an hour, Kate thrust her head out of the window.

'Put this on,' she ordered, handing out one of the two blankets that they had retained, and he pulled it across his shoulders, grateful for any covering from the thin, insistent drizzle. 'Matthew!' Kate gestured behind them, and he flinched as he saw a long column of horsemen.

'We can't outrun them,' he said. 'Let's hope they are not looking for us.'

He peered into the dark, hoping for somewhere to hide, but the horsemen were moving fast. They drew level within two minutes, cavalry with long cloaks covering their uniforms and rain dripping from the peaks of their helmets. Matthew raised his whip as the officer saluted with a wave of his hand. He watched the column trot past, their boots and spurs glistening as a hundred hooves spattered mud against the coach. Their gear jingled for a few minutes, and then they had vanished into the night.

'More troops for England,' Matthew said gloomily as he cracked his whip and pushed the carriage on. The thought renewed his energy and he did not spare the horses as he trundled and lurched onward at a steady four miles an hour. The rain eased just once, for a short twenty-minute spell, then returned with an intensity that forced him to huddle deeper into his blanket and haul on the reins every time the unicorn grey slithered in the mud.

'I thought France was a sunny place,' he shouted as Kate thrust a concerned face outside the carriage.

'Whoever said that had never been here,' Kate replied.

When they passed a small military encampment, Matthew pulled off the main road and plunged deep into rural France. He hoped that he was heading in the right direction as he passed through villages that looked nearly medieval in their condition, with streets of shuttered houses whose sagging roofs dripped water to add to the spreading puddles on the road.

'Have a rest,' Kate yelled, but Matthew shook his head and forced on, urging the tired horses with whip and voice.

'We'll keep going until dawn.' He indicated a grey band of light to the east. 'It shouldn't be long now, and we'll find somewhere to spend the day.'

Kate nodded. 'You look tired.' She extended a hand upward but could not quite reach. Matthew nodded, stretching back to touch her, and returned his concentration to the road.

'Careful now!' Matthew hauled the reins as the unicorn grey slipped for the second time in five minutes. He pulled on the reins, but the horse slid again, to crash down on its side in a flurry of kicking hooves and flailing harness. The coach slewed to the left, and banged into a halt in a deep rut. 'God! Kate!' He raised his voice. 'Are you all right?'

'I'm fine.' Opening the door, Kate jumped into the rain. 'Are you?'

They surveyed the wreckage. One horse thrashing in the road, the other two standing with heads bowed and steam rising from their flanks and the harness a tangled mess of ropes and leather.

'The screws are about done,' Matthew said. 'There's not many miles left in them.'

Kate cowered beneath the rain and looked around. They were at the edge of a sloping plain, dotted with the winking lights of small farms, and with a broad belt of woodland about half a mile ahead. 'If we can reach that forest we can shelter there for the day.'

Matthew nodded. At that moment the trees looked as far away as the moon. Bending to the grey, he tried to coax it upright, but the horse was no longer kicking. It looked up at him, eyes old and resigned.

'Beast's given up,' Matthew said. He whispered in the grey's ear, then loosened the harness and tried hauling it upright, but without success.

'Let me try.' Kate knelt down, breathed in the horse's nostrils, pulled at the collar and eventually, with rising frustration, slapped its shoulder. 'Come on, you stupid Johnny Crapaud!'

The horse seemed to settle further back into the mud, flanks heaving. Its companions looked on, dejected.

'Light a fire under it,' Kate suggested. 'I saw a carter do that once when his horse fell on the ice in Ashbourne.' The mention of the homely name increased their sense of isolation in this foreign land, and Kate stamped her foot and banged the closed fist of her left hand against the carriage. 'Oh, can't we just go *home*?'

'We'll try your fire idea,' Matthew agreed. He

did not like to maltreat the animal, but they had little choice. He had to get Kate to safety. 'See if you can find some paper.' He looked toward the trees in the growing light. 'Or anything that will burn.'

'There's the blanket,' Kate said. 'It might do.'

There was a tinderbox in the carriage, and Matthew struck a spark under the unravelled wool from Kate's blanket. He held the smouldering wool in the shelter of the carriage until the flames were strong enough to endure the rain, then carried it out to the horse and placed it beneath the animal's belly.

'Only another mile,' he promised, 'take us only another mile, then you can rest.'

The grey jumped at the sting of the flames, kicked weakly and subsided again.

'Oh, come on!' Kate knelt beside him, with the rain washing down her face. She pulled the collar of her smock higher, covering her chin and lower mouth. 'Try again. We must get to the trees.'

They were so intent on the horse that neither heard the sodden thump of marching feet, nor the clump of hooves.

'Madame?' The deep voice took them by surprise so that Kate jumped and covered her mouth, while Matthew looked up, blinking into the rain.

The man was tall on his horse, and some of the dye had seeped from his blue cloak onto the calf of his white breeches. He smiled down at them, one hand touching the brim of his helmet in salute. A small group of horsemen stood at his side, while a sergeant headed the column of infantry that stretched in patient misery along the road.

While Matthew felt despair slide sickeningly into his stomach, Kate stood up and spoke in rapid French, pointing to the fallen horse and their carriage. Matthew stared at her, stunned at her audacity; rather than urging the soldiers to move away, Kate was asking for their help.

The mounted man, whom Matthew took to be the officer in charge, clicked his tongue in sympathy as he dismounted. He spoke to Kate and knelt beside the recumbent horse.

Matthew moved aside, ignoring the officer's cheerful chatter as Kate joined them. The officer glanced at her, frowned, and then looked pointedly at the coach. He jumped to his feet, sweeping his helmet off his head and performing a most un-Republican bow.

'Citizen Peltier!'

Matthew started and rose to his feet, prepared to grab hold of Kate and run, but he realized that the officer was looking directly at Kate. The other horsemen were sitting at attention, with one holding his sword in the salute, its hilt pressed against his lips. Suddenly Matthew remembered the golden P that was emblazoned on the door of the coach and cursed his slow mind. P for Peltier, of course, they had stolen Peltier's own coach. He glanced at Kate, who stood in some surprise, her head down and her chin tucked into her collar.

'Monsieur Colonel,' Kate began, and launched herself into a torrent of French that relaxed the officer in a minute. He saluted, remounted and shouted a volley of orders that resulted in two of the mounted men galloping away, their hooves raising great clods of mud that spattered the unfortunate foot soldiers.

'They think I'm Citizen Peltier,' Kate whispered, 'so I've sent them off to find better horses for us.'

'What?' Matthew stared at her. 'Just get them away as fast as you can!'

'Why?' There was mischief in Kate's grin. 'If they think I'm some important Frenchwoman, I'm going to exploit them all I can.' When her smile faded he could see the exhausted strain in her face. 'We're about dropping, Matthew. These horses can't last, and nor can we.' She shook her head. 'I can't, anyway.'

'You're doing well.' About to put an arm around her, Matthew prevented himself. Citizen Peltier's coachman would not do such a thing. Instead he contented himself with an encouraging nod.

Kate adjusted her collar to hide a non-existent scar. 'Let's see how well, shall we?' Walking up to the officer, she gave more sharp orders that sent him scurrying away, and within a few minutes a soldier ran to Matthew with a warm cloak.

He accepted it gratefully, watched as Kate donned another before she retrieved the full brandy bottle and threw it to the sergeant. There was surprised delight in his face when he caught it. When Kate spoke again, the sergeant marched his men toward the woods.

'No sense them suffering,' she explained,

slightly shame-faced.

'Even though they could be marching through London soon?'

'If Mr Black succeeds, and he should with our horse under him, the French won't be any nearer than Boulogne,' Kate said, and glanced at the rapidly lightening sky. 'I wish they'd hurry with the horses, though. What would we do if the real Mlle Peltier turned up?'

Matthew breathed out slowly. 'We would run,' he said. He looked back along the road, now a quagmire of muddy puddles. The rain was at last easing, and he could see the details of farm buildings that had previously only been vague shapes.

'Here's somebody coming now,' Kate warned as the officers cantered up with fresh horses. She pushed Matthew back, watching as a squad of soldiers hurried forward to quickly replace the team. They worked noisily but with more efficiency than Matthew had expected.

The horses looked lean and unkempt, as did most animals in France, but they stood with their heads high, and seemed willing to work. Kate thanked the officer, handed him their opened bottle of brandy, and pushed Matthew onto the box.

'Allez!'

Matthew cracked the whip and nearly fell backward as the horses jumped eagerly forward. Despite the clinging mud, the coach growled along the road, passing soldiers who stiffened in salute, and one who cheerily waved the nearly empty bottle. Momentarily forgetting her character as Citizen Peltier, Kate waved back, which brought a raucous cheer.

'I should have asked them for some food,' Kate said as they passed through the wood and thundered onto an open plain.

'Yes, and a case of pistols and a map of France too.' Fatigue made Matthew sarcastic, but Kate did not reply. Abandoning his original idea of sheltering in the trees, he drove on, now determined to use these fresh horses as long as he could. He did not know how far it was to the coast, but now he was moving again, he was determined to lessen the distance. He bowed his head, concentrating on working the horses to their maximum.

Since Black had deserted them, Matthew was less concerned about reaching Admiral Springer with the information about the tunnel, and more worried about getting safely home. Black seemed to be a clever, resourceful man. Travelling on horseback, he would move far faster than three people in a diligence, and would also be less noticeable. Matthew expected that Black had already reached the coast, and had probably found some method of crossing the Channel. He guessed that Joss Page had given them up for dead days ago, but there were other smugglers, other boats.

Matthew shook his head. Black could look after himself. Kate was his concern, and her injured arm only added to his deeper worries about her safety.

'Leave the road!' Kate's voice was tense. 'Leave the road now!'

'What?'

'Now!'

Matthew obeyed, hauling the team onto a track that angled off to the left. The lead offside horse floundered in the deeper mud until he guided it with the reins. 'What's the matter?'

'Back there!' Kate pointed behind her. 'It's Citizen Peltier, and she's coming this way fast!'

Fourteen

France
August 1805

'Lord save us!' Matthew looked around, desperate for somewhere to hide. Stretching ahead, the track curved toward a belt of tall trees. Unfenced fields spread forever on either side, dotted with placid cattle that grazed unheeding of the carriage that swayed past. He plied the whip, urging the horses onward. 'Are you sure it's her? Where is she?' The solid bulk of the diligence hampered his rear vision as he twisted on the box, trying to see behind him.

'About half a mile away, but riding like the wind, and she is not alone.'

'She must have seen us!' Matthew smothered a curse as the carriage thumped into a hole, throwing him high into the air. He swore again,

259

louder as he descended with a spine-jarring thump.

'Keep going!'

Momentarily freed of the coach's weight, the horses trotted down a steep incline, splashed spectacularly through a ford and dragged up the far slope, slithering in the mud so Matthew had to saw at the reins to keep them on the track. Geese scattered in front of them, wings beating the air in a frantic effort to escape.

'Whip, Matthew! Use the whip!'

The horses were willing, clawing their way up the muddy slope, and when they reached the trees, Matthew saw a small steading ahead. It was the only farm in this ravaged countryside, a confusion of low- and high-walled buildings clustered around three sides of an irregular courtyard. In the centre, a woman stared stupidly at this stranger in her secluded world. She had a yoke across her shoulders, with a pail of slopping milk suspended from either end.

'Inside,' Kate ordered. She glanced back. 'Hurry, Matthew!'

Shouting, Matthew guided the equipage towards the obvious dwelling, with green-shuttered windows and a low roof, ignoring the geese that honked their protests and flapped great wings. The milk-maiden gaped in peasant incomprehension, unmoving as the horses pawed the ground a few feet from where she stood.

Jumping from the box, Matthew nearly ran into Kate as she left the coach. 'What's happening?'

'It was Citizen Peltier, with two or three men. They were riding hard, as if they intended cutting us off.'

'Where are they now?' Matthew cast around for concealment. If Peltier came into the farm, she could hardly miss the massive diligence, although spattered mud had obscured her initial emblazoned on the door. He would have to hide the damned thing. 'Ask that woman if they have somewhere to put the coach.'

Kate did so, her voice sounding urgent. The milkmaid slowly placed her burden on the ground and pointed to the nearest of the outbuildings. She did not speak. Matthew ran across the courtyard and opened the door, discovering a surprisingly deep barn in which stood a single horse, saddled ready for use and munching a bale of hay. A pair of goats ran toward him, until they reached the end of their tethers and jarred to a noisy halt.

'It should fit!'

'No time,' Kate warned. 'I can hear her coming!'

Matthew swore. 'Come on!' Leaving the diligence standing in the courtyard, he grabbed Kate and pulled her toward the barn. 'Hide!'

There were shaded bays and a simple wooden ladder that provided access to a hayloft, nothing else. Matthew sped up the first few rungs, remembered Kate's injured arm and turned to help her. She stood at the bottom, her left hand lifting her skirt high to allow freedom of movement, and her right arm held close against her chest.

'Matthew!' Her whisper was urgent. 'I can't

get up.'

'I'm coming!' Jumping down, Matthew moved behind her, holding her steady as she slowly mounted the ladder, one step at a time. Two hens flopped away, cackling at the intrusion. 'Under the straw.' He cleared a nest for her, delving deep so she would be hidden, piled straw on top and lay at her side, facing the closed door.

'Matthew' – her left hand reached for him – 'I'm frightened.'

'It'll be all right,' he reassured her, and she frowned, shaking her head.

'Matthew...' Her voice trailed away as she forced a brave smile.

There was the sound of hooves, the unmistakable voice of Citizen Peltier and a harsh male reply. Matthew felt Kate shiver. When he looked at her, she was staring at the barn door, her tongue licking at her lips. 'It'll be fine,' he said. 'Just lie quiet.'

He could hear the jingle of harnesses and more voices. Somebody barked an order and sharp footsteps sounded from the courtyard. The barn door crashed open and a man stood silhouetted against the light, the pistol in his hand cocked and ready. He glanced around, ignored the horse and concentrated on the ladders, calling out what was obviously a challenge as he pointed the pistol upward.

Wincing as Kate's nails dug into the palm of his hand, Matthew squeezed reassuringly. When she looked at him, eyes wide in a white face, he wished that he could hold her safe for eternity.

The soldier shouted something over his shoulder and began to climb, holding the rungs of the ladder with his left hand as his right thrust forward the pistol. The sound of his boots was very loud. Kate gave a tiny shudder. Matthew released her hand and balled his fists; once the Frenchman reached the loft, he could hardly fail to see them, despite their covering of straw.

Matthew felt the nausea as he tensed, preparing to jump as the soldier ascended the ladder. He took a deep breath. He had never thought of himself as a fighter, or even a brave man, but he could not leave Kate to be captured and guillotined. If he acted now, he should be able to knock the soldier to the ground. That would gain him a pistol, and at least a fighting chance with the others.

The Frenchman moved closer, each footstep a second taken from Matthew's freedom of choice. He closed his eyes, gathering his nerve. If he created enough of a diversion, perhaps Kate could escape. With her knowledge of French, she would have a better chance of getting to England than he had. Taking a deep breath, Matthew began to move.

The shout came from his left as a figure erupted from the straw. Matthew saw only the flash of movement, and then a confused struggle of flailing arms and legs as the man threw himself on the soldier. There was a roar of noise, the soldier shouting and the man swearing, and then the ladder tottered and fell, with both bodies hurtling to the ground. They landed with the horrible crack of broken bones. Somebody screamed agonizingly and the man rose, lifted his boot, aimed deliberately and smashed the heel down on the side of the soldier's neck.

There was a sickening snap and the soldier lay still. Light from the open door caught the man's face as he looked upward.

'Black!' Matthew said, rising to his feet, but Kate reached up, sliding her left hand over his mouth. She shook her head urgently, mouthing the word 'no' and putting an emphatic negative in her expression.

'What?' Matthew whispered as she eased him back down.

'Keep still!'

Black hunted for a second, lifted the pistol from the ground where it had fallen, calmly checked the priming and, without looking back, walked out of the barn.

'Why here?' Matthew asked. 'In all of France, why would he come here?'

'Where else could he go?' Kate touched his sleeve with a calming hand. 'Think on it, Matt; there was nowhere else for miles, save bare fields and trees. This farm is the only place he could have come!'

'I should have helped him.'

'No.' Kate shook her head again. 'He was here when we came in. He knew where we were, and he said nothing. He's playing a lone hand, Matthew, and I think it's best that we just leave him to it.' Her voice was calm but Matthew could feel her shaking.

'Why is he here? He should be at the coast by now – unless his screw foundered. I doubt he would treat it with any consideration.'

'That's probably it,' Kate agreed, 'and Citizen Peltier must have been chasing *him*, not us!' She looked toward the soldier, who lay with one leg twisted beneath him and his head at an acute angle. 'I think that man is dead.' She let out her breath in a long moan.

'I think he is.' Matthew did not say that he had been about to kill the soldier himself. 'Kate, I'll have to go and help Mr Black.'

'No. Leave him.' Kate's hand was firm on his arm. 'I have not forgotten that he deserted us.'

'Neither have I,' Matthew assured her, 'but I don't want the French to capture him.' If Black remained free, there was a greater possibility of getting information to Admiral Springer. Matthew could view Black's earlier desertion as ungentlemanly but logical.

Kate dropped her eyes. 'I'd prefer you to remain with me,' she said.

'I'd prefer that too,' Matthew assured her, 'but you stay hidden.'

As the ladder had fallen to the floor of the barn, Matthew had to climb down the beams that supported the hayloft. He dropped the last few feet, remained still for a second and glanced at the dead soldier. Flies already hovered around the corpse, some settling on the staring eyes. Matthew looked away, lifted a clumsy pitchfork from the ground and peered out of the door.

The diligence stood deserted with the horses still in harness and a lone goose pecking under the wheels. Three further horses stood unattended at its side, and the milkmaid had sensibly fled, leaving her pails and yoke unattended.

There was no sign of Black or Peltier. A cock called nearby, its raucous challenge mocking the morning.

Slipping stealthily from the barn, Matthew sidled along the outside wall, with his heart thundering and his breath coming in short, shallow gasps. The shaft of the pitchfork was already slippery with his sweat. He felt sick, wondering how he had got into this situation. Maybe he should just gather up Kate and run, leaving Black to fight his own battles? The Bow Street Runner, if that was what he was, seemed more than capable of looking after himself.

Even though he expected it, the sound of Peltier's voice made Matthew start. He shrank into the shadowed angle between the barn and the farmhouse. Appearing very efficient, Peltier emerged from the farmhouse with a cocked pistol in her right hand and her travelling cloak thrown back to reveal the sword at her hip. Buckskin breeches hugged her legs, while the cravat covered her scarred neck and mouth as she surveyed the courtyard.

Matthew stared; the sight of an armed woman in man's clothing was as scandalous as anything he had ever seen. Brought up to revere women as quiet, demure creatures that were talented in accomplishments such as painting and embroidery, he found it hard to reconcile his perceived image with the brutal reality of Citizen Peltier. On the other hand, Kate was hardly conventional either.

A soldier followed Peltier. He was walking awkwardly as the spurs on his glossy black boots chinked with every step, but there was nothing clumsy about the way he carried his short cavalry carbine, and the long-barrelled pistol under his belt looked dangerous. Feeling very foolish, Matthew clutched his pitchfork. The farm implement seemed very inadequate against a real weapon held by a professional soldier.

Peltier stared at the diligence as if she had never seen it before. Bending closer, she cleared the mud from the door so the golden P was revealed, straightened up and swore loudly.

'Monsieur Black!' Her shout rose above the noises of the farmyard and when there was no reply she pointed to the building opposite the barn. The soldier trotted over, holding his carbine at the ready. He hesitated at the door, lifted his boot and kicked it open.

The report of the pistol echoed around the courtyard and Matthew stared as the soldier staggered back, dropping his carbine and reaching for the wound that spread blood slowly across his chest. Black emerged through the white smoke that drifted from the door. Without hesitation he reversed his pistol and smashed the heavy butt on the soldier's head. The man fell, making small noises, and Black stood over him, lifted his boot and stamped hard onto the man's skull, again and again until there was no movement.

Black looked up, his eyes predatory and with the soldier's blood spattered across his boots and breeches. Stepping back to the shelter of the doorway, he began to reload his pistol. From beginning to end, the killing had not taken ten seconds.

'Monsieur Black!' Peltier strode to the centre of the courtyard, her cloak rippling from her shoulders and the sword hilt prominent at her hip. Without stopping, she pointed her pistol directly at his head.

Black dropped as she squeezed the trigger. There was a flare from the muzzle of the pistol, a swirl of smoke, and the sound of the shot rebounded from the surrounding buildings, but Black was untouched. He rolled across the straw-strewn mud, bounced to his feet and rushed at Peltier.

Throwing the empty pistol at him, Peltier flicked out her sword. Black checked his attack as she glided into the alert position, right foot forward and left arm balancing the slender blade that danced at his chest and face. Her reaction had seized the advantage, as she advanced slowly with her face immobile and eyes intense.

Black circled outside her killing range, still holding the clubbed pistol, still dangerous. Whipping off her cravat, Peltier gestured to the scar across her neck and mouth, shrieking at him in obvious reference to their previous encounter. Her laugh was high-pitched as she leaped forward, feinted at his eyes then dropped her blade to prick at his thigh. Black jumped back, countering the blade with his empty pistol. There was the dull clatter of metal on metal and Black backed toward the open door, mouth open.

Matthew prepared for a mad rush to impale the

Frenchwoman, but struggled with years of training that taught him gentlemen always treated ladies with respect. Men fought men, but women were unassailable: it was one of the cardinal rules of civilization, bred into him by habit and culture. Despite his best intentions, Matthew remained immobile, clutching the pitchfork as he watched uselessly from the corner of the courtyard.

Peltier feinted low, the point of her sword flicking at Black's groin, and when he doubled and leapt backward, she slashed upward, ripping the sleeve of his shirt. Blood spread, to drip from the point of his elbow. Her laugh was not pretty as she spoke again, taunting as the blade probed, forcing Black into a weaving, ducking dance that took him away from the sanctuary of the door and into the centre of the courtyard.

Twice more Peltier feinted, but there was no lunge, and Black circled, swearing softly, but still clutching his empty pistol, still looking for an opening.

Matthew knew that he had to do something. He could not stand and watch Peltier kill Black; if he could distract the Frenchwoman, it might help. A roaring charge might work, but if Peltier killed him, then Kate would be stranded, a one-armed Englishwoman in France. However, if he could throw something at Peltier, he might break her concentration.

But what then? Would Peltier focus on him, and more importantly, on Kate? Matthew realized that she was perfectly capable of killing them both, and realized also that Black would not help. Black saw his duty as saving Britain, not in making sentimental gestures.

Peltier lunged again, but this time her supposed feint continued; the point of her sword thrust into Black's shoulder. He yelled and dropped the pistol, and Peltier came forward. Her blade slashed, opening a wound on his chin, and she pulled back her arm preparatory for the final thrust.

Matthew levelled the pitchfork and opened his mouth for a yell, when the shot echoed around the courtyard. At first he did not see from where it came, but Peltier leapt into the air, her eyes open wide with surprise. Without any hesitation, Black snatched the sword from her hand, reversed it and thrust it deep into her chest. Even as the Frenchwoman collapsed, Black had mounted the nearest horse, kicked his heels into its ribs and clattered out of the courtyard. He did not look back.

Powder smoke drifted slowly from the diligence as the door opened and Anton Lamballe slid out. Stepping over the body of the soldier, he knelt beside Peltier and slowly withdrew the sword. Wiping the blade on her cloak, he shrugged and let both fall to the ground.

Lamballe stood up, carefully reloaded his pistol and thrust it in a holster inside his cloak. For a second a shaft of morning sun caught him, highlighting the jut of his jaw, and then he bent down and dragged the bodies of Peltier and the soldier to the side of the courtyard, adjusted his cloak and strode into the barn where Kate remained hidden.

Concealed by the shadows, Matthew started forward, determined to protect Kate, but Lamballe emerged a few seconds later, leading the horse. He mounted easily, kicked in his heels and trotted out of the courtyard.

Fifteen

France
August 1805

'I don't understand.' Kate was weeping as reaction set in. She lay in Matthew's arms, trembling as he held her face against his chest. 'There's havey-cavey business here, Matthew. What does it all mean? Why did Mr Lamballe shoot Citizen Peltier? Are they not both French? And why did he let Mr Black go free?'

Matthew shook his head. 'I do not know. Nothing seems to make sense, Kate. Nothing at all.'

'Unless you were mistaken, and Mr Lamballe was trying to shoot Mr Black, but missed.'

'No.' Matthew recalled the events. 'Citizen Peltier had wounded Mr Black and was about to kill him. She had the fight won. Lamballe deliberately killed her.'

Kate sighed, allowing him to pull her closer. 'Maybe Mr Lamballe is not all he seems.

Remember when we were escaping from the jail and we heard him arguing with Citizen Peltier? She wanted to kill Mr Black, but Mr Lamballe persuaded her to leave him be. He said: "This way is better." '

'I remember that,' Matthew said. 'But what did he mean? What way was better?'

Kate sighed and wriggled free. 'I'm sure that I don't know, Matthew, but I'll wager that she chased after Mr Black to kill him, despite what Mr Lamballe wanted. And it seems that Mr Lamballe thought it was important to keep Mr Black alive, even if Mr Dugua wanting to guillotine all of us.' She shivered at the memory.

'But why would Mr Lamballe want Black alive? He must know that we would tell Black all about the tunnel, and he will ride straight to England with the intelligence.' Matthew shook his head. 'There's something very smoky here, Kate, I am completely befogged.'

'Do you know what I think?' Kate sat up determinedly. 'I think that we should eat something, get back in the coach and drive like fury for England. We'll tell Admiral Springer everything that we have learned, including what happened here, and we'll allow him to make sense of it. That's what I think.'

Matthew sighed. 'You're probably right, but I do not like to present him with a mystery. I like things to be precise.'

'But nothing *ever* is, Matthew,' Kate told him severely. 'You still live by the rules of mathematics, while other people do not. Perhaps Mr Lamballe and Citizen Peltier were lovers once, and he killed her because she left him.' She shrugged. 'I doubt that we will ever know.' Tapping his shoulder with her left hand, she stood up. 'Come on; let's find some food and get on our way. Father will be wondering what has happened to me, away for so long and not a line of a letter written.'

Matthew nodded. It was typical of Kate to worry about her father the minute that she was out of danger.

The farm seemed deserted, with the milkmaid and any other residents having fled when the soldiers arrived, so Kate made free with the contents of the kitchen while Matthew removed the pistol from the belt of the dead soldier and cared for the horses. After a meal of goose eggs, bread, cheese and goat's milk, they drove the diligence a few miles closer to the coast before sheltering in a wood to debate their next move.

'Mr Black will reach the coast in a few hours,' Matthew said, 'and I doubt that he'll send anybody to look for us.'

'Probably not.' Despite her recent scares and the constant pain of her arm, Kate seemed quite content. 'But we'll find some other way home.' She looked up, eyes bright in a determined face. 'After we've come through so much, Matthew, I don't think a bit of water will stop us.'

'It's stopped Bonaparte,' Matthew reminded her.

'He's French,' Kate said. Standing up, she slapped his arm. 'Come on. Let's get home. We'll sort out all the mysteries later.'

By avoiding the main roads, they increased the

distance they had to travel, but the build-up of military traffic proved their proximity to the coast. They passed the occasional peasant, who stared as the diligence swayed alarmingly on the rough farm roads.

'Matthew,' Kate thrust her head from the open window, 'we are very noticeable riding in this thing.'

Matthew nodded. 'Maybe, but it's better than walking.' He swore as the diligence jolted into a rut.

'That last lot of soldiers were looking at us with great curiosity.'

'Let them. We've passed hundreds over the past few days.'

'Matthew. I would like you to stop for a few minutes. I want to talk about this.'

Recognizing her serious tone, Matthew hauled on the reins so the horses slowed to a lazy amble. 'We're nearly there, Kate. We should see the sea in an hour or so. I can nearly smell it.'

'Stop the coach, Matthew. Would you stop the coach, pray?'

'There's no need. We can talk like this.' Matthew shivered the reins so the horses increased their speed a little.

'There's every need, Matthew. I have a great desire that you stop the coach.' Kate sounded firm.

'Why?'

Kate sighed. 'It is necessary that I get off,' she said. 'Is that plain enough?'

Matthew stopped, looking away while Kate ran to the shelter of a copse of trees. He smiled fondly as she emerged, but she spoke first. 'I think we should walk from here. There are soldiers everywhere. Even on these country tracks.'

'It is easier to ride.' Matthew shook his head. He was used to driving now, and the prospect of walking was unappealing. 'Come on. We'll be at the coast soon.'

'We'll be in a French *prison* soon,' Kate amended. She climbed awkwardly into the coach, slamming the door to prove her annoyance.

Matthew's pleasure at having won a small victory was quickly replaced by guilt at having hurt Kate's feelings. He drove slowly, wondering how he could make amends, and how he could accede to her wishes without appearing weak; it was not easy keeping Kate sweet and happy while maintaining his pride.

'Easy, boys.' He looked ahead; the track seemed to disappear completely, to merge with the open, sparse field in which a score of women laboured with clumsy hoes. Matthew examined the ground for the best route and eased the horses into a slow walk.

There were wheel marks, a myriad hoof and boot prints, and other less salubrious evidence of the recent presence of soldiers. Matthew swore as the offside wheels thudded into a deep hole, throwing the diligence to one side. He heard Kate's voice raised high in complaint, cracked the whip and flicked the reins to urge the horse on. He swore again as the horses slithered sideways in the mud.

'What's happening?' Kate poked her head from the window.

'Mud's happening.'

'Well, get us out of it, then.' Kate looked around her. 'Should you not have kept to the road?'

'I would if there had been one!' Matthew heard the heat in his voice as he plied the whip again, shouting to the horses. They strained, but the wheels of the diligence sank hub-deep in the mud.

'It's no good,' Kate said quietly. 'We'll have to walk.'

'I think you're right,' Matthew agreed. He expected her to gloat, but instead she opened the door and stepped gingerly outside, pulling a face when mud sucked at her ankles. 'Oh! Come along, Matthew.'

He grinned to her in a surge of renewed affection. 'I'll set the horses free,' he said. 'Unless you want to ride?'

'Bare-backed?' She shook her head. 'We've already discussed that.'

Without the diligence to draw attention, the peasant women who hoed the fields barely glanced up as they trudged past. 'We'll be faster, now,' Kate said, but within half an hour she was limping as the wooden clogs raised blisters on her feet.

'Take my arm,' Matthew offered, and after an initial proud rejection, she assented, so they hobbled together. Leaving the country tracks with no regret whatever, they stepped onto a broad road that thrust, arrow-straight, toward the coast.

Apple trees lined both sides, and the occasional village seemed to have been picked clean of vibrant life. Only old men or wizened, brown-faced women peered from unglazed windows, while there were neither livestock nor ripe crops to be seen.

'Boney's soldiers have ravaged the place,' Kate said. 'God help England if they cross the Channel.'

'Mr Black will give ample warning of the tunnel,' Matthew reminded her.

'He *must* have seen us in that barn.' Kate stamped her blistered feet and winced. 'Yet he left us again. Lord, I want to tell that blackguard exactly what I think of him!'

The thought spurred them on, so they nearly marched through the next village, following the long, long road that seemed to stretch to infinity. Twice bodies of cavalry clattered past, kicking up gobbets of mud but not stopping, and once they had to step from the road to allow passage for a unit of artillery.

They smelled the encampment long before they saw it. The acrid reek of smoke mingled with the stench of men who had been long camped in one place. 'We're nearly there,' Kate said, and they slowed to a more manageable pace.

'We'll get to the coast and steal a boat,' Matthew decided. 'Once we're at sea, the Royal Navy will pick us up.'

'Easy as that?' Tension made Kate sarcastic. 'Won't the French notice?'

'Do you have another plan? Use a balloon,

perhaps?'

Kate's look could have curdled milk, but Matthew walked on, head bowed. After days of inactivity chained in the dungeon followed by long hours driving the coach, such concentrated walking had stiffened his legs, while every step seemed to jar the joints in his hips and knees.

'Stop.' Kate touched his arm. 'There's something happening ahead.'

There was a crowd on the road, infantry and artillery milling together, with the roar of voices underlying the sharper rattle of equipment. Matthew grunted, pointing, 'There's a cannon lying on its side. The caisson must have spilled.'

'Let's leave the road,' Kate suggested. 'I think we should head south, away from all the soldiers. It will make the Channel crossing longer, but it would be safer.'

They made slower time through the fields, pausing every few minutes to check their position and ignoring the few ill-dressed peasant women that they passed. The military seemed to have taken over this part of France, with tented encampments every mile or so, horse lines and parks of artillery. After half a dozen diversions, Matthew became worried. 'I'm not sure in which direction we are travelling,' he said. 'I can no longer see the coast.'

Kate glanced up, but lowering clouds hid the sun. 'I think we're still heading south.' She moved on, limping, favouring her arm but not complaining. They no longer cared about the mud through which they trudged.

'Trouble ahead,' Matthew sighed. A road

followed the margin of the field, and a dark-uniformed official was haranguing a grumbling mob of soldiers. 'It looks like a turnpike, except more official.'

Kate snorted. 'What happened to liberty and fraternity,' she wondered. 'I think we should try this way.' Turning at right angles, she headed toward the neighbouring field, until a regiment of cavalry trotted past.

'Back,' Matthew said. 'We'll circle around.'

With the route ahead blocked, they moved from field to field, keeping in shelter as much as possible. Soldiers occupied every building, with military wagons jamming the courtyards and men in diverse uniforms foraging wherever they looked. One group shouted loud comments as they passed.

'What are they saying?' Matthew asked.

'Just the same as British soldiers would say if they saw a woman,' Kate sounded tense. 'Keep moving and don't look round.'

Unable to cross the main road for the constant stream of military traffic and the ominous, dark-uniformed officials who questioned every civilian, they were forced to turn toward the coast. Matthew cursed himself for not foreseeing this situation. He should have headed north or south, not directly toward the invasion area.

'Down.' No longer loquacious, Kate spoke in short sentences. 'More soldiers ahead.' They heard the trill of music, the jingle of harness and ducked behind the trunk of a tree as another regiment marched past, heads high but looking tired with mud splattered on their white trousers and the blue of their coats already faded. Riding in front, the officers looked in better condition than their horses, splendidly gaudy with gold braid ornamenting their high-collared uniforms.

'Quite a contrast,' Kate repeated her refrain. 'So what about equality and fraternity?'

Every second field held an encampment, and the whole area echoed to orders and shouts, the tramp of marching men and the clomp of hooves, the grim growl of artillery caissons and the occasional rattle of musketry.

'Dear Lord, this is a nightmare,' Kate said as they crouched in the shelter of a ruined cottage. Nothing remained but the walls, for every scrap of wood had been looted for firewood, and everything portable had been carried away. 'How do we get through?'

'Lie low and wait for nightfall,' Matthew spread his cloak over her. 'We cannot move in daylight.'

Kate shook her head irritably. 'Behind us!' She motioned with her thumb and they ran on as a small group of infantry approached the ruin. 'We can't keep this up.' It was the first time that Matthew had heard despair in her voice.

'We'll be fine,' he told her. 'We'll get out of this at night.' There was a slight hollow ahead, with a small square building thrusting through a bank of nettles. 'Let's try there.'

Keeping low, they moved forward. 'What is it?' Kate wondered.

'No idea,' Matthew said, 'but I don't really care at the minute. Look behind you.'

A file of infantry was moving toward them,

long muskets over their shoulder as a moustached sergeant shouted orders.

'Oh Lord, oh Lord!' After a single glance over her shoulder, Kate moved closer, seeking the illusionary protection of close company. 'Is there anywhere we can hide?'

Matthew shook his head. 'Only that building, whatever it is.'

'Oh Lord, oh Lord,' Kate began to hurry, until Matthew took hold of her arm.

'Slow down. If we run, they'll wonder what we're doing.'

Taking a deep breath, Kate nodded. 'Let us complete the last act of this play, then.'

'And bow to an English encore, I hope.' Matthew kept his tone light.

The building proved to be taller than Matthew had supposed, and lacked a roof, but there was a small door that provided access. He looked behind him, to see the sergeant approaching, yelling at one of the more laggard of his men.

'Open the door,' Kate urged. 'He might think we have work here.'

Matthew nodded. He took hold of the handle, swore softly when it did not turn, and put his shoulder to the door. It juddered beneath his weight, but refused to open.

'Try again!' Kate sounded desperate. They threw their combined weight to the door, rebounding painfully from the stubborn wood. The sergeant raised his voice, shouting as he pointed toward them. 'Matthew! Do something!'

Matthew bent closer. 'We can't hide in there,' he said. 'They've seen us now!'

The sergeant rasped an order and two soldiers were trotting forward, muskets at the trail and long grass whipping at their legs.

'There's nowhere else, Matthew!'

They tried again, hurling themselves at the door in near despair. It opened with a bang and Matthew fell inside the building, tottering on the lip of a shaft that sloped downward into darkness. 'Sweet God!' he blasphemed, grabbed for Kate, missed and heard her high-pitched yell.

One-handed, Kate balanced on the edge with awful blackness sucking at her. 'Matthew!' For one horrifying second she swayed, left arm circling, and then she fell head first into the shaft.

'Kate!' Matthew heard her despairing scream, but could see nothing in the dense darkness. 'Kate!' Slipping over the edge, he began to inch downward, realizing that he was moving on some corrugated surface. Looking closer, he saw that it was cut timber, laid horizontally, so he could use the edges for hand and foot holds. 'Kate!'

He heard his voice echo, fancied that there was a reply, and moved cautiously downward, swearing when his feet slithered on the wood. Already the square of light at the surface seemed faint and far away, but still the shaft plunged onward. 'Kate!'

This time he definitely heard a reply, and moved faster, his shoes slipping on damp wood. 'Kate!'

'Matthew! Are you there?' Her voice was faint.

'Hold on, I'm coming!' Feeling his foot slide again, Matthew grabbed for the side, missed his hold and fell, rolling forever into the black with his hips, shoulders and head alternately cracking against the wooden ribs of the shaft until he came up hard against a surface of wet stone. He lay still, gasping for breath.

'Matthew!' Kate knelt at his side. 'Are you all right?' She was looking into his face, her eyes the only brightness in the gloom, but her voice caressing.

'I think so.' Matthew checked himself for broken bones. 'Yes, I am. Are you?'

'I have landed on my arm again, and scraped bits of me on these infernal pieces of wood, but I suppose I am well enough, considering that I have just fallen into the bowels of the earth.' Now she knew he was unhurt, Kate submitted to her anxiety. 'What on earth were you thinking of, bringing us down here? Where are we?'

Matthew sat up, shaking his head. He recognized his surroundings, with the incessant dark and the distant noises, the throbbing of a steam engine, the low murmur of voices and the rhythmic knocking, like an army marching out of step. 'We're in a mine,' he said flatly. 'I can hear the pump, and the noise of picks.'

Kate stood up, rubbing her left knee. 'I hear the noises,' she agreed, 'but I fear that you may be mistaken, Matthew. Consider the reason we are in France.'

'What?' Matthew stared at her, gradually understanding. 'We fell down an air shaft of Albert Mathieu's tunnel. We are in the tunnel.'

'I believe so,' Kate confirmed.

Matthew leaned against a wooden prop that supported the unseen roof as he wrestled with the implications. 'Good God,' he said. 'Now we're in a devil of a hobble. What do we do?'

Kate looked up the air shaft, but the angle blocked even the tiny square of light that should mark the entrance. 'We might try and climb up there.'

'You have only one arm,' Matthew reminded her. 'And other sore bits.'

Kate was quiet for a while. 'Leave me here,' she said at last, 'and get home yourself.'

Matthew could only guess what agony that offer had caused Kate, with her terror of darkness. There could be nothing worse for her than to be left alone in the black and hostile mine, with French slave miners somewhere ahead and untold horrors all around. He hugged her, but she broke free with an impatient, 'Not now, Matthew, for goodness' sake.'

'Is this not a tunnel?' Matthew kept his voice as light as he could.

'We know it is,' Kate said tensely.

'And is it not destined to finish in England?'

'Yes!' The impatience in her voice slowly died away. 'Do you think they have dug that far?'

Matthew felt a flush of unaccustomed madness. He grinned to her. 'Let's see, shall we? Think of it; we might be the first people to walk from France to England! Just imagine the expression on your father's face when we emerge a few yards from his parlour!'

'Yes, and just imagine Father's face when he

learns that I have spent the last few days wandering around France with a man to whom I am neither related nor married,' Kate scolded. 'He will be shocked beyond repair, and both our reputations will be ruined.'

Matthew considered for a few minutes. He knew that Kate was deliberately avoiding the real issue, but followed her conversation. 'Your father did know we were travelling together...' he reminded her.

'Yes, but in English inns,' Kate interrupted, 'not French dungeons!'

'Indeed. We must never let him find out what has happened,' Matthew said. 'Once we reach England, we must endeavour to keep the truth of these last days secret.'

There was silence that stretched for five minutes, and then Kate spoke again, her voice more sober.

'Let's concentrate on reaching home safely first, Matthew. How far is it to England? About thirty miles? I doubt that they have dug half that distance, but what other choice do we have?'

Matthew agreed. 'We cannot go back...'

'I could not climb back up that shaft,' Kate interrupted him. 'With one arm only ... no, it could not be done. But you could.'

'We cannot go back,' Matthew continued, 'not with the climb and the French army, so we must continue. It is our only choice.'

Kate was quiet for a minute and Matthew guessed that she was nerving herself for the coming ordeal. 'I don't want to die in the dark, Matthew. Not down here so deep under the ground.' Her hand sought his and held tight. 'Please don't let me die here.'

He pulled her close and when they embraced Matthew could feel the rapid beat of her heart. 'Let's go home,' he said softly. 'We have a marriage to arrange.'

'And a father to fudge.' Matthew heard the near-hysteria in Kate's voice.

They began slowly, testing each step on the damp rock, but after a few minutes their eyes adjusted to the lack of light and they moved quicker. Firmly clutching Kate with one hand, Matthew extended the other in front of him, feeling the way. Twice he had to stop as the tunnel changed direction, and he shuffled more slowly, always aware of the hum and gasp of machinery and the distant clatter of working men.

'How far have we come?' Kate's voice seemed to come from far away.

'Not very far,' Matthew replied. 'Quarter of a mile, perhaps.' He was surprised that the tunnel seemed to be getting larger. Rather than the single long and straight shaft with regular air vents that he would have designed, it seemed to be expanding both upward and outward, like a bell. 'Perhaps this is where the French army is to muster,' he said. 'Rather than marching in one long column, they might gather in certain areas to form up.'

'Perhaps,' Kate agreed.

The clatter of picks and shovel had increased, with other booming noises that Matthew did not recognize. He slowed, wondering what lay ahead, swearing as they paddled through ankle-deep water.

'This will quite ruin my shoes,' Kate said in a forlorn attempt at humour. Her laugh sounded close to hysteria. 'But at least we can see better now. Look.'

There was the flicker of light ahead, the deep rumble of machinery and a rising confusion of noises. Matthew stumbled as the tunnel changed direction again, used the wall as a guide and probed around a sharp bend.

'What the devil...'

'Matthew...' Kate hurried to his side. 'Oh, Lord.'

Where Matthew had expected to see a continuation of the tunnel, with a long shaft thrusting toward England, instead there was a vast cavern that extended in either direction. A score of lanterns threw pools of yellow light on a scene that could have come straight from the brush of Hieronymus Bosch. Black-uniformed guards yelled harsh orders to manacled, shaven-headed labourers who hauled at baulks of timber or hacked at the rock walls, while others hammered at great sections of iron plate.

'Matthew,' Kate shrank backward, pulling him with her, 'what is this? Is this activity normal for a mine?'

Matthew shook his head. 'Indeed, no. I have never seen the like before.' He looked again, searching for a pattern to the work and raised his voice above the incessant clamour. 'It is more like a blacksmith's workshop than a mine.'

'Let's go back. Please let us go back.' Kate's

voice was urgent. 'This is horrible. Awful; it is like the pictures in my mother's book.' Her hand tugged at his sleeve. 'I can't go on, Matthew; oh, Lord, I wish I had never come to France. Mother must have known that this would happen and she was warning me.'

Kate was reliving the worst nightmares of her childhood, sobbing her fears into Matthew's jacket. He held her, trying to soothe away her terror while his logical mind attempted to analyse the scenes just around the corner.

If Bonaparte was digging a tunnel, then this cavern must be the marshalling area. It was the only possible reason for so large an excavation. But what were those sheets of iron? Perhaps they were to strengthen the roof in case of a collapse? That would make sense, iron plates might provide greater security than the more normal supports of columns of coal or timber props.

'Kate.'

She clung to him, shaking with remembered terror and the strain of the past few days. 'No. No. Don't let go.'

'Kate.' Hating himself, he eased her hands free. 'We must press on. There might be a tunnel past this cavern, a way home.'

'No, I can't go through there.' When she looked up, her face was wet with tears that had coursed through the dirt on her face. 'You go on alone, Matthew. Please.'

'We're going together.' Putting his hands on her shoulders, he lowered his voice. 'We cannot stay here, Katie. We must keep going.'

She shook her head, sobbing. 'I can't, Matthew, I really can't.'

The first Matthew knew of the Frenchman was the sound of heavy breathing at his shoulder. When he looked up, the guard was peering at him through the glare of a lifted lantern.

'Matthew!' As Kate pulled back, Matthew acted instinctively, throwing himself at the man with all the pent-up frustration of the last few days. His first punch landed on the man's chest, his second on his face, and he followed up with a volley of kicks more vicious than anything he had ever delivered before.

Taken completely by surprise, the guard cowered before the blows, so Matthew continued, putting all his weight into every kick until Kate pulled him off, pleading for him to stop.

'Matthew, Matthew! You'll kill him!'

The Frenchman lay on the ground, blood oozing from his nose and mouth.

'That's our way through.' The decision seemed so obvious that Matthew did not wait for Kate's approval, but stripped the man of his uniform jacket and red cap. 'Now help me pull him deeper into the passage,' he ordered, 'and pile some of these loose rocks around him to make it look as if part of the roof collapsed.'

Although the man was slight, Kate was weak with lack of food; she gasped with the effort of dragging him.

'Now you put on the jacket,' Matthew ordered, 'and push me around as if I were a prisoner.'

'But they will see that I am a woman.'

'In this light?' Matthew shook his head. 'I doubt it. They'll see a uniform. Speak low, and the noise will disguise your voice.'

'You've no chains.'

'So bully me as if I was trying to escape.' Matthew forced a grin. 'We might or might not be able to walk to England, but we can get past this part, and there is sure to be another exit.'

Kate nodded. 'Oh Lord, Matthew, oh Lord.' She took a deep breath and tried to smile. 'Come on, then.'

Marching the 'Ça Ira' as if it were a talisman against the horrors ahead, Kate walked into the cavern, with Matthew shuffling before her. She held the lantern low so the light illuminated the floor of the mine and not their faces, but nobody even glanced toward them.

'Where are we going?' Kate whispered.

'I'm not sure, but the tunnel must continue beyond this workshop.' Matthew altered direction to bypass a group of men that were using long tongs to carefully pull a sheet of red-hot iron from a forge. 'Not far now,' he muttered, 'just a few more yards.' He watched as two men lifted a long piece of shaped timber, while others worked on what appeared to be miniature boilers.

'Matthew? What are these men doing?' Curiosity had replaced some of Kate's childhood fear.

Matthew shook his head, looking around. 'I'm not entirely certain, but this is certainly some sort of a workshop. These men are all engaged in manufacturing something. That group there,' he indicated six men who worked with the iron plate under the light of three lanterns, 'appear to be making a boiler, while these others are building a steam pump.'

'But why? And why here?' Kate shook her head. 'None of this makes any sense, Matthew. Why build a tunnel to use as a manufactory?'

Matthew sighed. 'I do not know. Perhaps they have devised some new mechanical method for tunnelling faster.' Aware that some of the guards were taking an interest in them, he lowered his voice. 'Push me, Kate, and keep walking.' He moved on, faster now, and then began to swear.

'Matthew?' Kate nudged him in earnest. 'Matthew! France has certainly taught you some commonplace language.'

'Pray accept my apologies,' Matthew said, sourly, and thrust out his hand. 'Look.'

The cavern ended in a wall of solid rock that extended to the roof. There was no passage to England, nothing but weeping limestone and a thick band of chalk.

'Where's the tunnel? Matthew, where's the tunnel?' There was panic in Kate's voice. 'Come, let's try in this direction.'

They scoured the cavern, walking the perimeter with little regard to the workers or their uniformed guards.

'There's no tunnel,' Matthew said after fifteen minutes of groping in the dimness. 'Just a shaft leading upward, which is no good to us. It ends here.'

'Why? It can't end here! That makes no sense at all!'

'Maybe there is another tunnel, somewhere else.' Matthew did not believe his own words.

'And maybe we've made a complete cake of

ourselves chasing moonshine with a fishing net!' Kate stood with her back to the wall, fighting back her tears. 'Think about it, Matthew, nothing in France has made sense. Why did Lamballe kill Citizen Peltier and let Mr Black go free? And why was her coach left in such an oh-so-convenient position for us to snatch? And there's more...'

'I'm sure there is, but not now,' Matthew said. 'But the guard is changing. They're all heading over there.'

Kate stepped closer, watching as the guards filed to one corner of the chamber. 'If there's no tunnel, we'll just have to go up that shaft. That's our way out, then. Come on, Matt!' Taking care to keep a respectable distance from the guards, she pushed him in the back, growled in deep-throated French and moved cautiously to the corner. Behind her, Hades' clamour continued.

Sloping gently upward, the shaft was wide, with enough headroom for Kate to walk upright. There was a steady stream of men in both directions, and the clank of chains provided a doleful background to the sharp shouts of command. Kate pushed Matthew toward one group that was struggling with a long metal cylinder.

'Join them,' she made a rapid decision, 'and I'll look fierce.'

The desperate attempt at humour failed, but Matthew grabbed hold of the rope and hauled alongside the shaven-headed labourers. It only took seconds for the sweat to start from his face, but, helped by the yells and prods of two uniformed guards, the prisoners dragged the object upward to another level. There was a wide corridor that curved out of view, and a doorway that led to another chamber, from which came the groan and hiss of a steam pump, and the clamour of hammer on metal.

An onslaught of orders besieged Matthew, and one of the guards pushed him toward the door. He stepped inside, helping the convicts to roll the cylinder against the wall, but when they clanked away, he remained, staring around him. Set around a steam engine, half a dozen men, free from manacle or restraint, worked busily on the hull of a boat. As Matthew watched, they lowered a small boiler inside, judging the position exactly while a tall man gave quiet, precise orders.

'Kate!' Matthew thrilled with a mixture of excitement and horror. 'They are building a steam-powered boat.' Momentarily forgetting where he was, he absorbed all the details.

The wooden hull was over twenty feet long, flaring toward the bow, but the boiler and engine occupied most of the space, leaving little for crew or passengers. There seemed to be no keel, while a slender funnel rose a full twelve feet above the deck.

'Kate, I must see more.'

'Not now.' Her hand plucked at his jacket. 'Later. We'll return at a more opportune moment.'

'No!' He brushed her away, unable to control his fascination.

'Matthew!' Her voice was urgent. 'Can't you see who that is?' She indicated the slender man.

'That's the engineer! Citizen Peltier's friend!'

Mathew switched his attention from the boat to the builder. About to swear, he restrained himself. 'Good Lord, Katie. So it is.'

'Come away!' She hustled him out, growling in French when one of the workmen glanced up.

While the guards kicked the manacled prisoners back down the shaft, Kate ushered Matthew along the curving corridor. 'In here!' She slipped into another doorway, turned the massive key that was in the lock and struggled to open the door. 'Help me, then!'

Constructed of oak and studded with iron, the door was immensely heavy but their combined weight opened it. As they stepped in, Matthew tripped over something soft, killed his curse and felt Kate pressing close. She lifted her lantern high.

They were in a storeroom, lined with barrels of various sizes from 40-gallon casks to 126-gallon pipes and huge 252-gallon tuns. 'Plenty of wine in here,' Kate said. 'Is it a base for smuggling to England?'

Matthew shook his head. 'I doubt that even Joss Page could carry this lot,' he said, 'even if he wanted to.' He moved further into the room, shining the lantern into every corner. 'This room is remarkably dry,' he said. 'It must have been specially lined.' They squeezed into a corner, seeking momentary respite. 'Kate, this is neither a tunnel nor a mine.'

'No,' she shook her head, 'you were right. It is a workshop. We have come to the wrong place.' He heard her catch her breath. 'Must we return and try again?'

'I'm not sure that we are in the wrong place,' Matthew said. 'Remember, we saw the French engineer...'

'Cusset,' Kate reminded him.

'We saw Mr Cusset enter the mine, and now he is here. I think we are in the same place. The mine leads here.'

'But why?' Kate scratched her head. 'Why dig a big hole in the ground just to make boats, and then build another in England? It makes no sense.'

'As you said already, Kate, nothing in France has made any sense. Why shoot Citizen Peltier? Why should Lamballe allow Mr Black to go free, when he knows about this place, and its lack of defences?'

'Mr Black will be in England by now.' Kate sounded very satisfied. 'And soon the entire Royal Navy will be here, blasting great broadsides to tear this place to pieces.' She looked up, bright eyes suddenly shaded. 'But Mr Lamballe would know that too. Unless he has some sort of dislike for the engineer? Maybe they were rivals?' She sank her head in her hands, and then looked up suddenly. 'No! I've got it, Matthew! Do you remember when you first knew Mr Lamballe? We all thought that he was an émigré?'

'I remember,' Matthew agreed.

'Well then, maybe he *is*. Maybe he is only pretending to work for Bonaparte and he's really on our side. A sort of double agent.'

Matthew nodded. The idea was appealing. 'That would explain a lot,' he agreed, 'but then, would Admiral Springer not be aware of him?'

Kate sighed. 'Yes, maybe he would. I don't know, Matthew. This whole thing is a mystery. It's too smoky by half, it really is. Oh God,' she raised her voice to the dark, 'how I wish that I was safely back home!'

'We will be,' Matthew promised. 'At least now we know why Mr Cusset is here. Imagine the French building a steam boat.' He marvelled at the idea. 'What *will* they do with it?'

'I always thought that the Scots would be first. Did they not build something similar recently?'

'They built a steam boat called *Charlotte Dundas*.' Matthew liked to keep in touch with all the recent engineering developments. 'It was too frail for open water, so they sail it in the Forth and Clyde Canal. It is used for towing barges.'

'Maybe the French are going to tow barges too,' Kate said. 'Or maybe they are going to tow these wine casks up to Paris.' She looked at him with her eyes suddenly wide. 'No, Matthew. They are not. They are going to tow the invasion barges across the Channel.'

'Oh my Lord.' Matthew felt the despair slide back. 'That could be it. If they have steam tugs, they do not even need a favourable wind. Indeed, they could wait until the wind blew the blockading Royal Naval squadrons away, and then tow the barges across.'

'That's it,' Kate said. 'But why the tunnel? And why the mine in Kent? There's more, Matthew, there must be.'

'We'll wait here until these men stop work,' Matthew decided, 'and then look around. The answer must be here, and I suspect that the steam boat is the key.' He forced a smile. 'I'd like to see what it's like, anyway. I've never seen a steam boat before.'

'Maybe they work night and day,' Kate said. 'They're only slaves.'

'Mr Cusset is no slave. He must rest. And the men with him were not shackled either, so they'll probably be treated better.'

Finding a small piece of black bread in the pocket of the guard's jacket she wore, Kate broke it in half, so they chewed a bitter supper before taking turns to rest. Matthew envied Kate her ability to sleep on demand, for one minute she was bright with ideas, the next she was curled up in a foetal ball with her left arm a pillow and her breathing as unconcerned as innocence. He looked down on her for a moment, wondering if they would ever get back to England, and if he would ever watch her sleeping in their own bed.

'Oh, Kate, this life of adventure is not for me. I want...' He shook his head, not knowing exactly what he did want, and not really caring, as long as Kate was there, and safe.

Unable to sit still, he inspected his surroundings, crunching over a gritty film that had formed on the ground and kicking aside the felt slippers over which he had tripped. This chamber was about eighty feet by fifteen, and was obviously used as a store. The barrels were lined neatly in rows, arranged by size and piled to the ceiling. Surprised that Kate had not already done so, he chose one at random and searched for a lid. There was none; the barrel seemed to have been extremely well sealed, but closer inspection found a leather bung, which he withdrew with considerable difficulty. He stood back, hoping for a flow of wine.

Matthew watched the coarse black powder trickle out for a few moments, before he realized what it was. He had opened a barrel of gunpowder. The next cask held the same, and the next, until Matthew sat down, listening to Kate's regular breathing as he tried to put the pieces together.

They were hiding in a room filled with barrels of black gunpowder. Tons of the stuff, and it would need just one spark to blow the whole place up. That gritty feel on the ground was spilled gunpowder, and the felt slippers at the door would be used by whoever worked in the room, to ensure that his footwear created no friction sparks. Matthew suddenly found that the hand that held the lamp was shaking, dancing short shadows around the lethal barrels. If he dropped that lamp, or spilled one drop of burning oil on the loose powder on the ground, the place would erupt. There would be nothing left of their bodies.

Matthew shook his head, feeling the chill sweat on his forehead and back. This room must be the powder store for Bonaparte's Army of England, but why hide it underground? And was there a connection with the steam boat just a few yards away?

Kate had speculated that the steam boats were to tow the invasion barges across the Channel, but Matthew was not so sure. The Scottish boat, *Charlotte Dundas*, was only fit to operate in the smooth water of a canal, and every earlier attempt had been even more unstable. No steam boat was seaworthy enough to face the unpredictable Channel, with its sudden squalls and savage tides. Perhaps the boat could operate in the smooth waters of this bay, but no further.

'Matthew?' Kate was standing over him. 'I think you should get some sleep now.' She listened intently as Matthew told her of the gunpowder, but rather than fear, she seemed quite amused.

'Gunpowder? Well, that means we should be quite safe in here. What rational man would come into such a dangerous place unless he had to.'

Matthew nodded. 'That's quite logical, in a perverse way,' he agreed. 'Just be careful of that lantern.'

She looked at him, her smile fading, and quickly extinguished the flame. 'Maybe I can face the devil of the dark. But stay close, Matthew.'

After another hour, they heard the rumble of voices and the tramp of feet in the corridor, and a few minutes later, Matthew cautiously opened the door. Peering outside, he saw only darkness.

'Has everybody gone?'

'It's so quiet that you could cut it into blocks and sell it at Ashbourne market,' Matthew confirmed. 'Bring the lantern, but don't light it yet.'

There was a sense of déjà vu in walking quietly along the dark corridor, opening the door of the chamber that held the steam boat and slipping inside. For a moment he was back in Kent, creeping through Lamballe's property, where this insane escapade had first started. Only when he was certain that the room was empty and the door securely closed did he allow Kate to scrape a spark from the tinder box, and applied it to the wick of the lantern.

The flame rose slowly, diffusing yellow light around them. The room was much larger than Matthew had at first thought, so the lantern illuminated only a small part. He saw the hull and tall funnel of a steam boat, and shadows that told of a second, a few yards further on.

'Kate. There's more.'

'There are,' she agreed. 'Let's see if we can get more light.'

It took only a moment to locate a second lantern, and Matthew gasped at what the gradual spreading light revealed. The room stretched for a further fifty yards, and there were four more steam boats, sitting in a line with their tall funnels nearly scraping the ceiling. Stepping closer, Matthew examined the first, gauging the quality of the workmanship and the size of the boiler and engine.

'But why?' Kate asked. 'What are they for? And how do they work?'

'You feed coal into this furnace,' Matthew showed her, 'which boils the water in the boiler, and the pressure of the steam powers this engine.' He explained further, showing her the complex system of levers that directed the power from the engine to the great wheel at the stern of the craft.

Kate shook her head. 'It looks very danger-ous,' she said at last. 'Would it not blow up?'

'No, no,' Matthew shook his head. 'I've hardly ever heard of a steam boiler blowing up.'

'Do you think that the French *will* use these steam boats to tow the barges across?'

Scrutinizing the nearest, Matthew shook his head. 'No. The Channel is too rough.' He came closer. 'See how low the freeboard is? These vessels were never intended for the open sea. They can only be used where the water is calm. A lake perhaps, or a canal, or maybe within the confines of this bay.'

Kate dismissed the steam boats with a con-temptuous shrug. 'They are not much good, then, are they? The Little Corporal can play with his little toy boats from Sunday till Christmas, but it will not concern us.'

Matthew walked around the line of boats. They were all of the same design, around twenty-five feet long, with the engine and boiler amidships, the wheel in the stern and the for-ward half empty. 'Perhaps that space is for cargo, or coal,' he decided.

Kate shook her head, frowning. 'Maybe I was wrong,' she said. 'The French are nobody's fools. They will know that these boats are only good in calm waters, and they would not have built them for nothing.' She walked away. 'You inspect these boats, Matthew, and I will see if there is anything else of interest.'

Every boat shared the same design, with the paddles in the stern and that long hold forward.

To judge by the size of the engine and the light construction, they would be fairly fast. Matthew wondered if it would be possible to mount a cannon in the bows, but decided that the scantlings were too fragile to bear the recoil.

He moved from the boat to a further bench, on which were a number of devices that he did not recognize. Lifting the nearest, he examined it with some interest. It appeared similar to the workings of a clock, so might be some kind of timing device, but he was unsure for what purpose. He inspected the mechanism, slowly working out its purpose. There was a small peg holding down a fairly powerful spring, but for what reason, he did not know. Unable to resist the temptation, he withdrew the peg and watched the spring gradually uncoil, with the release of tension drawing a trigger on something very like the lock of a musket. He watched the hammer snap down, and smiled.

'Ingenious.'

Presumably this device had some connection to the steam boat, but although he carried it over, he could not see that it served any practical purpose. He was still puzzling when Kate appeared.

'Matthew.' She was at his side, holding a folded piece of paper. 'Look at this.' Walking to a table, she cleared a space among the set squares, inkstands and sundry small pieces of wood before unfolding the paper. 'I think the Little Corporal plans a very nasty game with his little toy boats, but I am not sure what it is.'

The paper was a plan of the boat's construction, showing the dimensions of each piece of timber in the hull, and all the internal fixtures. In the cargo space forward, there was a picture of forty barrels, and a diagram of what could only be the small clockwork device.

'Oh dear Lord.' Matthew felt the blood drain from his face as he grasped the implications. 'I think you are right about Boney's nasty game.' He shook his head in reluctant admiration. 'But what an ingenious construction, and what a blackguard mind to devise it.'

'Is this not some sort of fireship, Matthew?'

Matthew nodded. 'It is a devilish device, Kate. Have you ever heard of Robert Fulton?' When Kate shook her head, he explained. 'Robert Fulton is an American engineer and inventor who tried to interest Bonaparte in an undersea vessel he called *Nautilus*. The idea was that *Nautilus* should approach a British ship unseen, travelling underwater, and attach a torpedo, a kind of bomb with a delaying fuse, to the hull of the British ship. When *Nautilus* had repaired to a safe distance, the torpedo would explode, sinking the ship.'

Kate shook her head. 'I was unaware of that.'

'So are most people. The French rejected the idea, but Fulton was not finished. He also designed a steam boat, which he sailed on the Seine, but the French said publicly that they did not want that, either, so he came to Britain and tried to sell us a thing he called an *infernal* or a *catamaran*, which was a long waterproof box containing explosives.'

'And what did this infernal device do?'

'Not a great deal, as it happened. Lord Keith

and the Royal Navy tried the infernals out against the French. He had boats tow them close to French ships and exploded them, but they were ineffective.'

Kate touched the plans as if they were contagious. 'But these things are different again. This is neither an underwater boat nor an explosive box.'

'Indeed not,' Matthew said. 'It was reported that Bonaparte rejected Fulton's ideas out of hand and scoffed at our infernals, saying that we were breaking the windows of Boulogne with English guineas, but perhaps the Little Corporal was only bluffing.' He tapped the plans that Kate had found. 'Instead, Bonaparte has built these devilish contraptions, combining the timing device of one machine with the explosive power of another, and then equipping it with a steam engine.'

Kate shook her head. 'I do not believe that it was Bonaparte that built these things, Matthew, but that engineer. Can you remember I said he looked familiar? Well, that is because he shares some of your mannerisms. He is shy, but intelligent, and he probably raises his voice before he lies, just as you do.'

'I do not,' Matthew denied, pleased to see some of her mischief returning.

'You do so. You spoke louder to reassure me when Mr Black left.' Kate gave her most smug smile. 'He is a dangerous man, Matthew, but what do they intend to do with these infernal devices? Sail them against the blockading ships?'

Matthew shrugged. 'Maybe; but I don't know how. These steam boats won't be able to leave the bay, and the Navy's not rash enough to come inshore, not with fixed batteries firing heated thirty-two-pound shot.'

Matthew knew that shore batteries had a massive advantage over wooden ships. Firing from stable positions, their cannon would be more accurate, and the huge cannon balls would do terrible execution. When the shore batteries possessed furnaces to heat the iron shot until it was red hot, even the Royal Navy would keep clear. There was little worse for a seaman than fire on a highly combustible wooden ship.

'Which shore batteries, Matthew?' Kate kept her voice conversational. 'We were there, remember? There were no cannon.'

'But the Royal Navy doesn't know that,' Matthew reminded. 'So they will hardly come in.' He stared at Kate as he realized the appalling truth. 'Until Mr Black tells them it's safe.'

'Dear Lord in heaven,' Kate said, softly. 'Oh dear Lord. That's what's going to happen, that's Boney's plan.' She stepped backward and sank on to a chair. 'Matthew, Mr Black will run straight to Admiral Springer with the intelligence that we gathered, and the Admiral will send the navy in to destroy the air pump for the tunnel. But there is no tunnel.'

'There is no tunnel,' Matthew agreed. 'But the navy does not know that. They will sail in to destroy the pump and other tunnel workings.'

'And then,' Kate's voice had sunk to a whisper, 'the French will send these explosive steam boats against them.'

'The navy will not know what they are,' Matthew continued. 'The French explosive steam boats will ambush them.' He lifted his chin, searching for reassurance. 'However, the navy is used to inshore operations; they always send in their smaller vessels – brigs, sloops and such like. The battleships remain further out.'

'Yes,' Kate agreed. 'They normally do, but they know that there is deep water in this bay, and no gun batteries, and a vital target.' She shook her head. 'They will want to ensure that the tunnel workings are destroyed, Matthew. Perhaps Admiral Nelson will come in person, with the Channel Fleet.'

'Twenty-seven battleships, the best in the world.' Matthew looked again at the narrow steam boats with the menacing holds, gaping for their cargo of gunpowder.

'And when the French blow them up,' Kate said, 'there will be nothing to prevent the French from invading. They will send over their invasion barges and land the Army of England in Kent. A hundred, perhaps a hundred and fifty, *thousand* veterans against our scattered Militia and few regiments of redcoats.' Her voice was hushed. 'Good God, Matthew, they played us like a fish, using the mine as a bait and feeding us titbits of false information one after another, just to destroy the Channel Fleet.'

'That is why Mr Lamballe shot Citizen Peltier,' Matthew said, equally quietly. 'She knew of the plan; after all, it was Peltier who allowed us to see the empty gun batteries, she nearly *showed* us the damned things.' He stared at her. 'But she hated Mr Black more, because he had killed her brother and scarred her.'

'And Mr Lamballe *had* to allow Mr Black to escape with his intelligence,' Kate agreed. 'So we were not so clever after all.' She smiled, wryly. 'The whole thing was set up for us to discover. The letter to Albert Mathieu that was left oh-so-conveniently on Mr Lamballe's desk, the use of Mr Houghton, a known French sympathizer, as a mine manager, Citizen Peltier directing us to the empty battery; everything was arranged for us to find exactly what they wanted us to see.'

'And it would have worked if Mr Black had not dallied with Suzanne Durand.'

Kate nodded. 'That was unforeseen. We were arrested and taken to that obnoxious little Dugua, who knew nothing about the plot. He would have killed us.'

'Happily,' Matthew remembered Kate's bravery in front of the guillotine, 'but we escaped.' He smiled. 'No, we were *allowed* to escape. Remember Mr Cusset was late? He was loosening my manacles, which is why they came so easily off the wall. Then there were virtually no guards, and a coach left waiting just where we wanted it.'

'Very clever people, the French,' Kate agreed. 'But now we know the truth, and we must get it back to England.' She looked at him with a hopeful smile. 'You are an engineer, Matthew. Can you not inflict some damage to prevent Bonaparte using these devilish devices?'

Matthew considered for a moment. 'There is an entire gunpowder store next door. I'll see what can be done, and you collect every document and plan that you can. We'll carry it with us to England. Think what the navy could do with steam-powered ships!'

'Not the gunpowder, Matthew.' Kate said, clumsily folding up the plans with her left hand. 'We are in here too, remember, and I don't want to be blown to pieces.'

Matthew felt momentary disappointment; he would have delighted in causing a huge explosion. 'You're right, of course,' he admitted, grudgingly.

'We still don't know the way out,' Kate reminded gently, 'and there are thirty miles of sea between us and England.'

'We'll find a boat,' Matthew refused to lose his optimism. 'If we have to, we'll take one of Boney's invasion barges.'

'You be careful.' Kate threw him a sobering look. 'If we're caught in here, *nobody* will save us from the guillotine.'

Once Matthew had worked out how the timing mechanisms worked, it took him only minutes to sabotage each clock so the explosion would take place seconds after the plug was released. The French steam boats would be in far more danger than their British targets. He eased under the nearest boat and began to bend the piston rod, when Kate hissed a warning.

'Matthew! There's somebody outside. Douse the lights!'

Sixteen

France
August 1805

'Not now!' Matthew scrabbled from beneath the boat and reached for the lantern, but haste made him clumsy and his knuckles rapped against the glass lens.

'Matthew!' Kate had doused her light and stood in petrified horror. 'Hurry!'

Matthew swore, and snuffed the light, but the door was already open. He heard a querying voice, a sharp question, twice repeated, and then somebody raised a lantern. M. Cusset moved slowly toward them, the high light casting shadows on his thin face.

Kate ducked behind the desk, but the movement attracted Cusset's attention and he swung the lantern toward her. He spoke again, glanced toward the desk as if searching for something, and lifted a long spanner from one of the workbenches.

Matthew shrank against the hull of the steam boat, momentarily unsure what to do. Should he attack Cusset, or grab Kate and run? Aware that any noise might bring a horde of guards, he began to move slowly, keeping outside the circle of light cast by Cusset's lantern.

Cusset spoke again, his voice sharp, querulous. He touched the lantern that Kate had just doused, retracting his hand from the hot metal. Keeping the spanner in his right hand, he lit the second lantern with his left. The light shone directly onto Kate, who produced a charming smile and spoke rapidly.

Cusset started, glancing from her uniform to her face. He pointed, said, 'Kate Denton,' grabbed hold of her shoulder and snapped a question, pointing to the bundle of documents she held. It was then that Matthew reached him, swinging a small hammer.

The Frenchman must have sensed his attack, for he parried with the spanner, and for a few moments they struggled together, matched in height and build. Matthew glared into the face of the Frenchman who was so much like himself, seeing equal fear and determination; each of them was working for his country, and only a few miles of water and opposing ideologies made them enemies rather than friends.

'Matthew!' Kate hovered nearby, her face frantic with fear.

Weakened by privation and lack of food, Matthew felt himself forced back, step by step, and it was sheer desperation that made him lunge forward with his head. The contact was sickening, but Cusset staggered back, dropping the spanner, and Matthew followed through with a bent knee to the groin that dropped Cusset in a writhing ball on the floor.

Kate hesitated, her face screwed up with a

mixture of pity for Cusset and relief that Matthew was unhurt. 'Come on,' she said, pulling him toward the door.

'The plans?' Matthew opened the table drawer and grabbed at the contents.

'I've got them,' Kate said. 'Come *on!*'

'Don't drop them!' Matthew warned. 'We don't know what's there!' He took a last glance, reluctant to leave in case there were further discoveries to be made. Slipping a small, flat box into his pocket, he lifted a final document, but swore as something grabbed at his ankle.

'Let go!'

Despite the agony that screwed up his face, Cusset swung his spanner against Matthew's shin.

Matthew yelled at the searing pain, unbalanced and fell, dropping the papers but keeping hold of the box. Cusset was immediately on top of him, swinging the spanner again. Matthew jerked to one side as the heavy metal crashed into the floor an inch from his head. He roared, kicked out and staggered free of Cusset's grasp.

'Matthew!' Kate hovered nearby, flinching in sympathy. She snatched up the nearest lantern. 'Come on! There's another door here.'

'I'm coming!' Matthew took another stride, but swore as Cusset's hands wrapped around his legs. He wrenched free, stamped on the Frenchman's arm, staggered and collided with the bench. Tools and papers cascaded onto the floor and onto Cusset. Matthew saw a double-barrelled pistol rattle under the chair, swooped for it, missed and moved on.

Kate's door was wide enough for a horse and cart, or a steam boat, Matthew realized, and scrambled out behind her. The lantern bounced shadows along a wide, smoothly carved shelf and glimmered eerily from rippling water.

'Sweet Lord above.' Kate stopped in shock. A long row of steam boats stretched before them, all berthed with their blunt bows facing the water.

'It's a whole armada,' Matthew said. He counted them. 'Fifteen boats; enough to sink half the Channel Fleet.' He looked closer. 'And the holds are already filled with gunpowder.'

'So they are all ready for Nelson,' Kate said. She looked from side to side. 'What can we do? Can we take one?'

The idea was instantly appealing. 'Why not?' Feeling suddenly reckless, Matthew moved to the nearest boat and looked in. 'We can't,' he said, 'it'll take a long time to get up enough steam to power the engine.'

'Well, get started, then,' Kate ordered.

The report of the pistol made them both duck, but the shot flew wide, ricocheting noisily from the funnel above Matthew's head.

'Kate!' Matthew grabbed hold of her arm and pulled her along the stone shelf, ducking into the shadows as a second shot ran out. Rock splinters showered them. Matthew glanced back, to see Cusset hastily reloading his pistol.

'We seem to have spent the chief of our time in France running,' Kate panted. She held the bundle of documents tightly under her injured arm and the lantern in her left hand.

'So let's keep running until we get home.'

Another shot cracked, striking the wall a few feet behind them. Kate screamed and ducked.

'We're giving him a fine target,' Matthew pointed out. Snatching the lantern from Kate's hand, he threw it hard toward Cusset. There was an instant of spiralling light, mad shadows dancing across the waterside, and then it landed inside one of the boats. Flame spurted briefly, then died to a muted flicker. 'Missed, damn it!'

Dimly seen in hazy moonlight, the stone shelf curved in front of them, with waves lapping at the moored boats to their left and the rock rising fifteen feet on their right. 'Matthew! This way!' Kate ran toward a wooden ladder that was fixed in the rock. She began to clamber slowly upward.

'Come on, Kate!' Matthew propelled her onward, regardless of dignity or respectability.

'Matthew! I've only one hand, remember?'

The pistol cracked again, Matthew winced, put a hand under Kate and nearly threw her upward, following her over the top, where the sheer rock eased into a gentler slope. Ahead of him stretched a moonlit hillock, a dome of coarse grass and rock, where a handful of scrubby trees moaned in a rising wind. When clouds returned to obscure the moon, Matthew was more aware of the steady throb of a steam engine.

'Where are we?' Kate asked.

Matthew looked around; the land ended in water in every direction. 'Sweet God in heaven, we're on Baie de l'Isle.' He had hoped to be on one of the headlands that overlooked the bay, but instead they were on the central island. Suddenly the logic was inescapable. 'Of course we are; it's a perfect base. The navy will sail in to destroy the pump, and the French will release the steam torpedoes from right under their noses. There won't be time for the ships to escape.'

There was the clatter of feet on the ladder, hard voices in the dark and the ghosting glimmer of a lantern.

'That's the army,' Kate dropped her voice. 'Some officer ordering his men to form a line and scour the island.'

'Let's move, then,' Matthew said, withdrawing quickly. 'Keep close.' He could hear the crunch of military boots and the rattle of equipment. Somebody was whistling softly, repeating the same monotonous six-bar refrain. There was a shouted challenge in the distance, quickly followed by the roar and flare of a musket. Matthew dropped, dragging Kate beside him, but the soldiers were rushing toward the sound.

'They're jumpy,' Kate said quietly. 'Firing at shadows.'

The officer was shouting again, straightening the bunched line.

'There's a gap,' Matthew said. 'Come on!' Grabbing Kate, he ran forward, head down and shoulders hunched. 'We'll get behind them.'

The rock was slippery underfoot, but they kept moving, sheltering behind a tree when somebody passed close, holding their breath when a soldier sat on a boulder to loosen a too-tight boot, gradually working their way through the straggling line of French infantry. Kate breathed

314

her relief when the moon slithered toward the horizon, darkening the sky, but they both dropped to the ground as a French officer loomed up. He sniffed the air, opened his mouth and bellowed a blistering reprimand.

'He's reminding them not to smoke,' Kate said. 'He said that it's dangerous with all the gunpowder so close.' She looked at him, forcing a smile. 'Well, he said something like that, but you are far too young to hear his exact words.'

Matthew nodded. 'You're probably right,' he said. 'Thank God it's night, or they'd see us for sure.'

'It will be daylight soon,' Kate reminded. She was right. Already there was a definite lightening of the sky to the east, and the sea, which had been virtually invisible save for the silver of surging surf, was already taking form.

'Tide's ebbing, though,' Matthew said. 'So we have more island on which to hide.'

He shook his head, trying to dispel the fog of fatigue. There were two choices: return through the tunnel to the mainland, or remain on the island and hope that the soldiers retired before full daylight. There was that whiff of smoke again, as some French soldier dared the wrath of his officer to puff on his pipe. 'God, Katie, what have I brought you to?'

'I brought myself, remember?' She patted his arm. 'We just need a boat, husband-to-be, and all will be well.'

Matthew grunted. He wondered if he should double back down the ladder and again try to raise steam on one of the torpedo boats. For a second he imagined the reaction in England if he arrived with a French steam boat as a prize of war and Kate at his side. What would the *Gazette* say to that? He shook away the day-dream; he must be tired to allow such fantasies into his normally logical mind. There must be a way off this island. 'Stay here,' he ordered, 'and I will see what I can find.'

'You'll find me, for a start,' Kate said, indignantly. 'You're not leaving me here alone with all these Frenchmen running around loose. What *would* Mrs Grundy say?' He recognized the hysteria in her giggle and realized how the strain must be affecting her.

'We'll stay together,' he decided.

The island was shaped like a turtle, with cliffs along the landward side, where the steam boats were berthed, but a gentle slope toward the sea. The air pump and other mine machinery was in the centre, where a convenient dip, or a dimple, as Kate insisted on calling it, provided cover from even the most observant of Royal Naval observers.

As the soldiers scrambled to the far side of the island, Matthew crouched in the lee of a seaweed-smeared boulder. 'That's England over there,' he said. 'Too far to swim.' Dawn was seeping life into the sky, highlighting the silver-white break of waves, catching the topsails of a distant ship.

'But maybe not too far with a plank to support us,' Kate pointed downward. 'Can you see it?'

The ebbing tide had revealed a shingled beach littered with the refuge of the nearby French army. There were abandoned boots, a tattered coat, pieces of weed-smeared cable and a length of timber, bobbing at the edge of the water.

'I see it.' Checking to ensure that there were no Frenchmen creeping up on them, Matthew moved closer to the plank. Around fifteen feet long and three wide and surprisingly free of marine growth, it floated high on the waves.

'Kate!' Matthew called her close. 'If we stay on the island, the French are certain to find us. If we go back to the tunnel, we might get out somewhere else, and then we can hunt for a boat, or' – he indicated the plank – 'we can push ourselves out on *that* and make for England.'

'Oh my Lord.' Kate sat down as she contemplated her choices. 'Oh sweet Lord.' She looked backward to the island, which grey dawn revealed as a barren hump of rock and thorn trees perhaps a mile in diameter. 'I can't face the mine again, Matthew. I don't want to go back to the dark, but to chance the sea on that...' She spread out her left arm. 'Oh, Lord, I don't know.'

It was the reek of smoke that helped them decide. 'There's that soldier at his pipe again,' she tried to laugh. 'Oh, God, what should we do?' She shook her head. 'Let's try the plank, Matthew. Better drowning than the guillotine. We'll be trying to do something, and the Channel is English, at least.'

Recognizing that he was playing advocate to his own devil, Matthew pointed out the dangers. 'It's about thirty miles, remember, and you've only one arm.'

'And you are the most perverse man in the

world,' Kate said, crossly. 'It was hard enough making up my mind once, without you trying to persuade me a second time. Come on, for God's sake.'

Keeping low, they splashed out to the plank, with seaweed clutching greasily at their ankles and the waves surging uncomfortably up their legs.

'Thank goodness it's summer,' Kate joked feebly as Matthew placed her face downward along the plank. 'The water's not too cold.'

Matthew nodded. Pushing the plank into the water, he paddled alongside as long as he dared before hauling himself on top in front of Kate. 'Now, paddle. The tide will take us away from the land, but we'll give it as much help as we can.'

'That won't be much,' Kate warned, thrusting her left hand into the water. 'Lord, Matthew, these French must be smoking like chimneys! I can smell them out here.'

The shout made them duck, and Matthew glanced back, to see a section of soldiers wading into the water as they aimed their muskets. The officer, gaudy in blue and bright gold, was pointing a curved sword at them.

'Paddle!' Matthew slid into the water, thrusting with his legs and pushing the plank with both hands. 'And keep your head down.'

The sound of the musket was muted, as if it came from a long distance, and Matthew did not see the fall of the shot. He heard Kate's hysterical laugh and pushed harder, hoping that the waves would provide partial concealment. One of the soldiers waded waist deep into the sea and began to swim, lunging arm over arm in a desperate attempt to reach them. There was another shot, and a third, and this time Matthew heard the rip of the ball above his head. The sound reminded him of somebody tearing a page from a book.

He felt the vibration first, as if a giant hand was stirring the water far beneath his feet, and then he heard the rumble.

'Matthew! Look at the island!'

The blast was unlike anything he had ever seen before, a mighty flash that encompassed the island and seemed to shake the whole world, accompanied a second later by a surge of sound so intense that it buffeted his ears and descended like a blanket, muffling everything. He tried to speak, but he could not hear his own voice, nor could he hear Kate, although her mouth was opening and closing in excitement.

Debris descended, pieces of rock and timber that splashed dangerously around them. Matthew yelled as a small stone cracked on his back and coughed as dust clouded thick around them, clogging mouths, ears, eyes and noses. Crawling back onto the plank, he placed a protective arm around Kate and gasped as the sea writhed and sucked them back toward the island.

Flapping a hand in front of his eyes in a futile attempt to clear the dust, Matthew saw white smoke rising, expanding until it covered the island. Again he tried to speak, but there was no sound, and he shook his head as the smoke billowed over the surface of the sea.

Kate rose to her knees, balancing on one hand as she stared toward the island and the rising wave that now raced in their direction. Blue and green, fringed with silver white, it rose high above their heads and carried them, spear-straight, away from the coast of France and out into the English Channel.

Holding tight to Kate, Matthew felt the wave thrust them deep under the sea, brought them back up and tossed them like a child's toy, among an accumulation of debris such as he had never imagined. He may have screamed, but he could hear nothing. One minute he was gagging and retching, with the water burning in his chest, the next he was thrown to the surface, hauling in vast quantities of air, and all the time he clung to Kate like a sinful man to a hope of salvation.

Twice some hard object smashed into him as the sea and sky continued to spiral, exchanging places, turning from blue to black to filthy brown, and there was Kate's face close to his, her eyes tight shut and mouth open, her right arm pressed close to her chest. Matthew tried to swim, to kick away from this nightmare, to reach England. He knew that if he kept moving he would be safe, for home lay just ahead. After all, Kate had said that the Channel was English, so he must be near sanctuary. And then the sea sucked him back under, where it was dark and cool and serene, save for a terrible bubbling roar inside his head and the crushing pain in his lungs.

Matthew began to relax, to close his eyes and allow the pain to take him to a painless place, but the sea spat him back into a maelstrom of noise and confusion and broken water.

'Matthew!' Kate was looking at him, her face white and anguished, and her hair flat against her head so even that always rebellious curl was straight.

He tried to speak, to tell her that it was all right because the Channel was English, but the words wedged in his throat and he could only stare, welcoming the sweet death that eased over him.

'Swim!' Kate's voice screamed. 'Swim! There is a sail!'

Matthew nodded weakly and kicked out. Of course there was a sail. Nelson would come to attack the mine and stop the invasion. He grinned, aware of defeat, but still supporting Kate with his right arm.

'They've seen us,' Kate said. 'Wave!'

Kicking with his legs, Matthew waved his left arm in the air and somebody in the boat responded. It was a low, raking two-masted craft with a dark hull and weathered sails, and it slithered close with a display of superb seamanship. Men clustered at the low gunwale, throwing lines for them to catch. Anxious, friendly faces peered at them, pointing, gesticulating, urging them closer.

The rope was rough in Matthew's hand, but he held on, looped it under Kate's arms and watched as she was hauled inboard. Wiry arms pulled her over the low gunwale in an undignified tangle of clothing, and he was satisfied. With Kate safe, he could sink back and die, his duty done; but somebody dragged him back to life's torment, barking his knees against the rough timber of the hull, crashing his head against the rail. Hard hands hauled him onto the deck and he lay there, spewing out vast volumes of seawater.

A man knelt beside him, touched his shoulder, and spoke to him. The words seem to come from far away, and they were in French.

Seventeen

The English Channel
August 1805

'Monsieur?' The man spoke again, repeating what was obviously a question. Matthew shook his head. After surviving so much, to be picked up by a French vessel was heartbreaking. He should have drowned.

The man tried again, but it was Kate who replied, choking over the words as she vomited onto the deck. There were murmurs of sympathy from the crew, somebody lifted her up and bent her over the gunwale so she was more comfortable. Matthew heard a change in the tone as another man approached.

'What have we here?'

'Two Frenchies, Captain. One's a woman in a uniform jacket, and I think the other's a deaf mute.'

'Let's have a look.' Ignoring Kate, the man turned Matthew onto his back.

Matthew stared into the brown face of Joss Page.

'Well, bugger me!' Page shook his head. 'I heard you were long dead, with the crows pecking at your eyes!'

'Not quite,' Matthew said weakly. 'I thought you were French.' Dust and salt water made it painful to speak.

Page shook his head. 'No. We thought the same about you, floating off France with explosions all over the place and the sea going crazy. What happened?'

Matthew shook his head. 'God knows.' Reaching out, he touched Kate's arm. 'But we're alive.' The realization hit him and he began to laugh. 'We're alive, Kate, and safe in an English ship.'

She straightened up, stained and sodden, with red-rimmed eyes and watery blood seeping from a gash on her cheekbone, and he thought that she had never looked so beautiful. 'I told you the Channel was English.'

Their frantic laughter changed to tears, and Kate fell into his arms, sobbing out the reaction to the weeks of horror and fear. They held each other close, shaking and crying together while the crew of *Tern* looked away, or patted their backs in rough, wordless sympathy.

'Matthew.' Kate loosened her injured arm and the packet of plans and documents fell to the deck. Stooping, she picked it up and placed it in his hand. 'I didn't drop them.' She spoke in a hoarse croak that Matthew found strangely attractive.

He stared at her for a long moment, then, bending close, kissed her again. 'I've never known a braver woman,' he said, and added an amendment. 'Nor a braver anyone else.'

'Wind's backing, Captain,' somebody reported, and Page rolled aft, giving a stream of orders that altered the set of the sails and sent the lugger away from the coast of France.

'We're going home, Kate,' Matthew said, holding her close. 'We're going home.'

'What *will* Mrs Grundy say,' Kate wondered, 'and more importantly, what will Father say?'

'Whatever it is,' Matthew comforted her, 'we can help the Channel Fleet. Once we tell Admiral Springer our intelligence, Nelson will not fall into the French trap.'

'You don't understand.' Kate was smiling, shaking her head and crying all at the same time. 'I doubt that there is much of a trap remaining. Look behind you.'

White smoke wreathed the island, spreading out to kiss the wings of the bay and send writhing tendrils drifting past *Tern*. As Matthew stared, flames glimmered, accompanied by an occasional rumble, and he shook his head. 'What happened?'

'*You* happened,' Kate said. 'Remember when Mr Cusset was chasing us and you threw the lantern at him?'

Matthew nodded. 'I remember. I missed.'

'And the steam boats were ready to sail, all loaded with barrels of gunpowder?'

Matthew was silent until Kate prompted him again. 'I remember,' he said softly. He thought of the soldiers searching the surface of the island, and the chained workers. 'Dear God; how many men did I kill?'

Kate's hand crept inside the crook of his arm. 'Only men that would kill you.' Looking at him, she amended her words. 'Men that would kill *us* without hesitation. More importantly, how many lives have you saved?'

Matthew stared at the spreading smoke, and thought of the horrors that must be hidden beneath. 'Dear God forgive me.'

'He will; if there is anything to forgive.' Kate pressed herself closer. 'Come on, now. Would you rather have the French blow up Nelson's fleet? And then cross the Channel?'

Matthew shook his head, unable to contemplate anything apart from the devastation he had caused. 'No; no of course not.'

'Kate!' Betsy Page looked as shapely and competent as ever as she grinned across to Kate. Producing a pipe from a hidden pocket, she thrust it, bowl downward, in her mouth. 'You look positively Hottentotish.'

'What?' Kate stared at her for a second, before putting a hand up to straighten her hair.

Betsy shook her head, laughing. 'Go down below, Katie, and get yourself tidied up.' She glanced at Matthew, grinned and leaned closer. 'You'd better look after him, Kate. You know how I like a nicely turned breech in a man.'

Kate followed the direction of Betsy's eyes, met her smile and placed her hand over Matthew's left buttock. He started and moved away, until he realized that his breeches had been torn at some point, revealing a section of white flesh.

'Does it matter all that much, Matthew? After all, I have seen you in the bath.'

Sobs mingled with their laughter as Betsy raised an inquisitive eyebrow. 'You're getting the right idea, Kate. We have to put up with men, so we may as well enjoy them.'

At one time Matthew would have considered such comments to be unladylike, but after the experiences he had shared with Kate, he no longer cared.

'You'd best go below, Kate, and change into something dry,' Betsy grinned. 'You can leave your man here.'

'He can change too, if you have something suitable,' Kate said, but she closed the cabin door very firmly in Matthew's face while Betsy allowed her the freedom of her wardrobe.

'Betsy, what do you make of that?' Captain Page passed over his spyglass. 'Dead astern.' The wind had moderated to a fluky breeze that merely rippled *Tern*'s sails, pushing the lugger slowly toward the visible coast of England.

Betsy focused for a moment before lowering the spyglass. 'Damned if I know what she is. I've never seen a rig like it.'

'Look again,' Captain Page said. 'Look aft.'

Betsy did so, frowning. 'Smoke,' she said. 'She's on fire.'

'That's what I thought.' Captain Page sounded

puzzled. He examined the sea, marking each sail with a small nod. 'There's nothing else unusual here, just the normal Channel traffic. Snows, ketches, brigantines, a cutter and over there is the Royal Navy.'

'Should we try and help?' Betsy asked.

'Of course we should.' Captain Page rattled out orders that saw *Tern* alter course and tack back toward France. 'I'll not leave seamen to burn to death.'

Matthew felt Kate's hand reach for his. 'I know we have to help,' she said, 'but I'd much rather go home.'

'So would I,' Matthew felt as if a prize had been snatched from him the second he came close.

Betsy had the spyglass directed on the burning ship. 'The smoke's increasing, but she's making good progress for a ship in difficulty. Even with the wind in her favour.'

Matthew's frustration altered to suspicion. 'May I trouble you for the spyglass, Miss Page?' Clambering on top of the bulwark for a better view, Matthew entwined one leg through the ratlines and focused on the strange craft. At first he saw only an orb of sky and sea, but as he grew accustomed to the motion of the lugger he found first the smoke and then the ship. She was long, and low in the water, with two masts, stepped far forward and aft, and a tall funnel on which were spread more sails and from which smoke emitted. His angle of sight prevented him from seeing the paddle wheel, but he knew there it would be aft of the mizzenmast, churning the

water to froth as it pushed the ugly vessel forward.

'Sweet Lord, but she's a masterpiece of engineering,' he said, and then the sick fear surged in
his stomach. 'Oh, God.'

'Matthew?' Kate tugged at his leg. 'What's
wrong?'

He raised his voice. 'That's not a burning ship,
Captain Page. She's a French steam boat.'

'A what?' Page laughed away the idea. 'Don't
be foolish, man! Steam kettles can't sail.'

'That one can.'

Kate was balancing at his side, the breeze
tousling her hair. 'Matthew! Will she have these
infernals on board?'

The thought was chilling. Matthew focused
again, wondering if he was witnessing the birth
of a new kind of sea power, something that
would render every ship of the Royal Navy
obsolete. A sea-going steam boat, armed with
these terrifying infernals, a machine that could
defy the wind, small, but powerful enough to
blow a three-decker out of the water.

'I hope not, Kate,' he said, soberly. 'Oh, God,
I hope not.'

Most of the crew had had left their work to
crowd aft and scrutinize this strange contraption.
Men were pointing and gesticulating, mocking
or swearing according to their natures. Some
were merely staring, unable to believe that a
steam-powered craft could float and move.

Matthew saw the jet of white smoke seconds
before he heard the muted crack. The tall pillar
of water rose two cables' lengths to starboard.

Captain Page grunted. 'Six-pounder! I don't know what she is, but she's certainly French.' He gave more orders to wear the lugger. 'If she had not fired she could have drawn us close, but now,' he laughed, 'there's no Frenchie built as can catch *Tern* before the wind.'

Turning even a small vessel was a complicated procedure, and the steam boat fired twice more. The first shot was well wide, but Matthew followed the passage of the second with fascination. As soon as he saw the smoke, he knew that the shot would hit. He saw the black streak for a fraction of a second, then the deceptively lovely feather of water as it skiffed the surface off a wave directly in line with *Tern*.

'Kate!' He pulled her from the ratlines half a second before a thunderous crash came from aft. He heard the high yell of pain, the snap as a line parted and saw, momentarily but horrifyingly, the deluge of jagged splinters as the cannon ball ricocheted from the deck to smash against the mizzenmast.

'Josh!' Matthew heard Betsy's scream of horror even as *Tern* shivered, momentarily in irons. He looked aft, to see Josh writhing on deck, then lying horribly still as blood oozed from his chest. 'No!' Betsy ran to him, kneeling at his side.

'Betsy!' Kate scampered across the deck. 'You attend to the ship, I'll look after Josh!'

'No!' Betsy looked up, her mouth and eyes wide and her brother's blood wet on her hands.

'Go on! Or we'll all be killed!'

When Kate gave her a little push, Betsy nodded, glanced at Josh and began to scream orders that set the crew to work.

The Frenchman fired again, with the ball smashing against the lugger's hull. *Tern* shuddered under the impact and Matthew wondered what damage a six-pound ball of iron, travelling at something over a hundred miles an hour, would do to two-inch-thick timber seasoned with years, pitch and salt water. In happier times it would have made an interesting calculation.

He saw Kate kneeling over the injured Josh, threw his weight to help a couple of seamen hauling on a line, ducked as the boom swung slowly across the deck and watched the lugger ease round to present her stern to the steam boat.

With *Tern* back on course, Betsy ran to Josh. 'How is he?'

'Hurt,' Kate said. 'There's lots of blood but he's breathing.' She looked up. 'You're in command now.'

There was another jet of smoke from the steam boat, another fountain of water beside the lugger. The sun caught the hanging droplets for a moment, creating a miniature rainbow, and then the wind blew away the image, splattering water across the deck.

Matthew carried Josh below, and helped Kate strip off his shirt before she washed away the blood and wrapped strips of linen around the ragged splinter wound. 'I'll look after him,' Kate decided. 'You get back on deck. You might be some use there.'

The steam boat was closer, with smoke gushing black and ugly from her funnel, partially obscuring her as it spread across the surface of the sea.

'Wind's dropping,' Betsy sounded worried. 'We're losing speed, but she's not.'

Matthew seized the spyglass and studied the French vessel, fascinated by the actions of a steam boat on the open sea. 'She's much larger than the others,' he said quietly, 'eighty or ninety feet long, and she's heavy too.'

'How heavy?' Betsy took the spyglass. 'How deep in the water?'

'I'm not sure. I haven't seen her before.' He made a rough calculation of her weight, guessing the engine and boiler size, and told Betsy his best estimate. 'Maybe ninety or a hundred tons.'

She looked at him. 'That heavy? She'll need depth, then.' She lifted the spyglass again, focusing on the waterline. 'There's not much freeboard.' When she looked up, her smile was entirely without humour. 'She's catching us fast though, with this fluky wind.'

'And this same wind will stop the navy from coming to investigate.' Matthew tried to hide his worry. He could see the steam boat clearly now, with a cluster of men around the cannon in her bow and a tall man scrutinizing the lugger through a spyglass.

'May I?' Matthew secured the spyglass again. The tall man sprang into focus and for one minute Cusset and Matthew stared directly at each other, eye to eye across half a mile of sea, and then a wave lifted *Tern* and Matthew was examining only an orb of clouded sky.

The cannon fired again, but the shot screamed

harmlessly through the lugger's rigging. Men cursed and ducked, with one shaking a futile fist at the Frenchman. Betsy flinched and checked her position with the coastline of England. The North Foreland thrust into the Channel a few miles to starboard and Deal Castle rose defiantly to larboard.

'Right, Johnny Crapaud,' Betsy said softly. 'Let's see if you are a kettle-boiler or a Channel seaman.' Raising her voice, she gave orders that altered the angle of the sails and changed *Tern*'s course so she was at right angles to the steam boat, with her sails momentarily flapping idly. 'Out sweeps!'

None of the men grumbled as they thrust the long sweeps into position and began a slow, rhythmic pull that eased the lugger through the sea. Betsy gave a succinct direction to the helmsman, 'Steer directly for Deal.'

He nodded, turned over the quid of tobacco in his mouth, and touched the spokes of the wheel. 'Right over?'

'Right over.' Betsy kept her voice level.

Twice more, Matthew saw the Frenchman fire, and each time he ducked. The first shot was wide, but the second skimmed the surface of the sea a few yards from the outstretched sweeps.

'Keep just under the surface here,' Betsy ordered, 'don't dig deep,' and the men grinned to her in immediate understanding.

'Why?' Matthew asked. 'Would it not be more effective to put the oars deeper?'

Betsy shook her head. 'Watch and learn, landsman.'

Kate emerged from below, blood staining her clothes. 'Joss is sleeping,' she reported to Betsy, 'and the bleeding has stopped. Sweet Lord!' She looked astern. 'That thing has nearly caught us.'

Men were coughing in the smoke and smuts that the wind blew from the steam boat across to the deck of *Tern*. Kate glowered over the few hundred yards of sea that now separated them. 'There's Mr Cusset, Matthew.'

'Well, Mr Cusset is not going to sink my ship,' Betsy said.

'He doesn't want to sink you,' Kate told her. 'We took something of his, and he wants it back.' She pointed to the cluster of men standing behind Cusset in the bow of the steam boat. 'I believe they are going to board us.'

'*I* don't believe so,' Betsy contradicted. Pulling her pipe from a pocket of her short jacket, she jammed it, bowl downward, between her teeth. 'Starboard the helm! Pull! Pull!'

The lugger increased speed, with the sweeps raising little feathers of white water.

'Wind's rising, Betsy,' an elderly, bald-headed man reported, 'and veering southward.'

'Pull! We need every ounce of speed!'

With a glance at Kate, Matthew slipped beside the bald man, grabbed hold of the oar and copied his movements, swooping forward and hauling back, feeling the drag of the water on the long sweep.

'Pull! Come on, lads!'

The steam boat was so close that Matthew could see the expression on Cusset's face as the French engineer shouted directions to the men that had gathered at his back. Most were soldiers in blue uniforms, with the white cross-belts more vivid than he had remembered; one or two were bandaged. There were also a few of the dark-uniformed guards, armed with muskets or pistols, and the remainder wore the loose shirts and wide trousers of seamen.

'Here it comes!'

Matthew had not noticed the squall approaching until the wind suddenly increased and rain battered from the sails and bounced from the deck. 'Larboard the helm!' Betsy raised her voice above the sudden moan of the rigging and the vicious slap of waves against the hull. *Tern* heeled, nearly unbalancing Matthew. He grabbed at the mizzenmast for support, and saw the bows of the steam boat rise up, a mere pistol shot away, and then abruptly stop as if the master had cast all her anchors simultaneously.

'Got you,' Betsy said quietly.

Wind-driven rain rattled from the rigging, diminishing visibility to a few yards as Betsy ordered the sweeps to be brought inboard and the sails reduced. Matthew could only watch as the seamen sprinted to their stations, working with a furious zest that he had never seen from any landsman. Kate came to his side, unblinking in the storm.

'Where's the steam boat?' She had to shout above the noise of the wind.

'Out there somewhere!' Matthew pointed into the murk, and then the weather abated as quickly as it had risen.

'Dear Lord,' Kate said. 'Look at it.'

Matthew looked, and swore, shaking his head. 'What a waste. Oh, what a waste of a master-piece.'

The steam boat was lying at an angle in the water, already mostly submerged, with one mast snapped and smutty black smoke belching from her funnel. Men were leaping into the water, some swimming toward the lugger, others strug-gling amidst the litter of timber, cordage and other debris that vomited from the stricken ship.

'What happened? Kate asked.

'We're above the Goodwin Sands,' Betsy explained. 'Matthew told me the weight of that steam kettle, and as there was so little freeboard, she must have a deep draught. I just steered for the sands, waited for the squall to blind her and led her on.' She shook her head. 'There's a nasty cross-current here, and a sharp ridge that will tear the keel from any boat.' She nodded toward the steam boat. 'I did not think that a real seaman would sail a thing like that, so it was as easy as jinking the exciseman.'

Tern's crew were pulling survivors from the sea and leaving them to drain on the deck when the steam boat gave a final lurch and disappear-ed, sliding sideways from the ridge into the sea. There was a bubbling roar, a sudden surge of water and then a confusion of litter burst to the surface.

'What in God's name was that?' Betsy had joined the crew in staring over the side. 'I've never seen a ship go down like that before. What was it?'

For a moment Matthew was as stunned as the

rest, and then he realized what had happened. 'That must have been her boiler exploding.'

Betsy shook her head. 'Well, bugger me. They'll not be building any more like that, I hope. And if they do, I'll not be sailing in it.'

There were bodies among the wreckage, dead men and pieces of men, spiralling and bobbing in the short, steep waves. Matthew stared in horrified fascination as one man bumped gently against the hull of the lugger, his eyes and mouth wide open and his arms outstretched in an obscene parody of a cross.

'Matthew.' Kate took his arm. 'That's Mr Cusset.'

Matthew nodded. He watched as the French engineer bobbed alongside for a minute, then slowly drifted aft. Raising a hand in salute, he felt as though he were watching something of himself die as Cusset disappeared among the waves.

'Let's go home, Matthew.' Kate did not hide her tears.

Eighteen

Realizing that he could not invade England, Bonaparte consulted with Talleyrand, his Foreign Minister, over the international situation. 'Once I raise my camp on the ocean, I shall not be able to stop myself; my plans of maritime war will have failed.' Abandoning his intention of marching on Great Britain, he said, 'I shall invade Germany with two hundred thousand men. I shall stop the Austrians and Russians from uniting. I shall beat them before they can meet. Then, the Continent pacified, I shall come back to the camp on the ocean and start to work all over again for peace at sea.'

By the 28th of August the Army of England had left its positions along the Channel coast and was marching toward the Danube. On the 2nd of September, Bonaparte left Boulogne to join them. He never again seriously attempted an invasion of Britain.

Kent
September 1805

'Did you hear that Boney has withdrawn his army from the coast?' Admiral Springer put down his glass of brandy and water and looked up at Matthew. 'He's marching full tilt for Germany with horse, foot and cannon.'

'No, sir,' Matthew said. 'I had not heard.'

'Aye. He's claiming that he will conquer Europe and then return, but I think we know differently, do we not?' His wink was as ponderous as everything else about him. 'So this tunnel thing was only a hoax all along?'

'Indeed, sir.' Matthew agreed. He looked around the table with its contingent of grave-faced men. Major Sir John Jones had taken notes, writing rapidly in a small hand, while Mr Reeves had tapped his fingers on top of the table as if conducting an invisible orchestra. Kate sat in demure silence, her arm still bandaged but perfectly useable and her face more tanned than was fashionable.

'That is not what Mr Black reported.' Reeves sounded dubious. 'Mr Black was adamant that there were tunnel workings, with a vulnerable steam pump and dummy gun emplacements.'

'I am afraid that Mr Black was unaware of the true extent of the operation,' Matthew said, as diplomatically as he could. 'The entire French plan was based on deception. They knew that you would be watching Mr Houghton, with his radical ideas, and Lamballe, of course, and they used them to lure us into Ottin Hall, where the incriminating letter to Albert Mathieu was left in plain sight.'

'And we took the bait,' Jones said. 'We followed every breadcrumb in the trail.'

'We did, sir,' Matthew agreed. 'We found the French mine, as we were meant to do, and

Citizen Peltier directed us to the batteries, with their false cannon, so we could see that the bay was undefended, and so, therefore, was the mine.'

'But I do not understand,' Reeves frowned. 'If the French wanted so badly to deceive us, why were you all arrested?'

Matthew glanced at Kate, who shrugged in a most un-English manner. 'You say,' she said.

'Things got slightly complicated,' Matthew started. 'We were staying in the farm of Mr and Mrs Durand, and Mr Durand thought that Mr Black was too friendly with his wife.'

'Oh?' Admiral Springer leaned forward in his seat. 'What made him think that?'

'I do not know, sir. Kate ... Miss Denton and I were inspecting the gun batteries at the time.'

'I see.' Looking disappointed, Admiral Springer subsided in his seat. 'So what happened next?'

'Mr Durand created a commotion, which alerted some French soldiers. Mr Black managed to escape, but Miss Denton and I were captured and taken to Paris to be interrogated.' Matthew spoke of Dugua and the threat of the guillotine, and Black's rescue. 'But we were captured again.'

'I am surprised that they did not just let you escape, if that was their intention all along.' Reeves sounded cynical.

'Yes, sir. I believe that there was some history between Mr Black and Citizen Peltier; it seems that he had killed her brother in battle, many years ago.'

Reeves grunted. 'I see. And she wanted revenge.'

'Yes, sir.'

'Very well, carry on, Mr Pryde.'

'Mr Lamballe arrived at the place we were being held, and he must have persuaded Dugua to let us escape. They loosened my chains, and when we left the dungeons, there was a coach waiting, apparently deserted. It took us a long time to travel across France, because we used the side roads, and Citizen Peltier still wanted revenge.' Matthew decided not to mention Black's desertion. 'She caught us and would have killed Mr Black, but Mr Lamballe shot her.'

'Good God!' Admiral Springer topped up his brandy, obviously enjoying the story.

'Indeed, sir. Together with the ease of our escape, that act alerted us that things were not all they seemed. It was Kate, Miss Denton, who worked out all the connections.'

'Miss Denton,' Reeves glowered at her, 'I fail to understand why you were in France at all.'

Kate gave her most charming smile. 'I was the translator,' she explained. 'Matthew can't speak French.'

'So we worked our way to the tunnel,' Matthew continued before Reeves asked too many probing questions, 'and discovered that it was, in fact, a workshop for making steam infernals.'

There was intense silence as Matthew outlined the French plan for luring in the Channel Fleet to destroy the tunnel workings, before releasing the explosive infernals. He produced the plans and blueprints that Kate had retained throughout the journey, unfolded them on top of the table, apologized for the seawater damage and pointed out the strengths of each device.

'Good God in heaven,' Springer said. 'Steam-powered boats that can carry forty barrels of gunpowder.'

'Indeed, sir.'

'And of sufficient explosive power to destroy a First Rate line-of-battle ship?' Reeves looked up, eyes questioning.

'Yes, sir.'

'I see.' Reeves scanned the uppermost of the plans. 'An infernal device, Mr Pryde. Would you not agree, Admiral Springer?'

'Infernal indeed, Mr Reeves.' Springer riffled through the paper, selecting a sheet at random. 'And this one? A steam-powered warship, no less. In your opinion, Major Jones, would such a device be practical?'

Jones spent a few minutes examining the drawing. 'It would appear so.'

The Admiral looked serious. 'And are there more of these, Mr Pryde? More steam boats, more infernals, ready to be launched at the navy?'

'I believe not, sir,' Matthew said. 'There was an explosion as we left, and I would doubt that any of the steam devices were left.'

'What Matthew means, Admiral,' Kate was unable to keep silent for so long, 'is that he destroyed them. As we left, Matt— Mr Pryde threw a lantern among the barrels of gunpowder. Mr Cusset, the French engineer, was firing at us at the time.'

'Oh?' Admiral Springer raised his eyebrows. 'You seem to have experienced some interesting times, Miss Denton. And you, Mr Pryde, are an extremely unconventional man, but your methods seem to work, somehow. Tell me, can this Cusset produce more of these things?'

'Mr Cusset is dead,' Matthew said shortly. When he lifted his glass of brandy, only Kate knew that he was making a silent tribute to the French engineer.

'That is well,' Springer said. 'So the French have no more steam vessels, and no enterprising engineer capable of building them, while we possess the plans.'

'Yes,' Kate said. 'Mr Pryde has been most successful.'

'Good.' Springer glanced at Reeves. 'So, Mr Reeves. I do not believe that we need these things.'

'No, sir.'

Lifting the plans, the Admiral ripped them across, doubled them and ripped them again. Matthew stepped forward, one hand outstretched to prevent such an act of destruction, but Kate grasped his arm, shaking her head.

'Have you heard of Her Majesty's gun-brig *Stubborn*, Mr Pryde?' Admiral Springer continued with his tearing, until he fed scraps of the plans to the nearest candle.

'No, sir.' Matthew watched the work of French genius curl and blacken in the flames. He thought of the thousands of hours of labour that must have gone into the plans, the heartache and work, the scientific progress and mechanical advances. 'You are a Goth, sir, if I may say so.'

'You may, sir, because you are correct, but on this occasion, I am happy to be so. *Stubborn* disappeared off the coast of France earlier this year. There were reports of an explosion, but no survivors. My nephew, Lieutenant Pole, commanded her, and I believe she was a victim of one of these infernal machines.'

'Perhaps so, sir.' Matthew pulled gently free from Kate's grasp. 'But if we build such machines, we could have a steam-powered Royal Navy, the first and finest in the world...'

'No, sir. We already command the sea. We would be the greatest fools that ever existed to encourage a mode of warfare which we do not need, and which others might use to wrest that command from us.' When Admiral Springer looked up, Matthew saw the resolve.

'As you wish, sir.'

Major Jones nodded. 'That would be best, Mr Pryde.' He narrowed his eyes. 'You seem to be a useful sort of fellow, and might make a half-decent engineer, given some proper training.'

'He's not joining the army, Jones,' Mr Reeves interrupted. 'Indeed not. We'll keep you in employment, Pryde, if we ever have to forestall Boney's designs again.'

'Thank you, sir, but I have no intention of acting the spy again.'

Reeves glanced at Admiral Springer. 'I'm glad to hear that, Pryde. It's no job for a gentleman, is it? Certainly not for Maidhouse College men like you. We'll leave that sort of thing to the Mr

Blacks of the world.' He looked up. 'So what do you have in mind, Pryde?'

Matthew looked at Kate. 'I have a marriage to arrange, sir.'

'Good God, man,' Springer muttered, 'is fighting the French not bad enough, that you must strive also for warfare at home?' His laughter exploded around the room, and he wrapped a massive arm around Kate. 'You could not find a better wife, I am sure, nor Miss Denton a better husband.'

'Thank you, sir,' Matthew said. 'As long as her father approves.'

The Admiral looked up. 'I am sure he can be persuaded,' he said. 'You leave Charles Denton to me.'

'Well met, Matthew.' Charles Denton looked up from the table. 'Admiral Springer informs me that you have both been busy with some military engineering business?'

'Yes, sir.' Matthew was unsure how much Mr Denton knew, so thought it best to say as little as possible.

'So it would be a quieter trip than you had planned, then. No adventures down northern coal mines, I wager?'

'Not quite, sir.'

Mr Denton chuckled. 'Not quite, sir. My daughter was injured, sir. She has hurt her arm in some fashion, so you had best appear solicitous. She pretends not to like attention and sympathy, but women...' He smiled, a man sharing a secret with his soon-to-be son-in-law.

344

'I will pay her all due attention, sir,' Matthew promised. He did not like to keep secrets from this kindly old man, but thought it better in this case.

'You seem to have been in the wars yourself, Matthew.' Mr Denton pointed to the fading bruise on Matthew's head. 'I trust that you are not seriously hurt?'

'Not at all, sir,' Matthew said, 'although Mr Lamballe's mine is no longer in operation.'

'I had heard as much,' Mr Denton said. 'Will there be some other employment?'

Matthew nodded, thankful that Mr Denton did not press him about his recent adventures. 'I believe so, sir. There is a Major Jones of the Royal Engineers who wishes a civilian engineer to help him build a canal in the Romney Marsh. He has promised me work, there or elsewhere.'

'Than that is well.' Mr Denton smiled. 'Here is your intended now; I will leave you alone, for you must have much to talk about, with so many arrangements to make.'

Kate emerged from the bookstore beneath the shop, holding a single volume in her hand. She bobbed in a far-too-formal curtsy. 'Good evening, Mr Pryde. I trust you are well?'

'I am, Miss Denton. I trust that your arm is healing satisfactorily?'

'Very, thank you,' Kate assured him.

'In that case, may I present you with a small gift?'

'I believe that I may allow you.' Kate curtsied again, then laughed. 'What is it, Matthew? What have you bought for me? Something foolishly extravagant, I hope?'

'Quite the reverse,' Matthew said. 'Indeed, this small trinket cost me nothing at all.' Removing a box from his pocket, he handed it to her. 'A small souvenir of France.'

'That's the box you found in the workshop.' Kate's eyes shadowed. She prised open the lid and held up the contents. 'It's a medal. A victory medal.' Dated 1804, one side of the bronze disc showed the head of Bonaparte, decked with laurel leaves, and was inscribed *Descente en Angleterre, frappi a Londres en 1804*, while the other showed an image of Hercules crushing the sea giant Antaeus.

'Not much of an engagement present,' Matthew began, but Kate pressed two fingers to his lips.

'It's a symbol of what we can achieve. I will treasure it always.' Sighing, she secreted it away in a pocket of her skirt. 'I was about to complete a small errand, Matthew. Would you care to accompany me?' She lifted the book that she had brought from the storeroom.

Taking a single lantern with her, Kate brought Matthew to the small yard at the rear of the property. Placing the book on the ground, she moved the lantern so it illuminated the title. Dante's *Inferno*.

'That was *the* book?' Matthew asked.

'That was the book with which Mother tormented me, and which has haunted me all these years,' Kate confirmed. She opened it, and slowly, deliberately, began to tear out each of the illustrations. Her shoulders began to shake at one particularly gruesome picture, but when Matthew moved to help, she shook him away. 'No, Matthew. I must do this myself.' Closing her eyes, she ripped downward and lifted the picture. 'This one is still in my dreams, but now I have seen the reality.'

'And defeated it.' Matthew remembered Kate's bravery in front of the guillotine. He began to hum 'Rule, Britannia!', but she stopped him with a gentle pressure on his arm.

'Not yet, please not yet.' She looked into his face, but quickly lowered her eyes. Only when all the pictures were in a small pile on the ground did Kate open the front of the lantern. Her hands shook as she ripped out the front page from the book and put it to the flame. When it was alight, she used it as a taper to light the pictures.

'Burn,' she said softly. 'Burn away all the memories.' Blowing out the lantern, she stood beside the flames, gradually feeding in the remainder of the book until every page was blazing fiercely and shadows jumped and leaped from the enclosing walls. There was no smile on the devil's face as his picture was the last to be burned.

'Now, Matthew,' he heard the sob in Kate's voice, 'I am ready to be your wife. We have cleansed the burden of the past.'

Matthew pulled her close and kissed her. He did not hear Mr Denton's footsteps as he withdrew into the house. 'Now you're sure, Kate,' Mr Denton said. '*Now* you're sure about your man.'

Author's Note

The Channel Tunnel

The idea of a tunnel under the English Channel was first mooted in 1750, but the technology available was not equal to the task. In 1802 a French mining engineer named Albert Mathieu again proposed a Channel tunnel, with one half being dug from France and the other from England. The tunnels were to meet at an artificial island that was to be built at the Varne sandbank, eight miles south of Dover. As one of the major problems in any mine was ventilation, long chimneys would thrust from the tunnel above the surface of the sea. Bonaparte was said to be in favour of the idea, but the resumption of war in 1803 after the brief Peace of Amiens ended any speculation. Contemporary British and French cartoonists capitalized on the idea, drawing pictures of vast armies of French soldiers either crossing the Channel by balloon, or marching through a tunnel to emerge behind the defending British. As far as historians are aware, there was never any attempt to build an invasion tunnel during the Napoleonic Wars.

Steam Power and Infernals

At the beginning of the nineteenth century, steam-powered shipping was very experimental. The Scotsman William Symington had floated a very frail vessel on Dalswinton Loch, and by 1802 a steam tug named *Charlotte Dundas* was hauling barges along the Forth and Clyde Canal. Meanwhile an American, Robert Fulton, displayed his steam-powered boat on the Seine in 1803, but after some consideration the French rejected the idea. Crossing the Channel, Fulton next offered the British Admiralty his device of a 'catamaran', although others knew it as an 'infernal'. This invention was little more than a floating box, twenty-one feet long, with forty barrels of gunpowder and a clockwork timing device. The idea was for small naval vessels to tow the infernal close to the enemy fleet, prime the timer and allow the tide to take the explosive device close to a moored vessel.

When the Prime Minister, William Pitt, ordered that the devices should be tried, Admiral Lord Keith attacked the French vessels at Boulogne with infernals, but with negligible results. Admiral Lord St Vincent gave his view quite succinctly: 'Pitt was the greatest fool that ever existed to encourage a mode of warfare which those who commanded the sea did not want and which, if successful, would deprive them of it.'

The world would have to wait for steam ships and mechanical torpedoes.